ALSO BY CAMILLA BRUCE

In the Garden of Spite

ALL THE BLOOD WE SHARE

A Novel of the Bloody Benders of Kansas

Camilla Bruce

BERKLEY
NEW YORK

BERKLEY
An imprint of Penguin Random House LLC
penguinrandomhouse.com

ISBN: 9780593102602

The Library of Congress has cataloged the
Berkley hardcover edition of this book as follows:

Names: Bruce, Camilla, author.
Title: All the blood we share: a novel of the bloody benders of
Kansas / Camilla Bruce.
Description: New York: Berkley, [2022]
Identifiers: LCCN 2022021599 (print) | LCCN 2022021600 (ebook) |
ISBN 9780593102596 (hardcover) | ISBN 9780593102619 (ebook)
Subjects: LCGFT: Novels.
Classification: LCC PR9144.9.B78 A45 2022 (print) |
LCC PR9144.9.B78 (ebook) | DDC 813/.6—dc23
LC record available at https://lccn.loc.gov/2022021599
LC ebook record available at https://lccn.loc.gov/2022021600

Berkley hardcover edition / November 2022
Berkley trade paperback edition / October 2023

Printed in the United States of America
1st Printing

Interior art: Ink splatter © paseven / Shutterstock
Book design by Alison Cnockaert

ALL
THE
BLOOD
WE
SHARE

1.

KATE

Labette County, Kansas

1871

WHEN WE DEPARTED the train on that January morning, all I could see was a bleak sky stretching out in every direction. It was freezing cold with not so much as a draft in the air. Dust coated everything around us, making it seem lifeless and dull.

This was a cursed land for sure.

In the bustle at the train station, I saw men with hard faces, baked and set by a scorching sun that had now sadly departed for the winter season; several of them chewed tobacco and wore wide-brimmed hats caked with dust. They were bowlegged from riding and filthy from the barn; their eyes reminded me of specks of glass set upon the skin of wrinkled old fruits. The women, too, looked haggard, all wrapped up like little presents in dresses of calico, their faces swallowed by voluptuous bonnets whose strings trailed under their chins like wattles. Children's hands were clutching at their skirts; the toddlers' faces were stained with grime and snot and their eyes were soft with pleading. The station smelled strongly of horseshit and smoke. A few scrawny stray dogs sniffed along the rails.

Of course, there was no one there to help us with the trunk. We had to carry it between us through the throng. Both Ma and I were huffing and puffing. Not one single gentleman stepped in to lighten our load. I looked around for a boy eager for a coin or someone from the railway company but could not see any of them either. There were only those weatherworn men, chewing their tobacco, their eyes as dead and docile as those of cows. Perhaps they spent more time with such creatures than their fellow men and had taken on some of their traits. I knew longhorns from Texas were shipped north from Kansas, so that was certainly something to look forward to as well: stray wild beasts and the occasional stampede—as if the prospect of the wolves and coyotes roaming the prairie was not horrible enough.

It *was* a cursed land, and no one could convince me otherwise, least of all Ma, whose judgment was entirely in question at this point.

We were both close to exhaustion by the time we had escaped the crowd and entered calmer seas. The hem of my new dress was caked with dust, and underneath the fabric I was drenched in perspiration despite the cold. I wondered when I would have the opportunity to bathe again. How could Ma ever believe that this would be our salvation?

I had been opposed to Kansas from the start, but Ma had been adamant. It was better, she said, to lie low for a while, and what better place to disappear than out on the prairie? The landscape was vast and empty, with only lonesome travelers passing through. We could keep to ourselves there, she said, as if that were a glorious, miraculous thing. Keep to ourselves until all was forgotten, and then we could emerge again, as new and fresh as lambs in spring.

She did not seem to grasp the implications: I could hardly fulfill my aspirations in hiding. The foolish plan that she and her husband had cooked up did nothing but slow me down, and I was not thrilled about it. But then, she always knew how to have her way, holding guilt above my head like a sharpened blade. It did not much matter that I was a woman grown, twenty years last spring. She would hold me enthralled until my debt was settled, and should I fail to satisfy, she would surely feed me to the wolves.

Finally, we caught sight of them. Pa and John had opted to stay with the wagon rather than come to our aid. Not even when they saw us come around the station building with our heavy load did they move into action, but remained there, watching. William, in his black hat, leaned against the weather-beaten side of the vehicle, while John sat at the reins. His shoulders were hunched and his head bowed. A stupid little smile played on his lips. His straw hat was new and made him look like a fruit farmer.

Neither of them smiled or even greeted us properly. There were no signs of relief on their drab features. Nor did Ma express any gratitude for the reunion, but set the trunk down and scurried at once to get up on the wagon's dusty deck. A few barrels were there, and some rope, but nothing but some burlap to sit on, which had me fretting for the dress again. It was a pretty thing of silk, striped in a lovely raspberry hue and a deep, clear blue.

William had noticed my new attire. "You're on the prairie now, Kate," he said as he helped Ma onto the wagon. "Nothing will do but some plain calico."

"She dresses like those whores she befriended," Ma said, huffing as she sank down on a sack of potatoes. "It's all so shiny on the out-side with them, while on the inside there's nothing but rot."

I rolled my eyes at her silly statement—we were hardly ones to pass judgment—and then I climbed onto the wagon as well, needing no help, though my skirt snagged on splinters in the rough wood. I winced when I felt it happening, but I would not show it.

I was not about to prove William right.

Our journey thus far had been long and trying, and the rest of it promised to be just as bad. Ma and I had suffered hours upon hours in a cramped, hot train carriage, surrounded by gaunt and tired faces. The air had reeked of smoke, sweat, and a hint of manure, and not even the sweetness of the apples Ma had brought for us had been able to chase the foul taste of defeat from my mouth.

"Stop sulking, Kate," Ma had said when I put my fruit away. "You'll feel better once we are settled in our new home."

"I know what to expect," I replied, speaking in German like her. "More *toil*; that is what." I refused to be anything but honest. "More delays and regret—"

"Well, we would not be in this predicament if it hadn't been for you." She spoke in a cool and even voice, even as her gaze wandered restlessly around us, taking in every face. She meant to shame me by saying such things, but it never worked.

"I had nothing to do with *them*," I said, thinking of the Vandles, of course. "My *God*, woman, I was outside in the wagon with you!"

"Oh, be quiet, Kate," she snapped at me. She huffed and sat back in her seat, holding the basket of fruit and beer close to her chest. Her traveling hat was a tattered thing: old when bought and rarely used. The brown ribbon at the pull was unraveling, as the silken butterfly pinned there had lost a wing. "If it hadn't been for you, we would never have met them in the first place."

I could hardly argue with that, and neither did I care to. Instead, I leaned back on the tattered seat and continued devouring my apple, wrinkled and winter sweet, tasting faintly of the barrel.

"What is it you used to say?" I asked after a while. *"We take care of our own, and the rest can fend for themselves."* I did my best impression of her, making my voice sound sharp and shrill. "I honestly don't see why you're so concerned with what happened to the Vandles."

Ma sighed. "No, you wouldn't, would you? It's all so easy to you."

It was my turn to sigh. "You're hardly blameless, Ma."

"I know," she replied and sent me a cold look. "I raised *you*, for one, which has surely bought me a ticket to hell."

The train had continued at a steady pace, swallowing the miles to Ottawa, where Pa and John were waiting for our arrival. From time to time, the whistle burst out hoarse signals, and sooty clouds of smoke passed by the windows. No one in our carriage seemed inclined to talk much. It was not first class, so they were a ragtag bunch. I saw a couple of young boys in similar hats and coats, who looked about them fearfully, and so were most likely traveling alone. There were pale-faced men with well-trimmed mustaches, vests, and pocket watches, whose financial strains still showed in the worn patches of fabric in their clothing. Their ink-stained fingers made them out as clerks. A few farmers were there as well, in sturdy but unfashionable wear; their wives, too, in colorful calico dresses and unbecoming bonnets. There was also a reverend, all dressed in black.

The carriage was built to be impressive, with green velvet upholstery and dark wood, but it had all become tired and old. Brown spittle and pieces of food marred the carpeted aisle, and someone had spilled beer there, too, leaving a sticky puddle.

I sighed deeply when I noticed how Ma, once again, squinted at the passengers with suspicion written all over her features, raising a few eyebrows among our fellow travelers.

"Stop looking around," I scolded her. "The law is *not* on our heels, Ma. They have no idea where we went. Besides, I've sewn the holy letters into my dress like you said." I did not feel ashamed to lie.

"You have not." She spoke tersely and rolled her eyes. "You're a terrible seamstress."

"Nevertheless, I *did*," I insisted, if only to ease her nerves.

"As if you'd ever take a needle to that dress you're so proud of." She snorted and did not even look at me; her gaze traveled from the boys to the reverend and, finally, to a tired clerk.

She did have a point, however. I had bartered the dress from a prostitute in Louisville in exchange for a cure to restore lost love, and it was at present the prettiest thing I owned.

Not for long, though. I would make sure of that. To hell with lying low! No one looked too closely if only you put on a confident facade. Ma could fret all she wanted, but I still meant to have my due: the stage and the acclaim that came with it.

It was what I was meant to do.

2.

ELVIRA

THE HOUSE THE men had built was an ugly thing, erected in haste; nothing more than a wooden structure. There were windows—more than one—but that was the only good thing about it.

Inside, the single room had a stove to the left and an assembly of table and chairs in the middle. There was a brass bed, too, farther inside, next to a counter with cupboards for storing. The place was cold, though, and the floor covered in dust. It was not what I had been hoping for when they picked us up at the train station. I had been hoping for a hot stove and a meal—had foolishly been hoping for something other than disappointment.

William was mightily proud of his handiwork, though, overly so, if I was to be the judge. He kept showing us the abode's various features like a tawdry magician trying to dazzle a crowd. I, however, had never been fooled by tricks that relied on diverting attention and was offended that my husband thought me so gullible. All while he was showing off, I bit my tongue and curbed my anger, though I knew I would not be able to keep it inside for long. William had clearly betrayed me.

Kate must have seen it on my face, as she looked at me and chuckled while rolling her pretty eyes. "Won't this be a lovely home, Ma," she teased. "Just as good as the one we left behind—"

"Oh, quiet, Kate, please," I snapped. I had enough concerns without her gloating. We would not have been in Kansas in the first place if it had not been for her, and she'd better remember that fact. Kate, though, only laughed at my anger.

My stepson, John, made up the rear of our little group. He, for one, looked stung by her words. He had probably put both sweat and blood into the house's erection, and maybe a little bit of tears as well.

"Here's the cellar for storage." William lifted the trapdoor in the floor by a leather strap with such flair that one might think he was revealing God's eighth wonder. "And look, here's a back door. It will be very useful when we have vegetables growing out there, and to empty out the night pot." He spoke of the barn, too, which was at the time little more than scaffolding. "We were thinking it should be able to hold at least six horses," he said.

"We only have the two," I remarked in a very curt voice.

"Oh, maybe we'll get more," he said in a puzzling way that made me believe that he was holding something back. I looked around me again, at the plain walls, and the Osage Trail, which snaked by right outside the window. It was impossible to think that William had not been aware that he was making a terrible mistake.

"It is *very* close to the road." I gave him a pointed look. "How are we supposed to hide when we are dwelling in plain view? Were there no other claims to be had?" I did not even mention how it was situated disturbingly close to the town of Cherryvale.

William's face paled a little beneath the froth of gray beard. His gaze landed on the floor and stayed there as he stood before me like an abashed schoolboy. "I've been thinking we should take in travelers." He all but stumbled on his words, so eager was he to get them off his chest. "Nothing fancy! We could just offer them a meal and a safe place to sleep indoors. It seems stupid not to, with the road running so close by." When he finally lifted his gaze and saw my expression, he hastened to add, "They will be stopping here anyway, asking for directions. It seems foolish not to make some money off it—and your stew is so good that it would be a shame not to share it with others—"

"You foolish, foolish man!" I bellowed. "How is that to *lie low*? You planned this from the start, didn't you? That is why you built so close to the road! You have fooled me, William!" Spittle flew from my lips and landed on his hands, which he held up as if in surrender.

"Elvira! Please, listen to me—*no one* will look for us here! They wouldn't even recognize us if they did! I have grown out my beard and John has a new mustache, and we go by the name of Bender now!"

"Oh, you and your *greed*!" I cried, more angry than I remembered being in a while. "It will be the undoing of us all! We came here to hide, not to line our pockets, but you always were a weak man! So very, very weak!"

"No, no, Elvira, no." He still held his hands in the air. "There could be a good living in this! Mr. Brockman at the trading station asked if I'd take some of his stock on commission. We could build a store counter over here." He gestured to one side of the room, next to the iron stove. "We could put up shelving on the wall, and we would never run out of coffee," he said, feebly trying for a joke.

I would not have it, though. "It's not what we agreed on, William!" My breathing had become labored. "Why would we invite strangers into our home? It is a foolish plan! Stews and groceries . . ." I shook my head. "I think you must have lost your mind! Have you forgotten what we're running from?"

"No!" He looked much like a dancer as he stood there, wriggling his hands in the air. "Don't you see that we are different people now? The past is all forgotten, Elvira! This is a new life for us—a *prosperous* one!"

"The past doesn't go away just because you want it to!" I jutted an angry finger in the air, sliced it between us like a blade. "There is no 'new beginning' for us—not yet! We have to hide and keep our heads down. *That* is what we agreed on . . . It's what we said before you left. Why did you change your mind all of a sudden?"

"He finds it tiresome to farm." Kate's voice sounded slow and lazy. "He does not much care to break the ground."

"No!" he cried, trying to defend himself, but it was far too late by then. My faith in him had vanished. I grabbed the nearest chair by the back and swung it hard and fast. It made impact atop William's thighs. He bellowed. I screamed and swung the chair again. It felt so good—so glorious—to let my anger out in that way. To hurt him just like he had hurt me. To punish him for fooling me. The next blow hit his back as he fled. Then the chair went high, high up in the air, before coming crashing down again, hitting his back once more.

I could have kept at it all day.

"You are mad, woman! Mad!" William bellowed before slipping out the front door with John in tow. Gnashing my teeth, I saw him leave, and then I dropped the chair to the floor. My breathing came fast and shallow. Tears burned in my eyes. Kate silently picked up the chair at my feet, dusted it off, and placed it at the table.

"It doesn't seem to be broken." She tested its mettle by sitting down and moving around a little on the seat.

"A roadside inn?" I groaned, still standing. "It'll be our very undoing!" I shuffled to the table, suddenly feeling both worn and weary. "I suppose *you* are pleased, though. You won't be rotting in hiding after all." I slumped down in an empty chair.

"I don't think we are very well suited for hiding," my daughter mused with her elbows planted on the table. She looked, if anything, calmly amused. "You know I won't thrive here, Ma. How could I? *None of us* will get what we want if you insist on keeping me out of view." Her mouth twisted up with annoyance.

I gave her a dark look across the table. "We have been over this how many times, Kate? None of us *would have been here* if it hadn't been for you—all I try to do is protect your precious neck, and all you ever give me in return is this endless *disdain*." I spoke fast and angry and concluded with a sigh.

"You could have left me behind in Louisville, Ma, but you didn't, and the only reason why is because you want to settle scores. You *know* I'm the only one who can give you back what you lost. William will never be able to." She sent the closed door a cold smirk. "You mean to hold me captive by your side until I pay up, and that has nothing to do with *protecting* me."

I did not reply at first. I did not want to go there again. We had done little more than argue ever since the men left us in order to purchase the claim, and nothing good had come of it. She distrusted me as I distrusted her, and the Vandles were just as dead.

She was not entirely wrong, though.

"You know how you are, Kate," I said at last. "It is not your fault—merely a quirk of nature; a lick of the devil, perhaps—"

"Say *you*?" Kate laughed. Her pretty face lit up with mirth. "You just chased your husband out the door with a *chair*!" She pointed a long, straight finger in said door's direction. "Maybe it's not *I* who's touched by the devil."

"Well," I said, straightening up on the seat. "It's not *my* hands that are red."

Kate pursed her lips and tossed her head. "I won't regret what I did, Ma, no matter what you say."

"Be as that might." I shrugged. "But the truth of it is that you would've hanged if we hadn't fled, and I assure you this piss-poor piece of land is better than the noose by far."

She pretended not to hear me. "Pa seems to have had a change of heart and won't hide at all. Why else would he build so close to the road?" Her chin tilted upward in a challenging manner.

"Well, Pa is a fool," said I. "He always will be, too. You, of all, know very well how easily he's blinded by dreams of prosperity—"

"It was an *accident*, Ma," she snapped, "with the Vandles."

I did not reply. We both knew well that it was a lie.

WILLIAM CAME SLINKING back before nightfall, like a dog with its tail between its legs. John, too, came shuffling in from the unfinished barn. The young man wore his guilt upon his face and kept his gaze glued to the ground. He knew they had done wrong. I did not blame him, though. He would be hard-pressed to oppose his pa.

"I should like to have my back tended to," William complained as he sat down at the table. Kate and I had spent the rest of the day making the hovel habitable and had fried up some eggs and made hot, sweet tea. The men both relished the meal.

Kate had retired to the bed, where she lay upon the blankets, reading one of her spiritualist pamphlets. Next to her lay her best friend, the whiskey bottle, a quarter empty already. She was as shameless with the liquor as with everything else, and I shuddered just to see it.

I shoved more food onto the men's empty plates. "Do you think you *deserve* treatment for your back?" I asked William.

"You cannot be angry forever, Elvira," he mewled. "The house is built—it's done."

"It was not what we agreed on," I muttered.

"No," he admitted with a sly look on his face, "but it's what you got."

"I should give you a taste of the frying pan next." I was so angry inside that I shook.

"No one will look for us," he said, though he had been nervous enough himself before they left. It had to be the prairie getting to him, the endless plains and the vast blue sky. It gave him a false sense of freedom.

"You betrayed me, William." I stated the fact.

"No." He shook his head. "I'm merely saving you from wasting your time on useless worries. We have left Pennsylvania behind, and Indiana, too. This time it'll be different—you'll see." He scooped some eggs onto his fork.

I glanced at my daughter upon the bed, eagerly turning the page. "You cannot outrun the devil, William."

The best you could hope for was to make her pay.

3.

HANSON

I REMEMBER WELL when the Benders first arrived in their misshapen wagon, rattling and swaying up the road to the trading station. It was a fine day in late fall, and I sat outside, busy with cleaning Mr. Brockman's rifle. Mr. Ern and Mr. Brockman were inside just then, but when they heard the rattle of the wagon, they both stepped outside, eager for business.

Mr. Brockman had grown a fine, dark mustache that year, which he often fondled and twisted between his fingers when eager to make an impression. He did that then, while standing outside the door and appraising the newcomers. He wore a leather vest over his shirt, and his pants were only a little dusty, which surely was a feat on the prairie. Mr. Ern looked old beside him, though the two of them were of the same age. His curly beard had some gray in it, and where Mr. Brockman had a ruddy complexion and was broad across the chest, Mr. Ern was of the scrawny sort and had a wizened look to his face. Mr. Brockman said that was just because Mr. Ern had had ague as a child.

The wagon rattled to a halt, and I looked up from my polishing to see a burly old man with a bit of white beard sitting next to a fine-looking younger man, whose lustrous mustache rivaled even Mr. Brockman's. The younger man held the reins, and a stiff little smile was plastered to his lips. The older man had a black felt hat perched upon his head, while the younger one sported one of straw. They both wore heavy checked coats powdered with prairie dust. The open deck of their wagon was filled with crates and trunks; there were some items wrapped in canvas, and a barrel of salted fish. The old man removed his hat when he saw Mr. Ern and Mr. Brockman.

To my great dismay, the old man rose to his feet and greeted my employers in German. The conversation continued in that language, too, rapid as a wildfire, which made it impossible for me to follow, even if I had picked up quite a few words over the years. Therefore, instead of listening in, I could only sit on the log with Mr. Brockman's rifle, minding my own business, while Mr. Ern and Mr. Brockman spoke to the men for quite some time. I noted how the older man was the most talkative by far.

When they were all done talking, the strangers left without buying as much as a sardine, which I found a little curious. We kept a trading station, after all.

"Who were they?" I asked Mr. Brockman when they had traveled a fair bit down the road and the wagon's rattle had died down.

"Father and son," Mr. Brockman said and wiped his hands on his thighs. "They said their name was Bender, and that they've taken the claim next to ours." He sat down beside me; the rifle rested on the wood between us. "They're thinking of setting up a homestead there. Maybe an inn, the old man said. His wife is supposedly quite the cook." Mr. Brockman's brow creased with worry. "I just hope their business won't interfere with ours."

My head at once flooded with images of an unruly flock of children my age, trampling across the prairie like a herd of longhorns. The thought sent a delightful shiver down my spine. "Will there be children there?"

Mr. Brockman shrugged. "They both have wives, that's for sure—or at least they spoke of the *women* arriving as soon as there's a house."

"They did not mention children, though?" The disappointment erupted as a sigh.

"No." He shook his head. "They only spoke of the women, and about the inn."

"We could probably do with some neighbors," I said, mostly to console Mr. Brockman, who seemed less than thrilled by the prospect of the inn, envisioning perhaps how the old man's wife would serve a stew that far outshone the jerked beef that we sold.

"Of course." His thin lips curled into a smile under the fine mustache. "I am sure it'll be good to have more people nearby. *If* they stay, that is. We'll see . . ." It was not so uncommon for people to stake a claim and then change their minds once the hardships began. We had seen that happen many times before, and especially with city people.

The Benders seemed to know what they were doing, though. It did not take many days before Mr. Ern and Mr. Brockman were talking about how a large shipment of timber had arrived and was presently stacked on their land, just a stone's throw from the trail.

"It makes sense if you want to keep an inn for weary travelers," Mr. Brockman said to me. "The closer to the road, the better."

When I climbed onto the barn roof, as was my habit, especially at night when the stars were out, I could soon see the beginnings of a structure, a skeletal framework, growing sturdier by the day. The two men already lived on the plot, sleeping in their wagon and cooking on an open fire. Many a time, I would see the smoke rising in the morning as the two of them brewed their coffee. I found them to be very diligent.

As the weeks passed by, I grew bolder and often walked over there in my few idle hours. At first, I would stand a little on the side, close to the trail, while watching the two men work. The old man was very spry and easily wielded the heavy hammer as he nailed sturdy boards to the wooden frame of what looked to become a sizable cabin—though not quite large enough to match the image of the inn that I had conjured in my mind. I had been picturing something akin to the hotel in Cherryvale, with its elegant salon and three stories, but this was clearly nothing like that, just a humble building on the prairie, like ours. I knew that such places were not uncommon; travelers were more than happy to pay a little to sleep under a roof, even if the accommodations were sparse. Lots of settlers along the road earned a little extra by opening their houses and renting out floor space, and I figured that the Benders meant to do just that.

The younger Bender was slower with the hammer than his father, but more precise. He would often squint and measure with his eyes before nailing a board in place. He sometimes fumbled with the nails, though, dropping them to the ground, and then he spent ages looking for them down in the dust, while the old man told him off in German.

That was how I ended up working for them.

Though they had doubtlessly seen me hanging around before, neither of them had ever paid me any attention. They were too intent on their work to care if a scrawny boy showed up as a spectator. On this day, however, the two of them both paused and looked at me before speaking to each other for a while. When they were done discussing, the older man went back to work, but the younger one turned to me.

"Hey, boy," he called. "Would you like some money?" He spoke in a very heavy accent. I thought this was a peculiar request but slowly nodded, as I would, in fact, like some money.

"What do I have to do?" I called back, taking a few steps toward them while still eyeing them with some suspicion.

"It is these . . ." The younger Bender held up one of the rough iron nails they used on the boards. "They fall on the ground. You can pick them up." He nodded with vigor as if to underline the request.

That certainly sounded easy enough, and I shrugged to say that I would do it.

It was not much, this job, but to me it was thrilling. I liked seeing how the house came about; how the walls were erected and the floor came in place, complete with a trapdoor for the cellar. In time, I helped with stirring the mortar for the chimney and carried bricks, moved boards twice my length and hoisted wooden shingles onto the roof, where John Bender waited with the hammer. Though I could not speak with them much, I still found the men good company, and I always liked being useful. In quiet moments by the fire, under the open sky, old William would read his Bible while John and I played silent games of cards. If I won, he often gave me a treat: a piece of dried fruit or brown sugar.

Then, after Christmas, came the women.

By the time they arrived, I had given up the hope of other children, as Mr. Brockman had figured out they had none. I was still curious about the women, though, as I saw mostly men, and would not mind to have a little soft kindness around to brighten my days. I did not remember my ma, but I always imagined that she had been like that: soft and kind—and just as funny as Pa had been. I was curious to see if I could understand them, as John spoke little English and Mr. Bender even less.

Mr. Brockman had struck a deal with them to stock their shelves with goods from the trading station, so the Benders could do a little shopkeeping as well as serving travelers stew. Mr. Ern had not been thrilled to learn that Mr. Brockman had made such a deal, and without consulting him at all. They had yelled and screamed at each other in German for half a night, but since the deal was already done, Mr. Ern could do little but accept it.

It was because of those shelves of groceries that I first met the other half of the Bender family. Having won the argument with Mr. Ern, Mr. Brockman called for me just a few days later and told me to take some sacks of coffee and dried apples down to the Benders to stock their shelves. John Bender had been there before for beef and tinned goods, but now they were to expand their range.

Mr. William Bender sat outside when I arrived, which seemed very cold to me. He had brought out a wooden chair and was sharpening a set of knives laid out on a piece of hide on the frozen ground before him. He had the whetstone in one hand, a knife in the other, and a small basin of water at his feet. The knives he had already done lay to the left and the dull and rusted ones to the right. He wore his black hat as always, but had traded his coat for a leather shirt. His beard was so long that it reached almost to his stomach; it was tangled, too, so had not seen a comb for some time. I wondered how his wife felt about that.

Mr. Bender nodded and smiled at me from deep within his

beard; his hands never ceased working, but kept dragging the stone across the blade, even as he looked away. I was mightily impressed by that. Mr. Bender then nodded to the house in a way that let me know I was to go in. I could tell there were makeshift curtains in the windows, and someone had made flowers from newspaper pages and placed them in a blue vase on the windowsill. Being very fond of such printings myself, I thought that to be an encouraging sign.

"Kate!" the old man hollered from behind me as I hitched the mule to the post by the door. "Kate!" he hollered again, as if to warn her of my coming. I wondered if Kate was the old man's wife, or if she was his daughter-in-law.

The door flew open before me and revealed that at least she was young. She was also tall, fair-skinned, and with gray eyes so pale that they almost seemed to look through you. Red hair tumbled like a nest of auburn snakes around her shoulders, so she must just have removed the pins that held it in place. I was not used to seeing women with their hair down and found myself quite mesmerized by the sight. Her dress, I noticed, was of a fine material, striped in blue and pink. It did not look much like prairie attire, but more like city garb.

The woman—Kate—laughed when she saw me. "It's just a boy!" she let out, as if amused by the fact, which led me to believe that she had been expecting, or hoping for, something else. Her pale eyes fell on me; her grin was still wide and her lips very red, so likely painted on. "We've seen less customers than we like." Her hands were at the back of her neck, twisting all the hair back in place. "I was hoping you were a traveling man, but you are not, are you?" Her gaze shifted to the mule. "You're just the boy from the trading station."

Before I had time to be offended that I was so little in her eyes, her lips split wide in a fresh smile. "John has told me all about you. He thinks you are quite the devil at cards." This, of course, had me blushing something fiercely, and it did not let up when she said, "Your name is Hanson, isn't it? I'm your new neighbor, Kate." She held out a plump, pale hand for me to shake. "Come inside and meet Ma," she continued when we had properly met. She swung open the door I had helped put in place.

I had meant to go back to the mule for the groceries before going inside, but Kate got ahold of my shirt and pulled me across the threshold. "We can get those parcels later," she said. "There's water in the bucket, so your mule won't dry out." As soon as the door had closed behind me, she spun on her heels and spoke to an elderly woman in a rocking chair. She had a skein of brown yarn in her lap and knitted very rapidly. It was a sock, from the looks of it.

"This fine young man has come with groceries for us, Ma," Kate said by way of introduction. "His name is Hanson, and John speaks very well of him. He helped them, you know, with the house." She then repeated, I assumed, all that she had just said in German.

"How do you do, ma'am," I croaked. I was surprised, I think, by the unexpected commotion my arrival had caused. Then I suddenly remembered my manners and had my frazzled straw hat off in no time at all. I strode across the floor with my hand outstretched. The old woman looked up at me with dark eyes and paused her knitting long enough to give my hand a light squeeze. Her thin lips curved in a slight smile, which made me realize that she was not as old as I had first thought.

"The card player, huh?" she said with a heavy German accent, and looked to Kate for confirmation. The latter nodded.

"The very one. John was *so* grateful for your help." Kate placed a hand on my shoulder and gave it a squeeze. "It's a good thing that you're here," she continued. "We do need to stock our shelves." She motioned to the rough-hewn shelving that now sprawled on the wall to the left of the entrance. The tins Mr. Bender had picked up were there—lots of tobacco and beans—but the boards were far from crammed at that point. They had built a store counter of sorts, simple and unpainted, but it would do, and on the floor lay a piece of board that was surely destined to be a sign, spelling out *Groceries* in neat black writing.

I saw that other improvements had been made to the house as well. The room was cut in half, for one, by a large piece of canvas nailed to a roof beam, so you could no longer see the bed. I figured it had been done to keep the business part of their establishment apart from the private quarters, although the room was so small in the first place that one had to wonder about the efficiency of the act. The table and chairs stood on the business side of the stiff curtain, and I figured that was where the stew was to be eaten, once the customers arrived.

Mrs. Bender, in the rocking chair, motioned to the table with one hand. "Will you have something to eat?" she asked me.

I shook my head, too embarrassed to say much, but Kate shooed me in the table's direction anyway. "Sit for a while," she urged me. "We go stir-crazy in here with only each other for company." As I found my seat, she went about rummaging on the shelves and put a half-empty tin can of crackers down before me. The lid clattered and spun on the tabletop. She followed up the offering with half a cup of thin coffee; the surface of the brew was riddled with grounds. I, of course, drank it anyway. I was nothing if not polite. My gaze darted to the paper flowers on the windowsill again as I chewed the gritty coffee grounds, and Kate, plopping down on the chair beside me, followed my gaze to the unruly bouquet.

"Well, there's not many wildflowers to find around here," she complained. "I had to liven the place up somehow."

"We do have some flowers in summer." I did not want her to think that these were barren lands. "I like the paper ones, though. I think they are beautiful. You must be very clever with your hands."

"Oh, thank you, sweet Hanson." Kate beamed at me. "Maybe you can show me those flowers sometime. The real ones, I mean."

I promptly blushed again and set about eating a cracker. Mrs. Bender chuckled at my expense.

"Tell me," said Kate, "are they all churchgoing folks around here?"

"Sure." I nodded. "Or if they don't go, it's not because they don't want to, but the road is too long or they have crops that need tending. They are God-fearing, though. We all are." Now that I had started talking, I was gathering steam and found the prospect of being the young Mrs. Bender's guide delightful.

"Say, are there people who talk to the spirits around here?" She promptly ruined my confidence again.

"What? No—I don't think so?" I sputtered.

"No? Like a medium, I mean. At a séance. Nothing like that?" Her gray eyes were hopeful when she looked at me.

I threw my gaze down at the floor, where, to my dismay, I could see several crumbs from my half-eaten cracker. I was a terrible eater. I could also see how the hem of Kate's pretty dress was gray with filth and yellow with dust. She ought to wear something simpler.

"You're thinking about spiritualists?" I asked her at last. When she gave an eager nod, I shook my head in turn. "Not that I know of," I said. "Are you in need of one?" I had of course read plenty about the spiritualists in the newspapers I collected in the barn. Some called them frauds and charlatans, while others were convinced that they did indeed communicate with the dead. I myself had not formed an opinion.

Kate laughed at my question. It did not seem sincere, though, but more like a performance. "Oh no," she said. "I speak with the spirits just fine myself and have no need of another conduit. I heal the sick, too, and at a lower cost than any medical doctor. I was thinking of taking on clients, you see; that's why I asked." She had lowered her voice and sent Mrs. Bender a furtive glance. "I just wanted to know about the competition." She winked with her left eye and fingered a cracker. "The inn is not booming with business at present, and we do need to earn if we want to keep living."

Kate's gray eyes bore into mine and made me feel a little dizzy. "One ought to share such gifts as mine, don't you think, Hanson?" Her gaze did not waver even a little.

"Sure," I agreed. I saw no reason why she should not.

"Ma disagrees with me at present, but I think she's foolish to do so." She sent the older woman another furtive glance. "You yourself have quite a few with you who would dearly want to speak." She raised her head and fixed her gaze somewhere above my right shoulder. "I see a woman there, yes . . . and a man, too. They must be your parents, don't you think?" I went cold, even though I knew she could have learned of my circumstances from Mr. Brockman. It still felt so strange that she was saying that, as if my parents were indeed standing there just behind my back, although I knew *I* would see nothing if I turned my head to look.

"Thank you so much, Mrs. Bender, but I have no money to talk to spirits," I muttered, feeling that I ought to make her aware of this predicament.

"Mrs. Bender?" She laughed again, in that same way as before that made me believe she was not truly laughing at all. "Oh, but I'm not my mother yet, Hanson—and surely not married."

"Oh," I uttered in surprise. "I thought John was your husband." To my own great dismay, I was blushing again.

"Oh no." Kate rolled her eyes. "John is my *brother*, not my husband."

"He is?" I had been so sure that Mr. Brockman had said that John was waiting for his wife.

"Yes. He is my brother through and through." Kate laughed again. She lowered her voice as if telling me a secret. "I would *never* marry the likes of him." In the rocking chair, Mrs. Bender snorted, so she did understand a little of what was being said. "If we cannot speak to the spirits, what *can* we do?" she mused next. "Oh, I have it!" Her eyes were at once wide open, and her hands were little birds again, dancing in the air. "Wait here," she said to me before rising from her chair and slipping behind the canvas curtain.

Mrs. Bender looked at me with a grim sort of smile, while her knitting needles still moved in her lap.

A moment later, Kate was back, carrying a bundle of cloth in her hand. When she plunked it down on the table, I could see that it was a blue scarf or shawl with countless silken tassels, wrapped around something small and rectangular. "Shall we see what your future holds, Hanson?" New stars seemed to have been lit in her eyes.

"Kate," warned the old woman.

"It's harmless," she shot back over her shoulder, and then added with a frown, "How am I to get better if I never get to practice?"

I did not much want to know what the future held, as I was too afraid of bad news. I knew all my dreams were in peril of re-maining just that, as I was a poor boy with very few prospects, but I also found it hard to refuse Kate Bender as she sat there before me, all sunshine again. "Please," she said. "Let me see your left hand."

I was a bit ashamed of showing it to her, as it was filthy, cal-loused, and damp with perspiration, but when she cupped her own hands and held them out like a cradle, I nevertheless placed it in hers and watched as a frown formed upon her brow. She looked at my hand from every angle, it seemed, and her lips moved silently, as if she was speaking to herself. When she was all through, she wanted to see my other hand.

"The left is what you are born with," she explained. "The right is what you do with it."

I all but held my breath when she lifted her gaze and was ready to give me the verdict. "You are a reading man," she said with some surprise; it sounded a bit like a question. I nodded with vigor, some-what impressed, all the while trying to remember if I had men-tioned my reading skills to John.

"You have great ambitions, too," she continued. Again, it sounded a bit like a question. "I did not expect to find that in a farm boy." She gave me a flash of a smile. "I think it must be . . ." She murmured to herself as she got to her feet and moved a bit closer to my chair. "Yes, it must be . . ." Her fingers were suddenly in my matted, dusty hair, working across my scalp. Whenever she found something interest-ing, her fingers dwelled there, kneading and touching. I dearly hoped she found no lice up there. "You are *very* bright," she said at last, "and that, my friend, will be your salvation."

Kate slumped down in the chair again and pulled the bundle of cloth closer. "Now we just have to see how your gifts can help you achieve those grand ambitions," she muttered.

When she opened the bundle by untying the knot I saw that there was a deck of cards in there, immensely fine and with gilded edges, though a little faded and frayed with use.

I wondered for a moment if she meant we were to play, but then she said, "These are special cards, Hanson. They are meant for telling the future, not to play for sugar with."

When she turned them over on top of the scarf, I could tell that all the picture cards were like beautiful paintings awash in colors. The ladies' white hair was piled high on top of their heads and set with pretty flowers, while the men wore theirs in neat ponytails.

Since I felt—or *hoped*—that Kate was right about my brightness and ambition, I was now most curious to see how my dreams could possibly come true and waited with baited breath as Kate first shuffled the cards herself, and then handed them to me and motioned for me to do the same. It was a little tricky, as they were smooth with use and threatened to jump out of my hands, but I did manage, somehow.

When the cards were back with her, Kate placed the deck facedown on the tasseled scarf and had me cut the stack twice. Then she gathered the cards back up again and started placing them, one by one, into a pattern that reminded me of a rose. That done, she took a deep breath, and then her hands flew across the tabletop, turning all the cards faceup.

I could tell that there were two queens down there on the table, and a lot of hearts—which I figured was good—but spades, too, which I knew to be unlucky.

"All right," she said at last. "This is what I see: the losses you have suffered early in your life will be made up by what you gain later. I see a very happy marriage for you, and at least five children, though one may be sickly."

I was a little stunned by this revelation, as I had not up until that point thought much of having a family at all.

"I can tell that letters are your first love, though, not your wife, and that it's by those that you will make your fortune." She glanced up at me, and I reddened, but not from embarrassment at all. In my chest, my heart had started thumping out a wild rhythm—could it be that I would become a newspaperman? It was what I wanted more than anything else.

"Yes," Kate said, as if having come to a decision or answering my thoughts. "Your ambitions will come to fruition—not this year, and maybe not the next one either—but early in your life, and it's by the pen and the pen alone that you shall thrive."

"But . . . how do I do that?" I whispered, as my voice had suddenly failed me.

"I suppose you must go to the city," said Kate. "There's poor soil for words out here. Pa says we'll have to grow corn."

I laughed a little at that, faint and shivering.

"Your wife is light of hair," Kate added as an afterthought, "and your first child will be a son."

I let out my breath in a deep sigh. Mrs. Bender in the rocking chair chortled.

"How did I do?" Kate beamed at me, eager for praise, it seemed.

"Not so bad," I blurted out, my pulse still thumping in my throat.

"Wonderful." She gave a satisfied smile and rose to her feet. "I have a gift for you to remember your wondrous future by." I watched as she crossed the floor to the windowsill and picked one of the newspaper flowers out of the vase. "Here," she said when she came back, holding the flower out to me. "Keep it close to you always, Hanson," she instructed. "This little thing is your lucky charm!"

4.

KATE

SUMMER HAD ARRIVED and the weather was scorching. The sun beat down and left us sluggish and slow; the earth dried out and the livestock languished. The creek had run almost dry, and I could no longer rinse my clothes. We tried to stay out of the sun, but the house became too crowded with all of us in there, and so I often fled to the barn, giving some excuse just to lie about and dream of better times to come. It was a trite space, but the walls smelled new; the reek of dung had not yet become deeply ingrained. The horses were outside, and so there was only the cow and myself in there, suffering the heat.

When I looked out through the open door, I could see the dusty air shimmer. When I closed my eyes, I saw the stage, hung with curtains of velvet. I saw myself up there, well-dressed in silk and lace, speaking in the voices of the otherworld. I saw my hair piled high on my head and the black fur stole that would snake about my

shoulders. On my chest rested a brooch encrusted with black
jewels—a present from a grateful patron.

The wondrous medium, Miss Katie Bender.

I knew that I could do it, and Ma did, too; that was why she kept
me around, waiting for me to flourish. Sadly, it was also the very
reason why she insisted on me being hidden away, lest I fall prey to
the law. She was overly cautious, though. I did not think anyone out
here would recognize us, or even think that we had anything to do
with those deaths. A new name, that was all it took in a land filled
with immigrants, where people moved around all the time. I felt
certain that was why William had wanted us to go west, just because it was so hard to keep track. He saw opportunities where Ma
was blinded by fear. She wanted to keep me as a secret jewel, something to take out when she deemed it was safe, but I had no patience
to wait. I would do what I had to in order to have my way, sooner
rather than later.

Then I would pay Ma back and be free of her.

I would never forget her words when I had threatened to stay
behind in Louisville. "You *owe* me, Kate, you do—and either you let
me keep you safe, or I'll make sure that you're not!"

"What is that supposed to mean?" I had asked her.

"Oh, you think yourself so clever all the time, but if you don't
come to Kansas with me, the law will soon find you!"

I did not even have to ask if it meant that she would give me up,
as I knew it did.

I also knew that my mother was not one to bother with idle
threats.

I suppose I should be flattered that she believed in me enough to
think that I truly could give her back all that she had lost: farm and
livestock, lush woods and mountain skies . . . Small things, I

thought, but then, she had always had humble aspirations. I, however—I wanted it all: the silk, the lace, the fur stole . . . my likeness rendered on newspaper pages.

It would not be so hard to achieve. Women far more foolish than I had left their stoves and needlepoint behind to become celebrated mediums. All it took was some confidence and a knowledge of man—things I had in abundance. The prairie was not the best place for such an endeavor, however, scarcely populated and out of the way, but I would surely try to make a start. Mayhap it could be my story to tell: how my gifts had grown like an unblemished rose out of the harsh prairie soil. My patrons would like that for sure.

Again, I saw it so vividly: the stage and the velvet curtains, the black jewels glimmering on my chest, the enraptured audience before me, seated below the glittering chandeliers. They were all applauding me, even rising from their seats to express their awe. I saw diamonds flashing and sapphires gleaming upon their thick satin gloves.

When I opened my eyes, the barn was still there.

I turned my head toward the sound that had pulled me out of my reverie. John stood in the door, staring at me as I lay there slumped like a sack of potatoes. "What are you up to, hiding out here?"

"Nothing much," I admitted. "I'm *dying* from the heat."

"Ma is looking for you." He shuffled his feet. His hands were buried deep in his pockets. "She thought you might have gone to the trading station." His lips below the drooping mustache twisted into something ugly.

"What would I go there for?" I teased him, and stretched one leg in the air, waving my toes around. I wore nothing but a blue-flowered calico dress, but even that felt like too much in the heat.

"That was what *I* asked." His grimace turned into a satisfied grin. "Whatever would you go *there* for, if not to buy some candy?" He chuckled to himself as he came inside, fumbling with the hayfork by the door.

"They might have something cool, though, in that icehouse they have." I rolled over to my stomach to follow him with my gaze as he wandered farther into the barn.

"Pa says you are *making eyes* at Mr. Brockman." He meant it as a question.

"I'm not 'making eyes' at anyone," I scoffed. "Rather it's *he* who's sniffing up my skirts."

"As long as he's just sniffing." John wanted some reassurance, although he knew he would never get that from me.

"Mr. Brockman is a fine man," I teased him, "and I'd be a fool to ignore his advances." I grinned. "He might have money, too, and something to offer a wife."

"You said you wouldn't marry—" His eyes went wide with fear. "You said that it was *a cruelty* to tie yourself to one man."

"Maybe I was drunk then—or maybe I have changed my mind." I got up from the hay and brushed debris off my dress.

John's lips disappeared into a thin line of fury. "Pa would be angry if you did something to ruin his business." He spat out an idle threat.

"Ma would be furious, too." I chuckled. "She would spend all her time on her knees, praying for the poor man's life." And her mountain farm, too, for sure.

"I would not mind it if you cut him." John's eyes went dark and jealous. He lifted the hayfork up from the floor and slammed it back down so the tines sank into the hard-packed soil. It neither frightened nor impressed me.

"I thought we were done with bloodletting," I said. "Or didn't you *swear* to Ma that the Vandles were the last?"

"Things do change."

"Yes, they do." I lifted my chin. "Maybe I want to ride Brockman now—"

"Stop teasing me like that!" he bellowed and strode across the floor, still fuming. His face had become all red. "*I* would marry you, you know that." His voice cracked. "I would marry you in a heartbeat, Kate. I'm mad for you!"

I could not help but snigger at him as he stood there before me, all worked up. "Don't you remember what happened to the last man who said that?" Even as I said it, I recalled the blood, thick and warm, coating my hand.

"He was a fool," John said with a huff.

"*All* men are fools," said I.

"But what about the darkness, Kate?" His eyes became soft and pleading. "You said I was the only one you could talk to about what happened to Zimmerman—about how it made you feel—"

"Well, I'm done talking about it." I spoke with distaste and looked away; my gaze landed on the shovels stacked in the corner. "It's behind us now; it's a bright new dawning. I'm about to become a medium for sure and have no time for it—"

"You cannot quench a thing like that," he insisted. "You said so yourself, that you could not *help* what happened with him." John stood so close to me that I could smell the sour odor of his skin.

"That was before," I muttered. The darkness had no place in the new world I envisioned: the stage and brooch, a drawing of my face in a newspaper . . .

"So you never think about the blood anymore?" He said it just to challenge me, and I hated that it worked.

"No," I said, though I lied. "I don't think about it anymore, and neither should you, John. I reckon I won't think of it again *at all*, if only I have my way." I made an effort to imagine the stage again, the audience and the sparkling chandelier.

John stepped even closer than before, so close that I could feel his breath upon my face. "To have a man's life in your hands," he whispered. "His blood pouring out like a red, warm river . . ." He was parroting my words from not so long ago.

"I was very angry then." I spoke in a hoarse voice.

"You're still angry, Kate." He spoke quietly into my ear. "And I'm the only one you can share those red thoughts with—"

"It was all just youthful foolishness." My gaze flitted to the tips of his shoes. "Ma is right; I'm too precious to hang."

John sniggered. It was an ugly sound. "But you still think of it, though. I can tell that you do. You still dream of cutting another—"

"I'll cut *you* if you don't shut your mouth," I snapped. Without pausing to think, I dipped my hand down to John's belt and pulled up his well-honed knife. His sniggering stopped when I had the blade against his throat. "We won't speak of Emil Zimmerman again," I said, sneering.

John had paled before me; I saw fear flicker in his eyes. "You— you won't cut me," he stuttered. With every word, I pressed the knife deeper into his skin. I could not help but watch intently; the pulse throbbing and his Adam's apple bobbing under the thin skin; the metal of knife that marked the thin line between blossoming life and nothingness.

"Don't tempt the darkness," I muttered.

We both stood thus, tense and waiting for what felt like a very long while. My jaw was clenched and my hand that held the knife never wavered. "We take care of our own," he muttered at last. It was one of Ma's favorite sayings, and to his credit, it worked. My eyes snapped away from his throat and landed on his face, on the frightened look in his eyes.

"The rest can fend for themselves." I completed the sentence and lowered the knife. "We won't speak of the darkness again," I repeated, and I put the blade back in the sheath on his belt.

The past had no place in the future.

5.

ELVIRA

WE HAD NOT been long in our new home before Kate began skipping her chores to go up to the trading station to visit Mr. Brockman. By high summer, this happened several times a week and caused William some concern, as he worried that Kate would create a rift between our households by making promises she would not keep. I, however, thought he ought to be worrying about his son instead. I did not like the dark look of him whenever another man came close to Kate.

I just did not see the new dalliance evolving beyond mere flirting, though. Brockman seemed to me such a reasonable man—but maybe that was my failing as a mother. I did not want to see just how dangerous my girl could be, even if she had caused us terrible trouble before. It was nearly midsummer before I finally saw how she had turned the man's head.

The day had started out pleasant enough. A couple of gentlemen on their way to Independence had stopped by the inn and paid handsomely for breakfast. We were all happy to see them, as this new business endeavor had yet to become the gold mine that William had promised me, and we often saw whole days go by without customers. Kate was outside with the travelers in the yard, happy as a ray of sunshine, looking healthy as milk and apples in her blue-flowered calico dress. Her red hair was up at the neck but had already escaped its confines, and tendrils slick as snakes fell down her back.

I watched from the window as she had the men seated outside on the ground and went between them with hot coffee, fresh biscuits, and crisp golden bacon. She offered to read their fortunes, too, grasping playfully for their hands, but apparently they refused. She laughed a lot; they laughed, too, and looked up at her with that special shine in their eyes that Kate so often coaxed forth in men, besotted and bewitched. The devil walked so close in her shadow that I would not have been surprised to see a glimpse of a cloven hoof under the hem of her skirt. It was her curse, that beauty, but perhaps, when it was safe, it could also become my salvation.

Behind her, by the barn, John skulked, pacing back and forth, half-heartedly moving some buckets around on the ground. He had pulled down his hat, but I could still see how his dark eyes followed the goings-on in the yard. He looked quite the thundercloud on an otherwise fine morning. Not for the first time, I found myself wishing that Kate would just cut the boy loose and not string him along like an adoring puppy.

I felt for my stepson, I truly did, and his infatuation gave me a bad feeling. I had spent the early-morning hours reading in my book—the special one I kept hidden in the double bottom of my trunk—hoping to find a cure for his affliction. If only I could curb his ardor, I figured, life would be easier for all of us. It was, however, hard to find something that could be given in secrecy, and I felt certain that he would refuse my help if offered. I needed something that would have his desire curdle like spoiled milk, or shrink and toughen like a dried peach.

So far, I had not found it.

When the men in the yard paid and left, I think both John and I let out our breaths.

Kate's good mood had not diminished by the time we walked up the road, headed for the trading station. She always blossomed for a while after having received attention. We both had empty baskets, which we hoped to have filled with eggs, mackerel, and honey upon our return, things that were so far not to be found on our own meager grocery shelves. We only had the two horses and the cow to help us get by, and William would not splurge on more livestock—not even a few scrawny chickens—having spent all we had on the house.

The trading station was not much, but quite the castle compared to our own humble home. The house was squat and weather-beaten, with a roof that sagged a little. Sour, dark smoke poured from the chimney, drifting on the breeze. The porch was crowded with barrels and wooden boxes; a few pelts hung from wooden pegs set in the timbered wall, just below the sign that spelled out the business's purpose. There was a log for sitting out there, too, placed by the wall, next to a hitching post and a watering trough. The boy, Hanson, was outside before the barn, readying a horse with a fine-looking saddle. When he saw us coming, he paused his work to lift one hand in greeting. Kate lifted her hand in turn to give him a cheery wave.

The trading station was not large, but at least there was a proper wall with a door separating the store from Mr. Brockman's and Mr.

Ern's sleeping quarters. The round-bellied stove stood in the middle of the floor, crackling with fire, among barrels filled with brooms, brand-new butter churns, and even a few straight-backed chairs for sale. The large counter was heaped with fabric, colorful gingham and calico; from the ceiling hung cloth-wrapped hams, black pots, and kerosene lamps. The walls were adorned with metal signs, most of them advertising fine tobacco. The shelves at this establishment were as crammed as ours were gap-toothed and sparse: coffee, tea, whiskey, vinegar, pieces of earthenware, and striped candy in glass jars. A narrow table was set especially to house heaps of lustrous pelts.

Mr. Brockman and Mr. Ern were both there, dressed in vests and shirts; Mr. Ern's golden spectacles rested on his nose. He had made no secret of his misgivings in regard to William's agreement with Mr. Brockman, and I could see as soon as we entered the store how his lips tightened and his gaze hardened. He looked at my daughter as if she was something foul, a piece of dirt or dog shit, dragged onto his clean-swept floors.

Mr. Brockman, on the other hand, lit up like a dry wick on a candle, and a soft, rosy glow settled on his cheeks. He was nothing but smiles and shiny eyes when he came out from behind the counter to greet us.

"Kate." He held out his arms as if wanting to embrace her but stopped short of that, of course. "Mrs. Bender." He turned to me, still smiling. "How is Mr. Bender? How is John?" Over his shoulder, I could see Mr. Ern roll his eyes.

"Good, good," I muttered, not feeling quite as cheery myself.

"What a lucky day for you to come visit." Mr. Brockman spoke eagerly. "Mrs. Tanner was just here with some cake—loveliest sort! Come, have a taste—and some whiskey to go with it!" He waved us farther inside, happy as a pup with a fresh bone, and Kate followed him, laughing all the way. The treat was there on the counter: a fragrant brick of marble cake upon a piece of muslin. Mr. Brockman cut it with a blackened knife and handed out pieces to Kate and me, but not to Mr. Ern, as he had left through the back, apparently not in the mood for a treat.

Kate took the soft cake and bit into it. She closed her eyes to express her enjoyment. "It's marvelous, Rudolph," she let him know. "Mrs. Tanner sure has my approval."

I nibbled on a piece myself, feeling a little guilty. Mrs. Tanner, a widow, had surely not been traveling to this den of bachelors with her scrumptious cake in the hopes that Mr. Brockman would share it with my Kate, and my heart bled a little for the unhappy widow, even as I ate the spicy treat, flavored with cinnamon and cloves.

Mr. Brockman poured whiskey in green-tinted glasses and passed them out. It turned out that he was right; the smoky liquor went well with the cake.

"Oh, this is glorious," Kate exclaimed. "Isn't it, Ma? Just glorious! You are spoiling us, Rudolph, and it's only a Tuesday—nothing special about it." She quite shamelessly traipsed behind the counter and sat herself down on a barrel there. The effortlessness of it told me clearly that she had been behind there many times before.

"Any day is a special day when I have such charming company." Mr. Brockman flirted and lifted his glass to Kate, not even sparing another glance for me, the crone stranded by the oven. "We should make this a party," Mr. Brockman said, "a celebration of the magnificent luck that brought a creature such as yourself to these parts."

"Yes, it does seem unlikely." Kate sent me a pointed look. "It sure must have been a funny twist of fate that brought me here." With my inner eyes, I saw a bloodied hand. The ghost scent of burned flesh teased my nostrils and made me abandon what was left of the cake.

"Mayhap your supple feet were never meant to walk on cobble-stones, but rather on prairie soil," Mr. Brockman crooned.

"Oh, but the cobblestones would sure miss me, then." She continued spouting nonsense for her audience of one. I cleared my throat, wanting to say something about the purchases we came to make, but neither one of them even heard me.

"Mayhap you are destined to bring some elegance to these parts," he flattered her. "That sure is something to celebrate!"

I swallowed my whiskey and thought to myself that John was perhaps not the only one who needed help to curb a worrisome ardor. Looking at Mr. Brockman standing there so radiant and happy, I felt my belly lurch with worry. The poor man did not know how my Kate could be.

Shortly after, the two of them started singing some lighthearted German folk songs. Kate drummed out the rhythm with her heels on the barrel, the half-eaten cake in one hand and Mr. Brockman's fingers in the other. She lifted her chin to expose her white throat, and her lips were deep red with young blood. Mr. Brockman, poor soul, blushed like a youngster before her as the song between them rose.

I went outside. The bell above the door chimed merrily, but I do not think either of them even noticed me going. I found Mr. Ern sitting on the log, nursing an ill-smelling pipe, and sat down next to him with my still-empty basket perched upon my lap. We could still hear them singing in there, only interrupted by bouts of unbridled laughter.

Mr. Ern picked up a bottle from the ground, tipped it into his mouth, and then passed it on to me. I could tell from the smell that it was gin. The bitter taste felt like salvation.

"She is just bored," I told the man beside me, the air, and myself. "She is not usually this raucous," I lied. "If only she had something useful to do with her time—"

"She would be bored here as well," Mr. Ern interrupted me. "If he had his way, they would both be incredibly unhappy. Not at first, perhaps, but later."

I did not get his meaning at first, and then when I did, I felt cold all over. "It surely won't come to that," I said, mostly to reassure myself. "It will pass, like a flu."

"A man in love is a dangerous thing—utterly witless," sounded Mr. Ern. His face creased with worry and he clutched the gin bottle tightly. I found that I liked him a little better than before. "Should they marry, my days here are numbered. I will *not* stay to witness it all fall apart."

"Surely it's not that serious—"

"Ever since she started visiting, he can speak of little else."

"She is a willful thing," I told him, "but she isn't stupid. She'll grow tired of him before long." I dearly hoped it was the truth.

"I just hope there is something left of him to salvage when that day arrives."

"He's a grown man and ought to be able to guard his heart." That much, of course, was true, but my Kate could be hard to resist for a man.

"Perhaps your daughter has *taken* that skill from him." Mr. Ern mirrored my thoughts.

I got a sinking feeling inside. It reminded me too much of Pennsylvania. "My daughter is no witch, Mr. Ern," I scolded the merchant and pried the gin from his hands. "Shame on you for saying such a thing."

"Well." He arched his eyebrows. "She is *something*—"

"You should not speak so ill of someone you hardly know. It's *not* becoming, Mr. Ern." Kate was for me to worry about, not some stranger on a trading station.

My stern words seemed to have rattled him a little. "My apologies, Mrs. Bender. You are of course right. I spoke out of turn. I just worry for my friend."

"I'll talk to her," I said, if only to calm his heart a little. Kate rarely listened to my advice.

"I appreciate that," said the man beside me, and rose to his feet. I noticed that the singing had died down in there. "If you would follow me back inside, we can see about your purchases."

I nodded and joined him, a little fearful of what we would find behind the door, but everything looked calm and peaceful when we entered. Kate was perusing the fabrics, and Mr. Brockman was polishing the brass of a lamp.

"There you are, Ma," Kate said when she saw me. "We better get to it. We don't have all day."

When we finally walked back toward the farm, both of us with heavy baskets, I turned to her and said, "You should stay away from that man."

"Ma? What is this? I thought you had better sense than to agree with Pa—"

"We're not here for your amusement; we're here to hide."

"Well, you don't want me to work, so what am I to do? I cannot spend all my time at home with *you*."

"Oh, you'll work," I told her, "just not yet. When it's all died down—when it's all forgotten, then you can work all you want; use all your clever tricks, but not yet, and not on our neighbor. It won't amount to anything but pain and despair."

"I won't cut Mr. Brockman, Ma." Her voice had gone quite cold.

"Well, you did not plan on cutting Mr. Zimmerman either, but here we are, and the Vandles—"

"I had nothing to do with that—"

"So you say." I did not believe her for a moment.

"Mr. Zimmerman called me a whore," she muttered, petulant as a child.

"So you say," I repeated with a snort, "but that is hardly a good reason to take someone's life."

"I thought it was," she replied, sounding haughty all of a sudden. Her pretty face had twisted up in a sour expression. Our feet beside one another on the road kicked up little clouds of dust. We were walking at a brisk pace, each of us annoyed with the other.

"What if Mr. Brockman should happen to offend you? What then, Kate?"

"Well, I'm hardly a child anymore. I'm sure I can stay my hand." She snorted.

"It's only been three years. I don't think you have learned any lessons at all."

"Well, Mr. Brockman would never treat me like Emil Zimmerman did." She dismissed my worries offhandedly. I gave a deep sigh, pondering if I was to continue the argument or not. It seemed like such a waste of time.

"Don't forget that you owe me," I said. "I won't have you hanging before your debt is paid in full."

"Not to worry, Ma." Her voice was brittle and bitter. She had turned her head away from me. "How could I *ever* forget?"

6.

KATE

THE YEARS HAD not been kind to Ma, or so she would have you believe. Four husbands in and nothing to show for it, just as the ravages of time made her options fewer. She had buried five children and I was the last, begotten by husband number two, who had lived out his sorry days behind bars.

She had been a simple woman once, she said, with simple aspirations. She had arrived in this country as a young woman, yearning for land to call her own, but somehow never made it farther than New York. My childhood was spent in cramped tenement buildings and cold rooms, pilfering goods and pickpocketing, trying the best that I could to make sure we all survived.

Then along came William, with his farm in Pennsylvania. Ma had met him as he visited New York to attend the funeral of an old friend, and to claim a team of horses that the deceased had left him in his will. He and Ma had met in church, and he surely seemed a salvation to her after years of hopeless missteps and failures.

Once they were married, we left the city to live with him, and there was no denying that his place was a beauty, situated high up on a rocky hill and surrounded by dense, lush woods. The house was no castle but far better than what we were used to, with logged walls and a loft, where I slept all alone on a cot. The cattle in the barn were fat and healthy, the pig was a happy giant in the sty, the horses' coats gleamed with health, and the spatter of chickens about the yard left large brown eggs for us to find. The woods were rife with game as well, and William and John were apt hunters. To add to this already abundant supply, there were plenty of fish in the river. I had never eaten so much or so well in my life.

At first, the surrounding farmers looked upon us newcomers with scorn. Neither Ma nor I understood the local dialect, and it was clear to all that we barely knew what was the front or the back of a cow. I was used to going my own way, though, and did not think it so bad at the time if people showed a little apprehension. Perhaps I should have. It might have served me well to be better prepared when it all came to a boil.

In the beginning, it was good, though, and Ma flourished. She had the life she had been yearning for at last. She even made a friend, a midwife like herself, and under her patronage, she was able to start peddling cures to the locals. I remember her from that time as happy and bustling, with a ruddy glow about her cheeks.

When she lost it again, because of what I did, I reckon it was only natural that something in *her* broke as well. She would never forgive me for losing that farm, and she meant to have me pay. Another farm just like it, hidden away on some lush mountain, with livestock and a clean river, was what I was to deliver, as soon as Ma deemed it was safe. She, too, had noticed as we fled Pennsylvania, how people flocked to séances, how the mediums were celebrated,

and how their performances rivaled even those of the most celebrated actresses, and she, too, knew that I could be just as good as
them. After all, there was nothing special about those women; they
were just as we were, only white-limbed and coifed, styled in the
latest fashions.

We both knew that I was an excellent performer. Back in New
York, she herself had helped me create an act of confidence where I
pretended to be a girl of some means, confused and lost. Gentlemen
on the streets will always come to such a creature's aid, if only to
guide them to the nearest church, not noticing until later how
their pockets are empty. A few times, they even brought me to their
homes, where I breakfasted with their wives and played with their
toddlers. When they eventually alerted the authorities about the
lost girl they had found, I made sure to be long gone, preferably
with some of their silver. It was Ma who sewed my lovely frocks
from pilfered silks and velvet, but it was I who learned how to speak
and act in order to perfect the ruse. It had kept us fed and clothed
for a while.

As she herself grew older and more tired by the day, she knew
that I was her best option if she was ever to achieve her humble goal
again. With what little we had, there would be no new farm of an
equal size unless I could make it happen. I was not opposed to it
either, if only to have her gone from my life, as I did not much like
her threatening me, but it was the waiting I could not endure. I
thought her overly cautious—surely no one would look for us in
Kansas. The Vandles had died in Indiana, and Emil Zimmerman
had drawn his last breath in Pennsylvania, so surely the law would
not think to look for us here.

I knew that Pa agreed with me, but still Ma held fast. "Not yet,"
she said. "Not yet," whenever I spoke of taking to the stage or oth-

erwise making myself noticed. I was bored out of my wits, eager for my new life to begin, so the dalliance with Brockman was only to be expected.

A few days after we had been to the trading station together, I told her so over dinner.

"If you want me to stay away from Brockman, you must let me work."

John looked alert at once; Ma looked appalled; only Pa seemed calmly interested, scooping up stew with a piece of bread.

"It's not safe—" she started saying before I interrupted.

"It only makes sense to let me work. We make a pittance here and barely get by. *One of us* ought to earn."

"Oh, but I make a little something," she muttered, while heaping her plate anew. She had taken to selling cures out the door, salves and suchlike, for udders mostly.

"That's hardly enough." I snorted. "It's bad enough that you make me live out here, but I *won't* live in squalor," I argued. "I don't have to take to the stage—not at once—and I'll be careful who I befriend, but I must acquaint myself with the locals in Cherryvale. You know that it only makes sense." My heart had stepped up its pace in my chest. Surely she would not threaten to give me up—not now, not here, while we shared the same roof. She might as well be tattling on herself . . .

"Do I?" Ma smirked and arched an eyebrow, but Pa, to her left, nodded, while his jaws worked relentlessly, chewing the stringy meat.

"I could offer only private sittings at first," I said. "It will take time to build a name for myself; they won't write about me in the newspapers just yet."

Ma drew a deep breath. "You know nothing about keeping yourself safe! You are reckless, foolish, and the reason why we are *in* this pickle—"

"But you need me," I said with as much calm as I could muster. "How else are you to ever escape this sorry life? None of you are young anymore, and if I go and marry Brockman, you have nothing at all."

A sound like a pig being slaughtered rose to my right. It was John, of course, venting his displeasure. I gave him a dark look and told him to be quiet.

"But, Kate—" he whined.

"Not now!" I barked.

"But surely you won't—"

"Oh, shut your mouth!"

Ma started laughing on the other side of the table. She lifted her glass, filled to the brim with fermented cider, and drank it all down. "Are you threatening me, Miss Kate?" she asked when she was quite done. "Maybe I'll whisper some words in the groom's ear, then." An ugly smirk had appeared on her lips.

"I'll tell him you are mad." I smirked right back at her. "Half the county thinks so already, what with your potions and your cures . . ."

Ma laughed again; dry and brittle. "As if speaking to the dead is any better—"

"At least it lends a certain elegance to the proceedings," I argued. My hand shook but a little when I poured the cider from the bottle. "People pay good money to be in the company of angels."

"Maybe I'll whisper some well-chosen words to someone else, then, someone in authority." Her eyes narrowed as she threatened me, but I only shook my head.

"You won't do that while you're all still living here, next door to the trading station—and where else are you to go? You have no means for another hasty departure." I only spoke the truth as it was. Her threats might have worked when it was Louisville I wanted, as then a well-placed tip might have seen me arrested while she herself would be long gone—but now we were trapped here together, and I was not so easily spooked. I knew well how far she would go to save her own hide.

"It might not be so bad, Elvira." Pa came to my aid. "It's as she says: she can start out small. We would not want to silence the angels." As much as Ma had tried, she could not make Pa discard his belief in me and yet keep his faith in her cures. It was all the same to him. Deeply religious all his life, he went blind when it came to spiritual matters, gobbling it all up, no matter how outrageous. In better times, Ma and I had laughed about it behind his back, but the time for such amusements was long over. We were at war now, Ma and I.

"What about the inn?" she asked him, slicing a piece of potato in two with her knife. "What are we to do about the guests if Kate is out 'acquainting' herself?" She was thinking of the language, of course. Most of the travelers spoke only English.

"I'm sure you'll manage," I said tersely. "It's not as if they are flocking to our door—"

"What do the angels say?" Pa asked. His blue eyes looked watery in the smoke-infested air.

"Oh, the angels have told me to start working for some time now," I replied, adding some warmth to my voice. "It's certainly what *they* want."

"The *angels* . . ." Ma snorted, but I think the threat about marrying had gotten under her skin. I would be out of her clutches then, and she could not have that. "Only private sitters," she said, "and I won't have you flaunting yourself." She wet her lips nervously with the tip of her tongue.

"The money will be good," I offered as a final argument. The sour cider suddenly tasted sweeter in my mouth.

"We surely need some of that," Pa muttered, just as Ma relented with a sigh.

7.

KATE

THE HOTEL IN Cherryvale was a brown brick building with ornate white window frames that made me think of gingerbread houses. The inside was grand enough for such a small town, with flowered wallpapers in green and pink, and furniture of polished oak. There were only three stories, with twelve rooms in all, but the hotel was rarely full. Downstairs was a kitchen, a small dining area, and a salon where the guests could read newspapers in front of a fire. In my new position as a maid, I arrived there every morning at dawn, with my hair pinned high and my eyes red from lack of sleeping.

John drove me most days, bleary-eyed and surly himself, while I sat next to him in the wagon, finding my courage in a bottle. It seemed I could not find it in me to go through the workday sober. It was better for all of us—employees and guests alike—if my mood was a little mellow from drinking. Besides, the liquor made it easier to speak in spirit voices, which was the point of the whole affair. I meant to build myself a reputation as a "prairie medium"—the very first of its kind—but in order to do so, I needed to advert myself through word of mouth and had decided that the hotel would be the best place to start. There was no other place in town where I could meet as many potential clients.

Sadly, though, I had learned early on that I was not the only one peddling elusive voices.

"Julie Hassler comes here next month," my new associate, Laura, said one morning while shaking out a pillow. She was a plump girl with big blue eyes, and skilled, too, in the things I was not, like dusting and airing heavy mattresses. I was lucky to be paired with her in my new occupation, as she rarely noticed if my going was slow, if my breath smelled of liquor, or if my scrubbing sometimes left much to be desired.

"Who is Julie Hassler?" I asked while half-heartedly beating a pillow of my own.

Laura's eyes widened. Clearly, I was supposed to know the name. "Oh, but she is *so* gifted, Kate. She is the best there is! Mr. Fisher has been trying to get her for years, and her calendar is already full upon arrival."

"So she is a medium?" I could not help it if my voice revealed some disgruntlement.

A concerned look settled on Laura's features. "Oh, not to worry, Kate. I'm sure many people will come to see you, too, in time. It's just that we have heard of Miss Julie for years and have been looking so forward to this—"

"I don't care that you want to see Miss Julie. I would very much like to see her myself." I gave as much of a smile as I could muster. It just will not do to let people see the maggots that crawl inside you. "It's always useful to meet another with the same gifts as one-self." If I sounded a little strained, I hoped Laura would blame it on the task we were performing, turning the large horsehair mattress over in the brass bed. "For us who can see beyond the veil, it's such a relief to discuss with another who knows how it is. It can be hard on the soul," I told my wide-eyed companion. "It's not for the faint of heart."

"Oh, but you should come with me to meet her! She is to give a séance at Mr. Fisher's home on Sunday. I'm sure I can secure you an invite. I'll just tell Mr. Fisher that you work with me." She gave me a bright smile, so very happy with herself.

This was not what I had wanted. I had even been a smidge dis-mayed to learn that there *was* a small group of spiritualists residing in Cherryvale. Not only had they formed a tiny circle with the re-tired lawyer Mr. Fisher at the helm, but they had also assembled a list of celebrated mediums that they dearly longed to meet. What-ever hopes I had harbored of being a godsend, the one to bring spiritualism to this town, had been severely squashed and disman-tled ever since I met Laura. I had been hoping to dazzle and charm with the novelty as my strongest weapon but had since been forced to realize that I would not be anyone's "first" in Cherryvale. The believers had all met mediums before—and mediums with estab-lished names, no less.

Still, I knew that in order to get anywhere with any of my plans, I had to get into their midst.

"That would be wonderful, Laura. But only if it isn't any trou-ble," I chirped, ignoring the bile that rose in my throat.

"No trouble at all." She gently grasped at the medallion that rested on her chest, displaying a lock of braided gray hair. "I'm hoping for a message from Ma," she said. "Maybe Miss Julie can find her."

"If not," I said, shaking out a sheet, "you can come to me, and we'll sort it out."

She gave me a look tainted with doubt, and I could hardly blame her for that. The mediums she so admired did not change sheets or empty night pots. "I've just had some bad luck, that's all, but I swear to you that I had quite the name before."

"Couldn't the spirits have warned you, and saved you from that bad luck?" My head snapped up and I examined Laura's face for signs of malice, but there were none. Her eyes were just as innocent as before, and she had not meant any harm by her question. I busied myself with the sheet again.

"Oh, they did, of course, and I warned Pa not to invest in that spinning mill, but he did it anyway—and so did I, thinking that perhaps the spirits were wrong. That's what you get, I suppose, for trusting man over spirit." I was quite proud of myself for inventing that failed investment; it would explain why we were living so poorly. "It's hard to see one's own fate," I added. "The sight too often gets clouded with all sorts of hopes and desires."

"Maybe Miss Julie has heard of you already." Laura gave me a reassuring smile, but I, of course, knew that Miss Julie had done nothing of the sort.

"She at least ought to recognize a kindred soul." And if she did not, I would make it so. The more I thought about it, the better it seemed. In fact, it was just what I needed to set myself up: an endorsement from someone the circle already admired.

When Laura and I were not turning down beds, we scrubbed floors, beat carpets, or worked in the kitchen. I hated all of it, but that was all right; I did not plan on staying there for long—just until I could get myself established. Laura had been lucky for me in that respect as well, being such a devoted spiritualist.

"Devil's luck," Ma called it, and maybe she was right.

WHEN THE SUNDAY of the séance arrived, I met Laura early in the morning by the church. It was a white-painted wooden building at the outskirts of town, with the tiniest little bell tower protruding from the roof. The weather was chilly, but not too cold. We were both wrapped in thick woolen shawls and had donned our bonnets, ugly as they were. Attired thus, we made our way through town on a dusty track between rows of storefronts adorned with painted signs. They were all closed, as it was a church day. Laura was nervous and chatted endlessly. I did not pay much attention, intent as I was on the day's task ahead, which could have such an impact on my future.

Mr. Fisher owned a proper farm some way out of town. It was a fine place, large and well-kept; the fields were shorn for winter. I could not help but wonder if he worked the land himself. It seemed a strange thing to do for a retired lawyer.

A hush fell over my companion as we neared the house. It was as if she walked on hallowed ground. Laura tugged at her shawl as if craving its warmth for comfort, tightened her lips, and lowered her head, as if she were walking the aisle toward Holy Communion.

I found it a curious thing.

There were several vehicles before the timbered two-story dwelling; some of them were small, others large enough to carry corn crops. Laura had told me that the spiritualists came from all walks of life, and that was apparent when looking at their modes of transport. The hitching post was crowded, too, with beasts of various ilk: glossy mares and burly stallions; a spatter of humble mules.

The tall front door was open, inviting us inside.

In the hall, all the drapes were closed shut, and candles had taken the place of daylight, which did nothing to disperse the illusion of something sacred taking place. I memorized all of it, adding it to my store of illusions. Judging from Laura's behavior, creating a church-like atmosphere was surely effective.

A gray-haired man, who spoke to us in a whisper so low that I barely understood a word, greeted us. He was all smiles and patience, his blue eyes so mild they could have belonged on an angel's face. He gestured to an open doorway, which led into deeper darkness. The scents of hot tea, sweat, and candle wax wafted toward us. I went in last, letting my companion lead the way. It would not do to appear too brash.

It was very crowded in there. Except for the oval table with its dozen chairs, all furniture had been pushed to the sides, and twenty people or more stood against the walls, clutching fine china cups filled with steaming tea. They were all staring at the table, where, in that particular moment, nothing much was happening. Yet the air hummed with anticipation, a vibration of barely contained excitement. The windows in this room were not only shrouded with heavy curtains but hung with thick black cloth as well. It could just as well have been midnight outside. Two silver candelabras on the table held five candles each; the hot wax dripped on the lace tablecloth, building magical castles and snow-covered mountains on top of the delicate fabric. There was also a silver bell at the table, a piece of parchment, ink, and a pen. At the end of the room, a staircase wound its way up into more darkness. Not a sound could be heard but the clattering of china, the slurping of tea, and the lowing of a discontented cow in the barn.

Laura and I served ourselves tea from a side table, where an impressive-looking samovar was balanced among the stacked china, then took our place among the assembled. My stomach was cramping, so I had been hoping to find something stronger than tea, but I was sorely disappointed in that regard. My hand shook when I lifted the cup.

Out in the hall, the old man closed the front door and then entered to join us. We all let out our breath. Things were about to start. He kept moving through the room, mumbling excuses as he gently pushed weeping women aside and sidestepped wiry farmers. He dropped out of sight when he reached the other side of the room, where there was a small piano next to the stairs. Soon the old man was playing a hymn, and all the gathered started singing—except for me, as I did not know the words, though they seemed to be about death and the afterlife, which was not surprising.

When the singing was all done with, we could see a faint light come seeping around the bend in the stairs, and soon the hem of a dress appeared next to a pair of polished shoes. It was Julie Hassler at last, on the arm of an elderly man whom I took to be our host, Mr. Fisher. They walked down the stairs as slow and regal as royals. Miss Hassler, a middle-aged woman with faded blond hair, wore a black dress with a cameo fastened at the throat, and a pair of pearl earrings dangling from her earlobes. She looked suitably demure and had powdered her skin to a pale shade. I took note of all of this for future use.

Miss Julie gave her escort a grateful look before sliding down into a chair at the end of the table, just where the oval tapered. Again, the assembly acted as one and let out a deep sigh.

Mr. Fisher said a few words in welcome, but I barely listened, being too preoccupied with wondering just who would sit in the other chairs. Was there a ranking order that decided? Would there be a draw? I was so busy with these thoughts that I almost missed the crucial part where he told us to make room as Miss Julie would now walk among us and select the eight to join her at the table.

I knew that I had to be one of them. None of my boasting would do any good unless Miss Julie recognized me as a peer.

My heart stepped up its pace when the celebrated medium rose from her chair and started walking the room, touching foreheads and shoulders as she went by, sighing a lot and sometimes closing her eyes as if listening for a message. I had to admit that she was very good.

The chairs had started filling up: there was a tall farmer with a thick black mustache, a ruddy-faced woman in a silk dress, a young boy of about fifteen, and a scrawny-faced old lady with very poor teeth. For each seat that was claimed, my heart jolted a little.

Finally, Miss Julie reached our side of the room, and, though it was a trick I had only performed on men before, I took a step forward with the teacup clattering on the plate in my hand and boldly snagged her gaze. Miss Julie, as easy as anyone, gave my shoulder a light tap and nodded toward the table. All the while, a slight smile played upon her lips. Perhaps she had resorted to such trickery herself in the past. I did not mind either way; the important thing was that I had been chosen.

I handed my cup to Laura, whose excitement on my behalf shone brightly in her guileless eyes, then I approached the oval table and claimed the nearest empty seat. By the time the séance began in earnest, I had learned that the large man next to me had breath that smelled like rotten onions and that the lady on my other side had the sniffles. Yet I did not hesitate at all when Miss Julie sat down at the head of the table and bade us to hold each other's hands. The man's was rough and callused, the woman's soft and small.

"I will now attempt to enter a trance," said Miss Julie in an airy voice. "While I am so suspended between this world and the next, in what we call 'the veil,' I will call upon spirits to join us. I will do so with the help of my special spirit, Ingot, who is very old and very wise. He will guide us through this séance." She did not look at any of us as she spoke, but kept her gaze trained on the steady flames of the candles. All around us, there was shuffling, rustling, and a clattering of china, as those who had not been fortunate enough to get a place at the table came closer, eager to hear and see all that was going to happen.

Miss Julie looked around at us chosen few and said, "You must not let go of each other's hands; it is important that the circle is closed. Whatever happens—even if you are afraid—you must not let go. If you think you may not be of a suitable constitution to keep up this task, I ask that you now step away." Predictably, no one did. "Good." Miss Julie smiled and slotted her own hands into the ones flanking her on either side. "Now, as we proceed, different spirits will speak to us. Some of them you may know, others might be strangers, but what is absolutely certain is that each one of them has a message to someone in this room." One could almost feel how those last words unleashed another surge of excitement among the assembled. They all so dearly wanted a message of their own.

Miss Julie took a couple of deep breaths before closing her eyes and bending her head so her chin rested on her chest. We all waited in agony as we watched her chest rise and fall, ever more slowly, until it almost looked as if she was sleeping. Then—suddenly—she threw her head back and her eyes popped open.

"Ingot! I can hear you!" she cried. "Ingot, I can hear you loud and clear!" She lowered her head a little, staring once again into the flames. Her eyes were wide open, her pupils dilated. Mr. Fisher, who had so far stood behind the medium, shuffled a little closer, as if to be at hand should she need aid.

"There are so many spirits in here," Miss Julie cried. "So many who want to commune with the living—I can barely hear the words for all the chatter. Give us a sign!" she cried out again. The lady on my left, caught up in the scene, squeezed my hand with surprising strength.

"Let the living know that you are here!" bellowed Miss Julie.

Then it began, quiet at first, then increasingly louder: a rapping from under the table, as if someone lay on their stomach on the floor and used their knuckles to make the sound. A woman behind me gasped. Then the little bell, still sitting on the table, started to chime from within. It did not levitate, which was a disappointment, but the sound was very distinct.

"Ingot, get them in line," cried Miss Julie. "Get them in line . . . one at a time . . . one at a time!" Sweat beaded on her upper lip, and her eyelids fluttered madly. Slowly the rapping became less insistent, the bell became quiet, and after a short while, the room fell silent again.

Miss Julie's eyes looked more normal, but she was drawling terribly when she spoke. It was as if the words were stuck in syrup. "*Mary* . . . I have a message for Mary . . . Is she here?"

"I am Mary," said the elderly lady beside me, in a voice that both quivered and shook. I stared at her intently, mesmerized by her excitement.

"Yes." Miss Julie nodded to herself as if having confirmed something that she already knew. "The message is from a lady, someone who shares your blood . . . could it be your mother?" Miss Julie seemed to listen to the ether.

"Of course it would be dear Mother," said Mary as a tear slid down her cheek. She squeezed my fingers again, so hard that it hurt. "What does she want to say to me?" Her mouth hung open in anticipation.

"She says that she has sent you someone—a friend? Do you have someone new in your life, Mary?" Miss Julie's eyes gleamed in the dim light.

"No . . ." She seemed unsure. "Well, there's the puppy! I had not planned on another dog, but he just wandered into the yard—"

"Yes!" Miss Julie's voice slapped like a whip. She arched her back in the chair for a moment before falling quiet again. "The dog!" she exclaimed. "She sent you the dog to be of comfort. She knows you feel sorrow sometimes."

"Tell her 'thank you,'" said Mary, all overcome with emotion. Since she could not let go of our hands, her tears dripped undisturbed down onto her knitted shawl to soak into the wool. I could not help but smile a little. The woman was truly gullible.

Miss Julie gave her a gentle smile and then she went as stiff as a board as another message slipped through the veil. I caught myself holding my breath while waiting for the next message to come pouring out. "Stevens . . . Stevens . . . Is there a man called Stevens?"

No one answered.

"Is there someone who knew a Stevens that has passed?" I stifled a giggle, thinking that Miss Julie had hit upon a dead end, but it turned out that I was wrong.

"I . . . I do," stuttered a man from the gathering behind me. "I knew a man named Stevens, long ago."

"Did you work with him?" Miss Julie had her head cocked to one side as if listening in on the ether. I had to stop myself from following suit.

"Yes! Yes, I did." The man sounded utterly astonished. "We worked together at the mill."

"Well, he would like you to know that he never cheated at cards," said Miss Julie, and a blast of laughter sounded from the crowd. "Except for that *one* time." Miss Julie had to speak louder to be heard above the raucous laughter. She, too, was loosening up, grinning widely, reveling in the moment. I smiled, too, enjoying the rise of anticipation. "He wants your forgiveness for that." Another burst of laughter followed Miss Julie's statement.

"Of course! Of course!" The man was as happy as a bubbling brook. He slapped his thigh with his palm and could barely stand still.

"Good," Miss Julie said, all satisfied, and made ready to relay another message.

It was then, when the excitement in the room was at a peak, that I finally found my moment. I took a deep, calming breath, then threw my head back and closed my eyes with such vigor that my chair clattered against the floorboards. I could not *see* what effect this had, but I could hear that a fresh hush had settled in the room. I scrunched up my face as if I were in pain and started breathing heavily. When I spoke, it was in a man's voice.

"I am Mr. Black, and I come to you from the great beyond. I have a message to relay from a man called Thomas . . . or Tom. The ring is between the boards in the cupboard in the house that he lived in. He hid it there before he left."

I heard a gasp, then a thump, followed by a quiet bustle, as if someone had swooned to the floor and was attended to by others nearby.

Only then did I open my eyes to see the circle of people staring back at me. Including Miss Julie, even paler than before, and with a glint of steel in her eyes. I knew then that my luck had turned.

My future looked suddenly bright.

8.

ELVIRA

I COULD NOT help but feel duped.

This always happened when Kate had her way; if you gave her an inch she always took more, and I felt as if my carefully constructed scheme to keep her—and *us*—safe had already somewhat unraveled.

What was this business with the hotel in Cherryvale? She never mentioned *that* when she pleaded with me to let her take sitters. Sure, she had mentioned becoming acquainted with the locals, but how had I been supposed to know that she meant to take a position in town?

"But it's the best way to do it," she had argued when I confronted her, acting all innocent, as if it should be obvious that this had been her plan all along, and how much of a fool was *I* not to have seen that?

"It was not what we discussed!" I raged, but she just smiled and threw out her hands.

"It's how it has to be, Ma, if I am ever to succeed—or would you rather stay here and rot for eternity? What about your farm in the mountains?"

"If they find us, you'll hang," I barked at her.

"If they find us, we'll *all* hang." She smirked.

I did not even bother to tell her just how aware I was of that fact. Neither did I deign to remind her that was just why I wanted us all to lie low—for a while. She was infuriating, that girl, and had it not been for what she owed me, I would have cut her loose the very moment we left Pennsylvania behind.

The money she earned as a hotel maid was much needed, though. That, at least, was true, but her working away in town came with its fair share of challenges. Brockman was mentioned less often, so that was good, but then we were supposed to be an inn, and though the rest of us did the best that we could, none of us could speak English as effortlessly as Kate. Sure, we could sell a pound of sugar and a quart of coffee, or heap some stew upon a plate, but the guests always stayed longer, and *paid* better, when she was around, chattering and laughing with them, making them feel welcome. With only the rest of us there, we mostly fell into sullen silence when some rider sat at our table sating his hunger, or we resorted to speaking to each other in German. Something Kate had told us repeatedly *not* to do, as it was not very welcoming.

I spoke to William about my fresh woes one morning. He, having been a baker in the old country, was making the bread, while I sat back and sipped my coffee. Outside the window, John was readying the wagon to take Kate into town. The latter was standing nearby, impatient and in a foul mood. She stomped her feet to stave off the cold and wrapped her arms around her torso. The light was pale so early in the morning; it looked almost as if the sun was freezing, too, withholding its fiery gold.

"Surely it would be better if she stayed here," I said to my husband while rocking gently in my chair. "It puts a strain on us all with her working in Cherryvale."

"Oh, I don't know about that." William was kneading the dough at the table. "Brockman seems to be less on her mind now, and John is in a better mood."

"He isn't in a better mood; he is just in a poor mood where you cannot see it. He is hanging around the hotel, as Kate tells it, scrutinizing the guests, just as he did here before." It had been a problem for us how he would skulk around whenever Kate entertained visitors, sending our patrons looks of pure doom. "What good is he to us if he isn't here to help? It seems to me that we have lost them both to Cherryvale."

"That isn't true," William argued. "He does the work he is supposed to."

"He ought to spend his time building a home of his own, rather than hanging around Kate's skirts."

"There is no point in John building if we aren't to stay," said William. He had been talking of the city again of late—had already grown tired of the prairie. I could not entirely blame him; it was an inhospitable place. Too cold or too hot. The dirt was hard to break. "We won't go far without money, Ma. That has always been our curse."

"Isn't that right," I muttered. The coffee tasted bitter on my tongue. I remembered with a start just how we had solved the money issue the last time we fled, and the scent of burned flesh came back to haunt me. I often forgot in the hustle and bustle of daily life that the very walls around us were paid for by the Vandles. I steeled myself against the thought and recited quietly in my head: *We take care of our own. The rest can fend for themselves.*

Outside the window, the yard was empty. Kate and John had gone. "She barely makes a pittance." I huffed and leaned back in the rocking chair with my cup. The drink was mostly there to warm my fingers as the morning was so cold, and I had woken with both hands feeling stiff and painful.

William had bent to stoke the flames and was looking up at me from below. "I agree that her earnings from the hotel are meager, but what of her talent—her speaking to angels. People are generous if you can make their lives a little better."

"Well, that is what we're all banking on, isn't it? For Kate to speak to the angels and make everything all right." I could not help that I sounded terse, even as it was true for me as well. Kate could sell anything, bend every will, if only she put her mind to it. She was a gold mine, that girl—but worth nothing to us dead. "If she would only wait a little—"

"The angels think it's time," said William.

"I don't want us to go back to the city, husband. I want a farm like the one we had before," I said, refraining from discussing "the angels." It was better for us all if he believed.

I could not have him crumbling under the weight of a guilty conscience.

KATE INSISTED ON bringing the medium Julie Hassler to visit, and it turned out to be an inconvenience for all of us. My daughter was quite the beast in the few days leading up to the call, pacing the floor like a caged animal. It was a relief when she had to go into work, although that, too, came with much agony and a gnashing of teeth, as working as a maid was no longer convenient, she said, and it just would not do in the future.

She seemed to think that this Hassler woman was some sort of godsend, a key to unlock the future, but I had my doubts. It was not good to have a visitor with such a wide circuit seeing us four together, I figured. Perhaps she would hear about our crimes on her travels and piece it all together. Kate only laughed at me, though. John was not to be seen, she said. As far as Mrs. Hassler was to know, she had no brother.

I thought it all a terrible—and unnecessary—gamble.

On the day of the visit, Kate took the wagon into Cherryvale to pick up her guest at the hotel, while the rest of us stayed at home to prepare for the medium's arrival. The whole morning had been taxing, with Kate's many preparations. She had hung the plain walls of our simple abode with esoteric clippings from her books and pamphlets, and even ruined the floor with a design she had found in a tome on astrology. She had also brought out candles instead of kerosene lamps and hung pieces of canvas before the windows to block out the daylight. William and John had been tasked with emptying the little cellar—setting my milk and cheese out back to fester—to make room for John to hide down there to make rapping sounds from below the floorboards. I thought this was a foolish idea and told Kate as much. "What if he sneezes?" I asked. "What if he cannot help but clear his throat? Then you will have neither milk nor sitters."

"Your milk will be *fine*, Ma," said she, with the brazen confidence of youth. "And John will not sneeze, will you, John?" She looked at him from under her lashes and added the sweetest of smiles. The sight of it made me groan.

"I will not sneeze," John promised, though I could not see how he could make such a vow. "We practiced all last night," he said, with the undignified excitement of a boy Hanson's age.

I knew that he was telling the truth, though, as their knocking and chatter had kept me up half the night. "When I ask, 'Spirit, are you there?' you will answer with one loud knock," Kate had instructed, then demonstrated with her knuckles to the floor. "Then I will ask you to reply one knock for yes, two for no . . . I will say it all in English, of course."

"But won't Miss Hassler, being a medium herself, think of hidden compartments?" John had asked—unusually bright for him.

"Oh, but it's all about the performance," said Kate. "People need to hear and see things for themselves in order to believe. It's not enough for them just to get a message from the beyond delivered through a medium's mind. Miss Julie has her own illusions to dazzle her audience, and she'll expect me to have mine. If I don't, I will appear quite inept."

"So it's all lies?" asked John, dumbfounded.

"No!" Kate spoke loud enough to startle us all, though I believe it was William who was the intended receiver of her message. "The voices are as real as you and me, John! It's just hard for someone who isn't gifted to understand that unless they hear or see something for themselves." She really sounded quite convincing, like a preacher in a pulpit. "I know this, and so does Miss Hassler." I heard the sloshing of the liquor as she lifted the bottle.

At that point, I had reached under the pillow for William's Bible, pulled the canvas curtain aside, and hurtled it through the air. When Kate uttered a sound of pain, I lay back down, quite content.

I could still hear them whispering, though, long into the night, scheming and plotting ways to impress the discerning Miss Hassler.

When William and I—sitting there in the candlelit darkness, wasting the best daylight hours—finally heard the wagon pull up in front of the house, I let out a breath of relief. The affair had taken up too much time already, and it would be a blessing to have it all be over with. I warned John of their coming by thumping my foot against the floorboards and heard a light knocking in reply. It all seemed so foolhardy, but even I realized that should this ruse come off as somewhat convincing to Miss Julie, it would surely fool those eager to believe. Despite my annoyance, I saw that it was a clever scheme, especially since the trapdoor was on the other side of the canvas curtain, and thus hidden from view.

"Remember," I told William as we sat there, waiting, me in the rocking chair and he in a chair pulled up before the stove, "we are true believers now. We belong to the spiritualist faith." I rolled my eyes. I could not help it.

William chuckled silently and nodded to me; his hands were busy with whittling a spoon, sending thin wood chips flying into the fire.

The door creaked open, and there they were: Kate, wearing her best dress, but with her hair hanging loose like a tart; and a slightly older, blond woman, who looked around her with shock written all over her face. I did not think she was very impressed with the quality of our home.

Kate spoke rapidly in English, cocking her head as she entertained her guest, while pulling off the silly little silk gloves she had bartered for in Louisville, and flinging them onto the table.

I rose to my feet and put on a meek, gentle smile. "Welcome to our home, Miss Hassler. It is not much, but enough for us. We came here to live a simple life, and left all desire for riches behind." Now that Miss Hassler was here, foolhardy though it might be, we all had to do our part to see the ruse through.

While Kate translated my words, I shuffled over to take Miss Hassler's soft, plump hand in mine. "Please, sit down," I said. "We don't get the honor of entertaining gifted individuals such as your-self very often, besides our Kate, of course. We are all so thrilled that you decided to visit." Kate repeated in English, and I led Miss Hassler by the hand to the table, and was not satisfied before her ample behind, wrapped in layers of dark blue satin, was firmly seated on a chair. Then I went to fetch coffee and pear brandy for our guest, while the women fell into incomprehensible chatter at the table.

"She says 'thank you,' Ma," Kate said from behind me. "She is honored to be invited."

"Doesn't seem much honored to me," I remarked, feeling more assured now that the woman did not understand me. "She might just as well have stepped into a fishmonger's store, and not one of the good ones either."

"She is just used to different rooms," said Kate, with a timbre of bitterness tainting her words.

"I'm sure she is." I put the glasses down before them. Miss Hassler smiled up at me; her eyes were large and bottle green. "I *said* this was a foolish idea." I smiled back at the medium and poured them both some brandy. I could hear William coming up behind me, risen from his chair at last. He reached out a bony hand to gently shake Miss Hassler's. The latter seemed appalled as she looked upon my beastly husband, who had not shaved for some time. He greeted her in German, putting on a friendly face, but that, of course, hardly showed because of all the hair.

I shuffled back to my chair, picked up my knitting from a basket on the floor, and kept working on a pair of socks for William, while the women drank and chattered at the table. I wondered how John was doing down there under the trapdoor. I hoped he was not freezing to death. For his sake, I hoped the séance would soon be under way.

"They are not friends, those two," William said when he joined me, looking at Kate and Miss Hassler.

"How can you tell?" I asked, astonished to hear him being so observant. He usually did not notice such things.

"Just look at them," said William. "They are like two vipers watching each other, both of them ready to strike."

"Oh, nonsense," I said to put him at ease, though he was not wrong. When I looked at them again, so animated and cheery, I could not help but think of dogs baring their teeth at each other.

Finally, a hush fell over the table. "Ma," Kate said. "Pa, will you be as kind as to lend us your hands?"

I got up again with some fussing with the yarn, and William rose, too, leaving the knife behind as he pulled the chair with him across the floor. I sat down in a vacant chair and so we were suddenly four, gathered by candlelight, clasping hands on the tabletop.

"I am about to go into a trance," Kate informed us in German, looking first at me, then at William. She had taken on a serene expression, but her gray eyes burned when she looked at Miss Hassler, whose green eyes burned right back. In the circle of our arms, the brandy bottle stood half empty. They had certainly been enjoying themselves.

Kate started breathing heavy and slow; she closed her eyes and threw her head back so her red hair spilled down the back of the chair. We sat like that for a long while; then, all of a sudden, all the muscles in her body seemed to tense up at once and she started speaking in a dark, gruff voice that I recognized as "Mr. Black,"

Kate's invented spirit guide—a former sailor with a salty tongue and vast knowledge of the spirit world he inhabited.

What she said was mostly unintelligible to me, but I could see Miss Hassler's face light up with interest, so it had to be something sound. Then came the knocking from under the floorboards: one at first, then several more, as John did his part in the charade. They went on thus for quite some time: Kate spoke and John answered with rapping from under the floorboards. Miss Hassler seemed most amused; a little half smile lingered on her lips.

Across from me, William watched Kate with a rapt expression. My husband's face seemed lit from within as he watched, even if he could not understand the words. Kate threw her head back again, her breathing came labored, and beads of sweat studded her forehead. It was a most impressive performance—even Miss Hassler had wiped the smile from her lips and seemed to listen intently.

Mr. Black spoke for a very long time, and then he suddenly stopped. By chance or miracle, that was just when a stack of canned beef on a shelf behind the store counter came tumbling down, giving us all a start, and a glorious ending to Kate's performance.

Miss Hassler laughed loudly from the startlement and pressed white-knuckled fists to her ruffled chest. Kate—always so aloof—calmly kept her wits about her and acted as if she was not startled at all, which certainly worked in her favor. John, too, had kept mum, even when the cans rolled across the floor.

"How did it go?" William asked in German. His eyes were wide and his mouth hung open. "What did Mr. Black say?"

"Oh, all sorts of things," Kate told him with a slight smile, before throwing herself into a new, rapid discussion with Miss Hassler.

"Nothing of any importance," I told my husband.

Of this, I was most certainly sure.

"THAT WENT WELL," I remarked when Kate returned from ferrying Miss Hassler back into town. I was alone inside the house then, as William and John had gone to tend the barn.

"No, it didn't," my daughter said with a sneer in reply, and it was then that I noticed her thunderous expression. "She could not stop talking about the state of this place," she said, slumping down in a chair. "All the way to town she kept at it, complaining about the draft and the filth . . . She could not understand, she said, how anyone wanted to live like us."

"Well"—I looked up from my knitting—"that's no surprise."

"But I'd told her that we lived like this for a *reason*, yet I fear that she didn't believe me. I wouldn't be surprised at all if she showed up here tomorrow with a charity basket." Her lips twisted up in the sneer she always wore when irked. "Maybe she won't endorse me now—who wants to send sitters to a 'house of squalor'?"

"She probably grew up in a place just like this," I said, trying to calm her down. "It's always those with something to hide—those who are a touch too familiar—who are the first to condemn another. If you looked into it, I'm sure you'd find that I'm right."

That tickled a real smile from her. "You should have said so *before* the séance," she told me. "Maybe I could have 'seen' it."

"Maybe you still can," said I, "if someone asks."

Kate grabbed the brandy bottle off the table and took a swig. "I don't like it, though, having her out there, speaking of how I live in a pigsty—"

John came in just then, so eager for Kate's praise that the door crashed loudly against the frame and set the windows rattling. He was with her in two long strides. "It went well, didn't it? I knocked when we agreed?" His eyes were almost pleading, as if he were a child or a dog. I huffed and let my gaze drop to my knitting again. I always found it painful to see a grown man debase himself.

"You could have rapped louder," said Kate with something sharp in her voice. She had a knack for that sort of thing, fashioning her voice into a blade that cut. "We could barely hear you at times. You could just as well not have been there at all. It was all such a waste."

"Now, Kate—" I started, but she cut me off.

"You knocked on the same board every time. The spirits move around; that's the charm of it! You should have moved around down there, knocked on different boards—!"

"It was dark," he said, trying to defend himself.

"Well, you ought to practice if you are to do that again," said she. "You're of no use to me if you cannot follow my instructions." She rose to her feet, got the bottle off the table, and strode toward the door.

"Where are you going?" He stood left behind, looking much as if he had lost his best toy. Had he not been so pitiful, I might have felt sorrier for him, but it is hard to truly feel for those who refuse to grow a backbone. Kate would not have treated him thus had he not allowed it to happen.

"I'm taking this up to the trading station," she said, lifting the bottle high up in the air. "Mr. Brockman is always good company." Without another word, she was gone, letting the door slam behind her.

"Damn that Brockman!" John cried at the closed door. His face was all contorted with anger and his coloring dark with fury. He grabbed one of the empty brandy glasses off the table and hurtled it at the offending wood. It exploded, of course, and dozens of tiny shards drizzled down upon Kate's peculiar design on the floor.

"That was mighty clever of you," I remarked. "Now we have

one glass less, and more to clean. I do hope some of it ends up in your foot and festers there for a while."

He did not even answer, but only sent me a look of utter fury before striding out of the house himself, leaving me to sweep up the mess.

I did not much like it, though, the anger in that boy.

9.

KATE

THE NIGHTS BECAME chilly as the days counted down to winter. I sat beside John in the wagon, on our way back from the hotel, wrapped in both a shawl and a blanket. He had brought lanterns for the wagon in case the darkness should fall before we made it home, but so far the sky was merely bleeding to dusk. It was a rickety journey, though. That wagon had never been hale.

I was still irked about Miss Julie—I worried that I had made a great mistake. No medium worth her salt lived in poverty; the spirits were supposed to keep such worldly worries at bay. If she went talking, it would be a tarnish on a reputation I had yet to gain—unless I became wealthy fast; then it would seem as though the spirits worked in my favor.

With all these bothersome thoughts swirling through my mind, I had no patience for John and his woes. On these homebound journeys he always wanted to speak of the guests at the hotel, worried that I would find myself a lover among them. It was annoying beyond belief when he strived to learn whom I had spoken to throughout the day, and he would not let up either, until I had answered.

"They are all men," he said with a huff as the wagon rattled along. "Why is it that all the guests are men?" He did not look at me but at the road ahead. His drooping mustache and knitted brow gave him a somber appearance. His hat was new, though, wide and black, looking much like Pa's.

"Men *do* travel more," I offered in reply, though he did not quite deserve an answer. It was getting more than tiresome, this constant suspicion—and especially when he aimed his arrow so wrong. Listening to John, one would think the hotel was nothing but a brothel.

"Well, did any of them speak to you?" he prodded.

"Nothing more than usual." I shrugged. "What is it to you? I am *not* your wife, John."

He swallowed hard and kept his eyes on the road. When he did not speak at once, I thought perhaps the inquest was over and that I would have some peace, but then he opened his mouth and said, "You know my flesh is weak, and my will is, too. If I could—" his voice suddenly broke. "If I could, I would rather not have to think of you another day."

I could not help but smile. "If I married Mr. Brockman, you wouldn't have to see me every day," I teased, knowing very well how it would hurt him.

He gave a short, barking laugh. "You would hardly be far enough away for that to count. I'd see you every time I went up there for cider . . . I don't see why you won't marry *me*," he burst out next. "Half the town think we're married already. It would be better, don't you think? We would be rid of Brockman and *all* of this nonsense—"

"They only think so because you said so before I arrived," I snapped. "It's been awfully inconvenient with people thinking me a married woman. It's not what we agreed on before we came here! We said we would be brother and sister!" Fury had started building in the pit of my stomach—how *dare* he lay a claim on me?

"Inconvenient how?" He sent me a dark glance. "Does it make it hard for you to dally with other men?"

"John!" I looked around my feet for something heavy to hit him with, a bottle or some such, but found nothing of use. "That's just *why* you said it, so that everyone would think that I was taken—and *no*, I won't marry you, not today or any other day!"

"*Why* won't you get married, Kate?" He had started crying; he sat with his head bent over the reins while tears slowly slid down his cheeks. "Is it just so you can be free to marry someone rich? Someone like Brockman?" His voice rose to a high pitch as he said our neighbor's name.

"Brockman is hardly *rich*." I rolled my eyes. "He is barely better off than us."

"Someone else, then?" He wiped his eyes with the back of his hand, clad in a gray fingerless glove. "Is it so you can be with others? Have you *been* with others?" His eyes looked wild as he turned toward me. "Have you been with *Brockman*?"

"That's none of your concern, John." Seeing him so pitiful did nothing but make the bile rise in me. "If I have been with Brockman, it has nothing to do with you!"

"Well, *have you?*" he all but shouted and smacked the horses with the reins; the poor beasts before us stepped up the pace. "Have you been with Brockman?" Unexpectedly, one of his hands shot out and caught hold of my wrist. It hurt and I yelped, mostly from surprise.

"Don't you dare lay a hand on me," I hissed through gritted teeth and tried to pull my hand free. "Do you want to end up like Emil?"

"You *will* tell me!" He shook my wrist so hard that my whole body shook with it. The horses ran wildly, barely controlled by his one hand on the reins. "You will tell me if you have been with Brockman!" While he was shouting, more tears came pouring from his eyes.

"*If* I have been with him, what will you do, John? What will you do with that knowledge?" I placed my fingernails against the hand that held me and sank them into his flesh. I could see the pain cross his features, but the oaf would still not let go. The wagon wheels clattered below us, and I worried that the vehicle would shake apart.

"So you *have* been with him!" John bellowed, and I used his distraction to grab hold between his legs, squeeze, and pull. He howled with the pain of it, and his grip on my wrist loosened.

"You idiot!" I screamed at him. "How dare you lay a hand on me? The last man who wronged me got a knife in his gut!" I wrestled the reins from his fingers and pulled. I would not die on this dirt track because he was fool.

John lay back on the seat, teary-eyed and clutching his crotch. I had never seen anything more pitiful in my life.

My wrist hurt, and my dignity, too.

This simply could not stand.

We already saw the farm before us by the time I captured the reins, and so the rest of the drive was thankfully short. I did not dally outside but left it to the sobbing man to dry off the horses, which *he* had exhausted, and see to the wagon. I only went inside briefly, to fetch a bottle and get my shawl. Then I trotted up the road to the trading station in the dusky night, muttering and cursing to myself, drinking all the while. My wrist throbbed and hurt and my mouth tasted of bile. By the time I reached my destination, my breathing had become labored and my knuckles around the bottle's slim neck were white. The darkness in me swelled. It was like a great wild animal opening its maw. Every time I blinked my eyes, I saw flesh pried apart with a knife. Ma's voice was booming in my head—*We take care of our own; the rest can fend for themselves*—but that could be a hard creed to live by.

I took a moment to compose myself before going inside the trading station. I did not want Brockman to see my fury. I brushed the hair back from my forehead with my hands and tied the shawl at the small of my back. It was either this or killing John. There were no other options.

The trading station was warm and welcoming, smelling of ground coffee, kerosene, and fur. Brockman was still behind the counter, going over numbers with a bottle of gin beside him. I could hear Mr. Ern behind the closed door to the back, moving around on the creaking floorboards.

"Kate." Brockman's face lit up when he heard the bell and looked up to see me standing there. "What a delightful surprise."

"I should hope so." I gave a short laugh that was meant to be flirty but came out a little shrill. "I missed you," I said, lowering my lashes. "I was hoping you wanted to walk with me."

"Now?" He sounded amused. "It's late—dark, and cold."

"I can keep you warm." I lifted the bottle. "The air is crisp and lovely," I promised, though it truly was bitingly chilly.

"Wouldn't you rather stay here?" He lifted his own bottle off the counter to tempt me. "We can stay warm *and* have our fun."

I looked toward the door to the back. "Mr. Ern would hardly appreciate it."

Brockman shrugged. "We can be quiet—like mice." He whispered the last part and winked at me.

I laughed as if amused, though the anger in me made it impossible to feel true joy. "I should like to speak to you," I said, "alone."

Brockman saw my wrist then, as I pushed some hair away from my forehead. I had not meant for him to—it was an accident. I never much liked for others to see me hurt. The smile curdled and died on his lips. "What happened to your hand, Kate? Did one of the guests do that?" I did not know if he spoke of the guests at the hotel or the guests at the inn, but it did not matter. It was a good cover either way.

"Sure," I said. "But it has all been sorted. He was drunk and meant no harm—"

"No harm? But, Kate—"

"It was not what I wanted to speak of." I was starting to lose my patience with him. "Are you coming or not?" I huffed and took another swig from the bottle.

He must have sensed my annoyance, for he did come then, stepping out from behind the counter and bringing his coat with him. As an afterthought, he brought the gin as well, and a lit kerosene lamp from a hook in the ceiling.

"Where do you want to go?" he asked when we were both standing out on the porch and our breaths formed smoke in the cool air.

"To the barn," I said.

"The barn?" His eyebrows rose. "But Hanson sleeps out there."

Just as he said it, I could see the faint light from the boy's lamp glittering between the boards of the building. "The icehouse, then."

"That's even colder—"

"Well, where would *you* go if you had a desire to rut?" I fought not to roll my eyes at him.

"To *what*?"

"You heard me." I gave him a lazy smile.

"Kate, I—" He seemed utterly bewildered.

"You have wanted it long enough," I said, "and here's your chance to have it. Do you want it, or not?" I lifted a hand to let my fingers trail his cheek. "We have kissed often enough," I continued, "but I want something more from you tonight . . . To tell you the truth, it has kept me sleepless. I have an itch that I just can't—"

"To the icehouse, then," Mr. Brockman decided and captured my hand in his. I could see the lust on his face already, in the scarlet flush of his cheeks. We were both laughing as we ran out into the night, the bottles and the lamp dancing in our hands. His laughter was happy and carefree, rife with anticipation. Mine was angry and hard, but he did not hear that.

We arrived at the icehouse but did not go inside. Instead, we stood leaning against the small building's earthen walls, kissing in the light from the lamp on the ground. The flame within the glass casing flickered, painting our faces in many hues.

"Finally," I muttered to urge him on. "Finally, I shall have you." It was not Brockman I thought of, though, but John. Every touch and every caress I gave our neighbor was defiant—an insult—and a smack in John's face. Who was he to guide my actions? How dare he even try? Every kiss that night fed the darkness—appeased its hunger, I hoped. Inside, I felt like a string pulled tight, all too eager to snap.

Had he not been kin to me, I would gladly have cut John up.

"Oh, Kate," Brockman uttered. "I have *never* met a woman like you—so bold, and so brash—"

"Only with you, Rudolph." I snuck a cold hand under his shirt. "Only ever with you. I just cannot seem to behave myself—"

"And neither do you have to," he assured me, placing a kiss on my palm. "You can be as free as you wish to with me. I cannot tell you how flattered I am that—"

"Do it," I whimpered, pressing myself close to his body. I thought it was going too slow. What was the use in all the talking? I was there to save John's life.

Brockman groaned then, like a beast, and I thought it must have been some time since he last was with a woman. He squeezed my breast through the cheap calico and undid the knot of my shawl at my back. I still thought he was too slow, and lifted my skirt up over my hips to present him with the real object of his desire.

"Here," I said, guiding his hand. "It's all yours for the taking."

He finally lost his head when he felt me, and became a whimpering flutter of fabric, buttons, and suspenders, until his prick was released and knocking at the gate. I lifted one leg to let him in. He went at it like an eager pup, rutting the best that he could.

"Oh, you're so wet," he marveled.

"Only because I want you so," I whispered, and turned my head so he would not see how I rolled my eyes. "Please, quench the thirst in me, Mr. Brockman!"

He kept going with renewed effort after that, and it was not long before he buckled against me. His mouth went slack in the throes of release, and his eyes closed shut for a blessed minute. I myself felt better. Not sated like him, but the fury had cooled and the darkness receded, and that, at least, was something.

Brockman, it turned out, was one of those men who is overcome by feelings once they have spent themselves. He cradled me close and pressed wet, sloppy kisses to my skin.

"Oh, Kate," he muttered. "Kate . . . you surely are a marvel—"

"I think that we should marry," I said with his lips on my throat. "Wouldn't you agree, Mr. Brockman?" I smiled as I said it, thinking only of John. It surely would drive him mad. As much as I would relish to harm him bodily, a cut to the heart would smart even longer. It would surely teach him for trying to rule me.

Brockman laughed, but not unkindly. "I thought that *I* was the one who was supposed to ask—"

"Well, I'm an impatient woman when I see something I want." I kissed his soft earlobe. "Don't tell me you haven't been thinking of it."

"Of course I have." The words came tumbling out in a hot rush of air. "I think of little else."

"Then you should ask me," I said while catching his prick in my hand, coaxing the softening flesh back to life. Mr. Brockman moaned softly, like a hurt animal.

"Will you marry me?" he groaned between soft sighs and moans.

"Yes." I placed a wet kiss on his lips and squeezed the fragile thing in my hand just a little bit more. "I most surely will." My heart beat wild and fast with glee.

WE ALL ATE dinner together the next day. Ma and Pa, John and I. On our plates were bread and pieces of bacon burned to a crisp. Our guests had emptied the pot of stew, and so this was all we had for our meal. It was not so bad—we had had far worse.

"Mr. Brockman has proposed to me," I said, bursting with my triumph.

"Oh, that poor man." Ma slapped a hand over her own mouth as if to stop the laments that were eager to follow.

William kept his gaze on the table, chewing a piece of hard bacon. He said nothing but made a sound in his throat.

Opposite me, John had gone pale. He slowly, gently lowered his fork to the plate. "What answer did you give him, Kate?" His voice was very calm, though a little out of breath.

"Oh, surely she hasn't answered *yet*." Ma started prattling, voicing her own hopes. "She needs time to think about it, don't you, Kate?" She glanced at me, to warn me, perhaps, against saying something rash. I could tell from the set of her jaw that she was tense. William, too, seemed uncomfortable, still chewing with his gaze on his plate.

"I did answer." I toyed with my fork, drew lines in the grease on the china. "I said yes to him, of course."

John was on his feet so fast that the table jumped, sending plates, bacon, and cups to the floor. "Damn that Brockman!" he shouted. His face was no longer pale but had taken on a flaming hue. "Damn him to hell!" he cursed, and set out for the door. "I will kill that bastard!" he cried. "I will kill him!"

William got to his feet then, too, and tackled his son from behind. "You will not do anything of the sort," he bellowed and brought them both crashing to the floor.

"Don't you dare touch Brockman, John!" I rose to my feet and added my concerned voice to the ruckus, though inside I was aflame with excitement. "It has nothing to do with you!"

"The hell it doesn't!" John cried back. He peeked up at me from under his father's strong arm, which held him in a vise grip. His face looked all contorted; his hair was slicked to his forehead, and he huffed and puffed as he struggled to free himself. Seeing his pain brought me great pleasure. I barely even felt the aching in my wrist.

"Brockman fills these shelves," Pa lectured his son, still holding on. "There will be no threatening of Mr. Brockman, and certainly not any bodily harm."

"Will you stop, both of you, at once?" Ma had finally found her voice. She was halfway to the corner already, going for the broom. It had always been her favorite mode of punishment. Before she got there, however, John had managed to break free of William's hold and was throwing an ill-advised punch at his father—promptly repaid threefold. Suddenly, it all erupted in a terrible melee of flailing limbs, smacks, and groans. It did not end until Ma was there with the broom, delivering blows where it hurt the most.

"Will. You. Stop!" she cried.

Finally, they did. John's nose was dripping with blood by then, and his eye was already swelling shut. Pa's knuckles looked sore. He staggered to his chair, lifted it upright, and sank down on the seat. John was still on the floor, heaving for breath with his back against the wall.

"Better you hit me than Brockman." Pa tried to laugh it off, but none of us joined in. He was rubbing his knuckles with his left hand. Ma was already rummaging in her trunk, looking for her special ointment.

"You better sleep out in the barn tonight," Ma said to John as she dipped her fingers in the jar. "But if you take the horse or run, I swear I will shoot you myself." Her lips were set in a grim line. She gently dabbed the ointment onto Pa's hand. She delivered a final warning: "Don't you *dare* test me, boy."

John staggered toward the door and gave me a look so dark that I almost took a step back. "You must be enjoying yourself immensely, Kate, having me act the fool."

"You're in every way poor entertainment." I smirked, though of course he was right.

"Damn you to hell!" he cried in parting, before slamming the door shut behind him.

10.

HANSON

MR. BROCKMAN HAD asked me to take the mule down to the
Bender place with some tobacco for their shelves, though I had already done so just a few days before. As I was readying myself for
the short trek, Mr. Brockman came out in the yard, looking a little
strange in the face. I expected that it had to do with Kate.

"Look around you while you are there," he said to me. "Let me
know if something looks out of sorts. Listen to what they say, too,
if any of them mentions . . . a marriage."

"Mr. Brockman," I said with wide eyes. "Have you proposed to
Kate?" It was the best news I had heard in long while. I knew that he
had been pining for her almost as long as they had been in our parts.

"I have." Mr. Brockman straightened up and dusted off his vest.
"Her father has not been to see me, though, and neither has she
been, since. I would like to know how the family feels about the al-
liance."

"Maybe Kate hasn't told them about it yet," I suggested, in an effort to comfort Mr. Brockman, but it was not what he wanted to hear.

"*Of course* she has told them," he said in a huff. "We are to be married, after all."

Still, Mr. Brockman must have had his doubts since he sent me there to spy. Maybe he had not spoken to Mr. Bender about it first and felt bad about that.

Kate was at home when I arrived, which was a surprise, as I had expected her to be at the hotel. I had taken some pity on the Benders ever since she had started working there, and sometimes stopped by if I saw that there were riders at the door, to help things run a bit smoother, with them not speaking English so well. It certainly did not hurt matters that Mrs. Bender always was kind to me and fed me lumps of sugar or a bowl of stew as a reward for my assistance.

There were riders there that day as well, a couple of burly men who sat at the table with their spoons deep in soup. Kate was with them, occupying a chair and topping up their cups with fermented cider every time they tasted it. It seemed very wasteful to me, but I supposed she wanted to be a good host. In her lap rested her new puppy, Rosie—a small black mutt with a very loud voice—seemingly oblivious to the noises in the room.

"Good morning, Hanson." Kate sounded thrilled to see me, but then, she always did.

Mrs. Bender was in her rocking chair with her knitting, and as soon as I had hoisted the tobacco onto the store counter, I made my way over to her and pulled out a wooden stool to sit at her feet and feed a few more chips into the fire.

"How are you today, Hanson?" she stammered in her broken English. She was better at it than she let on, but one had to be patient while she searched for the words.

"Good enough." I shrugged and gave her my best smile. She tousled my hair then, as if I were a small child. I picked up William's whittling from the floor—the knife and the wood that would soon be a spoon—and worked on it a little. I knew he would not mind.

Behind me, Kate was entertaining the guests. "Well, yes, it is true," she said in a boisterous manner. "I *am* to give a talk to the spiritualist society. I will have you know that I am *special* in that regard. I know quite a lot that others don't." She said it in a teasing manner, as if daring them to believe her.

"Is that so, Miss Kate?" One of the men had swallowed her bait. "What can you tell me that my own wife doesn't know?"

"Oh, that depends," said she. "I would have to consult your hand first, then the shape of your skull, then the shape of—" She cut off and drew a sharp breath, which caused the men to roar with laughter. Mrs. Bender shook her head.

John came slinking out from behind the canvas curtain that cut the room in half. I startled a bit, as I had not known that he was there, but also because of the way that he looked. Half his face had been beaten blue, and one of his eyes was as swollen as a plum. An angry red mark traced the shape of his chin. I thought that something terrible must have happened at the Bender place, and perhaps that was why they had not sent any word to Mr. Brockman.

John merely nodded in greeting when he saw me sitting there, and entered the room with a dark look on his face. When he passed me by, I could smell the fumes of strong liquor. Mrs. Bender shook her head again but did not say a thing. He stepped behind the store counter and started stuffing a pipe. At the table, Kate was laughing so hard that the puppy woke up and yawned. It teased a smile from all of us but John, who just stood there as morose as a midnight sky, looking out into the room with glazed eyes.

The door opened then, and in came Mr. Bender, looking much like a thundercloud himself, with his tangled beard and heavy frame, his face set in a scowl. He, too, carried the markings of a recent tussle, with green-blue bruises upon his face. His hand, I could tell, was wrapped in strips of cloth, and that unsettled me more than anything else, as I figured it was he who had beat up John, and done it with such force that he had ruined his hand. I found it all very chilling and thought that I did not know my neighbors at all.

Mr. Bender, too, slipped in behind the store counter, and then followed a string of German between the two men, delivered in a tone that reminded me of angry dogs barking at each other.

Mr. Bender must have said something to upset John, as he threw the pipe down on the store counter and pushed past his father and out of the cramped space in a rush. Then he went for the door and slammed it hard behind him as he disappeared outside.

At the table, all fell silent, even the little dog.

"Oh, never mind him." Kate broke the silence, pretending as if nothing was amiss. "He is always in such a hurry. He will take good care of your horses, though. He is good at that sort of thing." Her fingers were laced in the puppy's soft fur, rubbing its pink belly.

"But he's not a medium, like you?" one of the men said, lifting his cup of cider.

"No, not at all," said she. "My brother is about as sensitive as a turnip."

"Looks like he has taken a tumble, though," the other man said.

"A tumble? Yes, for sure," said Kate, though we all knew that was a lie.

It was not long after that I decided to take my leave. I was unlikely to learn much more for Mr. Brockman, and John's appearance and demeanor had left an ugly feeling behind.

I could not help but wonder what had really happened.

As I stood outside the house, readying the mule, John came staggering out from the barn. It was even clearer than before that he had been drinking. He paused very close to me, and though I had always liked John, I did not much like having him so close. Perhaps it was the way he was swaying on his feet, or the dark expression that he wore.

"She has been asked to give this talk," he said in his peculiar accent. "Now she's the *Queen of Sheba* all of a sudden." This was the longest sentence I had ever heard him say in English, and I thought that he maybe ought to drink more often, if only to keep the words flowing. "Spiritualists," he said, spitting on the ground between us. "How is your master?" He abruptly changed the subject, lifting his gaze to mine. "He is happy now, isn't he? He got what he wanted, with *her*." He nodded to the door of the house.

"Oh, I wouldn't know," I lied, finding it best not to agitate him.

"He better be quick." John seemed not to have heard me. "Maybe she'll find herself another *man*!" He shouted the last word, stomped his feet, and nodded to the house again, referring to the patrons, no doubt. "Many men stop here. You should tell Mr. Brockman that."

I did not think that was a good idea but nodded anyway before I hastened to take my leave. I had not liked the look of John at all, and we had come quite a far bit up the road, the mule and I, before my breathing was as easy as before.

There had been something—something about his eyes—that had me thinking of animals in traps; of something terrified and mindless.

11.

ELVIRA

THERE WAS NO warning before it happened.

The day was just like any other; I rose at dawn to a cloudy sky and a fine sheet of ice covering the windows. The fire had all but gone out in the night and I spent some time getting it going, all while rubbing my aching hands and blowing at them to get the blood flowing. I was thinking of the link of sausages I had procured, and how to best make them last.

William's hand had healed up enough that he could once again make the bread in the morning. I found this to be an immense relief. I had more than enough with the cooking and the cleaning, trying to make the shack he had built look like a dwelling for decent people, so that travelers might deign to pause. He was at it while I tended the fire and had the coffee going, smacking the dough supple and slick.

"Is John out in the barn?" I asked.

William nodded. "He prefers it these days. He's still mad about the beating."

"It was a bad beating," I stated and poured a handful of beans into the coffee grinder. That, at least, was a good thing about keeping all those groceries at hand; we would rarely run out of dry goods like coffee and flour.

It turned out to be a busy day. First, a single rider stopped by to rest and get some supplies. He had no money for a meal, though, so my stew remained untasted on the stove. Kate handled the man with the grace of a buffalo once it became clear that his pockets were empty. I did not have to understand all the words to notice the chill in the air.

Next, a German woman from town came riding in on a mule. She was pale about the gullet and had dark smudges under her eyes, so I figured she had come for a cure. Word of my services was slowly spreading, and my callers had become more frequent. I chased Kate outside and had the woman seated at the table. Then I sat down in front of her and took her hand in mine.

"You have an ailment," I told her. "What is it that gives you grief?"

She grimaced and looked away; a sadness flickered across her face under the brown bonnet. She was younger than she looked, I thought. Of childbearing age.

"Is it in your stomach?" I asked. Women are often reluctant to speak of such things, even to other women.

"I had a little one some weeks ago," she told me at last. "Everything seemed fine at first, but the blood hasn't stopped."

I nodded and let go of her hand. "I have seen this many times before," I told her, "and I know exactly what to do." I rose from my chair and went behind the curtain to rummage in my trunk. I found the herbs I was looking for stored in a glass jar, and brought it with me to the table with a few pieces of paper, my ink, and a pen.

"You should take a spoonful of this with hot water," I said. "It might hurt and bleed a little more after that, but then it will all clear up." I gave the pale woman a reassuring smile as I scooped some of the jar's contents onto one sheet of paper and folded it. Then I scribbled the proper words onto the other piece of paper and handed it to her. "If it doesn't stop within a few days, place your hand on your stomach where it hurts and say these words. It should slow the bleeding." Just as she was about to take the paper, I withdrew it to give her my warning. "Do not share this prayer with anyone, or it will stop working—or the bleeding will get worse." It was important to keep secrets that people were willing to pay for, and my warnings were usually heeded, as no one would risk getting worse.

Unlike Kate's spirits, my cures were tried and true; their power did not stem from some magic, but from God himself. I had grown up with such cures back in Germany and often found use for them in my work as a midwife. I also had ample opportunity to learn more while we lived in Pennsylvania. I had a friend there, Gretchen, who taught me much and gifted me special books on the subject. Unlike Gretchen, however, I did not put much trust in the prayers and the sacred words—though I often used them anyway, just to be on the safe side—but I knew without a doubt that my herbs worked wonders in ailing bodies. I also knew, with an equal certainty, that faith could work wonders as well.

My customer nodded solemnly, sniffled a little, and fished a leather pouch out from her sleeve. "How much do you want for it?" she asked.

"What is it worth to you?" I asked back.

She gave a quick smile and put her coins down on the table. All of them, from what I could tell. "Thank you," she said, and I felt I had done God's work that day.

Little did I know that I would also do the devil's.

No other patients came by that morning, only travelers for the inn. A man journeying with his boy of about twelve was the first one to ask for a proper meal. A little later, a reverend paused and asked for the same. None of them complained about the stew—or if they did, Kate never mentioned it to me. She was on her best behavior with the reverend, all but sat on his plate to suck up every word he said. She saw him as a peer, perhaps, another dabbler in spiritual matters.

Back in Pennsylvania, anyone talking to the dead would have been deemed a witch, and it still did not sit quite right with me that this was my daughter's chosen profession—even if her spirits were made up. I suppose it made me nervous to think that someone afraid of such powers would look too closely at her—at *us*. Then again, I could not deny that in the wake of the civil war, it *was* a lucrative profession. Almost every family had a dead soldier, and many of the mourners had a desire to speak to their lost.

I, too, realized how the "spirits" could be our salvation—if only Kate did not go and do something foolish, like marrying Rudolph Brockman.

The last guest arrived just as night was setting: a lone traveler in a thick coat and a pair of fingerless gloves protecting his hands from the night frost. His hat was dusty, and so were his boots. He said that his name was Jessup Jones.

That much, at least, I could glean from the conversation.

Kate placed him at the table and draped herself over the chair opposite the man. She leaned in across the wood, resting on her elbows, and watched his lips move with a rapt expression, all while making sure that his eyes were on her breasts—no doubt to annoy John, who had just come inside after taking the traveler's horse to the stable.

My husband was inside as well. He sat whittling by the stove, as was his habit at night. We were all waiting for the guest to have his fill, so we could split what was left in the pot between us. My belly was aching, and I could hear William's rumble, too, yet our guest seemed most comfortable just sitting there talking to Kate. I brought out the cider and placed the dusty bottle on the table with a glass. Kate poured for him and smiled. Talked some more.

"He will have the stew now," she said to me in German, still with that cloyingly sweet smile plastered to her lips. I let out a breath of relief and went for a plate.

"Mr. Jones is on his way to Independence to file a land claim," Kaye said behind my back. "He means to settle, I think."

John had slunk in behind the store counter and stood there with the morose expression that had become his everyday wear of late. He was cleaning out his pipe, drizzling soot all over the counter.

"Is his horse settled in?" I asked him while heaping stew onto a tin plate, just to have the boy think of something else but what was going on at the table.

"Of course." John looked at me as if I was stupid.

"Will he spend the night?" William's question was aimed at Kate. He twisted his neck to get her within his sight.

"I'll ask," Kate promised, and then her gaze was back on Mr. Jones, her lips once again curled into a smile. When he spilled a little bit of stew down in his beard, she bent forth and wiped it off with the hem of her apron, smiling all the while. Even *I* had to look away at that, finding the gesture intimate—shameless.

John said nothing but left his post at the counter to slip behind the curtain.

Kate laughed and filled the cider cup. William whittled. I busied myself with the kettle, thinking we could all use some tea. Mr. Jones spoke to Kate in a voice that had grown more boisterous as the cider went in. He laughed when she laughed. His face was shiny and red; his hair was tousled; his eyes shone like bits of mica. The candle between them on the table flickered.

Suddenly, his head met the plate with a crashing sound, splattering stew all over. The cup of cider toppled and spilled its contents down on the table, then to the floor. The candle went out when it followed suit, leaving behind an acrid smell. The room, now bathed in the glow from the kerosene lamp perched upon the store counter, seemed suddenly to have shrunk. There was another scent there, too, mixed in with that of stew and woodsmoke: pungent and heavy, laced with iron.

"What did you do?" Kate cried out. "What did you do?" At first, I thought she asked *me*, but then I realized it had to be John.

William and I reached the table at the same time. William bent over Mr. Jones and tried to force his head up from the plate.

"Calm down, Kate," I cried. "He has taken ill, that's all!"

William looked up at me from his examination of the guest; his eyes were shiny and dark as night. His hand, when it left Mr. Jones's head, came away red. It was covered in it.

Now it was *I* who cried, "What did you do, John? What did you do to the man?" My voice was shrill and panicked, my heartbeat as fast as a rabbit's in my chest.

John came out from behind the canvas curtain. His face was as white as chalk. He held the large hammer in his limp hand, and now I could see the grisly smear upon the curtain, just where Mr. Jones must have rested his head.

"Is he dead?" I cried to William. "Is the man *dead*?" William shrugged and threw out his red hands. He did not know. "Find out if he is dead!" I cried.

"I cannot tell," William replied to my question. "I cannot feel his breath, but—"

"Get your knife!" Kate's voice sounded calm. "If we do not act now, all is lost."

William scrambled across the floor to the stove for the whittling knife. John just stood there, staring without truly seeing the scene before him—the havoc that he had wrought.

"What were you *thinking*?" I shouted at his unmoving face. "Have you gone and lost your mind?"

William approached with the bone-handled knife in his hand, and Kate presented him with an open palm, waiting for it.

"No, no, no!" I cried when my daughter's fingers closed around the bone, but everything was happening too fast, and I could not prevent her from taking it.

I looked around me, trying to think; sweat dripped from my forehead. "Get rid of that hammer," I hissed at John. "Open the trapdoor to the cellar!" All I could think of was to hide the man away.

At this demand, John seemed to gather his wits somewhat. He placed the hammer almost gently upon the stool by the stove, and then he slipped back behind the curtain. A moment later, I heard the creaking sound of the trapdoor moving on its hinges.

William was back at the dead—or dying—man, using more force this time while prying his head from the plate.

"Help him!" Kate said to me; the knife shone dully in her hand.

Sniffling and cursing, I did as she asked, and made my way to
the other side of the table, where I laced my fingers in the mess of
hair and blood and stew. William and I lifted his head back and up,
exposing a hairy throat. At the time, I did not see just why we were
doing this. I thought, at first, that we were just going to hide him.

John, for all his stupidity, was no fool, and was already pulling
the curtain aside to expose the black hole behind Mr. Jones's chair.

"Tip him back," I said then, "we cannot have more blood spill on
the floor." The scent of it was strong already, mingled with a whiff
of piss. The floor at the man's feet was flecked with a dark substance, but I thought that it was mostly stew.

"Can you do this, Kate?" William's face looked gaunt in the dim
light from the kerosene lamp.

Kate did not hesitate. "You know I can."

A chill ran through my bones when I finally realized just what
they were thinking.

"But he is dead, is he not?" I protested.

"He might still be alive," Kate said, though if he was it was hard
to see. His mouth hung slack and his eyes were closed; bits of stew
dripped off his face. The shape of his head seemed wrong.

"If he is, he cannot stay that way for long." William sounded
both frightened and impatient. We all knew the implications of this.
If Mr. Jones should live, we would have to run again, with nothing
but the clothes on our backs.

"Do it, Kate," John cried from the other side of the cellar trapdoor, looking like a tall, pale wraith in the darkness. "What if another guest arrives?" He sounded much like a little boy all of a
sudden, frightened out of his wits.

William started kicking at the chair's hind legs so the furniture
tipped backward. Suddenly, we held Mr. Jones at an angle, above the

gaping cellar hole. The man was certainly heavy, and our arms shook from the strain.

William's gaze met mine over the slumped body. "We have to be *sure*," he said in a pleading voice. "We have to be *sure* he is dead."

"Do it, Kate!" John cried again.

I swallowed hard and nodded once. My face was slick with perspiration, my chest was heaving, and my limbs shook from the strain.

My daughter, though, was not in pain. She pushed the table aside, then crossed the short distance with the knife at the ready, brandished in her hand. Her gaze was fixed on the man's pale throat. *Her* hand shook, too, but not from fear. There was a sort of glow upon her face, and her eyes shone as if in rapture. She grabbed ahold of Mr. Jones's soiled hair.

"We'll tip him in the cellar right after," said William.

"Do it!" John cried again.

She lifted the knife and cut.

12.

KATE

THERE MUST STILL have been some life in him, for his blood came rushing out like juice from an overripe plum, coating the steel, coating my skin, emitting the smell of a slaughterhouse.

The gash I made ran clean across his throat, and a gurgling sound rose as his spirit left its shell. I thought I could feel it in the air for a moment, a lingering, cloying thing, wanting to glue itself to me. Then the man was gone.

I looked at him in the second before Ma and Pa tipped him into the cellar. His flesh was already turning white; his gaze was crushed and broken. Ma was wrong when she said that I did not feel a thing, for I felt very strongly in that moment—just not the regret that she wanted me to feel. The darkness is like that: heady and strong. Better than the world's finest liquor. I felt as if I were to burst from my skin myself when looking at the corpse of the man I had slain. I was in awe of the power in my hands.

It had been far too long since I last felt so strong.

I had fought the darkness ever since Pennsylvania—I *knew* it would not serve me to have it unleashed, and yet . . . I threw my head back and laughed. I felt much like a child again, giddy and free. Next, the laughter turned into a howl, like a wolf's, and I threw the knife in the air, just to catch its slippery handle when it returned, laughing all the while.

John laughed, too, as he closed the trapdoor with his foot. Ma did not; she looked pale. Pa, always so serene in the midst of upheaval, shuffled to the corner for the broom.

The floor was indeed a mess.

"Get out of here!" Ma sent me a look of utter contempt. "I cannot look at you, Kate."

"Why?" I was still laughing. "It was John who hit him—I only served the man cider."

"Get out of here!" she bellowed. "I cannot look at you now—and not you either." She looked at John. "Get out of here, the both of you!" She was white in the face and shaking all over.

"They have to help with the cleaning," William interjected, but Ma would not have it.

"Get out!" she screamed at John and me, and I, for one, was more than happy to oblige.

I got my shawl from the peg by the door and strode out into the calm night. The sky high above was black as tar and freckled with stars. The air around me was cold and invigorating. I lifted my hand to my nose to smell the blood just as I heard the door slam behind me, and John's footsteps sounded on the dry, cold ground. When he came up beside me, he cocked his head and smiled, though I could see the insecurity lingering in his eyes. He did not know if I was still mad at him.

I took his hand in mine as we rushed toward the barn. It was the only place to go with it being so cold outside. I felt as though I was flying across the ground, was still beset with a ridiculous joy—a sense of triumph that reverberated deep within my bones—as I flung the barn door open and entered the musty dampness inside.

I waited impatiently while John lit the kerosene lamp dangling from a hook in the ceiling. There was not a sound but our breathing and the shifting of the animals. Once the wick lit up, John and I caught each other's gazes and laughed again. I did not see a fool in him just then, but a savior. Who would have thought that his bothersome jealousy could ever lead to *this*?

"John." I laughed. "John! You truly know how to make me happy."

"Did you really like it that much?" He sounded both delighted and astounded. "Had I known that you would like it, I would have done it much sooner. Killing that Brockman, for one," he boasted.

"Shut up, John," I said, still smiling, and slumped down in the hay. "It was a brave thing you did tonight, smashing his head with the hammer. I do think you deserve a reward."

"Do I?" He sounded as delighted now as he had been angry before. "What is it?" he asked, in a voice full of anticipation.

I searched with my hand in the hay until I found the neck of the bottle I had hidden there. His face fell a little when he saw it; I suppose he had been hoping for something else.

"You sure like to cut." He chuckled nervously while I myself had a drink before handing the whiskey to him.

"That I do," I agreed, still savoring the feeling, riding high on the relief from the cut. It was the best that I had felt since Pennsylvania; ever since Emil Zimmerman.

"It's the darkness, isn't it?" he asked. "It's that feeling you were telling me about when we fled? The one that's always tempting you."

"It sure is," I agreed, remembering only too well how I had tried to explain it all to him back then, while we slept under the wagon, hiding in unfamiliar landscapes. I had recalled Emil's death and how it had made me feel. "It was as if I was the most powerful creature in all the world—as if Emil was nothing but a beetle under my shoe . . . It must be how God feels," I had told him. "It felt like the sweetest victory." I had also shared with him how I could not help but think of it since; how my mind so often strayed there, remembering every moment and recalling every sensation.

How I longed to feel that way again.

I did not think that John had hit Mr. Jones to please me, but he had pleased me nevertheless, and though I had often regretted sharing my feelings about the darkness with John, as it felt sacred, almost, I was glad of it now, as I would not have to hide my feelings.

"Ma will kill us," John mused. He had sat down beside me in the hay and handed the bottle back to me. He sounded pleased, though. Pleased and amused. John had never had any qualms about causing damage, and especially not when he felt threatened somehow.

"She'll be even more afraid now, for sure," I agreed with a chuckle. The whiskey tasted smoky and strong; it fueled the fire already burning in me.

"Was it as good as last time?" he wanted to know. "Was it as good as with Zimmerman?"

"Sure," I said, laughing again. "It was even better, because this time, if we play our cards right, we won't even have to run."

That whole mess with Emil Zimmerman had started out as nothing much—just a silly infatuation. Emil had been a farmer who had lived not far from us back in Pennsylvania. He came to Ma one day seeking a cure for a wound that would not heal. He said that he had been chopping wood, struck wrong with the axe, and hit his calf. I was at home when he arrived, and I helped Ma clean and bind the damaged leg. I admit that I liked the look of him. He had dark brown eyes and thick brown hair, and he smelled of fresh sweat, pine, and tar. He had a golden sort of complexion that I had never seen the likes of on any man.

He came back several times that spring to have his wound treated, and it was easy to see how he did not mind my hands upon his skin as he sat there on the chair with me on the floor, washing out the pus with a damp cloth. While I rubbed in the ointment, he told me tales from when he was fighting in the war. Once, he pulled down his pants to show me a scar upon his hip, where a bayonet had struck. It looked ugly still, like a vein of winding tallow, yet that little glimpse of him caused me many a sleepless night.

Not even when Gretchen told us that Emil had *not* been careless with the axe, but had taken part in a drunken brawl over property lines, did it make him any less in my eyes. I could not chase that man from my mind, but neither did I try very hard. As he got better, I often went to watch Mr. Zimmerman work in his field, innocently strolling by on the dirt road with a basket in the crook of my arm, as if I had been out for herbs for Ma. Sometimes he came to talk to me, while wiping his brow or refreshing himself with a drink of beer. We would stand under the blazing sun, jesting and laughing, until his wife, Louisa, came outside. Then I found it was time to go.

When he was done with his work in the fields that spring, he moved on to the woods, chopping down trees for firewood. That was when things got easier. Louisa would bring him food at noon, but otherwise Emil was working alone, with no one else in sight. I, of course, happened to stroll by with my basket, and it was easy after that.

For a few heady weeks, I went to see Emil every day. Our trysts were quick and rough, and often left my back red from scratching against tree trunks or the naked ground. I cannot say just why Emil Zimmerman lost his luster for me, but he did so early on. Mayhap all I had truly wanted was to see if I could have him. Mayhap I had done it mostly to irk John, who was a menace already then.

Once the deed was done, however, I found that I felt nothing at all.

I went to the woods less often, and when I did I would not linger, but have my fill and go. I thought that surely I could find another man just as fine-looking who could provide me with a little more than swift company.

I do not know how the rumor spread. If it was Emil himself, who drank too much and boasted to a neighbor, or if we had been seen. Whatever the cause was, the secret was soon no longer ours alone, but spread like a creeping wildfire. I could see it reflected in people's eyes whenever I crossed their path. No one said anything outright, but neither did they have to. No one came to Ma for cures anymore, unless they could do it in the cloak of night. Pa was warned by other men to keep his daughter in check. It did not help one bit that I stopped seeing Emil in the woods; the damage was already done.

"It will pass," Pa said when Ma complained about the neighbors' unfriendliness. "They cannot afford to hold a grudge for long. We depend too much on each other up here." Maybe he was right, too, that it would have blown over in time, had it not been for Louisa.

It so happened that, just as the secret crept silently from farm to farm, one of the Zimmermans' cows took ill and lost most of its weight within days; it also happened that what little milk the cow gave came out red. It did not take long, then, before Gretchen came to tell us that Louisa Zimmerman claimed that it was Ma—or even I—who had put a hex on the creature, as revenge for Emil refusing me. I was livid when I heard the accusations. Not because I feared Louisa, but because she had said that *her husband* had refused *me*, when I knew that to be wrong.

Ma, however, had other concerns.

"It's a terrible thing when suspicions like that are being voiced," she said as we ground up herbs for a poultice. "You may laugh at it, but in a small place like this, it's no laughing matter. You know how they are *terrified* of witches around here, even as they love their cures."

"Maybe they deserve to feel a little fear," said I.

"No, no." Ma shook her head so hard that some locks of her hair fell out of the pins and danced around her face. "It's no laughing matter, Kate. People become dangerous when they're afraid. Gretchen said they are spinning tales where the two of us are danc-ing naked in the graveyard, invoking the devil himself."

"What for?" I frowned at her. "Why would we do that?"

Ma only shrugged. "I'm sure they have many ideas."

"Pa says it'll blow over."

"Let's pray that he is right," she replied, though she knew I was bad at that—and in the end, no prayers could have saved us, I think, when the wind blew up to a gale.

Louisa Zimmerman took ill on a Monday, lying in bed with stomach pains. On Tuesday, they sent for Gretchen, and when her remedies did not help, they sent for a proper doctor to come, even if it was costly. The doctor could not say what was wrong with Mrs. Zimmerman, though, and people of course knew who to blame.

Now all doors were suddenly closed to us. No one would barter or buy anything we had touched. Even Gretchen saw fewer people coming to seek her aid, and her friendship with us became a secret overnight, conducted in hushed conversations in dark rooms. Ma and I would make our way after nightfall, and Gretchen would let us in through the back door to huddle before the smoldering stove. She dared not light a lamp or even a candle for fear that the people she depended upon for her livelihood would see her consorting with witches.

Dead crows started showing up on our doorstep. They were shot and left, bloody and ruined, for us to find. Ma scoffed at it at first, calling it pranks, but then they never stopped. Every day there was a new one, and their message was more than clear. None of us slept very well but for the nights when Pa kept watch on the porch.

When this had been going on for some weeks, we were all wrung out from the ordeal. It was bothersome—and humiliating—to be barred entrance to other people's homes. I was forced to spend my days at the farm again, with John's eyes always upon me, just for fear of what could befall me if I went outside alone.

Then they set fire to the barn.

It was never a large fire, as we caught it in time, but it spooked the horses and reduced some hay to cinders. It happened in the early hours, and had not John slept out on the porch with the rifle, we might not have seen it before it was too late. The arson had been done by the outer wall, and it still smelled strongly of kerosene where the flames had eaten through the timber.

Pa raged and wanted to go after the culprits, but since we did not know who that was, it simply could not be done. Ma, always one to look to prayers and magic in her hour of need—and only then—made crude poppets out of wood, hollowed them out, filled them with matter, and spent a whole day hammering nails into their wooden forms, a trick she had learned from Gretchen. Their only true purpose was to ease Ma's anger and fear, as they would surely not bring death to our enemies.

I thought that it was time that I spoke to Emil himself, and asked him to put a stop to the rumors. He would surely know that it was not *I* who had made his wife sick, and should stop her from spreading her lies. It seemed to me that if anyone was to be punished, it was him, as it was *he*—not *I*—who was married.

I did not tell anyone that I went, as I was sure my family would object. They did not know Emil as I did, though. I had had him between my legs, and felt his breath upon my lips. He had taken great pleasure in our meetings, so surely he would have to listen to me.

It was dusk when I arrived at his farm. He had a sturdy-looking house with a wide porch where a white cat was slumbering peacefully. I could see candles burning in the windows, so they were likely holding a vigil for the sick.

I had meant to go straight to the green-painted door and knock, but before I had even entered the porch, their large gray watchdog came upon me, barking something fierce. I took a few steps back and waited instead, certain that the ruckus would draw someone out. After a while, it did, and Emil himself was suddenly there before me, filling the doorframe with his broad shoulders. He looked a little haggard—likely from having a sick wife. His cheeks seemed hollow, and black half-moons fanned out below his eyes, which were glossy with drink and fatigue.

When he saw that it was I, dread settled upon his features, and he quickly stepped outside, pulling the door closed behind him.

"Kate," he hissed, "you cannot be here."

"Sure I can," I said. "I need to talk to you."

"Not here," he hissed again, and stepped down from the porch. "We'll talk in the orchard." He nodded toward a cluster of gnarled apple trees on the hind side of the barn.

He told the dog to stay, and then we made our way to the apple grove, each of us huddled and grim in the face, keeping ample distance between us. Neither of us wanted to be there. It was late and dusk had settled, painting the world in dark shadows. Beneath the apple tree branches, we were invisible to the world.

We stood facing each other like strangers.

"You have to stop your wife's foul tongue," I said. "She's causing all sorts of happenings up at our farm."

He grimaced and looked a little sick himself. "My wife is ill—"

"Not so ill that she cannot poison every one of our neighbors against us. We can barely feed ourselves—"

"I can't help you with that, Kate."

"Sure you can." I lifted my chin. "You better tell her, and everyone who listens, that you did not have me, and I did not curse you."

"Well." I could only just make out his smug face in the dim light. "I *did* have you, so that would be a lie."

"I don't think your soul would be further tainted by one small lie." My voice had grown hoarse with scorn. It bothered me a great deal to think that this man who was nothing to me still yielded such power over my well-being. I *loathed* to be at his mercy.

"Perhaps my wife's illness has made me change my ways." He still sounded calm, still sounded smug—and more than a little bit drunk, too. "Mayhap I'd rather be inclined to tell it like it is," he said.

"Really?" I arched an eyebrow. "You'd tell her that I grew tired of you—that you couldn't properly serve me?" I smirked.

His pale cheeks got some color then, and his face twisted up in a sneer. "I'd tell her that you're nothing but a *whore*, Kate—maybe not a clever witch, but surely a *whore*, but I won't bother my sick wife on your account!"

I had brought my knife, but I had not thought to use it. Up on the mountain, it was always there at hand, dangling from my belt. I used it to cut herbs and twine, twigs and burlap. Yet when the anger at his words came rising like hot champagne, I did not even think twice before whipping it out between us.

"What is that?" His mocking voice rose in the night and he swayed a little on his feet. "Will you stab me now, Kate? Well, I suppose that's what *whores* do, if they do not get their way." He laughed as if it was all so very ridiculous. He did not fear me at all.

I stabbed him then. I did. All the way to the hilt, just where I knew the belly was soft and likely to easily yield. When the knife was in and he screamed with pain, I jerked it upward. I have found that if one is fast enough, one can easily make up for a lack of strength and it does not much matter if your opponent is large.

Before his hands had even reached mine to wring them away from the knife, his belly was slick with blood, and he had to fight a long time before he got the knife out. He should perhaps not have removed it, because as soon as he did, he went down to his knees— then to his side, cursing like a sailor all the while.

"Help me," he uttered in a broken voice when he realized that things were not going his way. "Help me or I'll die!"

I thought that a foolish threat to make, as I had clearly *meant* for him to die. "You got better than you deserved," I said, then kicked him where he bled and left him behind to die in peace.

I felt nothing but cold fury until I was halfway home. Then it all shifted in me, and instead of the rage, there was the darkness: heady and blissful—better than being drunk. The euphoria was so strong in me that I took off from the path to find a tree stump to sit on and remained there for a good long while in the dark, warm night, laughing until my belly ached, then screaming into my hands. I did not leave before the rush had subsided and the mirth had settled to a dull glow.

Then I went on home.

My family was not as amused as me. They were all still up when I arrived, filthy and drenched in blood. They were gathered at the table, where a single candle burned.

"Where have you been?" Ma rose to her feet.

"To see Emil Zimmerman." I spoke calmly, though my voice was hoarse from screaming.

"You foolish girl," said Ma.

"Did he hurt you?" John sounded frightened.

"Not at all," I replied, smiling at them. "He won't help us squelch the rumors, though. He won't do anything much at all."

"For heaven's sake, Kate." Ma came striding across the floor. She grabbed ahold of my arm and shook me. "Did you leave him alive? Did you?"

"Yes." I met her eyes with mine. "But I do not think he'll last."

John, at the table, started giggling. Ma's lips curled into a hard line.

Pa rose to his full burly height and said, "I'll go and ready the wagon. We must be gone by dawn."

We left then, that night, and had been running ever since.

13.

HANSON

THE BOTTLE EXPLODED in a glittering shower as my new friend Bruno Weissbrod threw the stone. He and his brother, Max, had just moved from Missouri to a homestead nearby, and to my utter delight they quite often came to spend a little time with me, or to beg some boiled candy from Mr. Ern and Mr. Brockman. They were of the same age as myself, tall and strong from farming, and had hair the same shade of brown as our mare. I liked the younger one, Max, the best. He had a very freckled nose and was not as brash as his brother, who tended to always think himself the better judge.

On that day, we had lined up several bottles behind the barn and were competing to see who could destroy the most. I was never a strong marksman and had resigned myself to fill the role of the loser early on. I still participated, though, thrilled to have the company of other boys, and taking heart in the knowledge that I likely was better at my letters than the Weissbrods. Every night before going to bed, I dreamed of what it would be like to be a proper newspaper-man and touched Kate's paper flower for luck.

The Weissbrod brothers were serious competitors, though; they squinted their eyes as they took aim and hurtled the pebbles through the air. They reeked of it, too, a strong, sour smell of sweat, as if the excitement of the game came pouring from their skin. I was happy not to share in that particular reek. On that day, their minds were not entirely on the mark, however. They, like the rest of us, had heard the rumors from town about the body that had been found in the shallows of the river, with its skull bashed in and its throat cut.

No one knew who he was.

"His neck was cut from ear to ear," Bruno said as he took aim again. "There was barely any blood left in him."

"Ma says he must have been emptied of it before he went into the water," Max added.

Their ma seemed to be a bloodthirsty sort who reveled in such gruesome descriptions. I had seen her many times, as she came for canned beans and loaves of sugar, but you could not see it on her. She looked much like everybody else, with a long, lean body and a face etched with lines from sun, wind, and rain. Mrs. Weissbrod preferred to speak German and would gossip with Mr. Brockman at length while partaking of sweet tea and maybe some cake. She was sure to enjoy having a dead man to occupy her mind.

"Why would they empty him before he went into the water?" I asked, unable to see any practical use for human blood.

"Some people like to drink it." Bruno shrugged and hurtled a rock, reducing another bottle to shards. "They think it makes them strong."

"Ma says that if you have developed a taste for it, nothing else will do," said Max, instantly adding to my growing menagerie of things to fear in the night.

"Surely no one in Cherryvale has such appetites," I said, shuddering to think it could be one of our patrons.

"It doesn't show on the outside." Bruno laughed, which brought me no comfort at all.

"I'm sure he was killed for his money, not his blood." I half-heartedly threw a pebble of my own. It landed just in front of its intended mark.

"Ma says that you never know what people are capable of." Max weighed another rock in his hand.

"Maybe the man was a robber himself." Bruno inspected the ground for something else to throw. "It could have been a brawl between thieves."

"Nah," said Max. "Pa said there were no marks on his knuckles, just the holes in his head and neck. He did not look to have been in a brawl." Mr. Weissbrod had been one of the first to see him, having passed by just as some men from town carried him from the river. It seemed such an ugly thing to me, to die like that and be tossed away like any old chunk of bad meat.

As if he were worth nothing at all.

"It's like he was killed thrice," Bruno mused. "First the blow to the head, then the cut to the throat, and then, lastly, the drowning—though he was sure to be dead by then."

"Someone wanted him *really* dead," Max added with an ounce of glee.

"Someone sure wanted his cash," I said, still eager to rule out a blood-drinking fiend.

"They got *that*," said Max, "and his pants besides, leaving him with nothing but his drawers."

It sure was a greedy murderer.

The Weissbrod brothers were not the only ones to speculate. The dead man was all people seemed to talk about when they came to the trading station. They detailed the damage to the body and wondered about who he could be. He had to be a victim of robbery, they said, as there were no valuables left on him, and barely any clothes. Many people went to see him after they had fished him out of the water. Some were mostly curious, I think, while others wanted to solve the mystery of the dead man's identity. I did not go, and neither did Mr. Brockman or Mr. Ern. The first was much too heartbroken over Kate's silence to find even a spark of curiosity left in him. He worried that something had gone wrong between them but could not say for sure, as Kate did not come to visit anymore— but neither had she broken off the engagement, so none of us knew quite what to make of it. Mr. Ern, on his side, found such voyeurism tasteless—or at least that was what I thought at first.

"Maybe you *should* go," I said to Mr. Ern one morning as we were sharing some eggs. "Maybe you'd recognize him. Maybe he's been *here*, stocking up on supplies." Many of the patrons at the trading station were more than willing to share a little about who they were and where they were to go, so this was not unlikely at all. I had been thinking hard myself, trying to remember what the different riders had said of late. I could not think of it for too long, though, as the thought of the dead man in the river left a cold feeling in my chest. It was as if nothing was safe anymore and even the mundane seemed suddenly riddled with danger.

"I don't think I should get involved in that ugly affair," Mr. Ern said. He had placed his beat-up tin plate on the store counter and was shoveling his eggs with a long-tined fork. The coffee he had poured himself sent swirls of smoke into the cold morning air.

I was seated on a wooden stool close to the stove, which had just about gathered up steam. Inside its iron belly, it crackled and hissed as the flames chewed at the fuel. I had my own plate of eggs balanced on my knees. "But what if you could tell them who he is?" I said between mouthfuls. "Maybe you could solve a mystery." That thought was very compelling to me.

Mr. Ern shrugged. "He died in such an ugly way, and though they say it was a robbery, we don't know that for sure. Perhaps it was someone known to him, and the murderer wants to keep the victim's name a secret. I don't think it's wise to aggravate someone with such a thirst for violence. Maybe he'd come for the tattler next."

"But what if someone is waiting for the dead man back home?" I asked.

Mr. Ern gave another shrug. His jaws were working fast and efficiently as he chewed his breakfast. "The truth will always come out in cases such as this. If he has kin, they will certainly come here as soon as they hear of the finding."

"But what if he has *no one* at home? Or what if they think he is safe somewhere else?"

"Then they will live blissful in that conviction, until something happens to shatter the delusion." Mr. Ern finished his eggs with a couple more forkfuls and went out back with the greasy plate.

I thought this was all very strange, as I would have been thrilled to be of help in identifying the man, but I suppose Mr. Ern was too frightened of the evildoer. Just the month before, shortly before Mr. Brockman's engagement, we had a man stopping for some jerked beef whom Mr. Brockman later informed me was a known horse thief by the name of Handsome. I had been a little shaken after that and had decided to sleep on a mattress inside the station instead of retreating to the barn. I still slept inside, though I missed the sounds of the animals at night. It was getting colder, so it was not just the horse thief—or the *blood drinker*—that had chased me inside. I much preferred the little warmth from the dying embers in the stove to the sharp sting of cold in the morning.

I kept thinking about that horse thief, though, and if *he* could have something to do with the dead man. Mr. Brockman had fretted some because he had stopped at the Benders' after he had been at the trading station, and so he had feared for Kate's safety. I had thought that a little silly, as we had all known by then that she was more than capable of holding her own, being supported by the spirits and all. Now I decided to go and see them, though, as, even if Mr. Ern and Mr. Brockman refused to look at the nameless body, maybe the Benders would. He could just as well have stopped by *their* place, I reckoned, and I felt quite the Pinkerton agent as I walked with the mule down the road.

I found Kate outside the house, at it with a plunger in a tub of dirty water. Under the gray-tinted surface, I saw pieces of white cloth swim in the churn like little pale fish. Plumes of steam rose in the cold air, so she must just have added some hot water. Her brow looked sweaty, and some of her hair had come undone, coiling like serpents on her shoulders. A thick brown shawl was wrapped around her torso.

"Hello there, Hanson," she called out in greeting. "Is this fine, cold morning treating you well?"

"Very well, Miss Kate," I chirped in reply, acting far more cheerful than I felt. A strong scent of woodsmoke permeated the air around us, creeping out from the chimney.

Kate paused her eager plunging, straightened up, and stretched her back. "What brings you here so early? Are you running errands for Mr. Ern?"

"No," I admitted. "I just wanted to see how you were doing, with the news from town and all." I had meant to be more furtive about it, but since it was so strongly on my mind, I ended up blurting it out at once. Perhaps I was not a very good Pinkerton.

"What news?" Kate furrowed her brow.

"About the dead man," I said. "The one in the river."

"Oh, that." Something like annoyance flared across her face, as quick as the flap of a bird's wing. "I haven't really thought much of it," she said. "Such things happen. There's a lot of bad men on the roads."

"Sure." I took off my hat and scratched my head, feeling a little puzzled. "Some travelers stop by here, though," I said. "I thought maybe you were worried because of that."

She shrugged. "What can you do? We cannot spend our time worrying and fretting, and I am well protected, as you know."

I felt a little calmer when she mentioned that fact. "Has Mr. Bender been to see the dead man?" I asked. "I'm curious to know if he ever stopped by here—if you happen to know who he is."

Kate shook her head. "Pa hasn't mentioned it. There's a lot of people stopping by, so of course he *could* have been here . . . it's hard to say." She had picked up the plunger again and stared down into the tub's murky depths.

"Maybe Mr. Bender would know him if he saw him," I prompted eagerly. "Perhaps he could help find out who he is—"

"*Was.*" Kate corrected me with surprising sharpness. "He is dead now, so he isn't anyone anymore."

"Well, who he *was,* then," I agreed.

"Why are you so curious to know?" She looked up at me from her bent position, pale eyes framed by auburn coils of hair.

"Oh, I . . . I just wanted to know if he was a bad sort is all." If he was, I could maybe sleep a little better at night, as it diminished the likelihood of a random murderer prowling in the night.

"All men are bad one way or the other." A slight smirk curved Kate's lips. "You only have to look close enough and you'll see it. There's nothing like true innocence in this world, Hanson. We're all guilty of *something*."

I wanted to say that I thought she was wrong, and that I for one had very little on my conscience, but then I thought better of it. I was not there to flaunt the purity of my soul. "The Weissbrods think he might have been a scoundrel himself," I blurted out. "They think it could've been a matter between thieves."

"The Weissbrods, huh?" Kate was working the plunger again, creating a noisy torrent in the tub. "I have seen those boys around, crossing the property for no good reason . . . I think they're a nosy lot."

"They sure are." I shrugged. There was no point in denying it.

"Well, it's perhaps not such a good idea to come snooping around here," Kate said, her mouth twisted up as if she were sucking on something sour. "Pa can be short-tempered, and he always has his rifle nearby."

I thought that did not sound much like Mr. Bender as I knew him, but perhaps he got particularly irked by boys like the Weissbrods, who could indeed come across as aggravating. Even *I* could tell as much. "I'll let them know," I said.

Kate paused her work again to give me another look; this time her eyes were soft. "You shouldn't worry so much about that man," she said. "Travelers are often destined for unhappy fates. You're not, though; you're special, Hanson. You'll live far into your nineties, as I see it." She laughed and winked at me.

I shuddered a little to hear her speak such a prophecy as if it was nothing at all—and even if she said I would grow very old, I still did not like having my own death predicted.

"But what about that horse thief?" I tried once more to coax some interest from her. "He who was here before . . . Mr. Brockman was very concerned for you then. Do you think he could have something to do with the dead man?"

Kate chuckled a little at that. "You'll sure make a fine newspaperman one day," she remarked, and I felt a hot swelling in my chest. "I don't know about any horse thief, though. I don't think that he was here." She paused again and drew a hand across her brow to wipe off the fresh shine of sweat. "How *is* Mr. Brockman? I haven't seen him for some time."

I did not think it was my place to explain how Mr. Brockman had been disappointed after his proposal and the subsequent silence from the Benders, and how Mr. Ern may have gotten to him, whispering his doubts. "Oh, he's fine," I lied. "Only very busy."

"Maybe you can take a message to him?" she asked. "I'll write him a note."

"Sure." I agreed at once, as it was sure to cheer him up.

"Wonderful." Her face lit up in a smile. "You know, if they really wanted to know who that dead man was, they should come to me," she said as an afterthought. "I'm a coveted medium, you know. They have even asked me to demonstrate at the hotel in Cherryvale. Mr. Black could tell who he was in no time at all. He's already whispering as we speak. He says the dead man was indeed a bad sort, so you were right about that, Hanson." She gave a nod of surety, but I could not shake a feeling that she was saying it mostly to comfort me. "I'm sure I could give them a name just as easily if they were willing to pay for the answer," she added. "Mediums make for fine detectives."

I thought that it seemed more practical for Mr. Bender to just go and have a look at the body but deemed it wise not to say so. "Mr. Ern won't look at the body either," I complained instead. "I just think that someone *should*. It's not unlikely that he came through here."

Kate sighed and placed a hand on her hip; once again a flare of annoyance crossed her features. "You ought to let it go, Hanson. It has nothing to do with you or me. Why don't you step inside for a bit? I think Ma has some soup on the stove—the good kind with lots of meat." She said it to tempt me, and it worked as well, as my belly was growling with hunger. "Everything will be fine," said Kate. "What is dead is gone, and there's nothing we can do to undo it."

"I just wish the murderer would get caught," I said with a heart-felt sigh, feeling the wish settle deep in my bones.

"Well, yes," said Kate, sounding a little impatient; her lips had become a thin line in her face. "I do understand that, Hanson, but we cannot always get what we want."

14.

KATE

WE HAD HAM for dinner, buttered potatoes, and pudding. We could afford all that now; we were rich—or at least better off than before. We had just bought a calf, a piglet, and a handful of chickens. Things were looking up at the Bender place.

The ham was so tender and pink, the butter so salty and golden. I had not eaten anything like it since we arrived in Kansas, and I felt as though I deserved every bite, every morsel of savory flesh.

John, too, exhibited an excellent appetite, shoveling food into his maw with much joy and relish. A little grease glistened in his mustache.

"Wonderful food, Ma," he complimented our cook. "The best meal we've had since we got here." Pa, next to him, nodded his agreement, armed with knife and fork. His face was red from all the strong cider he had drunk, on top of a fair share of whiskey. Only Ma remained sour as a bottle of vinegar. Her disapproval curled though the room like smoke. She ate her food, but from the looks of it, it could just as well have been cold potatoes and old fish on her plate. I rolled my eyes and sighed when I saw it—she always knew how to make every occasion all about her and her mask of righteousness. I could not stand it. I never had. The woman was rotten through and through.

Ma's head kept swiveling in the door's direction, her gaze darting to the window. She was listening for sounds of horses out in the yard. It was not inn guests she feared, but riders from town. The county trustee, Mr. Leroy Dick, and his men had come to the farm a few days before, wanting to know if we had served the dead stranger. I was the one to deal with it, of course, which had been simple enough: a shake of the head and an utterance of shock, and they had been on their way. They did not even look around but only took my word for it. It is both the blessing and the curse of my sex to never be seen as a threat.

It had been lucky for us that Jessup Jones had traveled loaded with money. Lucky, too, that Pa had thought to strip him down, claiming it a waste if we let him meet his grave without saving whatever was on him. Shoes, socks, belt, pants, and vest—he could think of a use for everything. Most joy was derived from the man's money belt, of course, cleverly strapped to his waist. Jessup Jones had indeed been out bargaining for land, it seemed, as much of his savings must have been in there.

Now it had bought us new livestock.

"Don't look so glum, Ma." I lifted my cup and drank deep. "I swear to you that no one knows who the dead man is. It's a mystery to all of them, something to keep them occupied."

"It was a foolish thing to drop him in the river." She kept her gaze on her plate and shook her head with such vigor that her jowls quivered. "You should have known that he would wash up." She raised her gaze to look between the men, who had seen to the disposal of Mr. Jones.

John put down his utensils. "It was hard to get him far enough out to be submerged," he admitted, sounding somewhat petulant. "We were in such a rush, worried we'd be caught red-handed."

Pa nodded solemnly. "It was the best we could do that night, lest we'd still have him festering in the cellar."

"I can't think to store my milk down there again," Ma lamented. "The floor is drenched in blood."

"He bled a lot," I agreed. The memory teased a smile to my lips. I, for one, had felt better ever since the man went down in the cellar. The darkness was sated and I was strong.

"I think that he most certainly was dead after the hammer," Ma said, as if to convince herself. I did not understand why, as she had not known Jessup Jones and had no reason to grieve for him. It annoyed me greatly how she would always make such a spectacle of her woes and suffering. She had benefited from his death like the rest of us—just as she had from the deaths of the Vandles.

"It was cunning how we did it, don't you think?" Pa sounded proud, unable, as always, to properly sense Ma's mood. His face was flushed with excitement, his demeanor like a dog with a bone, inflamed by inspiration. "He didn't see John coming at all," he continued, marveling at it all. "That curtain is a blessing—a man can hide behind there for however long without detection, and the man in front, eager with his meal, he won't know a thing before the blow. He won't have time to defend himself, and then with the trapdoor, there's very little spill—"

"What are you saying, husband?" Ma's voice cracked in the air like the snap of a whip.

"We made more from that strike than we do in a year," he stated as his eyes glittered and shone below the bushy eyebrows. "The kind of savings we will need to start anew are hard to come by, Elvira, and Kate and the spirits will still need some time . . . If you want to leave here soon, we ought to think about it." Content with his speech, he set his cup aside and lifted his knife to slice into the tender meat.

"It's not safe to leave," Ma muttered, though I could see the greed come alive in her eyes. "They haven't forgotten the Vandles yet."

"*No one* is looking for us, Ma," I said, although it was a tired tune, uttered too many times to count. There was simply nothing to do for it; the fear had crept in under her skin and settled. Before we left Pennsylvania, she had been so bold and brash, but ever since we had to flee, she had become different, erratic and simpering. It was nothing to me of course, if she had not insisted on keeping me close, tethered to her with an iron grip. I was the last child alive, the one to make it count, all that she had suffered. I was to pay her back, not just for the farm but for everything else as well: the life that she had lived and deemed so unjust. She thought I should pay her for the damage I had wrought just by being born.

"It's too soon!" she replied, another old tune.

"But when you deem it is safe"—Pa sounded utterly undeterred—"we ought to be prepared! Line our coffers with gold so we can make a fresh start and set up a proper farm for you, high up in the mountains."

"Have you all gone and lost your minds?" A sheen of sweat had erupted on Ma's pale face. "Do you want to turn our home into a slaughterhouse?" She promptly set to filling her cup anew; the cider fizzed and danced down there.

"Oh, Ma." I sighed, exasperated by her display. "You care no more for your fellow man than *I* do—maybe even less. We take care of our own; the rest can fend for themselves."

Suddenly, she was on her feet and promptly emptied her cup in my face. The fermented apple juice hit me like lukewarm rain. I just could not help but laugh, even as I gasped, cursed, and wiped at it with my sleeve. It seemed like such a foolish thing to do—so unlike Ma, who was usually swift to go for the broom.

"Shame on you for speaking to your mother in that way." Ma stood before me; scolding me in a hoarse voice. The empty cup was in her hand, dripping onto the floor. "Stop laughing!" she demanded.

"It's all right, Elvira." Pa's voice was calm and steady; he rose from his chair and shuffled over, placing a calming hand on her shoulder. "It was a hard thing for all of us, what happened, but we got through it, didn't we? Mr. Jones has been found, but no one looks to us; they are blaming some unknown evildoer for it. We'd be stupid not to think if we could do it again."

"Are you all so cold?" She shrugged Pa's hand off and sank back down onto her seat. Her lament did not sound sincere, however, not to me. I had known her for far too long. I only rolled my eyes at her, then rose and went behind the canvas curtain to find a scrap of cloth to properly dry off the cider, still with a smile of amusement playing upon my lips.

While I was back there, I noted the trapdoor in the floor, and all sorts of wonderful sensations came upon me as I remembered the man, how he had bled; the scent and the sight—and how good I had felt, wielding the blade. I did not regret it at all. I had not known Jessup Jones, and did not *care* to know anything about him either, so I had stayed far away from the investigation in Cherryvale. It was better not to know a thing and let him remain naught but a warm body that passed through our door. I had not hated him like I did Emil Zimmerman, but he had sufficed just the same.

My thoughts at night were dark of late, but deliciously so—I remembered every second of the kill. I had saved a button from Mr.

Jones's coat and hidden it in a box in the barn. It was a pretty box of metal, made for cigars and smelled like it, too, all fragrant and strong. It had a painting of a ship on the lid. Sometimes I would go out there alone just to look at its sole treasure and hold it in my hand; it was made of brass, and a swirling pattern was etched into its dome. I often traced it with my finger.

It was not wise, keeping such a trinket around, but I could not seem to help myself. Besides, the world was awash in buttons, and who would ever look to me—to us? We were hardly outlaws or vagrants, and people were easily fooled. I had learned so early on.

"Not all travel with cash strapped to their bellies," John mused just as I returned to the table, still wiping at my sticky face; I had gotten some of the cider in my nose, and so everything smelled like yeast and apples. "How would we know who to choose?" John asked. He was picking his teeth with a piece of bone.

"Well, we do have a proper medium in our midst." Pa, back on his chair, smiled with something like pride on his face. "I'm sure Kate's angels can help with that—right, Kate?" He beamed at me, and I could not help but chuckle.

"For sure, Pa." I played along as I sat myself down, pretending not to see Ma's furious gaze. "I'm sure they can be of use."

"We were going to lie low," she complained, kept singing that old, sad song.

Pa shook his head. "Our mistake before was to harm someone we were known to have had an argument with. It's different with these strangers." He combed through his beard with his hand; a thoughtful expression had settled on his features. The thought of doing it again sent my head spinning as my heart started racing.

"You want the farm, Ma. I know you do." I took care not to let my excitement show, as it would doubtlessly unsettle her anew.

"Why should others prosper while we suffer?" I asked, as I knew such musings irked her. She always felt shortchanged in life, as if some glorious fate had escaped her. It had made her both greedy and bitter, and such emotions are easy to stir.

Ma went quiet for a long time. We were all watching her, John with the bone still protruding from his lips, Pa with his hand cradling his beard, and me with the cider-stained cloth between my fingers. "And if we get caught?" she asked at last. I suppose it was her greatest fear, to never again have the share she deserved but draw her last breath in the noose's embrace.

"We won't." Pa sounded certain; a wide smile had appeared upon his lips. "Not with Kate's angels and your cures on our side." He chuckled, content as he leaned back in the chair.

I smiled, too, though for other reasons. It also did not escape my attention that if the travelers could provide us with ample cash, I might not be forced to pay for Ma's farm after all.

I could be free of them all before long.

15.

KATE

Labette County, Kansas
1872

I WAS STANDING in the very same hotel where I had, only months before, been toiling with soiled bedding, delivering a speech from the beyond.

"We who have passed aren't silent because we desire to be so, but because we have not found the right conduit to make our voices heard!" I spoke in Mr. Black's thundering voice. The crowd before me was enthralled.

"If you open your minds and your hearts to create the right atmosphere, your loved ones need not be lost forever once they pass behind the veil, but can still be a part of your lives . . ." Mr. Black stomped across the scuffed floor with his hands behind his back and a light stoop. "Imagine," he said, drawing a hand through his invisible beard, "in a few years, visiting with a medium will be no different from calling on a doctor or a barber! It will be an everyday part of life. Rather than visiting a grave to feel close to a departed, you can speak to them directly and have their answers in turn. It will be a *glorious* dawn for humanity once you learn to accept that life and death are merely two sides of the same coin!" I paused to catch my breath and have a sip of the whiskey Mr. Black insisted on having at hand. The liquor sloshed gently against the sides of the tumbler, lit to an amber glow by the candles burning in sconces on the walls.

Before me, on rows of simple benches, sat the believers first and the curious next. My old friend Laura was there with Mr. Fisher. I recognized other faces from Julie Hassler's séance as well, but some of the crowd had to be from out of town, as Cherryvale did not sport so many believers. Maybe some had come just to see a woman turn into a man. There was a freedom to this ruse that could not be found anywhere else; good women did not speak in front of a crowd lest they be thought lewd or insane; neither did they drink liquor or smoke strong cigars, but as Mr. Black, I could. They listened to me then; they soaked up my words; they looked at me with admiration, not scorn. It was no wonder many women had taken to the profession.

"The human spirit is made of a substance too airy and light for us to see or touch," said Mr. Black, continuing his speech. "In the same manner, the spirits' voices are too high-pitched for your flawed ears to hear. Some mediums, like Miss Katie Bender, can loan her voice to the departed. This is not superstition," he promised, "but merely a science in its infancy. In only a short few years, we will know as much about the human spirit as we now know about the forging of metals, or the mechanics of a steam engine. The spirits are already here." I threw out my arms. "We are just waiting to be heard!"

The skeptics that dwelled in the back looked at me with narrowed eyes and arms firmly crossed over their chests. Unlike the believers, who readily saw the old sea captain cross the floorboards, *they* saw only a young woman who should have stayed at home mending socks. They were men, most of them, though there were also a few tight-lipped wives. I thought I recognized a late reverend's widow. Mayhap she was there just to show her scorn, but just as likely she was sitting there nursing a seedling of a hope that she might speak to her departed husband again. I had seen such things happen at séances before—the disapproval never quite reached their eyes.

The men around her were not as weak; the scorn in *them* reached all the way to the bone. One or two of them chewed tobacco, and one man even spat on the floor. They thought it ungodly to speak with the voices of the dead and meant to stare me into silence. They did not scare me, though. With some flourish, Mr. Black found the cigar that lay next to the whiskey bottle on a table and lit it from a candle. He puffed with great relish, having been deprived of his vice for so long. The shocking act caused a spatter of gasps and a titter of voices to rise among the assembled. It certainly was not every day they saw a woman in satin skirts blow plumes of fragrant smoke into the air. The scent reminded me of my button box.

"Why is it that only a mere handful among you can be a conduit for heavenly voices?" Mr. Black asked, waving the smoking cigar in the air. "Are those with such gifts merely blessed? Are they special or chosen? Is it God who, in his wisdom, has placed such individuals among you so you will not lose touch with your dead?" As I spoke, I could not help but ogle a man in the front row, for no other reason than his fine looks. He was broad shouldered and tall, with honey-colored hair and an angular face. His dark eyes were what captured me the most, as they seemed to smolder with heat as he watched me.

If I recalled Laura's gossip correctly, the man was a widower called Morrin, who farmed not far from town. To my recollection, he had two young daughters and a third one in the grave. His expression of rapture continued as I kept up the speech, and I reveled in his admiration. I was relieved that I so wisely had asked Mr. Brockman not to attend the meeting, telling him how it would upset my delicate balance if I knew that my fiancé was in the room. If he had caught me looking, it would surely have caused a tantrum.

John was there, though, somewhere, waiting for me while I gave the lecture. At first, he had been pacing in the back of the room, gnawing on some dried plums. He made no nuisance of himself, merely gave me the occasional dark look from under the brim of his new hat. When the meeting took too long for his liking, he had stepped outside, to stay with the horses, I reckoned. I did not mind his departure at all, and hoped he would continue to stay away.

"It *is* God, or the all-encompassing spirit," Mr. Black declared, "who bestows the ability to speak for the dead, but the gifted are not cut from a different cloth from others—no! It is merely a trait, much like one's temper or the color of one's hair, which can be inherited like countless others. It is simply a part of the human tapestry—a colorful thread, to be sure, but the medium is not divine! She is made from flesh and blood," I stated, and looked at Mr. Morrin all the while. "Miss Bender is merely a woman with a rare set of skills!" The crowd erupted in applause. The skeptics in the back twitched on their seats. "She is offering up those skills," Mr. Black continued when the applause died down. "She offers them up for you to use—to *aid* her fellow humans!" I dropped the cigar to the floor and stepped on it. "The dead are not a secret to be kept," I told the crowd. "The dead should be available to all!"

At this, the applause would not end, and I threw my head back and convulsed as Mr. Black departed. Mr. Fisher was there at once to steady me as I made a show of coming back to my senses. He was red-faced with happiness and offered me a glass of lemonade, though I would rather have kept at the whiskey. All around me, I saw smiling faces turned on me; some of their eyes were glossy with tears. The sound of their acclamations were as sweet as a cat's purr to me. I soaked it up, every bit of it—every clap of their hands.

After the lecture, most of the crowd stayed in the dining room to savor the day's excitement. Some had coffee, others tea; a few had tumblers of the whiskey that I craved. I had sworn to be more careful, though, and not let the thirst get the better of me. I had seen plenty of wretched women at the tenements of my childhood wasting away under the pull.

Laura came to speak with me but seemed shy all of a sudden, having perhaps realized that I *was* something special after all. She shook my hand and thanked me for the wonderful lecture. Everyone wanted to offer me something: a seat, a glass, or a flattering word. Finally, Mr. Fisher caught up with me again and introduced me to a handful of elderly men whom he described as his friends. They were a very tiresome lot who took great pride in their knowledge of spiritual matters, but I could not in good conscience ignore them—not if I wanted to be invited back—so I let them snare me into their circle, where I stood, half listening, while sipping my tepid lemonade.

I had been fretting after Julie Hassler's visit that my career in this town would come to naught, but as it turned out, Mr. Fisher had been very impressed with my abilities after the séance in his home, and so Miss Hassler's endorsement had been superfluous. I still did not know if she had given it. Neither did I know if the fainting woman from Mr. Fisher's dining room had ever found a ring in her cupboard. It did not matter if she had, though. All that mattered was the performance.

"Miss Bender." One of Mr. Fisher's friends addressed me. I recognized him as the little man who had played the piano at the séance in Mr. Fisher's home, but I could not remember his name. "Would you be so kind as to share your thoughts on the use of spirit cabinets? Have you ever used such a contraption yourself?"

"I have surely thought about it," I replied, but I did not share how I had dismissed the idea. Usually in such performances, the medium was tied up inside the cabinet, while an accomplice moved around the dark room pretending to be a spirit. I had no one I trusted to fill such a role. John would for sure have been a disaster; he could barely manage to knock under the floor. "Though I *am* a physical medium as well as a mental one, manifestations of spiritual beings are trying," I said instead. "I could do it for sure, but why would I exhaust the spirits and myself in such a way? They are as real as you and me and should not have to prove themselves." I added a little laughter at the end.

"Very wise, very wise." Mr. Fisher nodded. "What about apports? Have you ever manifested objects from the spirit realm?"

"Of course," I said, though I was not entirely happy with this line of inquiry. Why could they not be satisfied with what they got? Surely Mr. Black was more than enough. "I have received many a flower from my spirits," I told them nevertheless. "I have also received various fruits—all of them out of season." The latter was a particularly popular trick among my peers, and the men around me sighed with awe. What better way was there to prove oneself than to manifest an anomaly? No one ever had to know that the fruit was made of wax, frozen, or bought at horrid expense. "They arrive with the scent of roses," I added with a shy smile. "Heaven's own fragrance . . ."

"Tell us, Miss Bender, how did you first discover your wonderful gift?" a third man asked; he was tall and round-bellied and sported a heavy steel-gray mustache. Mr. Fisher had introduced him as Mr. Cooper.

"Oh, I have always had it, I suppose." I smiled my sweetest smile. "Yes, I have indeed heard the spirits around me all my life."

"But how did you train?" Mr. Cooper's blue eyes were filled with wonder.

"Ah, I . . . I read about others who had taken up the profession in newspapers and such, and then Mr. Black came and told me that I should do the same—to share my gift," I clarified. "To help the bereft." It *was* true that I had started reading about this curious new thing in the newspapers as we fled from Pennsylvania, and had sought out many performances whenever we dwelled near a city, or when our path had crossed a medium's circuit. It had not taken me long to realize that it was something I could do and do well—better than most, in fact, as I was an excellent performer and an equally good deceiver. Ma had taught me well in that respect.

I scanned my surroundings and let out a breath of relief when I still could not see John about. It was better that he was not there when my knees buckled just as Mr. Morrin passed me by.

"Miss Bender? Are you all right?" He put a warm and steadying hand on my elbow.

"Just a spell," I assured him, giving him a grateful smile while savoring the touch of his hand. "I'll be fine in just a moment."

This brief exchange had alerted Mr. Fisher and his friends to the idea that I might be unwell, and suddenly there was no shortage of aid, as they came to pat my shoulders and ask after my well-being, fetching glasses of water and smelling salts. No whiskey, though—not for the lady.

"Give her some air," one demanded.

"Get her a chair," cried another.

"Was it the spirits that moved you?" Fisher wanted to know.

All through this, Mr. Morrin was by my side as a gentle presence. He was still holding on to my elbow, and I could feel the heat of him through the satin. I was wearing my very best dress that day, the one from the whore in Louisville.

"I'm not usually so frail," I told him with a downcast gaze.

"It was a wonderful lecture," he said in a deep, warm voice, "though I'm sure it cost you much strength."

I took one offered glass of water and waved away another. "I am quite myself again, gentlemen," I told the concerned spiritualists. "It was merely a spirit passing through me that caused a moment's weakness."

"Oh, who was it?" a plump older woman wanted to know. I recognized her from the gathering at Mr. Fisher's house. She, too, had been sitting at the table.

"I cannot tell for sure," I said. "The spirit did not linger, but it was surely a woman, and she did belong to this room."

"Oh," they exclaimed like a choir around me.

"Who could it be?" said one.

"It has to be Martha," said another. "She cleaned these floors more than once."

They all looked to me for the answer; their eyes shone with anticipation.

"Yes." I satisfied their need. "I do believe it *could* have been Martha." The circle around me had by then become a small crowd, which erupted in eager chatter once I had given my verdict. The plump woman's pale cheeks glowed a rosy red from the excitement. Mr. Fisher laughed aloud from joy, while the old man beside him chuckled.

"You cannot tell for sure, can you?" Morrin spoke into my ear, not without amusement.

"No," I whispered back. "But it surely thrills them to think so."

"I am Nicholas Morrin." He let go of my elbow to take my hand. His warmth lingered behind where he had touched me. "I came here today as a seeker, and I think I found my answer." He gave me a most charming smile.

"Is that so?" I was intrigued.

"I would like to come and call on you, Miss Bender, if it is convenient. My wife passed a few years back, and I—"

"Of course." I placed my hand on top of his. "Stop by the inn anytime," I told him. "I'm quite positive we'll get her to speak. I can feel her in the air even now."

"Do you really believe so?" His beautiful eyes went wide.

"Oh, I am sure of it," said I. "I think she has a lot on her mind."

He could not thank me enough after that, and stayed close to me for the rest of the meeting, fetching fresh glasses of lemonade and even a small glass of sherry when I asked him to. "To fortify myself," I said.

Before he left, he pressed a kiss to my hand—in gratitude, for sure, but perhaps also just to feel my skin against his lips.

I did not mind it at all.

IT WAS NIGHTFALL before we arrived back at the inn. John had been sullen and quiet in the wagon, but that was not unusual when I had been out, and especially not if there had been other men about.

As we neared the farm, he turned to me and said, "I agree with

Ma, Kate. You shouldn't stick your neck out as things stand. We don't want to draw attention to ourselves."

"This was always the plan," I told him coolly. "Nothing has changed in that regard. I always said I would work as a medium—"

"Things *have* changed, Kate. We have a secret to protect now."

"As did we before," I retorted. I could barely remember a time when there were no dead bodies shared between us.

"No." He shook his head. "This is different. We never killed anyone *here* before, and not so recent either—"

"Be quiet!" I hissed, looking around us in the darkening night. "What if someone hears you?"

"Who would that be?" He sounded amused. "It's a clear road, Kate."

"Still . . ." I would not have him ruining everything just because he was irked.

"Pa is waiting on you," John reminded me. "He wants to know who to look for next." At this, he gave me a look of anticipation.

"The last one is barely cold," I teased him, even though it had been a few months, surely long enough for people to start to forget the man in the river. The thought of another red throat surely made the darkness stir and open its great maw of *need*. It was not as if I did not long for it, every day and always, and especially at night. The only thing that held me back was the fear of it interfering with my ambition. I worried that we would have to flee again, just when things were going my way.

"Why cannot Pa choose for himself?" I asked—that way I did not have to decide.

"You know why." John snapped the reins. "He likes to think

there's some purpose to it, that it's blessed somehow. I guess it makes it less about his greed."

"And you?" I looked at him.

"I don't much care how it comes about." Our eyes locked for a moment.

"I'll have an answer for Pa real soon."

16.

KATE

JANUARY BROUGHT A terrible blizzard that raged on for days, and we found ourselves housebound with only each other for entertainment. Nary a soul was foolish enough to travel in such weather. We rarely went out but for the most needful things, and in no time at all—and despite the gale that blew through the walls—the house soon reeked of us: sweat, blood, urine, and yesterday's stew clotting in a pot.

We played cards; I reread pamphlets on astrology and palmistry; Ma knitted a new shawl for herself. Every once in a while, John would pull on the heavy fur coat we all used when we went outside and make the short trek to the barn to tend to the animals. When he came back, he always fretted that it was too cold for them out there, and perhaps we ought to bring them inside. Ma would not hear of it, though, saying there were enough animals inside, and she was not speaking of Rosie, my puppy.

In the corner of the room stood the grandfather clock that William had bought with some of the money we had taken off Jessup

Jones. It ticked out the seconds painfully slow, measuring every minute of the blizzard. I rather wished that he had not bought it at all, because it made everything move even slower than before. He had purchased it to appease Ma, to give her something pleasant to look at, and an inkling of what was to come. She had said very little on the subject, only scoffed and pursed her lips, avoiding all our gazes.

On the third day, I was nearing my wits' end.

"Come here," I said when John stepped in behind the curtain, where I was lounging on the bed with a book and a bottle. His face lit up at the request, and he slumped down beside me, settling in to read the pages alongside me, as he used to do back in Pennsylvania. Sometimes he would even turn the pages, knowing my pace so well. On that day, I found it hard to concentrate, however. The darkness was too strong in me. I could not help but think of Mr. Jones—of how it had made me feel. The desire to have that sense of power again burned as well as any liquor. I tried to think of my future—the stage—but kept seeing again the gaping flesh of a ruined throat. I tossed and turned and sighed upon the bed, unable to exorcise the desire.

I gave in with a sigh and a deep sense of relief.

"It won't be long now," I whispered in John's ear. "The first man who comes through the door will be marked." Just saying the words made a delightful rush of power course through me.

"Should we tell Pa?" he whispered back.

"Sure." I took his hand and squeezed it. "Tell him that *the angels* have spoken."

THE MARKED MAN arrived two days later. The blizzard was still raging, and yet he rode to reach Independence. He paused for a meal and a warm place to sleep: his horse was exhausted and so was the man. He was strong-looking and well-groomed, and refused to take his coat off.

He was also not alone.

There was another man with him, tall and lanky, wrapped up in a pelt coat. This man did *not* refuse to take off his coat, shake out the snow, and hang it before the fire, so I supposed he did not carry the money.

From my place before the stove, stirring the pot, I looked to Pa to see if he had noticed, too, but he did not meet my gaze. He was behind the store counter with a stupid smile on his lips, acting the feeble old man. He had the broom back there with him, and once in a while he would take it and sweep a little about his feet. Ma was fussing with the plates at the counter in the back, clattering with the china, while John was outside, defying the blizzard to get the men's horses to shelter.

The guests themselves sat at the table, partaking in some whiskey to thaw their frozen bones. Their faces were red from the cold, and there was a steady drip of water on the floor when the snow that had nestled in their clothing melted. The exhaustion on their faces increased as the warmth of the room caught up with them. I hoped it would make them feel calm and drowsy.

My heart raced as I stood there, stirring, not sure what we were to do next. Were we to attack the men? If so, how? We had struggled enough to get *one* man down in the cellar—how were we to take on two?

"You must be *starving*," I said over my shoulder, offering our guests a sweet smile. "Your meal will be ready in no time at all. It'll fill you right up." Before me, the fire in the stove's belly raged; outside, the wind howled.

Those men sure were lucky to have found us.

"We almost rode straight by," said the man who had no money. His name, he said, was Finch. "The snowfall was so heavy that we could barely see the road."

"We found a dead horse some miles back," said the man who *did* carry the money. He had given his name as George Brewer. "The beast was frozen solid. Someone must have given up on it and left it there to die."

"Maybe the wolves will make a feast of it," his companion suggested.

"It has to thaw first," Brewer muttered.

Neither one of them had said why they were traveling in such foul weather, but neither did I much care. I could feel my face flush but could not tell if it was from the heat from the stove or from the excitement I felt. I looked to Pa again: he was still grinning and twirled the broom in his hands. Occasionally, he would step out from behind the counter to top up the men's tin cups. He wanted them weak, I thought. He wanted them exhausted and drunk. The thought made me feel giddy with excitement, but I took care to hide it well.

"I suppose you will be spending the night," I said. "We have some blankets to spare."

"Certainly," said the one.

"Much obliged," said the other.

Ma came up beside me with the plates, holding them out so I could scoop a little stew onto them. There were some pieces of ham in there, I saw.

"It must be awfully hot with your coat on," I said to Mr. Brewer as Ma served them food. The latter wore a grim face; her movements were a little too quick, as if she were in a hurry. She must have been wondering, too, about the fate of our guests.

"Oh, I got some bad chills," Brewer answered my question. "I better keep the coat on lest I end up like that horse." I turned away to hide a smile. He was traveling with money for sure.

As they lifted their forks to start devouring, John came back inside and stomped his feet against the floor to get rid of the cakes of snow. He took his hat off, too, speckled with white, and even shook his head to get the snow out of his hair. The air shifted once he was inside; it was as if the dim light grew denser. The current of excitement that had been there ever since the men arrived seemed to thicken and grow stronger.

"It smells like there's food on the table," he said to me in German.

"Get yourself a plate," said I.

"Those two idiots have taken the only good ones that are clean."

The men did not stir at all, so likely they did not understand, which was certainly good news for us. "What do you think?" I asked Pa.

"Let them eat their fill," he said, "then we should play a game of cards."

We were going to do it.

My whole body tensed up with pleasure at the thought—but wariness, too, because we had to do it just right if we were to overcome two grown men.

Ma's rocking chair creaked as she sat down, picking up her knitting from the floor. She wanted no part in what was about to happen, her demeanor said. I could not help but smile when I saw it. She would certainly enjoy the spoils.

I left the stove at last, wrapped my shawl tighter about my torso to better show off the swell of my breasts, and sank down in a chair by the table. I poured them both—and myself—more to drink.

"So," I said with my very best smile. "Tell me why two hand-some fellows such as yourselves are crossing the prairie in a storm."

John sniggered behind me, and then he came to the table as well, sporting a worn deck of cards in his hand. Behind the store counter, Pa swept the floor. Ma's rocking chair creaked. In the stove, the fire was feeding with a fury.

"Maybe we should play," John said in his broken English and sat down beside me. "When you have finished the stew."

The men, with their mouths full of meat and bread, nodded their agreement, loosened up already by the whiskey.

"It's a shame that you were waylaid," said I, "but we'll do our very best to make it a memorable night—you shall not regret stop-ping at the Bender place." My mouth felt as dry as the prairie in high summer, and my lungs fought to breathe under the shawl. My skin was slick and hot.

"Nothing but the best for our guests," muttered Ma in her chair. She said it in German, so the message was only meant for us, laced as it was with her resentment.

None of us deigned to reply—we had other things on our minds.

When the grandfather clock had measured out another two hours and darkness had swallowed the white fury outside the win-dows, Finch and Brewer were good and drunk. The atmosphere had become rowdy by then; our guests were laughing and stum-bling through stories about this neighbor or that who had done something foolish. John and I laughed with them and poured more to drink.

Finch finally had to step outside to relieve himself. He was sway-ing on his feet as he staggered toward the door, and fetched his heavy coat on the way. I looked to John as he looked to me, and then we both looked to Pa. John got a sly look in his eyes, like a viper about to strike. I straightened up in the chair with a tightening in my belly. Pa stepped out from the store counter and came to stand by the stove, still acting all innocent, stoking the fire with a poker.

I smiled at George Brewer until my cheeks ached.

John rose from the chair and whistled a tune as he stepped behind the canvas curtain. There was nothing strange about that, as the card game was on hold until Finch had done his business outside. Ma's knitting needles clicked. I barely flinched when John struck with the hammer through the canvas, making Mr. Brewer wail and clutch at his head.

The blow had not been hard enough.

He sure cried, though—bellowed—and his eyes were wide with shock and fear. Rivulets of red ran down his neck as he staggered to his feet with such force that the table lifted from the floor. I was up, too, stepping away from the bleeding man as John threw the curtain aside and stood there with the hammer, looking all white in the face. Before Brewer had thought to turn around to face him, John was there again, delivering another blow to his skull, moving the tool in a wide arc.

This time, the man went down. He sank to his knees between his upended chair and the table. Then the door opened, and Finch entered, already alarmed by the ruckus, and shouting with all his might as he lunged toward John.

He had not seen Pa, who stood behind the door, brandishing the poker.

At once, he was on Mr. Finch, delivering a blow to the back of his head. The man howled and spun around, just as Pa struck again, hitting his temple.

"The knife, Kate!" Pa cried out, and I slipped the newly sharpened blade out of my shoe and unsheathed it. Pa had the man in a grip by the neck by then, and was forcing his head back to expose the throat. Mr. Finch himself seemed delirious, from pain or shock, I did not know, but his head was bleeding profusely.

"Watch the floor!" Ma was on her feet, too. She looked most aghast at the sight of all the red spreading in a puddle beneath him.

"Cut him, Kate," said Pa, and, taking a deep breath, I stepped up to the struggling beast and placed the steel against his skin, as white as the snow outside. It did not take much force at all; he split like a taut, ripe pear.

Ma would be scrubbing the floor for days.

On the other side of the table, John had been successful in silencing his prey. The man lay limp at his feet, moaning softly. I went over there next and handed the knife to John, as a gift, all while admiring the gleam of Mr. Brewer's silver buttons.

We both stood over the fallen man when John made the final cut.

17.

ELVIRA

THE URGE TO flee was upon me again. Unlike the others in my family, lounging about as if nothing were amiss, I feared that we wove a net about ourselves that would eventually trap us. I did not trust the peace at all; it was as if the earth beneath me shivered. I waited every day for some rider to come and tell us that William and John had been seen out in the blizzard with corpses in the wagon, or that the dead men's horses—still in our barn—had been recognized.

Just as I had done after the Vandles' demise, I turned to the cures Gretchen had taught me and drew markings upon the chimney and stitched letters of holy words into my clothing, just in case it should work, but I still did not feel safe. I cursed Kate in my mind for being so foolish as to welcome sitters to our home, as I thought that we should hide, not advertise. It was bad enough, I felt, with the inn guests coming and going. There was no stopping her, though, not after she gave that lecture. She would have her way, come what may.

We had had a terrible argument about it, just days after Mr. Brewer and Mr. Finch had been killed. Kate was waiting for a sitter, a widow from town, and was readying our abode with candles and thick curtains, which she had procured in town. I was in my chair, as usual, but could not help but complain when I noticed a rust-colored stain on the floorboards.

"You are baiting the law," I told her, "by bringing all these people here. Sooner or later, one of your sitters will notice something amiss."

She twirled around the floor, and her eyes seemed very dark, though that could have been due to the dim lighting. "It is now or never, Ma. If I ever am to make a name for myself, I must make the best of it when I have the chance."

"But things are different now," I complained. "Surely with this new scheme you and the men have cooked up, you can wait just as I told you to. There's no longer a need for you to stick your neck out—quite the opposite. We should be more careful now than ever before."

She laughed at me then—laughed! "*Our* scheme, Ma? You're just as much a part of it, even if you don't wield the knife!"

I shook my head with vigor. "I never wanted anything to do with it—"

"Well, neither did you stop us," she hissed. "You don't fool me, Ma—you never have. The greed in you will always be much stronger than the compassion, and you mean to have your way just as *I* mean to have mine. The only difference between us is that I'm not afraid to get my hands filthy to get there." She barely paused to draw her breath before continuing with her tirade. "This has always been your way, Ma—hiding in the back, simpering—wringing your hands and leaving others to do the ungodly work for you—"

"Whatever do you mean?" I burst out. I could feel my face grow hot from anger. I was no longer knitting, but just sat there with the yarn in my lap, looking at my furious daughter, whose eyes shone with menace.

"Oh, those frocks you made me—the ribbons for my hair. Do you remember when you brought me to those fine establishments to learn to sip tea like a lady?" She lifted an accusing finger and pointed it to my chest. "You meant to make money off me even then—well, now I *am*—I *am* making you money, Ma. I'm *slaughtering* for your comfort, so I would rather not hear you complaining!"

I meant to go for the broom then—I truly did. I meant to give her a lashing for speaking thus to her mother, but my resolve quickly faltered before it even bloomed. I had found it hard of late to punish my daughter, ever since the killing of Jessup Jones. Perhaps I no longer trusted her not to turn the broom back on *me*.

Then there was the issue with the horses.

After Jessup Jones's death, John had taken the man's horse, a black mare, to the sinkholes. We could not think of anything else to do then, as we figured we could hardly keep the beast. It did seem a terrible shame, though, for the animal to meet such a fate when it still had many good working years left. She would have fetched a good price for sure if we had only found a safe way to sell her. Thus it had been utterly foolish to kill yet *another* man without a proper plan of disposal in place—and this time it was *two* beasts taking up space and chewing feed in our barn.

William had a solution, though, but I did not like it one bit. The year before, just a few months before Jessup Jones had died in our house, a man called Jack Handsome came to stay the night. "Handsome" was clearly not his given name, and neither did it reflect the state of the man, who was both filthy and uncouth. He had a tall, wide frame, and his red-brown mustache was so wild and unkempt that it covered his mouth like a curtain. In addition, he sported a black eye that did nothing to add to his charm.

Jack Handsome did speak German, if stilted and with a strong accent. He used to live among Germans before, he had said, though he never did tell us where. What skills he had with the language were enough to get him on William's good side, however, and my husband plied the man with drink and games of cards, filling his plate many times over.

It was in the morning that we realized we had a problem on our hands. I woke up to a terrible ruckus on the other side of the canvas curtain and rose at once on my aching legs to go and see what it was. The light was bleak as it filtered in through the soot-speckled windows, but I did not need much illumination to see John and Jack on the floor out there, just between the door and the table, with fists flying everywhere.

Kate was already up, standing by the stove with her brown shawl loosely draped over her shoulders, holding it together with a hand at her chest. The kettle was boiling behind her, so she must have been up for a while, making our guest some coffee, perhaps. Rosie was at her feet, yapping at the tumble with her small ears twitching. Then William came staggering out behind me, tall and ungainly in only his long underwear, and so we were a complete set, all of us dreadfully pale in the dusty morning light.

"What is going on?" I demanded to know. "What is this, John?" I obviously thought that Kate had been caught dallying with the unsavory man, or that he had said or done one thing too much, setting off John's awful jealousy.

I had not expected Kate's answer.

"He will not pay," she said. "John and I caught him sneaking away. I had just put the kettle on when he went for the door, to piss, he said, but then John demanded to see payment before he let him outside, and Mr. Handsome went into a rage." She delivered the news in a very cool manner. Then William stepped back behind the canvas curtain, and I already knew what would follow next.

"Go behind the counter, Kate. It's safer there," I said, just as William came back with the rifle. He was quite the sight, standing there in his drawers with the rifle aimed at the grunting pile of wriggling limbs on the floor.

"Get out of my way, John!" William shouted, and then, when John seemed not to hear him, he lifted the rifle and fired a shot into the wall, just a little away from the men.

We all startled and I yelped. I stepped back so fast that I crashed into the stove and had a burn mark on my hand for days. Kate, behind the store counter, toppled over several cans, which clattered to the floor in a ruckus of their own.

The men on the floor stopped fighting when the shot went off. John's lip was split and bloody by then, and Jack Handsome's face was even less handsome. Rosie stopped her yapping.

"Get up!" William barked. He looked at Jack, not John. My husband's face seemed much as a thundercloud, just about to erupt. He motioned to the stranger with the rifle, telling him thus to hurry it up. Both fighters staggered to their feet; John wiped his lip with his sleeve. Jack Handsome swayed a little. "Are you out to cheat me?" William asked the man he had so dearly embraced the night before.

Jack gave a sound that might have been a chuckle. "Yes," he replied, nodding, "but then you caught me at it, so now we're at a standstill." He summed up the situation quite nicely.

"I better take your horse, then, if you have no coins to pay me with." The rifle was still aimed at the man.

At this, astonishingly, the man started laughing in earnest, showing off black molars. "Oh no, old man," he replied. "I don't think you want that. The horse is stolen, you see, and it would only get you into trouble."

"I think you're lying," William growled; the rifle did not waver one inch.

"I do not." The man still seemed dizzy, staggering some to regain his balance. He drew a hand across his sweaty forehead. "You're new here, or else you would have known. It's what pays my way in life, and I am much despised." He said the latter without self-pity. "I only came here because no one else will have me."

"How come you're not hanged, then?" Kate sounded amused. She had gathered up the little dog from the floor and pressed it to her chest.

"Luck and some goodwill." Mr. Handsome shrugged. "There's always some man in charge who needs a good horse thief from time to time. Maybe you will, too, someday."

"Do you mean to settle with a favor I might not ever need?" William asked, but I could see that the rifle had drooped some and pointed more to the floor than at flesh and blood.

Jack Handsome nodded. "I'm the best there is," he said, quite shamelessly. "I have a woman some hours away by horseback; she is widowed, lives alone, and often takes messages for me. I shall tell you her name and where to find her."

"As if I could ever trust your word," William said, but in the end, there was not much else to do. Beating the man would not get us our money, and a ransacking proved that he did not carry cash. If the horse truly was stolen, we did not want it, and none of his clothes were worth much.

"You don't seem to me as if you have much luck with your trade,"

Kate said after patting him down. "If these poor threads are all you can afford, perhaps you're not such a wonderful thief after all."

"I don't travel with my gold," said Jack, quite unfazed. "I make it a point to not stand out—but you're right, I lost my purse in a bar fight." He lifted his hand to his swollen eye, the one that John had not punched. "I was drunk and foolish and had only a few coins left on my person when I finally sobered up. I only have to get back home," he pleaded. "I swear I'm not a bad man to have in your debt. I can solve many issues to your satisfaction."

Since he had nothing else to give us to pay for his stay and the food he had eaten, we let him leave after that, though we all doubted that his word was worth much. *I* certainly never expected to see his debt settled—but perhaps William had kept him in mind all along and remembered Jack Handsome even before the hammer fell to Mr. Brewer's head. At least he was quick to suggest Jack when we wondered what to do with the horses Brewer and Finch had left behind.

I, of course, wanted nothing to do with such a man but could hardly protest when John rode out to see if he could find the woman, Georgina Weiss, and leave a message for Jack. It must be said that William had made inquiries at the trading station by then, and had much of Jack Handsome's story confirmed by Mr. Ern, so we did know that he was indeed a horse thief. That did not mean that he could be trusted, of course; rather the opposite, I thought. Fraternizing with such an individual seemed ill-advised even at the best of times and most certainly when we wanted to lie low. It could do nothing but cause more trouble, but then we had those horses in the barn . . .

It was all such a tangle, and we really had no choice but to go into business with Jack Handsome, or at least that was what William said.

I, for one, thought it was a mistake.

18.

HANSON

THEY FOUND THE men when the snow melted: two of them, dumped together, with their heads done in and their throats cut. It had to be the same murderer as last time, they said, and my nights, which had taken on some normalcy with me falling asleep when the sun set and rising with its dawning, found me tossing and turning again, listening for sounds that ought not to be there, like footfalls, a cough, or a whisper.

People were more worried now than last time, maybe because the new discovery made it less likely that the man in the river had been a bad sort himself. Now it seemed more certain that there was a hungry villain about. One with a taste for blood.

When the townspeople entered the trading station, their faces were somber with concern, and they spoke in hushed voices over the counter, as if they did not want anyone to listen in. As if what they said was dangerous. I could not help but listen, though, even if what I heard left me pale. They speculated something fierce, the men, wondering if there had been others found in other towns in such a dreadful state, or if the murderer was local to Cherryvale. That was what they feared more than anything else—that the murderer was one of their own.

"Not very likely," Mr. Brockman said when I brought it up to him one afternoon. We were alone in the store just then, sharing some coffee and biscuits. "There are a lot of outlaws roaming the prairie, and most of them we don't ever see. They set up camp somewhere and hunt for food, but if they need something special, like ammunition, they'll rob the next poor fellow who crosses their path. It's nothing personal in it."

Mr. Brockman did not look so bad that day, though his eyes were slightly bloodshot. He had been having more doubts about Kate. She *did* come to see him now, though not very often. Sometimes she was as sweet as a kitten, and the two of them huddled behind the counter to share a few kisses and a drop of liquor—but other times she acted cold toward him, looking almost grim in the face when she arrived, and dissatisfied when she left. I once heard her tell Mr. Brockman that they *were* still engaged, but that it was difficult with her family, who relied on her for income.

"I am sure we can find a suitable arrangement," he had said then. "As a son-in-law I would surely do my part."

Kate only fretted, though, and asked him to wait. "Once the stars are more favorably aligned," she said, "and the farm yields some produce."

I did not think that Mr. Brockman was inclined to wait for long.

I brought my mind back on the murderer. "I think it sure seems personal," I noted as I sat there on the stool by the stove, held the poker in my hand, and stoked the embers from time to time, trying to bring the fire back to blazing life. "He could just have shot them, couldn't he? Why all that blood?"

Mr. Brockman gave me a look that said I knew nothing at all. "A gunshot is too loud if one wants to avoid detection. A knife is very quiet," he informed me.

"But how could he take them both at the same time?" I wondered. "Where did their horses go?"

"With the murderer, I presume." He paused to rub his nose. "There's no doubt at all that it was a robbery."

"Is that so?" I still was not convinced, though I ought to cherish the thought, as it certainly meant less risk to me. I had nothing a robber would want, unless it was my life. "The Weissbrods say that it has to be someone in Cherryvale who has done it," I said next. "They say that's why the dead men are all strangers. It's less of a risk that way—no one will miss them for a time."

"So that's what the Weissbrods say." Mr. Brockman sounded amused. "They know it all, don't they? Those clever little boys . . ." He was only speaking about them in such a way because Max and Bruno had been teasing him about Kate, saying Nicholas Morrin had been calling on the Benders day and night. They claimed that everybody knew he had been meeting with Kate. When Mr. Brockman had asked her about it, she had replied that Mr. Morrin was just a sitter, eager to hear from his late wife, and Mr. Brockman could hardly argue with that. He got annoyed with Max and Bruno instead, which was a bother for me, since they were my only friends. It was hardly pleasant to have them visiting when Mr. Brockman gave them grief for every little thing they did, and looked at them as if they were as welcome to him as a nest of mice in his mattress.

"Why do you even care who visits with Kate?" I had asked the brothers. "She has sitters all the time now, ever since she gave the spirit lecture."

"Oh, we don't." Bruno had shrugged. "Ma does, though. She is good at keeping track." The road was close enough to the Weiss-brods' place that they could see who came and went. Furthermore, they could see who took off from the road and entered Bender land.

"Why does your ma care?" I wanted to know next.

Bruno shrugged again. "It keeps her occupied."

"She doesn't like surprises," Max added. "She wants to know what's going on."

"Maybe she is bored," I suggested. I could hardly fault her for that. Usually nothing much was going on in our parts. It was only recently that terrible things were being discovered.

Things that made it hard to sleep at night.

"I wish they found out who the men were," I said to Mr. Brockman and went at it with the poker again, as if to punish the embers for our lack of answers. "Maybe the new men were villains, too." There was some hope, at least.

"Oh, I don't know." Mr. Brockman pondered by the counter. "It seems more likely that there's someone robbing travelers . . . It does strike me as foolhardy, though, to pick a set of two."

"What about that horse thief?" I asked. "The one who was here before. Maybe he has something to do with it."

"Jack Handsome?" Mr. Brockman looked surprised. "I never knew him to be of the bloodthirsty sort, but you never know, I suppose."

"Maybe we should tell someone about him."

Mr. Brockman laughed. "They're all well aware of Jack; it just seems that no one cares to do much about him."

"Why is that?" I had given up my eager stoking of the fire and had my gaze fixed on Mr. Brockman's face.

"Aren't you the little newspaperman already?" said he. "If you truly want to be a writing man, you have to learn to handle bad things without losing heart," he added. "Newspapermen write about such horrors all the time, and they cannot afford to lose sleep over it." He brought out a piece of cloth and set to wiping down the counter even though it was already spotless.

"I'm not afraid," I lied, even as I shuddered.

Mr. Brockman tutted. "I can hear you moving around at night and complaining in your sleep."

"What about you?" I asked, looking up at him. "Why aren't you afraid?"

"I learned a long time ago that being afraid won't put food on the table. One cannot live as if every day could be the last. If a man should come in here and aim a rifle at my chest, then I'll be afraid, not before."

"What if it truly *is* someone from Cherryvale?" I said, unable to share in Mr. Brockman's stoic calm. The hand that held the poker shook a little. "Maybe it's someone who comes in here every day." My mind was racing with the possibilities.

"No one comes in here every day." Mr. Brockman remained unfazed.

"What if it's someone we know?" My eyes went wide and my lower lip quivered just from the horror of thinking about it.

"Of course it's not someone we know." Mr. Brockman rolled his eyes a little. "One should look to the drifters, those who are here for only a short time. Men with little to lose."

"The Weissbrods say—"

"I don't *care* what the Weissbrods say. Those boys are dripping with gossip and lies." His lips became a sour twist under his fine mustache. "Spreading rumors like that . . . it can be damaging to a woman's reputation, Hanson. You should not let them go on telling such stories, and especially not about a friend of yours. Kate *is* your friend, is she not?"

"Sure she is," I murmured. "I'm sure they mean no harm."

"Of course not," said Mr. Brockman, "they're only silly boys, but that doesn't mean no harm will be done. It's often such foolishness that sets things ablaze, and once a reputation is tarnished, it doesn't matter if the rumor was true to begin with. People will always suspect."

I thought it perhaps was his own reputation he worried about the most. If he was to marry Kate and she was somehow sullied, it would surely rub off, and I did not think Mr. Brockman would like to be called a cuckold. I did not worry about Kate that much; she seemed to care very little what people said. Perhaps speaking to spirits did that to you: people's meddling had to seem such a petty little thing compared to the mysteries of the afterlife. It made her almost holy in a way—untouchable.

Maybe that was why Mr. Brockman so seldom complained when he went days or even weeks without seeing his betrothed. Perhaps that was why he did not protest when she preferred to send notes rather than seeing him face-to-face. It was such a silly arrangement—it took no time at all to go between the houses, and yet they sent *me* flitting between them like a homing pigeon with folded pieces of paper. I did not mind it, truly, or at least I did not mind it before. After the two men had been found, I ran the short stretch as fast as I could, clutching the paper with sweaty hands, afraid that I would see something if I turned and looked back. A rider in black, maybe, or a man with sharp teeth; a blood drinker salivating at the sight of me.

I only wished that they would find and hang the culprit.

"I need you to take a message to Kate later." He spoke as if he had been reading my mind. "It's not just a letter, it's—" Suddenly, he seemed not as much a grown man as another boy, stumbling in his words. "I got this— No, I better give that myself. I could write it, though, that I have something for her, something she will adore, I hope." He fumbled through his pockets, blushing and smiling a silly smile of embarrassment and delight. Finally, his hand emerged with a small package; something wrapped in velvet. "I should not— maybe you could describe—" He muttered while making his way from behind the counter and over to me by the stove. I was utterly mystified but could do nothing but look on as he kept trying to string the words together.

"I don't know why I'm showing you this—you're just a boy, but maybe you could—it's such a pretty thing." While he spoke, his fingers were working on the velvet, exposing a rather unremarkable cardboard box, small and square. What was inside it was rather precious, though: upon another piece of velvet lay a ring, a smooth and golden band.

"Look at it—look!" Mr. Brockman demanded, as he held the small trinket up before the smoldering embers to have me look inside. *To Kate*, it read, engraved in the metal. "I do hope it fits," he fretted. "Do you think it'll fit?"

I shrugged, as I did not know, but he was not listening anyway. He was just staring at the ring as if it was the prettiest thing he had ever seen.

I, for one, was just happy I would not be tasked with taking it to Kate, as I felt sure an evildoer would be able to sniff it out from miles away. Gold was never safe on the prairie.

"She should have one, don't you think?" Mr. Brockman asked me, but mostly the air. "She should wear one now that she is to be married. She would want to tell the world that her heart is spoken for."

I nodded but said nothing, thinking to myself that Kate had

likely never thought such a thing. It would be good for Mr. Brockman, though, to give her that token—to brand her as his own with a shackle of pure gold. Perhaps it would make him sleep better at night, knowing that she wore it. Maybe he even thought that it would stop Mrs. Weissbrod's wicked tongue.

I hoped that she would take the ring.

19.

KATE

MR. FISHER'S DINING room was again draped in shadows, il-luminated only by candles, their flames flickering gently in the draft from outside. It was a cold day in early spring, but the wind had been strong enough to smart on our way over. I had taken the wagon my-self that morning, against John's protests, and picked up Laura, my old friend from the hotel, on the way. The latter was terribly excited for me, though I myself felt like this was nothing more than I deserved.

Today, it was I who sat at the head of the table, dressed in black and with my hair pinned up. On each side of me were the spirit-ualists: eight of them in all, perched upon the straight-backed chairs. They wore their Sunday best and appropriately solemn expres-sions. Mr. Fisher was there, of course, and a few of his silver-haired friends. There was also a widow called Braxton and a spindly little woman wrapped in a heavy black shawl, whom I had come to learn was Mrs. Fisher. Between the latter and Laura sat the most special guest of all, namely, my new friend, Mr. Morrin.

As an audience, it was not much—Mr. Fisher's abode was hardly a stage—but it was important nevertheless, both for my reputation and to duly impress Mr. Morrin. What I was not entirely thrilled about was the aim of this hastily assembled séance, but Mr. Fisher had felt it was our duty—or rather *mine*, for being a conduit to the otherworld—to try to help the town in its time of dire need.

Hands clasped, we all closed our eyes and tried to reach the souls of the dead men who had been discovered on the prairie just outside of town.

After a minute or two, I opened my eyes and started speaking in Mr. Black's raspy voice. "We are calling to the ill-fated lost souls who were found some weeks hence," I declared. "Come forth and state your names!"

I took a deep breath and waited; it would not do if the "spirits" arrived right away. There had to be some waiting, some heightening of anticipation. I did not much like to draw any attention to the dead men—and Ma had been aghast when I told her what I was to do—but it was better that it was I, was it not? It would not do if some other medium took the reins and spun this tale in an undesirable direction. If it was I at the head of the table, I might be able to steer them away. I had no doubt that no matter what was said during this séance, Mr. Fisher would promptly take it to the authorities. The man was obsessed with proving the existence of spirits and would not let a chance to impress men of standing pass him by.

Ma was a fool to think that cowering in fear would keep us safe—no, it was just by speaking up that we could build a good defense, and if I happened to impress the handsome widower while I was at it, that certainly did not hurt either.

"Come forth!" Mr. Black called again. "Make yourselves known!

You are safe here and among friends . . . Let your desire for *justice* guide your way . . ."

Around me, the congregated still had their eyes closed. I could not help but notice how Mr. Morrin's thick eyelashes fanned out on his skin. I knew he was there only for me; I had invited him myself. He had been to see me often of late and had become quite devoted, ever since his "wife" first spoke through me. I was hoping to soon replace the latter.

"Hel-hello." I changed my voice; made it lighter, smoother. "My name is Barnabas Groff. I think I might be the one that you're calling for." This was fairly unusual for me. I tended to let Mr. Black act as an intermediary so that he was the one who spoke to the spirits and relayed the messages to me, but I was out to impress, and so I had to make a better show.

Mr. Fisher, to my right, opened his eyes. A connoisseur of séances, he knew what was expected of him when the spirits spoke.

"Welcome, welcome, Mr. Groff. We are *so* delighted to have you here in our midst." His blue eyes shone with excitement. "Yet we are deeply sorry for your untimely demise," he hurried to say. "Such a tragic, tragic event . . ." He shook his head with a sad expression, while his fellow spiritualists mumbled their agreement. One by one, they opened their eyes to look at Mr. Groff—me—at the head of the table. Mr. Morrin's face wore a most satisfying expression of astonishment and awe.

"Grieve not for us, for we have entered another realm," said Mr. Groff. "Weep rather for those who are still suffering in this cold world. Death is naught but a portal one must pass through, and now we are beyond pain, beyond the fear of dying."

"But how did you get there?" Mrs. Braxton's shrill voice sounded in the dark room. "Who murdered you so cruelly?"

I took a deep breath and let my head fall forward, ignoring how the hairpins dug into my scalp. "He was a man," I said, seeing it so clearly in my mind: a specter with a bloody knife, a demon in a human guise. Just what they all wanted. "He never gave us a name, but he was tall and black of hair. He wore a coat of wolf pelts. He stopped us at gunpoint as we traversed these parts but butchered us with his knife."

"But why?" Mr. Fisher said, aghast. "Why would he do such a *horrid* thing?"

"He was after what little we had in our pockets; it was not much and hardly worth it to suffer for, but that man could not be stopped . . . He rode a red steed and had a scar like a cross upon the back of his hand." I lifted my head again, so I could see my audience.

The gathered exchanged looks across the table. No one of that description dwelled in Cherryvale, and I noticed how a breath of relief crossed many of their faces.

"He must not be local to us, then," stated Mr. Fisher.

"Rather a vagrant," said Mrs. Braxton. "A drifter, most likely—one fleeing from the law."

"Maybe the cross-shaped scar means something," Mrs. Fisher mused. "Perhaps he is a *marked* man." I could tell that she found some delight in that thought.

"He might be all of that," Mr. Groff agreed. "He does no longer dwell among you—that much is certain," I said to put their minds at ease. I would rather that the locals stopped worrying so much about the dead men. It made Ma nervous and me impatient, and all of it was only because Pa and John were terrible at hiding the bodies. "I see him in a large city," I declared. "He must have traveled north."

To this they all expressed relief and gratitude. There was much sighing and gasping among the women.

"Is there something we can do for you, Mr. Groff?" Mr. Fisher asked. "Do you have a message for someone still alive? A wife, perhaps, or a mother?"

At this, Mr. Groff shook his head. "I had left them all behind already. It was my one regret—but I would rather wait for them here in the afterlife and explain to them then how badly I fared. I should never have left my father's farm." My voice shivered with emotion. Had there been a larger audience, I might have asked them to seek out his sister or some such, but with the dire circumstances and Mr. Fisher so determined, I found it better not to risk it, as they might in fact follow through with a search.

"What was the name of your friend, the man who you were traveling with?" Mr. Fisher asked next, but I found that I had given them enough already, and did not deign to answer.

"I am weary," Mr. Groff said instead. "I shall leave you now."

"Farewell," Mr. Fisher said at once. I suppose they were all ready to be done with the spirit, so they could discuss the amazing discovery among them. "We are truly grateful that you would speak to us tonight. We are honored to have had you with us." Mr. Fisher looked both touched and solemn.

I gave a deep sigh to signal that Mr. Groff had left.

All the assembled, with the exception of Mr. Morrin, had been to such séances before, and knew not to let go of each other's hands just because the spirit had fled. They knew that the spirit guide had to be reinstalled and the delicate medium restored before the circle could be broken. So they remained seated and linked like obedient children. The candle flames still flickered; the room had grown increasingly hot due to our close proximity, and a musky scent of unwashed winter skin mingled with that of woodsmoke from the hearth. There was a sweet scent as well, emitting from a covered tray next to the Fishers' samovar. I supposed this meant that Mrs. Fisher had baked something good for the tea we would have after the séance. I could smell both lemon and cloves.

I don't know what came over me then—some kind of madness, perhaps. I had already done what I had set out to do: the spiritualists were utterly fooled as to what had happened to Finch and Brewer, and I could have ended it there, exited the trance and had some cake, and yet . . . Perhaps it was the thought of Mr. Morrin sitting there, the pleasure of his eyes upon me that did it. Perhaps it was something else.

My head fell back again, as another deep sigh left my lips. I felt, rather than saw, how the gathered tensed up around me, how their eyes sought me out anew. No one knew what to expect.

I slowly straightened up again, and spoke in Mr. Black's voice. "There is another," he told them. "There is another spirit here. She dearly wants to talk—she wants to tell you of a great wrong!"

Again, there was much sighing and gasping; their eyes shone toward me like glittering stars. Mr. Morrin's eyes, too, were alight with wonder, and his chest rose and fell heavily under his coat as the excitement of the moment moved him.

"Hello . . ." I spoke in the voice of a young girl.

"Hello, and welcome!" Mr. Fisher was there at once. "To whom do we have the pleasure of speaking?"

"Ada." I gave him the name of my youngest sister.

"Welcome, Ada," Mr. Fisher replied. I could detect how he was a little insecure; he did not know what to expect, if the newcomer was tied to the dead men or not. "Mr. Black tells us that you have a story to share," said Mr. Fisher, urging Ada on.

"I would . . . I would like to tell you all how I died," said Ada.

"Oh, sweet child," Mrs. Fisher burst out, already taken with the tragedy.

"How old are you, Ada?" Mr. Fisher asked.

"I'm . . . twelve," I decided, as that was my age when both my sisters died.

"Oh my, that's so young." Laura sighed.

"Please, Ada. Tell us," Mr. Fisher urged. I could hear a faint rumbling from his stomach and figured that he, too, was eager for some cake. He would never dare to interrupt a spirit, though.

I must have waited a little too long while searching for the words to begin, because next, Mrs. Fisher spoke. "Where are you from, Ada? Did you live here in Cherryvale?"

I shook my head. "I lived in New York when I was alive. I lived in a tenement building with my ma and my siblings. I had two sisters . . . there were three brothers, too, but they were already in the grave. I was the oldest one left."

"Did your ma raise you all alone?" Mrs. Braxton asked when I—again—seemed to struggle with the words. I already regretted starting down such a confusing path, but by then it was too late, and Ada would have to deliver. I took a deep breath and went on.

"Ma was married three times—or at least she *said* she was married, but I do not know if she ever stood before a priest. She was a midwife for the poor, immigrants and such, but never made enough to feed us all . . . She was a clever woman, though—very clever indeed. She would train me every night after we had shared a meager meal. She would hide certain items upon her body and then I was required to 'steal' them from her. She had been married to a thief before—her second husband, my father—and would often remark on how it was in my blood, that I was destined to thrive in such a trade. She also said that I owed it to her, for all her suffering and toil."

"Dear Lord." Mrs. Fisher sighed. "What a cold woman she must have been."

"Or *hungry*," remarked Mrs. Braxton.

"Terrible," said Mr. Fisher with a shake of his head.

Mr. Morrin watched me intently.

"After I had been trained," Ada continued the story, "Ma brought me out on the streets. We found easy marks at first, drunk people, mostly. I found that it was easy to pilfer what little money they had on them; I was quick and lithe and had clever fingers, and soon Ma would let me go out alone. She had no time to chaperone me, she said, having her hands full with my sisters and her work. For a while it went well; it was mostly how we made a living, and we ate better then than we had before." I remembered thinking of Lenora and Ada while walking the bustling streets, of how they would cry in bed at night if there had been no bread that day.

I cleared my head of unpleasant thoughts and continued the sordid tale. "After some time had passed in that way, Ma came up with a scheme for me: I was to pretend to be rich—or at least better-off—and present myself to well-to-do men, saying that I was lost, or that I had been robbed. I was then to persuade the gentlemen to give me money for a carriage ride home, or make them offer me a meal while I gathered myself. If the gentlemen had their wives with them, I was told by my mother to look endearing. 'You're a pretty child,' she said to me once. 'The least we can do is make some money off it.' My aim with this ruse was of course to get ahold of the gentlemen's purses."

Again, the ladies gasped.

"Did you ever feel remorse?" Mrs. Fisher asked. "I mean, stealing for a living . . . well, it's a *sin*."

I felt a sudden urge to laugh but quickly stifled it. "My ma would often say to me, 'We take care of our own, and the rest can fend for themselves.'"

"What a dreadful woman." Mrs. Baxter huffed.

"I suppose she was." I gave a wry smile. "Then it all went wrong." I promptly wiped the smile from my lips. "One day, I had gone with a man who looked fine enough from the outside. He was beyond his prime, with a little silver in his hair, and wore a nice, thick coat and a fine hat and carried a silver-tipped cane. The only thing that bothered me about him was that he seemed to have a terrible cough. He had promised to help me find a carriage and give me money for the fare. He was not a kind man, though, or at least he was not to a thieving child, and when he caught me with my hand on his purse, I had to flee for my life—or at least that's how it felt, as he beat me so badly with his cane." It had been shaped like a fox, with a vicious, sharp snout.

"Did *he* kill you?" It was Mr. Morrin who asked. He looked very worried for Ada. His eyes seemed to gleam with tears, but that could just have been an illusion conjured by the poor light.

I shook my head. "I managed to flee from the hotel where he was staying, but I was in a bad shape. I knew that it would be a terrible thing to come home empty-handed, but I didn't know what else to do . . . Ma showed no mercy, though. She was *so* angry that I had come back with nothing, but also because I had ruined the dress that she'd worked so hard to make. She said I was a terrible child who brought her naught but grief. She locked me up in the small cupboard." It was dark in there, dank and cramped. It smelled like mouse droppings and mold. I was still wet to the skin, as it had been raining outside, and the gentleman's cane had left angry welts upon my arms and legs.

For a moment, the silence in the room was complete, then Mr. Fisher cleared his throat. "Did you die then? In that cupboard?"

I shook my head anew. "I stayed in there for hours—all through the night. I wasn't entirely alone, though. My sister Lenora came tiptoeing across the floor after Ma had gone to sleep, and she sat outside the locked cupboard, keeping me company. We whispered through the gaps in the woodwork, and she even managed to push some bread in under the door. What none of us knew, though, was that the man with the fox cane had passed his sickness on to me, and as dawn arrived, I was already coughing. I was sick for many days after that."

"And then you died?" Mrs. Fisher's mouth hung open with astonishment; she had savored every word.

"Then I died." I nodded with a solemn expression. "And it was all because of my mother's greed." In truth, both Lenora and Ada died, having caught the man's sickness from me. At the time, Ma often complained that it was the wrong daughter who had survived, but I did not think she truly meant it. My sisters had both been too young and too plain to properly fool a gentleman—and so Ma had needed me still.

She had changed the scheme shortly after, though, and added soothsaying to my repertoire; we had both learned to read the cards from our upstairs neighbor, an Italian woman called Lucia. This was also about the same time that Ma would start peddling ointment and salves. Our room smelled like an apothecary, and the much reviled cupboard became the home to jars of herbs and steeping roots. I suppose she found the time then, when she no longer had my sisters to think about.

"What a dreadful, dreadful story." Mrs. Fisher's eyes were filled with tears.

"Can we do anything for you, child?" Mr. Fisher's voice shook a little. "Would you like to see your mother brought to justice?"

"Oh no," I said. "She is already dead—I would just like for my story to be known."

"And now we know it." Mrs. Baxter nodded with a serious expression. "We will keep it in our hearts, always."

"Thank you," said Ada. Then I threw my head back and gave another deep sigh, signaling that the spirit had left me.

They all waited for a while, anxious to see if another dead soul would step forth, but I was entirely exhausted. I straightened up in the chair and mumbled something incomprehensible in Mr. Black's gruff voice, then I opened my eyes as I pretended to come to.

"Phew, what a journey," I said, and could tell that there was relief on everyone's faces. None of them were ready for another sad tale. They were in awe of me, though, so in that I had succeeded. Despite all the acclamations, however, and the ample piece of cake that was shoved into my hands, I did not feel entirely satisfied.

I should maybe not have done it, I thought. It had perhaps been a reckless and foolish thing to do. It had touched Mr. Morrin, but since he did not know it was me I had spoken of, that truly did not mean a thing. Had that fleeting look of compassion on his face truly been worth reliving it again—why had it felt so important to move Mr. Morrin to sympathy?

I felt as though I no longer knew myself. My cheeks burned hot with anger, and I had no one else but me to blame.

20.

KATE

"ANDREA KEEPS TALKING about the beauty of the Summer-land," I told Mr. Morrin. The widower had come riding to the inn early in the morning, and now he sat before me at the table; our hands were entwined on the tabletop, our fingers braided in a tight grip. His skin was warm and dry, and his breathing came heavy, much like mine. He might as well have entered a trance himself for the passion he displayed. If I opened my eyes, I knew his would be right in front of mine, burning with dark intensity.

I only wished that it were me they burned for, and not his long-dead wife.

"What else does she say?" he asked in a husky voice. "Does she say something about Alma and Constance? Is Lavinia with her still?"

"Oh, she misses her girls terribly," I said. "It pains her a great deal to be away from them." I had given him that same message at least a dozen times before, but he seemed to crave hearing it—to get that reassurance. He feared for his daughters' future, I figured. He feared what was to become of them without a mother to steer them right. "She says that you're doing well." I bent my head and creased my brow, as if I was straining to hear. "She says that she is at peace now, because she knows that you will do right by her daughters." I had long since stopped making a real effort with Mr. Morrin. I knew very well what he wanted to hear.

"And Lavinia?" Mr. Morrin kept asking about his dead daughter as well.

"Oh, she is with her mama, held close to her bosom. You don't have to worry about the child." I really wished he would take it to heart. I had said that, too, many times before—and yet he kept coming, pressing coins into my palm and asking me to say it again.

I did not understand him at all.

At first when he came calling, I had thought the dead woman was just an excuse, but when he kept coming back without anything much happening between us, I started having my doubts. He liked me, I could tell as much, but he sadly seemed unable to do much about it.

I feared he was still married in his heart.

"She wants you to move on, Nicholas," I said. "She wants you to find happiness again. I detect a certain worry—nay, *distress* . . . She is determined that you look out for yourself and find some joy in life." I said this from time to time to nudge him a little, but thus far, it had not yielded much result. Ma chuckled in the rocking chair, amused, no doubt, by my performance, though she did not understand much of what was being said. I wished I could crack one eye open to give her an ugly stare.

It would not do, though, as I was in a trance.

"How?" my handsome sitter pleaded before me. "How am I to find happiness?"

"Oh, it might be closer than you think," I assured him. "Perhaps all you have to do is look up." It was a bold thing to say, but I did not hold out much hope that he would understand my meaning. Ma snorted in the chair, and I wished that she would find herself some other entertainment. John was gone for the day, though, which certainly was a relief. He was to help another German settler dig a well. It made for a poorer séance, of course, without him to provide the noises and such, but Mr. Morrin did not care for fancy displays anyway. He only wanted to speak to his wife, and his faith in me was absolute.

"She may be right." Mr. Morrin fretted. "I am often too burdened with worry to properly see the world around me. Last year, when Constance had the ague, I even forgot to eat. I cannot recall the last time I paused to appreciate the sunrise."

"You are a good man," I assured him, "and a fine father to your girls. You deserve to have a good life as well."

"Does Andrea say that?" His voice brimmed with hope.

"She certainly does—though I do, too," I hastened to add. "I can tell such things just from looking at a person."

"Is that so?" He sounded intrigued.

"Of course! That's why I can diagnose my patients with such accuracy . . . Lavinia is still playing with her doll." I smiled at Mr. Morrin with my eyes still closed. "The one you put in her coffin." He had revealed that detail to me himself, right after he had told me how his wife went into the grave with her wedding ring wrapped in a silk handkerchief. Mr. Morrin was a great romantic. "Andrea thinks it was a thoughtful gesture, putting that beloved toy next to the girl. She says Lavinia has met her grandparents, too. They think the child is delightful."

"Tell her to kiss Lavinia for me," Mr. Morrin whispered.

"I will," I whispered back, and tightened my grip on his hands.

"What luck that I found you," he said then, and I opened my eyes just to find his waiting, burning hotly. "All is not lost after all." He smiled. "Not when I have you to help me."

"Yes," I agreed, feeling faint. "Aren't you the luckiest man?" The stupidest, too, by far. "You should take your wife's words to heart," I advised him, though I did not hold out much hope.

I was starting to think that the problem of Mr. Morrin might require a less subtle approach. I found myself to be drawn to him, and not just because of his good looks. I was devising a plan; it was still new and raw, but I thought that Mr. Morrin could serve me well in the future.

If only he let go of his dead wife.

When Mr. Morrin had left, Ma looked up from her knitting to say, "It bothers you, doesn't it?" Her eyes gleamed with mirth.

"What does?" I pretended not to understand—not to see her pointed look—and busied myself with washing out a cup. I was of no mind to quarrel with Ma that day. I was far more concerned with pondering what to do with Mr. Morrin.

"That he doesn't take to you as other men do," Ma elaborated.

"I don't care one way or the other if Mr. Morrin likes me or not," I said, though we both knew that was not true.

"Of course you do." Ma started knitting another row. "You cannot stand it at all. The less attention they pay you, the worse you get." Ma chuckled, but it did not sound joyful. "Isn't it enough with those you already have sniffing around your skirts?"

"Who? Mr. Brockman?" I slumped down in a chair with the cup

and a bottle, mystified by this sudden onslaught. She had to be in a terrible mood.

Ma arched an eyebrow when she looked at me. "I'm surprised you even remember his name."

"What a cruel thing to say—we're engaged to be married." I could not help but laugh as I said it.

"You should talk to him." Ma did not share my amusement. "You should tell him the wedding is not to be. It's cruel not to."

I shrugged and looked away. "It's no harm if he doesn't know it. He's as happy as can be—"

"He's not, Kate." She gave me another stern look. In her lap, the knitting needles kept moving. "It never ends well when you start playing your little games; just look at what happened in Pennsylvania."

"This is hardly the same," I defended myself, annoyed that she would bring that up again. "And it was *you* who taught me to never close a door, as one never knows when it might be of use! I visit Brockman enough that he won't entirely give up, and so I know that I have him if I need him. Besides, none of my current suitors are married." I snorted.

"No, but Brockman thinks he will be." Ma looked as sour as a nun in a whorehouse.

"It cannot hurt to keep him for a while." Like a pickle in a jar. "Just in case."

Ma looked rueful. "These things never end well, Kate, you *know* that."

"Mr. Morrin—"

"Mr. Morrin is a *decent* man. You should leave him be. Think of his children if nothing else." She huffed and dropped her gaze to her knitting. "I hardly think you are fit company for those girls."

I rolled my eyes at that, seeing how she had treated her own lit-
ter of pups. "Shouldn't I redouble my efforts instead, if Mr. Morrin
truly is so *decent*?"

"No, Kate." Ma sighed. "You cannot have that—a decent man.
It's far too late for that." She gave me a dark look.

"Is that so?" In my chest, my heart started racing, for no good
reason at all.

"Your hands are dripping with red." Ma's gaze was as cold as a
blizzard, and just as merciless, too. "How can you be a mother to
his girls with a soul as foul as the devil's behind?"

"I'll find a way." I sounded sullen, and despised myself for it. I
just could not stand Ma telling me what I could or could not have—
if anything, it only made me want it more, if only to prove her
wrong. "Maybe it won't even be that hard."

"Oh, it will Kate." She was still cold. Not even a sliver of warmth
sounded in her voice. "You just cannot help yourself—"

"Help myself with what?"

"If you get angry—or not even that . . ."

"What do you mean by that?" I poured myself more whiskey
and slammed the bottle down on the table. It irked me even more
when she deigned to tell me who I was.

"You are a danger to any man, Kate," she went on. "Surely you
won't leave those girls orphaned—"

"I won't *harm* Mr. Morrin." The idea was ridiculous.

"You cannot *know* that. Maybe he'll say a wrong word to you, or
you'll simply grow bored—" Her fingers around the knitting needles shivered.

"Maybe it'll pass," I said. "This *affliction* of mine—"

"Oh no." Ma shook her head. "I don't think one can heal from
bloodlust."

I laughed again, but it sounded forced. "What do you mean for me to do then, Ma? Live out my days as a spinster?" Had it not been for my plans with Mr. Morrin, I might in fact have entertained such a thought. Many mediums lived alone and supported themselves through their work. The prospect was not a poor one, but rather tantalizing.

Ma shrugged. "Unless you marry John. He would certainly provide for you, right up until the day you hang." She gave a dry laugh in the statement's wake.

"But what about Mr. Brockman—?"

"Oh, him." Ma rolled her eyes. "He will always make you miserable. I don't expect him to live for long if he is to share bed and board with you." Her eyes lit up as she waited to see if her poisoned arrow had hit its mark.

"You truly have *no* faith in me." I smirked and tossed my head, then I emptied my cup in one long swallow—the arrow had entirely missed the mark. Ma was often small-minded and unable to think that others might have different aims than her. That farm she so coveted was nothing compared to my visions of the future.

"Just stay away from the handsome widower," she grunted from her chair. "We do still aim to keep *children* safe in this house."

I did not even bother to respond, although I did wonder what her true reason was for keeping me away from Mr. Morrin. I thought that she had one for sure—and it had nothing to do with his daughters. Her meddling had ruined the day for me, though, and so I brought the bottle with me and went into the barn to think about Mr. Morrin in peace.

There, on a roughhewn shelf on the wall, behind buckets of nails and coils of rope, was the thing I was there for, the one item to always bring me peace: the cigar box with its painted ship and rich

fragrance. I brought it out and shook it to hear the rattle from inside. Then I opened the lid and let the scent engulf me. There they
were, resting at the bottom, three perfect buttons: one of brass; one
of silver; and another, plainer one, of bone. Jones, Brewer, and
Finch. I often wished that I had a button from Emil Zimmerman as
well, but I had not thought of it then.

I fondled the buttons one by one, as was my habit. All the while,
I thought about their deaths: how they had looked; how I had hurt
them; the moment when they went.

The darkness in me stretched like a lazy cat and licked its lips.

I knew it was not wise, and that I had other—more important—
things to attend to, like paving my way to the stage or seducing the
stubborn widower, and yet the longing in me could not be denied.

The "angels" would speak very soon.

21.

KATE

EARLY IN SPRING, we killed a landowner called Edmund Mc-Crotty and buried him behind the house, on a patch of soil meant to become an orchard. Ma had wanted apple saplings for it, but now it had become a grave instead. We had found that it was better to dig them down on our own land rather than letting them lie out in the open. They were bound to be found then, and for questions to be raised. Pa and John had proven to be not very adept at hiding bodies.

McCrotty had been traveling with plenty of cash, so it had been a lucky pick, though I did not know anything about that, of course, when I whispered to John to get the next man wandering in through our door. Pa still believed it was the spirits telling me whom to choose, but in truth, the darkness seemed to ebb and flow with my bickering with Ma. The angrier I got, the more I craved it. It was certainly worth it, though, to spill the blood, as I knew that the more money Pa saved in the grandfather clock, the closer I was to getting rid of them all—and the darkness was soothed, too, for a while.

Edmund McCrotty gifted me a fine leather button for my box.

Not all of my problems were so easily solved, however, and it was only a few days later that it came to blows in the yard.

It was shortly before noon when Brockman came up to the house in his wagon, and his meek face annoyed me on sight. He did not look very good, even if the winter had thawed and the sun licked the soil with a fiery tongue, coaxing it back to life.

Hanson had brought me many messages of yearning of late; of flattery and annoyance, too, as Brockman would like to see more of me. He was also about to lose his patience, and dearly wanted to know—*exactly*—when we were to wed, though I had said to him many times before that the planets had to be in our favor. As I saw him come into the yard that day, I even wondered for a moment if Ma had been right, and that I should tell him that the wedding was not to be, rather than him becoming a burden of annoyance.

"Rudolph!" I exclaimed as I stepped outside the door, having wrapped the brown shawl about myself and hastily pinned up my hair. "What a nice surprise! Are you here to see Pa, or just my merry self?"

"You, of course." Though the man was clearly in agony, he could not prevent his lips from curling into a coquettish smile. He did not climb out of his wagon, though, but remained seated at the reins, which ignited some hope that it would be a brief visit. "What better way to celebrate a fine, clear morning than seeing the one I hold so dear?"

"Oh, you flatter me," I played along. "I'm so *very* sorry that I haven't been to see you—"

"Please, don't fret." He waved it away. "I know you are busy with your sitters, and that the séances take their toll. It's not easy being a conduit for the spirit world."

"No," I agreed, "it certainly isn't, but at least I was able to do some good and put some minds at ease." I put on my most solemn expression and saw his face light up with admiration—he truly was unusually gullible.

"It's godly, what you do." He nodded in agreement. "I just hope when we are wed that I can ease the burden some and give you a little more time to rest."

It was my turn to nod. "It's certainly not easy to find rest when one works as hard as I do, and also live with aging parents."

He shaded his eyes and squinted up at the sky. "Let's hope the planets are favorably situated soon."

"Oh, they will be," I assured him, and swatted at his calf in a playful manner, all while fighting not to roll my eyes. "Once the moon comes out of Jupiter's shade," I explained, "and when there's a better conjunction between Venus and the sun."

He took on a sage expression, as if he knew just what I spoke of, though I hardly knew it myself. "Of course! We would not want any celestial shadow to stand between us on our wedding day." He smiled and made merry, though a flicker of exasperation crossed his drab features.

"No, we certainly would not." I did marvel at the man's patience, even as I loathed him for it. What sort of fellow would let himself be led by the nose in such a way? Perhaps Ma was right, and he would not have lasted long in my bed. "I want our marriage to have the best start possible," I assured him.

"That is in fact why I am here." He looked all smug and climbed down from the wagon at last. "I . . . I have something for you." He fumbled a little with the words, and his cheeks suddenly flushed a dark scarlet. "I . . . I do hope you'll appreciate it . . . it's just a silly gesture . . ." His forehead broke out in sweat as his fluster increased, and I felt a growing sense of unease. This could hardly be good, with all the fumbling and breathing as he fought to get something out of his coat pocket. His hand finally emerged with a small parcel wrapped in black velvet. For some reason, the sight of it unnerved me. It had me thinking of black crows and funerals.

"Here." Mr. Brockman held it out to me. It was soft to the touch. "Please, do open it." He looked like a young boy standing there before me with his eyes alight with anticipation.

I unwrapped the thing with growing distaste, though I could not say just why, as I usually loved all manner of gifts. Mayhap it was because I sensed this particular present was a snare meant to bind me. Mayhap that was the death I saw in the rich velvet cloth: my very own self's demise.

Inside the velvet wrapping was a simple cardboard box. I breathed a little easier then, because how precious could the gift be if it was delivered in something so plain? Then I opened the box and saw the ring, that little gold band, and my stomach lurched.

"Oh, Rudolph! It's beautiful!" I croaked through the bile that filled my mouth. "How very thoughtful of you!" I could not meet his gaze, however, and now I could feel a fresh coat of sweat breaking out on my skin.

The planets would not align anytime soon.

I picked up the ring while Brockman stammered before me. "It's just a little thing . . . a token, if you will. I . . . I just thought you might like—I hope it's not too presumptuous. Since we must wait—"

"Oh, it's lovely!" I held it up to the sun and saw the letters engraved on the inside: my very own name spelled out in gold. "I will wear it always," I swore and rose up on my toes to place a kiss on his cheek.

"Oh, good! I'm so pleased!" His voice was brimming with relief. "Here." He took the trinket from my fingers and grasped for my hand, meaning to place the gold upon it. "Please, let me," he said. "I do hope it is a fit."

I never got to try it on.

"What's that?" John's voice boomed behind me. "What's that?" I turned my head to see him standing there with a pail of milk, fresh from the barn, which crashed to the ground a moment later when he came striding quickly toward us. "What do you have there?" he yelled as he walked. "What do you have there, Brockman?"

I stepped forth to stop him, as I did not want any trouble to erupt, but he rudely shoved me aside. He grabbed ahold of Brockman's wrist and squinted to have a good look at the ring. All the while, Brockman was chattering. "It's only right that she has some token . . . a symbol of the promise we made. I know we cannot wed yet, but it's—" He abruptly stopped talking when John hit him square in the jaw.

Brockman went silent for a moment. He just stood there pressing a hand to his face. Then he found his voice again, and his animation, too. "Are you mad, John?" he cried, waving with his free hand. "This is no way to treat a brother-in-law! What on earth has gotten you so enraged?"

John did not reply, but bent his neck and went for him, pummeling his face and torso with his fists, all the while groaning and breathing heavily, and with a mad-looking grin upon his face. He reminded me of an angry bull, singular in intent and beyond any reason.

"Don't be an idiot, John!" I cried out, but I did not expect him to heed me. "You'd better go!" I attempted to warn Brockman, but it was far too late for that, as the man had decided to defend himself, and so they were both at it with flying fists.

Pa would not be pleased.

"Have you gone completely insane?" Brockman cried to John between blows.

"You leave her alone!" John cried back; his voice was hoarse with strain.

"She is no child!" Brockman cried.

"You take that filthy ring and go!"

Next, they were on the ground, kicking up dust as they rolled about, panting and groaning. The ring itself, the apple of discord, lay forlorn in a dirt heap, and suddenly, I had had enough. It did not matter one fig to me who lost or won. I had another man on my mind and could not see anything worth my while coming out of that fight.

Without alerting the fools on the ground, I spun on my heel and went for the barn. I could see that Ma was watching from the window, but like me, she did not seem inclined to try to put an end to the fight. Pa might, but he was out hunting, and so the tussle would just have to burn itself out. Shortly after, I was on our dun mare, riding for Nicholas Morrin's place.

Neither of the men fighting on the ground even noticed that I left.

NICHOLAS'S FARM WAS neat and well-kept, with flowering fruit trees and freshly plowed fields. His glossy horses roamed in the paddock, and a flurry of white chickens fled under my horse's hooves as I came riding into the yard.

His two daughters were playing with wooden dolls by the well.

Both girls wore plaid dresses that were whole and clean. White bonnets protected their skin from the sun. I wondered if it was Nicholas himself who had braided their hair. The girls looked up when I arrived but deemed me of no importance, it seemed, as they quickly went back to the arduous task of giving their dolls a bath.

Mr. Morrin, too, had seen me coming, and stepped out onto the porch. He wore a faded shirt that was open at the neck and dark pants held up by thick suspenders. His hair was a little tousled from working outside in the sun. He gave me a curious look as I dismounted the horse and hitched it to a post by the water trough, then waited patiently as I approached the porch, lifting my skirt to avoid the horse droppings. I sure wished I had worn something different from my drab brown shawl, and had taken some care with my hair, but there was nothing to do for it. I would just have to do.

John and Brockman had driven me to it.

"I have had a message," I declared when I reached the porch steps. "And Mr. Morrin, it was so *imploring*! It was as if all the angels gathered by Andrea's shoulder to deliver it. Her words were soft, yet as clear as a thousand chiming bells!"

"What was it?" He urged me on, taking a step closer.

"They said that it is *I*, Nicholas. Andrea said that it is *I* who am to make you happy again." I closed my hand into a fist and pressed it to my chest. "Through all our hours together at the table, I never thought that—"

"*I* did." His words came fast and breathless. "I have thought it so many times, but then I could hardly go courting before the very eyes of my precious wife—"

"Oh, Nicholas." I sighed with delight. "It was what she wanted all along—she might even have been the one bringing us two together."

A softness had come upon Mr. Morrin's face. "And you," he said as if in wonder, "such a fragile and sensitive soul . . . Who could have imagined that I should be given such a treasure to keep?" The wonder gave way to a smile. "You'd better come inside, Miss Bender."

"Please, call me Kate," said I.

"Kate," he repeated, and never had the name sounded sweeter.

As I stood there in Nicholas's house at last, it was with a sense of deep contentment. This man was milk and honey, I thought. He was apples and all sorts of fruit from the orchard, fresh, wholesome, and ripe. He had a heart that was honest and true beyond the grave.

I would very much like to have him as my own.

22.

HANSON

IT WAS AS if a chasm had erupted in the earth between the trading station and the Bender place, one that no one but me could traverse. Whenever goods were to be transferred or money exchanged—even when a simple message had to be relayed—it was I and the mule that had to go, as no one else seemed to be able.

It ought to have made me feel special, but it only made me feel ill at ease.

Whenever I made the short trek, I hoped to find Kate around, as she seemed to be the only one unchanged by the recent discord. As far as I could tell, she was always her own pleasant, chattering self. I did *not* want to see John, as I did not care for him as I had before. Things had been so easy between us at first, with the card games and the treats, but nothing about him was simple anymore. The men at the trading station kept talking about him with curled-up lips and telling gazes, shaking their heads at his peculiar habits: the

way he muttered and laughed to himself and the temper that struck
for no reason at all.

After John's fight with Mr. Brockman, he was no favorite of my
employers either, even if Mr. Bender had been to the trading station
to apologize for his son, and also to return the ring Mr. Brockman
had bought for Kate, seemingly unaware of its significance. He had
only said that he had "found it in the dirt," and Mr. Brockman,
ashamed, had taken the trinket back and pushed it to the back of a
drawer. He had still been sporting cuts and bruises all over his face
when that happened, and was likely not inclined to go courting
anew. I figured he would give the ring to Kate again when they next
met, but things seemed to have taken a gloomy turn for him, and
so I could not say for sure.

Mr. Brockman and Mr. Ern had many disagreements in the first
few days after the fight, ones I was not privy to but could easily in-
terpret even without any vast knowledge of the German language.
Mr. Ern would chastise Mr. Brockman for not heeding his warnings, and Mr. Brockman, in turn, would defend himself, citing
Kate's virtue as evidence that his love had not been squandered and
there was still a future to be had with her by his side. He would not
relent, he said, before Kate herself told him that the engagement
was over, and thus far, she had not.

He might have been the only one to still believe that the wedding could be saved. Even I had lost most of my faith in their union,
especially with Kate being so happy all the time, and not even once
asking me how poor Mr. Brockman fared. Neither did she visit with
ointments and such, although I knew they had plenty of those in the
house. She just did not seem to care.

So I was not about to defend Mr. Brockman's stubborn love
when Mr. Ern sought me out in the barn one morning, after a spec-

tacularly loud argument the night before. I was just up then, and waiting on the cow to finish her breakfast, so we could get some milk for ours. Mr. Ern entered, hollow-eyed, having likely not slept much at all. His beard had not been carefully combed, as was his usual habit, and his glasses were specked with grease.

"What are we to do with that foolish man inside?" he complained. "He simply will not see reason!"

"Well, it's hard when Kate hasn't told him no."

"Oh, she never will." Mr. Ern spoke with a hardness to his words. His accent was much more pronounced than usual, so he was certainly very agitated. "That little minx, she will not let him go without a fight. She wants to keep him there on her dancing card even if she will never swing in his arms. He is foolish—deluded. She has no love for him!"

"But would she truly do that?" I asked as I settled on a stool by the cow's warm side and placed the bucket under the swollen udder. I just could not see any good reason for it.

"Ah! Who knows?" Mr. Ern lifted a hand to slap his own forehead. "It's madness, all of it! We should never have gotten ourselves tangled with that family. They are nothing but trouble!"

"Did Mr. Bender say *why* John was so mad with Mr. Brockman?" That question had been bothering me some.

Mr. Ern shook his head. "He only said that his son had a poor temper, and that he had been drinking, but Rudolph did not smell any liquor on his breath."

"Perhaps he thought Mr. Brockman had *offended* Kate somehow?" I mused.

"Perhaps that is what *she* said," Mr. Ern replied. "I wouldn't put it past that *minx* to lie just to get a rise out of someone."

That did not sound like the Kate I knew; she never did strike me as someone to do something for nothing. "I don't think she cares for such squabbles," I dared to say. "As Mr. Brockman said himself, Kate had already left the yard when Mr. Bender returned from his hunt and the fight ended. Maybe she's staying away because she's angry that Mr. Brockman fought."

"That is a very kind assessment," Mr. Ern remarked.

"Well, I see her quite often," I mumbled, implying that I might perhaps know her a little bit better than him. While I spoke, my hands were constantly at it, squeezing fat streams of milk from the cow.

Mr. Ern folded his arms over his chest and leaned against the timber wall. "You know, they say in town that John might not be her brother at all."

"What?" It took me utterly by surprise.

"Do you remember when they first came here, Hanson? I am fairly certain John said that he was waiting for his wife."

I, too, remembered hearing that but had long since deemed it a failing of my memory. "Why would they lie about something like that?"

Mr. Ern snorted as if to say that I was both young and naïve. "People have all sorts of reasons for lying—perhaps the Benders are hiding from something."

"Yeah? Like what?"

My employer shrugged and gave a sigh. "Theft, maybe? Fraud?"

"Oh, I don't believe that." I shook my head with vigor.

"They aren't much alike, though, Kate and John. They don't *look* like siblings," Mr. Ern noted. I thought of my friends Bruno and Max, who both had that same shade of brown hair, and had to agree a little. "It would make more sense," Mr. Ern continued, "if John attacked Rudolph because Kate is in fact already his wife."

"That just seems silly to me." Yet my ears burned and I focused intently on the milk hitting the bucket, just so my unease would not show. "Why would she agree to marry Mr. Brockman if that's the case?"

"I don't know, Hanson," Mr. Ern replied with another sigh. "It all just seems awful."

"Well, *I* don't think Kate is a liar," I declared, clinging to that belief with all my might.

DESPITE MY BOLD statement, I did not feel quite all right the next time I was sent to the Benders to pick up our share of the earnings. In fact, I felt increasingly insecure the closer the mule and I came to the Bender place. I dreaded seeing both Kate and John, as I feared that I would somehow give away that I knew of the rumors about them. I also dreaded seeing evidence that the awful gossip was true. What was I to do if I learned for sure that they had made a fool of poor Mr. Brockman? I could not quite see it happening, though. Kate never acted like a loving wife to John; rather, she treated him somewhat with contempt, much like a sister might, I figured.

But then there had been that awful fight.

It was a cold day, however, so, despite my misgivings, I did not dawdle for long outside the door, but quickly went inside, hoping for some hot soup, or at least a moment by the fire.

I was disappointed on both counts.

Kate was not there, and neither was John, and, strangely, even Mrs. Bender was missing from the rocking chair. A soft snoring gave the latter away, though—she was probably asleep upon the bed. *Mr.* Bender was there, however, whittling by the stove, though the wooden chips drizzled upon ashes that were cold. It seemed like an awful oversight not to light a fire when the air outside was freezing. Furthermore, a terrible smell of rot seemed to permeate the air in the room.

I could not help but grimace, and Mr. Bender smiled when he saw it.

"Ma left out the meat." He gestured to the back, where they kept a counter for storing and chopping. "Too long."

"It's very cold," I remarked, and made to hold myself and rub my upper arms while clacking my teeth to make my point.

Mr. Bender smiled again. "Fire is . . . expensive." He motioned to the stove with the knife in his hand. The blade looked very well honed. "Come back later, Hanson." He looked back down at the piece of wood in his hands, and I felt thoroughly and utterly dismissed. I did not much care, though, as the smell was so terrible. I figured it might very well be just why the fire was not lit, though surely they had thrown out the rancid meat by then.

How could Mrs. Bender even sleep in such a stench?

I thought I should ask Mr. Bender when Kate was expected back, or make my errand known somehow, but the air in there was simply too cold and foul, and Mr. Bender clearly wanted me to leave, and so I slunk back out again, deciding to tell Mr. Ern that Mr. Bender had not understood what I wanted. It seemed easier than explaining how the house that day had unsettled me.

I was a little relieved, too, as I returned up the road with an empty purse, as at least the blood-drinking murderer would not sniff out my wealth and come rushing with his knife to finish me off. Even if they had not found more bodies, the thought of the murderer still haunted me, especially when I traveled with valuables, so that at least was a silver lining. I worried about those old folks, though, sitting there in that reeking house, with nothing to warm their bones.

I sure hoped that Kate and John would be home soon.

Perhaps it was the same worry that had me turn my gaze on the Bender place that night. I had climbed up on the barn roof to look at the stars, as I often did when sleep was slow in coming. Not only did watching the sky calm me down, but I also felt safer up there. No murderer would think to look up, I figured.

That night I had brought a couple of horse blankets with me and sat huddled in the darkness like a perching crow. I looked at the stars that twinkled up there like a smattering of luminous pearls and wondered at how Kate could make heads or tails of their movements. It greatly amazed me how she could read them like letters and even predict the future from those tiny dots. Mr. Brockman had cursed them many a time as he waited for Kate to decide on a wedding date.

It was then that I saw something happening at the Bender place: a dot of light appeared behind the house. It was moving, so it had to be a lantern, a bright yellow flame that traveled through the night and then stopped at what was destined to be the Benders' orchard.

Then came the sounds of digging. It was faint and far off, but the sounds were unmistakable. There was the thud of the shovel hitting the dirt, then the rush of the soil drizzling from the blade.

Why were the Benders digging at night? Were they finally getting rid of the rancid meat? Surely, that could have waited until dawn if they had only put it out by the door.

Maybe they were afraid of coyotes . . .

I told myself that it was none of my concern when our neighbors wanted to work their own land, even if it was well past midnight, and yet I could not help but stare, squinting my eyes in the darkness. My ears were perked, listening to the sounds of digging. It went on for a good long while, and then other sounds appeared: male voices talking, discussing—though in German, and so fast that I could not understand a word. Then came a female voice, too, and I thought that it had to be Kate, as it was so clear. I could see the light shifting as the back door was opened and closed several times. Then it was open for a longer while, and I heard the sounds of grunting and groaning, as if someone was under strain.

By then I had to acknowledge a growing sense of unease, as I could not for the life of me figure out what they were doing. I tried to force myself to look at the stars and not the lights at the Bender place, but spectacularly failed at this. There were two golden dots in the orchard now; one of them was bobbing, so it had to be held by someone. Then came the sound of digging again, the thud and the drizzle of dirt. They were at it for a long, long time, before both the golden dots moved anew and the back door was opened, then closed.

It did not open again, but there was still light in their windows when I quickly climbed down the ladder and slipped inside the barn, not even daring to light my own lantern. For some reason that I could not name, my heart was racing madly in my chest, and my breathing came hard and fast. I told myself that it was just my imagination again, seeing evildoers everywhere, even in my own neighbors' orchard. This was *just* the sort of thing Mr. Brockman berated me for whenever I got the shivers.

I swore as I lay there in the dark, next to the chewing mule, that

I would forget what I had seen. If the Benders wanted to dig down some rotten meat, and make it deep to keep it from scavengers, it was surely nothing to me if they did it late at night.

Yet it gnawed at me—it did! I simply could not help it.

Something about it was wrong.

23.

ELVIRA

MY HUSBAND'S AND my pleasant mornings together had turned as sour as curdled milk. William would still make the bread, and I would still make the coffee, but we no longer saw eye to eye.

"It is madness what we're doing," I said—nay, *hissed* at him one day at dawn as he worked the dough at the table. "We have two bodies in the orchard now and three others besides. This is not what we agreed on, husband. We agreed to hide!" I sat on a chair beside him with my hands in my lap. Quite without meaning to, my fingers were moving nervously about like hungry hens, pecking and worrying at each other. I had lit a fire in the stove so we could make the bread, but it was not such a good idea, as the summer had come with a blazing crown, bringing a sweltering heat in its wake.

William worried about drought, while I—wretched thing—worried about the noose.

"It was bad enough with the Vandles," I muttered. "Now we have added strangers to the list—strangers that we know nothing about! Mayhap one of them has said something about staying the night with us, and a family member is turning their gaze upon us as we speak—"

"You worry too much, Elvira," said he, giving me a look of compassion. "We have made it thus far, have we not?" His long, bony fingers worked the dough with firmness. "I wish you would see it as I do, as a means to our salvation and not a ticket to damnation. We reap now to sow the future—"

"Poetry won't change the nature of our crimes," I told him. "Murder will be murder, no matter how you cloak it in words—and murderers *hang*, William, you know that as well as I do."

"*We* won't." He sounded so sure, so serene. He turned the dough over so it slapped against the table. "Kate's visions have brought us this far, and her angels won't let her come to harm—"

"You put too much stock in the girl," I snapped. "You think she can do no wrong, but Kate is no stranger to failure, husband. At the end of the day, she's nothing but a girl."

"Oh." He arched an eyebrow at me. "She is surely a woman grown, and she has still not steered us wrong. Her predictions have all proven true, haven't they? Every man we have slain has had pockets full of coins." He gave the dough another slap, and I rose to see about the coffee.

"Just luck." I snorted when my back was turned. "She is full of these tricks! I simply cannot believe that you buy into them." I sneered. "My own husband! What a shame!"

"Mayhap it is you who trust her too little," he suggested, seemingly unfazed by my outburst. "Have you ever let yourself truly believe that Kate is blessed by the angels—?"

"No angels would condone such bloodshed, William." I could not believe my own ears. "If anything, it's the devil speaking, and luring these men to our door." I measured out the coffee grounds and watched them getting swallowed by the black depths of the kettle.

"Who are we to say what the angels want?" His stoic calm was most maddening.

"Well, I never heard of an angel who put men in harm's way!" I left the kettle to brew and went back to my chair by the table.

"Maybe Kate's angels are special," he suggested, and I knew then that there would be no reasoning with him. He would believe what he wanted to believe, whatever could justify his bloody means.

"And what if you are wrong?" I asked him coolly. "What if they figure us out—what then?"

"I trust in Kate and the angels," said he, and lifted a flour-dusted hand to thump his chest. "I can feel it in here—we are protected."

I sighed deeply. "We are running on luck alone." I tried one last time. "We should flee *now*, while we still can."

"Run *where*, Elvira? With what? We'll need more if we are to buy another farm."

That shut me up, as I *did* want that farm. I *deserved* it, after all that I had suffered—after all that Kate had taken away from me. She *owed* me, that girl, for raising her with nothing and providing her with ample skills, but most of all for forcing us to leave Pennsylvania behind. At the end of the day, I had to admit, I did not much care *how* the money came about, as long as the debt was settled.

But I did not want to hang.

"What if Kate is wrong the next time?" I fretted. "What if the next man is the nail in our coffin?"

"You truly have no faith." He shook his head with a sad expression, which only infuriated me more.

"Madness, husband." I shook my head with disbelief. "My nerves were already frayed when we came here." I appealed to his compassion next. "Now they are as lit by fire, hounding me night and day."

"I'm sure you have a brew for that." I almost expected him to pat me on the head.

"Oh, I can barely take my teas anymore," I admitted. "I am too afraid that all the good has been purged from them as a punishment for what we have done." I did not, of course, but I wanted him to think so. William was a spiritual man and likely to understand such woes even better than common sense.

"Nonsense, Elvira. Had there not been a blessing upon this house, we would have hanged a long time ago, and our savings would have dwindled, not swelled."

"Is that what you all believe?" It hurt me to see how they were all so in tune, while I was left out like Thomas the doubter. "Kate is merely clever," I tried again. "More clever than most, that is true, but she is certainly not so blessed—"

"It is a shame that you, her own mother, cannot see her for what she is," said my husband. "Kate is divinely connected, of that I have no doubt."

"Of course you don't." I finally gave in with a sigh and went out back to get the chipped china cups we used for coffee. What was the point in quarreling? He believed that my daughter was all of that because it was what she wanted to him to. I had taught her how to turn a mind myself, and been poorly repaid for the effort.

"She is up to something, though." I gave him one last warning upon my return. "She's off at all times, and avoiding John. I think she's seeing that farmer much more often than she lets on."

This caught my husband's attention at last. "That's not good," he agreed, and his hands, deep in the dough, stopped moving. "An entanglement of the heart can bring on all sorts of trouble."

"Isn't that right." I gave another sigh. "We have just gotten rid of Brockman, and now this other one comes along."

"Brockman isn't gone," said William. "He's merely waiting for the tide to turn. Had he abandoned all hope, our partnership would have ended, too."

"He's an idiot, then," said I, placing the cups on the table with such force that they clattered together.

"That he is," William conceded, and we had some agreement at last.

"John cannot know," I warned him as I went for the kettle. "We cannot have another fistfight—not with Mr. Morrin. The man is a decent sort."

When I turned my head back, I could see that William nodded. "My son is better off in the dark. We surely don't need that sort of attention."

"Let him think Kate's heart is free and that she is merely riding to see about sick people, like she says." The scent of coffee was strong by the stove and, despite my agitation, I could not help but enjoy it. To have such mornings somewhere else—somewhere safe—surrounded by lush woods . . .

"And if he finds out?" William's voice sounded behind me.

"Then you better hope that her 'angels' are at the ready." I turned around with the kettle in my hand.

A flicker of annoyance crossed William's features. "He is a fool for her," he stated.

"That he is," I agreed, and so there was peace between us.

I could not find *my own* peace, though. For all the violence that he wrought, I found my husband to be hopelessly naïve, and that assessment was duly justified as the summer moved on.

The two riders did not seem like much at all when they arrived;

they were clothed plainly and covered in dust from the road. They both wore wide-brimmed hats to shade their faces from the sun, and shirts whose sleeves were rolled up to the elbow, as the day was very hot. Their cheeks were riddled with stubble, so I thought they had been riding for a while. They also both seemed to have outgrown their prime and gained some pale silver in their hair.

I had a stew simmering on the stove, and they wanted to take it outside. That was all fair and good, but as they started eating, sitting on the ground in the shade and resting their backs against the wall, I noticed a certain restlessness about them. They barely even chewed the food after scooping it into their maws. They also did not smile or jest between them, but retained their morose expressions throughout the meal.

I had a bad feeling.

"Those two may be fugitives," I told William as we stood by the window, looking out on them.

"I don't think so," said he. "Their clothes are very well made, and those leather boots are new."

"Well, they are very skittish, aren't they? Look at how their eyes move around."

"Maybe they carry valuables," said he.

"Don't you even think about it." I glared at him. "Kate has *not* marked those two."

"I thought you didn't believe in Kate's visions," he replied good-naturedly and sipped the coffee in his hand.

"I don't," I replied, "but you *do*."

William chuckled at this. "They tried to speak to me as I brought them the food, but gave up when I replied in German." William thought this was a relief, as he did not much like to speak to strangers. "I thought they said something about a man."

"What man?" I gave my husband another angry stare.

"A John, I believe," he answered serenely. "Not to worry." He offered me a glance. "There are many Johns about. Half of our guests are Johns." He chuckled.

"William!" I hissed. "We have at least two Johns out there in the orchard—"

"Well, it could be someone else." He drew a hand through his long gray beard. "They might not even have been asking about a man. I could have gotten it wrong." But I did not think so. Not at all. "There is Kate now," he said, as she entered the yard upon the dun horse, riding sidesaddle for once. That did not prevent her from exposing her calves to the world, of course, with the worn blue skirt lapping at her knees. Her hair, too, flowed freely down her back from under William's wide-brimmed leather hat, much like a river of red.

She had probably been to see Mr. Morrin again.

"Maybe *she* can make sense of them," William said, nodding to the men through the glass.

Kate did indeed speak to the men, and at first, I thought she had softened them up with her banter. Their eyes lit up and smiles appeared on their thin, chapped lips like the sun coming out following rain. She had that effect on men. Then, as I watched her standing there beside them, hitting her riding crop lightly against her thigh, she seemed to stagger, just a little, and so subtly that only we who knew her would notice. It still happened, though, and her face took on a touch of strain.

I knew that something was wrong.

When Kate came barging inside, the smile she had worn for the men's benefit was quickly wiped from her face. As soon as the door closed behind her, her lips drooped down at the edges and her nostrils flared.

"They are asking about the last one." She was whispering even though she spoke in German. "The old one—Johnny Boyle. They are friends of his."

"I thought you said he was a lonesome bachelor," I whispered back.

"Well, yes, but obviously he still had friends." She nodded in the men's direction through the wall. "They're likely of the same ilk as him, I reckon, lonesome old men with nothing better to do than pry into people's business."

"What did you tell them?" William still sounded calm, was still combing his bushy beard with his fingers.

"That we had not seen any Johnny Boyle around," said Kate.

"Was that wise?" I wondered. "What if he had told someone he was to stop at our place?"

She shrugged. "I can hardly be expected to remember all of our guests, and especially not one as unremarkable as Johnny Boyle."

I remembered how he had howled when John struck him with the hammer, and how his blood had smelled as it coated my arms.

William placed a hand on Kate's shoulder. "Go out there again, Kate, and offer to do a séance to locate their lost friend." He caught my expression of surprise and added, "There's no reason why we cannot make a little extra from it. The man will still be dead whether Kate puts on a performance or not. You won't actually talk to the angels," he said to her, looking mischievous all of a sudden. "You will just make as if you do. You can do that, right? It won't offend the angels?"

A ghost of a smile crossed Kate's lips. "No, Pa, it won't offend them. Is it wise, though? Should we meddle and not leave them well alone?" For once, I thought she asked good questions.

William shrugged. "It seems like a good opportunity," he remarked. "Just as when you spoke to those people in town." He was referring to Kate's séance when she had pretended to be one of the dead men.

I looked to Kate, curious as to what she would do. I am sad to say that I was not surprised when she squared her shoulders and plastered on a smile. "I can surely send them somewhere else," she said. "Massachusetts, maybe."

"That's good." William nodded, satisfied, while I groaned and hid my face in my hands. I barely peeked out again when she went back outside to make the men her offer. I could not help but hear her, though, her confident voice speaking rapidly in English.

William's hand landed on my shoulder. "It'll be all right, Ma," he said. "Just you see. Kate will have them fooled."

"But just the fact that they are *here*," I fretted, "searching for *that man*—"

"Now, don't you let the fear get the better of you." He aimed to soothe me. "We are still blessed, just you see."

I could do nothing then but put the kettle on to serve them coffee when Kate brought the men with her inside. They came scampering through the door, bringing with them a scent of sunbaked skin and musty perspiration. William was already by the window, hanging the heavy, dark curtains to block out the blazing sun.

The men looked nervous when Kate had them by the table; they clutched their hats with gnarled hands and let their eyes roam the room, though there was little to see with only a candle for illumination. I myself retreated to the rocking chair and folded my hands as if in prayer. We had found this put Kate's sitters at ease, especially when she told them how devout her ma was. Simple, old, and foolish—but devout. I never much minded this, as I would much rather sit in my chair through it all than take part in the dimly lit charade.

The séance seemed to follow the usual pattern, with some clever knocking from Kate under the table and some flickering of the flame. I looked to William across the room. He was standing by the grandfather clock, which bothered me some, as that was where he kept the knives. I did not think he would fall for the temptation and do something stupid, though, as John was in town for feed, and not behind the curtain with the hammer.

Kate sighed, jerked, and rolled her eyes, and I sat there as if in prayer for a very long while. Then she started speaking, rapid and unhinged, in Mr. Black's voice. Sweat pooled on her forehead and the candle flickered madly on the table. I thought I still could smell Johnny Boyle's blood, rising from between the floorboards, and gave a little jerk of my own.

The men looked at my daughter with rapt expressions; their eyes squinted in the poor light. It certainly did not help with the overall discomfort that the room was as hot as a baking oven. I could feel the sweat run under my clothes, and the calico plastered to my skin.

When it was finally over and Kate "came to," it was hard to tell from the men's expression if they were pleased. They did pay the agreed-upon fee, though, and seemed courteous enough when dealing with Kate. The latter looked appropriately dazed from the spiritual encounter, vulnerable and soft, as she pressed the men's hands between her own.

I was not sad to see them leave.

"I said he had fallen in love with a native woman," Kate said when they had left the yard. The two of us had taken the curtains down and were watching them ride away from the window. William, too, was out there, tidying up around the barn. "Is there any stew left?" she asked suddenly. "I'm starving."

I cannot say if the men truly believed Kate, or if the message they had gotten had left them bewildered. The encounter with Johnny's friends had shaken me up some, though.

I truly felt it was a bad omen that a search party had entered our house. It was as if the threat I had always sensed had come closer all of a sudden—as if the gathering clouds had moved in.

As any good grifter knows, people will be fooled for only so long.

24.

KATE

I HAD PERHAPS forgotten how luck could change in the blink of an eye.

I sure must have looked foolish as we stood there, gathered around Benjamin Brown's body, searching through his clothes, and there simply was no money. No pocket watch or jewelry, no weapons or leatherwork of any particular value. The man was as good as a vagrant. Even his buttons were a plain sort, nothing but simple wood.

"I thought the angels had marked him." Pa's gaze upon me was loaded with dreadful disappointment.

Mr. Brown's clothes lay in a heap on the floor; his eyes looked up at the ceiling, vacant and glass-like. His flesh was very white.

"His wagon is handsome," John remarked laconically. "I'm sure Jack can fetch us a fair price."

"It's not enough," Pa grunted. "What's happening, Kate? Are the angels tricking us?" His face bore a bewildered frustration. In his hand was the knife, glinting in the light from the candle on the table. The canvas curtain's smear of red was slowly turning to a dark brown stain that could be easily mistaken for dirt.

Ma chuckled from the rocking chair, finding us very amusing.

"Maybe it *was* a trickster," I said. "Not all spirits are pure of intention. I cannot always say which ones are honest." I noticed how my hands shook a little; I was still riding the pleasant wave that followed whenever I had wielded the knife.

"You never spoke of this before," Pa complained. "How come there are *liars* among them all of a sudden—" He stamped his foot and huffed.

"There never were before," I argued. "Mayhap it's your greed that has grown too strong," I accused him, to shift the blame a little. "Mayhap our knife is too hungry to satisfy."

"Mayhap your angels aren't what they pretend to be?" Ma suggested, and I wanted to throw something heavy at her.

"The wagon, though—" said John.

"Oh, but Jack Handsome *never* gives us a good price." Pa groaned and sank down in a chair. He did not look good; the disappointment was etched upon his features, and his skin looked clammy in the hot summer night. "He is *always* complaining," Pa lamented. "He says that his debt to us is surely erased."

"He is suspicious," croaked Ma. "He knows there is something terrible about the horses we bring him. He can sense that we did not just steal—"

"No, Ma! No." Now it was I who stomped my foot against the floorboards. "Don't bring up that nonsense again. *No one* knows what we're doing here!"

"Jack Handsome has no conscience." Pa snorted. "He would not care either way."

"Oh." Ma shot us a glance. "Not all are as callous as you lot."

"You're not so high-and-mighty yourself," I muttered, happy that we were no longer speaking of my untrustworthy spirits.

"At least I'm not dressing my wicked deeds up with angels and spirits." She snorted. "A murder is just that," she said, "and God doesn't care if the Benders thrive or not."

"Well, *someone* up there does," Pa insisted.

"Clearly not." Ma nodded to the carcass. "That one was nothing but labor and misery."

"We must get him in the ground." I shrugged. There was nothing else to do but cut our losses. "He'll smell in no time in this heat."

"I have to drive to Jack's before dawn," John mused.

"You better get out your shovels first," said Ma.

Pa shook his head with a grim expression. "I don't understand this at all."

Despite Pa's disappointment, *I* was still glowing with our bloody deed when I went into the barn later, just as the men were digging in the orchard. I had brought a glass-enclosed candle with me, as it was dark, but I just could not wait to be alone, and to put the scuffed, cigar-shaped button in with the rest in the box.

There were six of them already resting at the bottom: one of brass, one of silver, one of bone, and one of leather. Jones, Brewer, Finch, and McCrotty. Then there was one of wood with bone inlays from Mr. John Greary, whom we had slain in early spring. He had been a resident of Cedar Vale and traveled with ample cash in his pockets. I had been reading his fortune in the cards when John hit him in the head with the hammer. The card deck had been soiled afterward, and we had to burn it in the oven. I had not been happy about it as it had been my special deck, pretty enough to make my sitters gawk and be distracted by the colorful details.

There was also another brass button, sporting a simple flower that reminded me of a buttercup. It had belonged to Johnny Boyle, the man we had slain at the beginning of summer and who had proved to have such curious friends. The old bachelor had traveled on foot with plenty of cash to do some land buying. I had been car-less with the knife when I cut him, and Ma had me standing on a chair to clean the ceiling afterward.

Now there was a wooden button, too, just as unremarkable as the man who had carried it, and my collection had grown to seven, enough to hold in the palm of my hand and let drizzle down into the cigar box. They gave a most satisfying sound.

I brought the box with me down in the hay and lay back, seeing it all again in my mind: how Mr. Brown had entered and paused on the threshold, as if he felt for a brief moment that he was walking to his doom. How I had greeted him, pulled him inside, and seated him at the table—given him soup.

I had known already then that he was a scruffy sort; his clothing was plain and he had a lost air about him, as if he did not quite know what to do with himself. But it was already too late by then, as John was behind the curtain, "the angels" had marked him, and the dark-ness was strong and restless in me, clamoring for its due. He sure liked our whiskey, though, when I poured it.

He loosened up as the drink went in, and I told him of my work as a medium. He turned out to be a believer and hung on my every word. I was just about to offer to ask the spirits where he ought to go next to find good opportunities when John struck him and his head landed in the soup bowl. A waste, truly, of good food.

The darkness was upon me then, and I barely waited for John and Pa to come and lift Mr. Brown away from the table and tip his chair back so he slid down into the cellar, landing there like a sack of feed, heavy and still. I dearly hoped he was not dead yet, but then he moaned, and so I was satisfied. I lifted my skirts and jumped down there with him. Pa held up a lamp for me to see. Benjamin Brown had landed with his head tilted to the left, already giving me a tantalizing glimpse of the softness of his throat.

"Do you need help?" John asked me from above; he was antsy, as he knew the night was only so long, and we had much work to do before dawn. It was almost better if we managed to kill them by day, and then had a few hours to prepare before nightfall, while the body lay waiting in the cellar. It sometimes smelled, though, so that was no good.

"No," I called back. "I can do it on my own. He is bleeding badly from the head." We did not like that much, as it ruined the clothing. I grabbed ahold of his legs and pulled as I stood over him with one foot on each side of his body. He moaned as he shifted on the handpicked cellar floor, and his head fell back, exposing more of the throat. I pushed away a few greasy curls of hair to have a clean canvas; only the stubble of his beard marred the white surface of his skin.

Then I cut.

THE NEXT DAY, I rode into the Morrins' yard. I let Nicholas take the mare's reins and catch me in his arms as I slid down from the horse. His body was hot and damp in the heat, his honey hair plastered to his forehead.

"The girls have been waiting for you," he said, holding me just a little too long before letting me go, dazzling me with his brilliant smile. "We all have," he added with a wink.

"Kate! Kate!" The girls came tumbling outside. They both wore flowery calico dresses and their hair was neatly braided. Constance was clutching a wooden doll to her chest, and Alma, the eldest, had Rosie on her heels. The dog and the girl had taken a liking to each other, and I did not mind at all if Alma borrowed her from time to time. The dog was awfully spoiled at the Morrin farm, and always came home freshly combed. When John asked, I said that the dog had run off but that she always came back.

So far, he had not seen through my ruse.

I bent down to receive the girls' warm embraces. They both smelled of sweet milk and fresh bread. Alma led me by the hand as we approached the house with a thrilled Rosie yapping at our feet.

Well inside the handsome farmhouse, we all worked together to set the table with biscuits, butter, apples, and cheese. Before we ate, we held hands while Nicholas said grace. The girls were both very well-behaved and passed the food between them with polite remarks. Even Rosie fell in line and lay quietly in a corner in a basket Alma had readied for her use. The food there was, as always, delicious; the biscuits were soft and the cheese was fragrant. The cider in my cup was very sweet. The family around me was good to each other—none of them sported bruises or cuts. The girls had surely never been locked in a cupboard or forced to go with gentlemen only to steal their coins.

It was all so very perfect.

"Tell me, Kate." Alma's eyes, as dark as her father's, looked up at me with childish curiosity. "How is my mama today?"

I closed my eyes and pretended to listen. "Oh, your mama is very pleased today. She can see how you and your sister are so clean and well-behaved. She wishes she could be with you, but Lavinia needs her in heaven."

Alma gave a soft sigh in reply, half in yearning and half in satisfaction, and set to buttering her biscuit. "She must be happy that you are here with us, though. She must not have wanted us to be alone with only Papa."

I opened my eyes again. "Your papa is very good at taking care of you. I can tell that he loves you very much."

"Of course he does," said Alma, and I reeled a little at the sincerity in her voice—her absolute conviction that it was true. I thought I had never known such trust.

"Your mama is a little bit with us, though, when Kate is here. It's like she's visiting," Nicholas said.

"Only better," said Alma, "because we get a visit from Kate as well." She proceeded to offer me another brilliant smile.

"The food tastes better when Kate is here, too," little Constance declared and had her father laughing softly.

"That's because Kate is so sweet," he told her, with only a faint blush staining his cheeks. Both girls giggled at that.

To have this, I thought then. To have this man and this home, to be a mama to these girls. To have this warmth and this bustling life around me always. In Nicholas's fields, there was barley and corn; not a single human bone spoiled the earth. I could see it all so clearly: how I would continue to receive sitters, but in this wholesome house. How I would become a renowned medium, known for my virtue and strong faith. The girls would thrive under my care, Nicholas's heart would heal, and all would admire me for how I put this family back together again after their terrible loss. Twice a year I would go touring and give spiritual lectures, staying in fine hotels. I could be happy then—I felt sure of it. Surely the darkness would recede then, and I would never again long for it. I would bury my button box and never think of it again.

Surely, there had to be a way.

After we had finished eating and had rinsed all the plates, the girls and Rosie went outside to gather eggs and feed the chickens. Nicholas and I were finally alone. It did not take long, then, before he had me pressed up against the wall between the windows, and his mouth was on mine, hot and eager. His hands roaming my sides were strong and yearning, obviously aching to touch my skin, but staying above the fabric in an infuriatingly chaste manner.

"Oh, Kate," he moaned into my ear. "How come you have me so weak?"

"It's meant to be between us," I replied, equally aroused. "That's why it feels so strong."

"When will you tell Brockman that his wedding is off?" he asked against my neck; his hot breath tickled me; the scent of him left me feeling heady.

"Soon," I murmured through the pleasure. "When his pride has healed after my brother's attack."

"I would like for our engagement to be known," said he.

"It will, Nicholas. Soon," I swore, while wrapping my arms around his shoulders. The air around us was hot, but I was hotter still, and I could not for the life of me understand what possessed a man to choose such a righteous path, refusing to bed me before my previous engagement was broken.

I had told Nicholas about my brother's fits—how reason sometimes escaped him and how his temper could not be trusted. I had said that I felt guilty for what had happened to Mr. Brockman, as he had been harmed on my account, due to my brother's muddled mind. I had also told Nicholas how our newfound connection had made it plain as day that the marriage to Brockman would never happen. "I just need some time," I had said, "to settle things with

Mr. Brockman in a manner that won't further damage him." In truth, it was John who worried me, though.

He had not been thrilled when I left the house that day.

"Another appointment?" he had asked as I readied the mare in the barn. "I don't see why you so often have to ride out to them. Why can't they come and see you here?"

"They are sick people, John. I can hardly expect them to travel."

"Then why can't I go with you?" he complained. "It would be easier and more convenient for you with the wagon—"

"I don't know how long it will take, John, and I sure won't impose on their hospitality by having my surly brother in tow."

"*Brother*." He snorted. "I have never been your *brother*."

"Be as that might; I don't want you there while I work. People are afraid of you, John, after what you did to Brockman. You're just not good for business."

"What do I care what people think?" he said, but I could see that he had clenched his jaw, so he was not as aloof as he pretended to be. "Take Pa, then," he continued. "It's not becoming with you riding alone like this."

"Why not?" I asked as I fumbled with the saddle. "I am Professor Miss Katie Bender." I tried out the new serious title I had chosen for myself. "There's nothing strange about me riding alone. Everyone knows that I'm out to heal the sick."

"Do they, though?" he muttered, but did not wait for an answer. "Some may say you are a wild one."

"Well." I shrugged. "I cannot help it if they do."

"People will start talking." He gave me a pointed look. "It's just what Ma is afraid of."

"Says *you*, who beat up my fiancé in the yard." That had certainly set the tongues wagging.

"Well, I can't take that back, but you—"

"I ride alone," I snapped, and he did back down then, but I did not expect the peace to last.

John could never know about Nicholas Morrin and me.

If he did, all my plans would be overturned, and it would surely end in murder.

25.

HANSON

MRS. BENDER WANTED to give me some broth, but I did not feel like it. Perhaps the weather was too hot, or the broth was too cold, sporting a rind of fat against the iron of the pot. I did not think there had been a fire in the stove for some hours.

Ever since William had come to apologize for John, none of the Benders had come to the trading station, not even to bargain for a little corn. Neither had Mr. Brockman or Mr. Ern traversed to the Bender place. Yet I went—as I always had—with the mule, carrying goods and transferring money between the houses.

I no longer feared the blood drinker, though. He had somehow lost his power.

The Bender home, on the surface, looked as it had always done, if a little more dusty and untidy than before. I did not think Mrs. Bender swept the floor anymore, and a foul smell seemed to have settled within the walls. I told myself they were likely to have rodents—or one of the old couple had acquired the sort of illness that old people got. Sick rooms, I knew from experience, could often smell quite badly.

Kate was rarely there anymore. John said she was busy with visiting the sick, now that she had gained some renown. "They rarely pay her, though." He sniffed. "Or if they do, it is only in eggs and such." His English had gotten much better, I noted, but that did not make him any cheerier. He did not seem to like that Kate was busy with her patients.

Mrs. Bender, too, spoke to me more often than before, and I learned that her grasp of the English language was also better than I had believed. "You should not come here, Hanson," she often said, placing a hand on my shoulder as I sat by the table, eating a little something or sipping a cup of tea. Before the night when I saw the lights, I would have thought she said that out of concern because our houses were somewhat at discord, but everything had taken on a sinister cast ever since, and I could not help but fear that the Benders had a terrible secret to protect.

The house was often quiet; none of them was saying much. Despite the daylight filtering in through the dusty windows, a gloom seemed to dwell there always.

We never even played cards anymore.

Yet I still missed Kate if I had not seen her for some days, and often held the flower she had given me—the one made out of a newspaper page—before I went to sleep, thinking of what she had said about my destiny as a newspaperman. It seemed to me that before she had arrived, I had barely dared to dream of such a future, but ever since Kate had read her cards, it all seemed within my reach. She had a way of making anything seem possible—though sometimes it was a lie, as it had been for poor Mr. Brockman.

Mrs. Bender did not much mind that I did not eat her broth that day—she did not much care either way, I figured. I had noticed how her stews of late were mostly bones and gristle, and how she did not seem to care if the soup she served was warm or cold in the pot. She knitted even more than before, but I rarely saw her with the pestle and mortar, preparing some herbs for ointments or brews. She seemed to leave all the curing to Kate now, which I supposed was only fair and right, with Mrs. Bender being old, but the latter did not seem to thrive for it. Her posture had become a little stooped, and she often rubbed her aching joints. I wondered why Kate did not cure her ma, but then again I knew that some illnesses were harder to squelch than others.

If Mrs. Bender had become slower, her husband had become faster, jumping, almost, when he saw me in the room. I did not take offense, though, as I had seen him display a similar surprise when a customer stopped by for feed and lamp oil. He just seemed to be very restless and uneasy. He kept his rifle nearby at all times, even when he sat down with me.

I did not like it at all.

Only when Kate was there, some sense of normalcy seemed to return to the household and, thankfully, she did on the day of the broth. She came riding into the yard just as I was about to ready myself to leave, and as soon as she had led the mare to the barn, she came inside, smelling of hot skin and horse sweat.

"Hanson!" She ruffled my hair, greasy as it was. "How are things at the trading station?" she asked before going to have a drink of water from the bucket in the back.

"Oh, well enough," I muttered, not wanting to give away the sorry state of Mr. Brockman, who was both quiet and morose ever since that fight with John.

"Tell Mr. Brockman that I will come to see him soon," she

chirped. I could hear heavy fabric slap against the floor and figured she was changing her attire back there. The thought of it made me blush. "It has just been difficult—busy," she uttered, "with all the sick folks."

"I am sure he'll appreciate that," I replied, feeling that it was no lie.

"How is Mr. Ern?" she asked next. "He's not still about that silly business of wanting to end our partnership, is he?" Mr. Ern had sent a strongly worded letter in the wake of the yard tiff.

"I wouldn't know," I said, feeling uncomfortable. "He was mad at the time," I offered up.

"No wonder." Kate reappeared, wearing a dark purple dress that I had not seen before. It made her look all proper and nice. I wondered if that was where the money for the cures went—the ones that John never saw—into dresses and finery. The thought had me smiling despite everything. Kate frowned and sat down with me at the table. "I would have been mad, too, if John had mauled one of *my* friends in such a way. Just don't let August Ern ruin our friendship over John's foolishness," she begged. "It is many months in the past already. Don't you think it's time there was peace between us?"

I nodded in reply, even if I thought that the state of Mr. Brockman's face after the debacle certainly deserved a stronger term than "foolish."

"What has Ma given you?" Kate reached across the table and pulled the broth close. "Oh, Hanson, don't eat that." She wrinkled her nose. "Didn't Pa make any bread today?" She turned in the chair as if to inspect the room for said commodity. Her gaze fell on her mother in the rocking chair, and the two of them exchanged a rapid series of German words. They did not sound very friendly. "I'm so sorry, Hanson," she said when she turned back to me. "Pa didn't make any bread today."

"It's all right," I told her. "I was just about to leave anyway."

"MA SAYS THAT she has the devil in her," Max Weissbrod said, nodding toward the Bender place, where a few horses were hitched to the post outside. "She says that she visits Nicholas Morrin at night in the shape of a cat."

"A cat?" I snorted from the foolishness of the statement.

"Sure." Max sounded utterly convinced. "A black one. All witches can turn into cats."

"Kate is not a witch." I rolled my eyes.

"No?" It was Bruno who spoke. "What else is it but witchery that she's doing? Talking to spirits and predicting the future—"

"They make charms, too, the Bender women," Max interjected. "*I'm* sure she's a witch, and so is Ma."

I thought to myself that Mrs. Weissbrod seemed to me the sort of woman who believed whatever would make her day a little brighter.

It had been a few days after my last visit at the Bender place, and the Weissbrod boys and I were sitting behind the barn at the trading station, perched upon the plow, among tufts of hard green grass. I had been doing my very best not to think of the Benders since the day of the broth, as the sense of unease that had followed me home had been so hard to get rid of. I thought that I could taste the cold broth on my tongue for hours, even if I had eaten only a little of it, and had snuck a lump of sugar from the trading station's store as soon as I got home.

"Why would Kate go to visit Mr. Morrin as a cat?" I asked. "It seems terribly inconvenient; she could just have taken the mare." I said it only to tease them; I knew that the cat made for a better story.

"So that she can go in secret." Max gave me a telling gaze.

"Perhaps so Mr. Brockman won't find out," Bruno added. "Or that mad brother of hers."

The logic in this was sound, besides the part with the cat. "I don't think Kate can turn into a cat," I insisted. "Her dog wouldn't like it, for one, and I would've seen it myself by now."

"Really?" Max asked in a challenging manner. "I think there's a lot going on in that house that you don't know about."

"Is that so?" My heart had started racing, but I was determined not to let my unease show. I both dreaded and craved my friends' knowledge.

"Sure." Bruno sounded haughty. "Ma told us that Mr. Dickinson, the clerk, had gone over there to peek through the windows, hoping to catch Kate in the bath—"

"Ew," I interrupted with a grimace.

The Weissbrod boys both laughed at this.

"Anyhow," Bruno continued, "when he looked inside, he saw Kate and Mrs. Bender before the stove. They had hung some rags on a clothesline and was milking them."

"What?" I turned my head to look at Bruno. "Why would they do that?"

"Oh, witches do that all the time," said Max. "They steal milk from their neighbors in that way. The rags become the udders somehow. Mr. Dickinson said that he had told Mr. Angell, and *he* had said he had seen the udder of his own cow deflate on that very same day, before his very eyes."

"But the Benders have a perfectly good milking cow," I argued. "They don't need to steal milk from others."

"You can never have too much milk," Bruno declared.

"What did Mr. Dickinson do when he saw that?" I asked.

"Oh, nothing. He just slunk off," said Max. "Terrified, of course."

"Of course," I muttered, not believing them at all.

"She sure does look like a witch—the old Bender woman, I mean," Max said sagely. "Kate, too, come to think of it."

"We went down there after Ma told us the story," Bruno continued.

"Why would you do that?" I asked, aghast. I had warned them many times to stay away from the Bender place.

"We wanted to see if Kate was a witch, of course," Bruno replied, unabashed. "Ma had told us before that the trick is to have them sit on a nail. They can't feel it if they're a witch—"

"We only had some barbed wire, though." Max continued the story. "We went inside to buy a can of beans and then we put it on her chair when she rose to take our payment."

"And?" I could not help but be curious. "Did she sit on it?"

"She did." Bruno's cheeks had reddened some.

"And did she feel it?" I was holding my breath.

"Sure she did." Max burst out laughing. "She clobbered us both about the ears."

Bruno chuckled, too. "She sure went into a rage."

"Served you well," I muttered, though inwardly I felt a strong and sudden relief that Kate had passed the test.

The relief was short-lived, however, as it was still gnawing at me, that sense that something was amiss, even if it had nothing to do with witchcraft.

26.

ELVIRA

IT WAS THE gunshot that woke me up and had me staggering from the bed and out from behind the canvas curtain. The room was empty, as it was late in the day, and I had only been napping. I had often felt the need to sleep during the day of late. William said it was my age, but I thought it was just that I did not want to be awake.

The door was open, and so I stepped outside, fully expecting to see men on horseback with their rifles aimed at my William's chest. Maybe one of them even carried a noose—already tied.

This was not what I saw, though.

Out in the yard stood my husband with his rifle at the ready. The scent of gunpowder revealed that he was the one who had fired as well.

"What is this, husband?" I tore outside into the heat of a balmy fall. "What is this madness?" I looked around but could not see any culprits about, and so I turned my gaze on him again.

"I saw them—I'm sure of it! Those little scoundrels!" he spat.

"Sticking their noses into everything! One of these days we'll find them in the orchard with shovels—just you see!"

"Who on earth are you talking about?" I made to take the rifle from him, but he quickly yanked it away. "Who did you see?" I wanted to know. "What is it that has you in such a huff?"

"Those boys!" he bellowed. "Those nosy, awful boys!"

"Who? The Weissbrod boys? William, are you sure?" I looked around again but could see neither hide nor hair of them. Had it not been for the fact that such occurrences had become fairly common-place over the previous weeks, I might have just taken his word for it, and maybe even helped him look for the boys but, as it happened, this was not the first time I found William outside with the rifle, hunting phantoms. Usually it was men he claimed to have seen, though: dark-clad fiends hiding behind the barn; or Jack Handsome's crew circling the premises on horseback. No one else ever saw them, however, and so I had to chalk it up to wild imagination.

"William." I placed one hand gently on his arm. "There is no one else here, not the Weissbrod boys, nor anyone else. You have to give me the rifle now." It just would not do if he shot one of our guests, some wayfarer in need of tobacco or a meal.

He resisted me for a little while longer; his muscles were taut under my hand, and then all at once he seemed to slump as he gave in. His rigidness mellowed and he handed me the rifle without fur-ther argument. "Perhaps it was just a coyote," he muttered.

"Or a wolf," I agreed, and supported him as we staggered back inside the house, although he was hardly an invalid. "It's very warm," I said as the door swung open. "Mayhap the sun's glare blinded you."

"It will be winter soon," he complained. "What will we do with the bodies then?"

"Perhaps the ground won't freeze like last year." I did my best to comfort him. I placed him in a chair and went to get some coffee.

"Am I losing my mind, Elvira?" He sounded like a lost little boy.

"No," I replied, not just to be kind, but because I could not afford for him to. "It's just that you've gotten the fright in you."

"Why is that?" He looked at me with watery blue eyes.

"Because you no longer have the angels' protection." My lips curled up in a sour smirk as I crouched there by the stove, trying to light a fire.

"You were right all along," he complained.

"That I was."

"I cannot be certain of anything now."

"No," I agreed, "you cannot."

What had changed was that Kate's predictions no longer seemed to prove true. Not only had it been the disappointment with Benjamin Brown, but the next two men her "angels" had singled out, an Irish day laborer called Sconce, and another man called Weitzell, had also proven to travel with little more than the clothes they wore on their backs.

My husband's faith had been shaken by that, and now he no longer believed himself to be sheltered by angels' wings.

Had it not brought on such misery, I might have been relieved that the scales had finally fallen from his eyes, but with him seeing phantoms everywhere, it was hard to revel in the victory. The plan to earn enough for a new farm through these unsavory means had long since departed, as far as I was concerned. With what little we had gotten off the last few, we would have to kill an army to get it, and so I no longer saw much reason for any of it. William still clung to the notion, though, that murder was the way to our salvation. Had he not known all he did, I would likely have ended the marriage between us—but then he *had* left his home for us, and up until the day the Vandles died, he had been the best husband I had ever had.

"She doesn't even seem to care," he uttered next; his voice was bitter. "Kate just rolls her eyes at me when I ask her how come her angels now seem to always be wrong."

"She really *doesn't* care." I cleared that up for him. "Her attention is elsewhere now. She doesn't much care what happens to us—or what she owes." Now it was *I* who sounded bitter.

"But she, too, wanted to leave," William muttered.

"Not anymore," I told him as I rose to my feet and cleaned my hands on my apron. "She has other goals now. I think she means to marry that man." *All* her appetites were sated now—right here.

"Brockman?" William looked up.

"No, of course not." I made an impatient gesture with my hands. "The other one—the widower. Mr. Morrin." She had never said so, of course, but I knew just how her mind worked. The man was handsome; he had land and money—all of it clay for her to shape into her liking. If she truly meant to stay with him, or simply suck the marrow and be gone, I could not tell.

"Oh." William nodded as understanding dawned. They worried me, those lapses in memory that he had, but I told myself it was only the strain of living like we did, always prepared for the axe to fall. Again, I should have reveled in his fear, that he finally saw the world as *I* did, but the misery of it all took the joy out of my glee.

"Maybe we should just stop," I said as I came to sit by him. On the stove, the water in the kettle slowly came to a simmer. "We have made do so far, and no one has found the missing men yet. Perhaps we ought to stop planting them out there."

"How will we get a new farm, then?" His gaze seemed to have

regained some if its clarity. He no longer looked like a bewildered boy, or at least not quite as much. It was a relief to see it.

"We'll do as I said before and let Kate's work pay for it." If only I could turn her away from Mr. Morrin. I should remind her of her lofty ambitions, perhaps. Tell her how a husband would do nothing but hold her back. I was not very optimistic, however. Kate rarely did as I said—as the whole debacle with Mr. Brockman had proved.

"That might take awhile." William mulled over my suggestion. "And especially if she gets married." He echoed my own thoughts.

"She would want for us to stay if she does," I noted, and the thought upset me enough that I went behind the store counter for a bottle and some glasses. "This land is already broken, so someone else would want to move in if we left. They'd find them then—the men. Kate would get in trouble." I placed the bottle on the table and poured the amber liquid into the cloudy glasses.

William drank all the whiskey at once, then he wiped his lips with the back of his hand. "I was so sure that Kate—"

"Well, you always put too much faith in her." I swallowed a hot mouthful of my own drink. The warmth was much needed, a soothing balm for my nerves.

"But she seemed so sure about it all," he complained.

"That's certainly her way." I rose to my feet and shuffled out back to get our china cups. We could not fortify ourselves with whiskey all day. "They have been asking about him in town," I said over my shoulder, even if I was a little worried that the news would agitate him anew. "That Weitzell fellow, I mean. Apparently, he had friends."

"Well, they haven't been *here* to ask," William replied.

"Not yet," I muttered, but I did not say it very loud, as I would rather not see him storm back out again with the rifle. "They have no idea he was here," I said instead, "and John has done as we agreed on and told the other Germans of the band of riders."

"What riders?" William asked in a gruff voice as I emerged from behind the curtain with the cups.

I sighed at his faulty memory. "Don't you remember how we agreed to say there was a band of riders? We were to say that we thought they were robbers."

"What for?" The little boy was back in his eyes, and it pained me so to see it.

"So they will suspect *them*, not us," I clarified.

"Of what?" He remained confused.

"Of the *disappearances*." I sighed again, deeply, and went behind the store counter for the coffee grinder. "We were to blame the band of robbers, though there aren't any." I added the last bit to clarify.

"I think I saw Jack Handsome's men," he started. "They were riding around the property—"

"No, William, they were not."

"He is mad that we keep bringing him horses. He doesn't trust us to be honest thieves." He chuckled.

"I know that, husband." I slammed the grinder down on the table with a bang.

"But the angels have deserted us—"

"Oh, don't you start with that again!"

"We only need a few more, Elvira." He suddenly sounded like his old self again. "A few more with well-lined pockets and then we can leave this place for good."

"We cannot trust Kate—"

"No, I know. I'll find them myself, don't you worry."

"But if we left *now*?" Kate be damned.

"No, Ma. It has to be with *something* to start our new life with."

I shuffled to the shelf for coffee beans; the groceries from the trading station had started gathering dust. "We'll need new names, then," I muttered. "We cannot be the Benders anymore."

"There are plenty of names we could go by," he agreed. "They'll never find us then, if we have new names."

"Kate would sure be in a pickle if we left," I said, and could not help but smile.

27.

KATE

IT WAS A hot day in late August when I was riding out to heal a German man called Carl Becker, who was suffering from a stomach upset. Mr. Becker was so poorly, his son had told me when he sought me out, that he could no longer rise from his bed.

I saw it as a cause for optimism that they had thought of me in their hour of need. Perhaps the locals were finally starting to put some faith in my abilities. I could see this in my future as well: me riding around much like a town doctor, doling out powders and creams. Who was to say I could not do equally fine work? Though I was loath to admit it, Ma might have had a point when she argued that people around here had more use of cures than a channel to the afterlife.

Lucky for them, I was capable of satisfying *all* their needs.

The Becker family lived on a small farm much like ours. There were a few scrawny horses in a paddock, and their yard was littered with wooden boards and food scraps that served as feed for the chickens and one burly pig, who seemed to have made its home on their porch. A few spare wagon wheels rested against the logged outer wall.

I knocked before I entered the dark, smoke-filled room inside. There were no curtains in their windows, but the glass was so covered in dust that very little daylight found its way inside. I did not hold this against Mrs. Becker. The windows looked much the same at our place.

"Good afternoon." I greeted them while waiting for my eyes to adjust to the scant light. After a short moment, I could make out two wooden beds in there, behind the table and chairs and the smoking stove, one to the left and one to the right. The air smelled strongly of liquor, so I assumed that Mr. Becker had been trying to heal himself.

"Good afternoon." Mrs. Becker, a pale woman with a lined, tanned face, rose from her husband's bedside. She brushed her blue-and-white-striped dress free of debris before approaching me in an effort to look presentable. This pleased me greatly, as I saw it as further proof that they did indeed think of me as a doctor. Mr. Becker groaned in the bed—I suppose it was all the greeting he could muster.

"He has been like this for days," Mrs. Becker said after ushering me inside. "He won't eat, and what little he manages to swallow comes right back up again." She sounded both frightened and repulsed. "The doctor came two days ago, but he couldn't do a thing." She shook her head and her face took on a hard expression. She clearly had little faith in learned medicine.

"Not to worry, Mrs. Becker," I said in a calm and reassuring voice. "I have ample skills—and just as much knowledge as any doctor. I will see to your husband right away."

"Oh, thank you," she uttered with relief. "I'll put the coffee on . . ."

She busied herself at the stove while I went farther inside the murky darkness until I could make out my patient, lying upon the bed. The man was knocking at death's door, I could see that right away—his pale cheeks were sunken and his eyes were black pits—but that was beside the point.

I put down the sturdy leather bag I had acquired for instances such as this, filled with herbs and ointments, and also a few prayers and transcripts of holy letters, as many of my patients put great trust in them and were willing to pay a fair price to have them. Ma had been right about that as well. I also wore my new purple gingham dress, as I thought it made me look both serious and proper.

While Mrs. Becker bustled at the stove, I pushed my sleeves up over my elbows and started moving my hands slowly across the man's body, just a few inches from his flesh. He lay on his side, curled in on himself like an infant, likely to lessen the pain. One dark eye followed my every move, but he still did not try to speak. Perhaps words were already beyond his reach. I supposed he had a cancer somewhere.

"The magnetic fluids in his body are out of balance," I told his wife, as I figured it was she I had to impress—the man himself was too far gone. "Luckily, I'm an apt magnetizer and will adjust them promptly through the art of mesmerism."

"Oh," the woman said, standing with the kettle in her hand. "I thought you could give me a powder or some such . . . a brew, perhaps, or some holy words."

"You will have that as well," I replied, a little annoyed. It confounded me how hard these people were to impress. "Mesmerism is more efficient, though."

I ignored Mrs. Becker for a while and focused on moving my hands over her husband's body. I had closed my eyes and wore a serious expression, as I knew that she would be watching me keenly. Sometimes I uttered a little sigh or some such to convince her that I was hard at work.

When I felt that ample time had passed, I stopped and let out my breath. "His body is restored to strength and balance. You should see a great improvement tonight," I told Mrs. Becker, who was pouring coffee into tin cups. "If you don't, he isn't meant to live."

"What do you mean by that?"

"Only that sometimes, no matter how skilled the healer is, the Lord has other plans," I explained, while making a show of lifting a square white piece of cloth out of my leather bag and carefully drying off my hands. I had found it made the patients think that my hands were covered in invisible grime—the sickness itself, perhaps—and had to be thoroughly cleansed. I folded the cloth neatly before putting it back in the bag. Then I gathered the bag up and hoisted it with me to the table. It was time to bring out the herbs and the prayers—Ma's old cures, boring as they might be. While sipping her thin coffee and doling out herbs, I thought about reminding Mrs. Becker of my services as a medium, but with her husband at the brink of death, I decided it was better to wait until after the funeral.

It would not do to be accused of foreseeing such a tragic event. Some might even think I had caused it.

I was fairly pleased with myself as I rode back home. I thought that I had at least made Mr. Becker's last days a little more interest-ing, even if I had not saved him. His wife could tell the story of the mesmerism for years, and perhaps even entice others to seek me out. My good mood lasted for a good long while, but as I neared the inn, it was as if a cloud descended. I was sick of them all, the house was filthy, and Pa was losing his mind. There was no fun to be had there—nothing but complaints. It was as if the prairie dust had gotten into their heads and settled. Nothing waited for me there but boredom, misery, a sense of doom, and some freshly turned soil in the orchard.

Not even the button box brought me as much pleasure anymore—even if the collection now numbered nine, with the addition of one tin button stamped with a bird from the Irishman, Mr. Sconce, and one blue fabric button from Mr. Weitzell. Neither of the men had added much to Pa's savings, though both of them had satisfied the darkness at the time. It was just the misery the dead men brought that bothered me: Ma complained, and Pa fretted . . . It had almost been better before when we ran from our misdeeds instead of making our beds among the graves—and it was such a lovely day, too. It would surely be wasted at the inn.

I promptly turned the horse around and set out for the Morrin farm.

There, at least, there was laughter to be had. Nicholas was working in the barn just then, while the girls played out on the porch. They had found three small, gray kittens under the steps and had put them in an empty crate with a blanket. Now the girls were patiently waiting for the mother to arrive and be reunited with her offspring.

"She is probably out chasing mice," said Alma.

"She'll be *so* happy to see the kittens' new bed," Constance declared.

"They are the sweetest kittens I ever saw," I cooed before going in search of their father.

He was feeding the cows when I stepped inside, lifting the

loaded hayfork effortlessly. His skin was slick and he wore only a shirt. He sure made my mood perk up.

"Kate." He beamed as I stepped inside. "I thought you were healing the sick today."

"I was," I said. "I did, but then I missed you all, so I came here."

"Don't they need you at the inn?" He put down the hayfork and came toward me with a smile on his lips.

"I suppose they do, but I won't always be there, so they'll have to learn to manage on their own." I leaned my back against the wall and waited there until he arrived and pressed his lips against mine. "I daresay you are happy to see me," I murmured when the kiss had ended.

"I'm *always* happy to see you," he replied and placed another kiss on my forehead. "I'll finish up in here and then we can go inside." He took a few steps toward the hayfork.

"No, wait." I reached out a hand and caught the cotton of his sleeve. "There was something I wanted to talk to you about, without the girls listening in."

He turned back to me with a question written on his features. He looked a little concerned, too, which pleased me greatly.

"I'm worried about John," I said; my voice had dropped to a low murmur, and I arranged my face into a frown. "He doesn't seem to get any better . . . He's always muttering and laughing for no reason—and he's so easy to anger, too. Just look at what happened to poor Mr. Brockman."

Nicholas came to embrace me again, fold me into those strong arms. "Not to worry, Kate," he said into my ear. "I'm sure he won't do something so foolish again. It turned people against him."

"But I *do* worry—there's no saying what he can do! I no longer trust him at all. Just the other day, he was about to start a fight with one of our guests, and Pa had to manhandle him so he wouldn't ride after the poor fellow."

"What set him off?" Nicholas wanted to know.

"Oh, I don't know. He has always had a terrible temper." That, at least, was true. "It's living out here, I think . . . the solitude and the hardships . . . It might have become too much for him."

"Do you worry that he should turn his anger against you?" His brow knitted up with concern. I found it to be a tantalizing sight.

"Oh, I don't know," I replied. "He is out at night doing God knows what, and he won't tell me when I ask him what he has been up to. Sometimes he works, I think. I can hear him outside, digging." This was a daring thing to say, but necessary. "And the worst part is that the spirits won't answer me either. They won't speak of John at all. It's as if they all fear him."

Nicholas's eyes went wide with astonishment. "That's not good at all," he uttered. "Do you think he has turned away from God?"

"I don't know, Nicholas. I don't know." I leaned my forehead against his broad chest and inhaled the musky scent of his skin. "All I know is that something is wrong with John."

The dead men in the orchard had been on my mind of late, especially at night. I had always known that it would have to be resolved somehow but had not known quite how. *If* Ma should get the money for her farm in the mountains, they would all leave, and should the bodies be discovered then, I alone would have to answer for the crimes. That would not do, of course. The best way to solve it was if I left, too, but then I had seen a future here all of a sudden, and things had been going so well . . . Perhaps it was this more than anything else that had put me in such a terrible mood of late.

The darkness, of course, only responded by stretching and yawning to make itself known. The more I struggled to untangle the web of possible threats and protect myself, the more it hankered inside of me. I was no fool, so I knew this was not good. It seemed to me that the more I fought, it only got worse, as the darkness thrived on such misery.

But if people were to blame John . . . Why *wouldn't* they blame John? He had made nary a new friend since we arrived, and the townspeople found him to be peculiar. His reputation had also been thoroughly tarnished by the fight with Mr. Brockman.

Taking the brunt of the blame was nothing more than he deserved, truth be told, with the way his silly jealously had become such a liability. I could not stand it, the way he was trying to lord over me and following my every move. To hell with taking care of our own!

I would take care of myself from now on.

28.

KATE

IT WAS LATE in September when the news from town reached us. I had just made some meat and potatoes for dinner, as Ma seemed to have lost her appetite for cooking. She was picking at the food with her fork, her nose wrinkled up with distaste. Between us to my left was Pa, eating heartily as always, his beard glistening with grease. John, to my right, was slower in eating; his gaze kept darting to the windows and the door. Under the table, his legs bounced, humming with unreleased tension.

"They are searching again," he said between mouthfuls. He had just been in town, as we had to make all our purchases there ever since the blows to Brockman. "They said at the convenience store that they will send teams of men to search all the properties. They worry that the disappearances will reflect poorly on the area." He sniggered a little at this and lifted his hand to wipe food grease from his lips with his sleeve.

"And right they are," Ma muttered. "I sure wouldn't want to move to a town where men are disappearing all the time."

"They won't dig up the orchard." Pa, for one, sounded calm and collected.

"Why not?" There was an edge to John's voice. "How do you know they won't?"

Pa shrugged. "They won't have time for it. They have many farms to cover."

"That's quite a gamble," John remarked. "We don't know how thorough they will be. Perhaps they'll find turned soil interesting enough to bring out a shovel."

"Not very likely," Pa declared, stabbing a potato. "I know the men around here, and they're a lazy bunch. They only search so they have something to say when asked if an effort has been made."

"You put too little trust in your fellow man," Ma told him, pointing at his chest with her fork. "I think it's worrisome to people that men go missing from the road. They fear that they'll be next."

"They should notice that no local men have vanished," Pa said. "They ought to feel perfectly safe," he added with a benevolent smile.

"That only makes them think that the murderer is among them," I noted. It was just common sense. "In fact, it would be better if a local man *did* disappear—"

"We only need *one* more," Pa declared. "Maybe two, but likely just one, if his money belt is heavy. Then we could leave before winter settles and be safe up in the mountains when the lean months arrive. There's plenty of game there; we'd eat like kings."

"You always say that." Ma sounded sullen. *"Only one more . . ."* She lifted her cup and drank deep.

"Oh, but don't any of you realize?" John's face looked flustered as his gaze darted between us. "They are looking *now*! They might come knocking!"

"Then we'll say what we always do." Pa sawed a chunk off his meat. "That there's a band of riders about, and we do not like the look of them." It was a relief to hear him sounding so calm and reassuring. He had had several bad spells of late, running about the yard in nothing but his shirt, chasing ghosts with a hayfork. John had even taken his rifle and hidden it out of sight in the barn.

"That'll work for only so long," I mused nevertheless, while spearing a potato with my knife. "It *does* seem strange that there is a band of wicked men that no one but the Benders has seen—"

"That, and the fact that Jack won't take the horses anymore," John added. "It was bad enough before when he suspected us of foul play, but since Pa chased him off with the rifle, he refuses to even *look* at our cargo."

"What are you getting at?" Pa snorted. "I never did such a thing."

The rest of us exchanged dark looks. It was tiring how he never seemed to remember much about his bouts of confusion once his world had righted itself. Jack Handsome had come to settle with us after a successful trade but had never even made it across the threshold before he'd been rudely chased. John had had to ride after him to get our meager earnings. It had put an end to our partnership, though, and when John came back from the chase, dirty and disheveled, he fretted that Jack would give us up.

"The *moment* there is a reward." He had nodded as if to say that this he knew for certain. "Then he will stand at the county trustees' door, knocking."

"You don't know that," I had argued. "He doesn't truly know a thing, for one, and I would think he has good reason to keep his head down. Horse thieves are hardly upstanding citizens."

John had only shaken his head. "No one will hang Jack Handsome. He has friends in high places. That's why he wanted to get rid of *us*."

We had not killed another man after that, as we could not figure out what to do with the horses. I myself was happy for it, as it only brought trouble, but the darkness did not agree. It kept me awake many a night, flooding my mind with memories and filling my heart with aching. The worse it got at the Bender place, the hungrier it became.

"We should leave," said John. "Soon."

"We need one more," Pa insisted. "One with a heavy purse."

"Pa, you have not been yourself," said John. "Perhaps you should let Kate decide."

"Kate is the one who got us into this mess," Ma interjected, her face twisted up with displeasure. "I would not look to *her* for advice."

I rolled my eyes but let it go; I was in no mood for a fight.

"Those useless, useless angels," Pa lamented with a sigh.

"We have no time to squabble between us." John sounded increasingly exasperated. "What will we say if they find the bodies?"

"They won't," I said, hoping I was right. Though I felt confident that I could turn away any man at the door, frightened people were harder to predict.

"They might," said Ma, sending me a dark look.

"Who will?" said Pa, rising from his chair and looking around him with a wild expression. His hands were curled up in the air as if he was carrying the rifle. "Are they here?" he cried. "Jack Handsome's men?"

Ma sighed, I groaned, and John put down his fork to rise and soothe his lost pa.

Things were not good at the Bender place.

A FEW DAYS later, a man called Henry McKenzie stopped at the inn. He was weary, as he had traveled a long way and wanted both food and lodging. This made Pa believe that the man had coins to spare. He no longer asked about the angels, and I did not offer any advice either. I was happy enough to let him build his own confidence on the matter; it was bothersome to be blamed whenever things went wrong.

We had him seated at the table as usual, and heaped his plate with what food we had. It was not much, just some cheese and bread, but I fried up some eggs to satisfy his hunger and poured him plenty to drink. I smiled at him, too, as if he were the prettiest man on earth, though his long brown mustache could sure use a wash, and his face looked rather gaunt. I had also seen several teeth missing when he first came inside, yet I bent toward him across the table, speaking nonsense, and chased some blood to his cheeks.

Out in the orchard, John and Pa were digging.

Mr. McKenzie ate well and drank well, and I do not think he even felt it when the hammer came bearing down. He was out like a light at once, and the quick slash with the blade was likely superfluous and did nothing but cause more stains for Ma to clean. I waited for the sense of power to come rushing, and for my heart to start racing but, as much as the darkness had craved the violence before, it was not there to reap its reward. I felt nothing in that moment.

Mr. McKenzie, though, was good and dead.

We kept him in the cellar until past sundown, and then we hoisted him up again and onto the canvas. When he was all stripped down, John and I went through his pockets and saddlebags, while

Pa sat down with Ma to catch his breath. John fretted about what to do about the man's horse, a dappled gelding, currently chewing feed in our stable, unaware that his master's life had ended. He said it was a shame to kill the animal, but we could not give it to Jack Handsome either.

"Nothing," I said at last when all the man's pockets had been emptied. I was still kneeling on the floor behind the mound of white flesh that had once been Mr. McKenzie.

"He is poorer than we are." John let out a surprised little laugh. He kneeled on the other side of the corpse and peered into the dead man's purse as if his gaze alone could conjure nuggets of gold.

"There really is nothing of value on him." I nodded once, sat back on the floor, and wiped my hands on my skirt to get the blood off my fingers. Then I picked up the bloody knife and cut a yellowing bone button from Mr. McKenzie's discarded coat. This did not bring me much pleasure either, and I felt sorely disappointed.

"We need one more," said Pa.

29.

ELVIRA

THEY CAME THE next day around noon, five burly men from town. They seemed polite enough when they greeted Kate with tips of their hats and left their horses in John's care.

I watched them from the window with my folded hands pressed to my chest. It was not in prayer, exactly, but I was begging for help nevertheless.

William lay in bed; he had become so out of it that morning that we had to restrain him in the end. I was terrified to think that the men out there had a German among them who insisted on speaking to the man of the house. If William was still weary, I just did not see how that could go well. He would surely give us up in a heartbeat.

I heard Kate through the window, laughing with the men. She looked so young and carefree out there in the dusty yard, demanding all their attention. She had brought out whiskey and glasses and was pouring generously from the bottle, wanting them in a good mood. Sweet as chocolate. Candied apples. Just as I had taught her to be.

It had happened thrice now that someone had come to her asking about the lost men, trying to locate them through psychic means. She had been like that then as well, carefree and seemingly guiltless, as she spun the worried relatives a story about opportunities elsewhere and unexpected love. She had nerves of steel when it counted, and I could not decide if I admired her for it or if it scared me more.

William groaned in the bed, and I shuffled out to him. It was a relief to have an excuse to leave the window and the unsettling view.

"What's all that noise about?" William asked when I approached the bed. I was happy to see that his gaze was clear and devoid of any confusion. He wiggled his hands, still tied to the brass tubes of the bed. He had ceased asking why when he found himself thus. He knew that his mind sometimes fled but was reluctant to speak of it once he was sane again, much preferring to pretend that those embarrassing moments had never happened.

"They're here," I informed him as I set to work on the knots. "The search party, that is. They're looking for the missing men." My heart seemed to flip in my chest as I said those last two words.

"Is it Kate I hear with them?" he asked.

"Of course it is," I said, not without bitterness. "Who else can speak for us?"

"Oh, good." He sagged with relief. "She will surely mislead them."

"Of course," I said again, just as we heard them come around the house to the orchard. William cursed in the bed. Then we both fell silent, afraid to make a sound to draw attention. We certainly did not want them inside—the stink from the cellar was bad, though it had grown fainter as the weather cooled down.

I heard Kate through the wall, saying something about apple trees, I thought. Likely telling them our agreed-upon story of how we had started preparing for saplings last spring but had not gotten as far as we had hoped, thus the heaps of soil out there. Her laughter sounded loud and amused through the wall.

"I hope they won't go poking," William whispered, rubbing his released wrists.

"So do I," I mouthed back. We had dug them deep, but I still worried. I feared that the smell was out there as well, rising up from the dirt.

Kate said something else that I did not properly hear, or perhaps it was my understanding of the language that failed. The men muttered something back in turn, but there were no sounds of digging— at least not yet.

I sat down on the edge of the bed and clutched William's hand in mine. His wrist was raw where the rope had chafed. My heart was hammering painfully fast in my chest. I did not properly breathe before we heard the party move back to the front of the house again. Kate was still chatting merrily. She would no doubt pour them another taste of the bottle, and maybe even read their palms or sell them a cure. She never let an opportunity for business pass her by. Just as I had taught her.

She had even had advertisements printed and had been plastering them in store windows all over town.

PROF. MISS KATIE BENDER

Can heal all sorts of Diseases:
Can cure Blindness, Fit, Deafness and Dumbness.

The girl clearly did not know what it meant to keep one's head down. When I said as much, however, she only retorted that it was better to "hide in plain sight," suggesting that no one would suspect foul play of an upstanding member of the community. I took it that she meant herself, though I had never seen her cure either fits or dumbness.

My husband relaxed beside me as the voices faded. "See," he said and squeezed my hand. "They did not go poking. Kate took care of it."

"Sure." I relented as my heart returned to a steady beat. "Not this time," I added, "but maybe next time they will."

"We just need one more," said he, looking ashen against the sheets.

"We should just go—"

"No! One more, then we'll go."

I nodded before I freed my hand and rose to my feet. What use was there in arguing with a madman?

As I made my way to my chair and my knitting, I kept pondering how it was that *Kate* took care of everything all of a sudden—how it was the men both looked to *her* for guidance in everything.

How it was that I myself found it harder and harder to speak against her.

I wondered how it had happened, but also *when* it had happened, and I suppose it all had started with the Vandles.

We had first met the Vandles after we had left Pennsylvania and set our course west. We had nothing then besides the horses, a wagon, and our trunks. By the time we reached New Albany, Indiana, we had sold what we could of William's books and other trinkets he had collected over the years: a compass, a silver walking stick, and an opal in the rough. We knew we had to pause, if only to fill our coffers, and used what little we had left to rent a small place outside of town. It was no better than a shack: the wind passed right through the walls and the roof was about to fall down. The horses had nothing but a roof to shield them, and barely even that. Though the place had been vacant for quite some time, the mouse droppings were plentiful. A scrawny crow had taken up residence in the chimney and had to be chased off with the broom.

William had found work with a cobbler, as that was something he had done before. It did not pay much, but enough to keep us from starvation. I started trading my teas and ointments whenever we needed eggs or a pound of wheat, having nothing else left to barter with, and soon it became known that I knew a little something of ailments and their cures. I was often called upon when needed.

We had been in New Albany for less than a year when I befriended Gertrude Vandle. She was an elderly woman who lived on a farm not far from ours with her husband, Otto, who was suffering from gout. Having had some luck with my ointments, she often came to see me to barter for medicine, but also to share a moment out in the sun with a cup of coffee or a lick of brandy. It suited me well, as I had missed a grown woman to speak to since we'd left Gretchen and Pennsylvania behind, and I much appreciated her advice on how to best work the land there.

In the winter after we met, Gertrude suddenly fell ill. She lay in bed with a terrible cough and a raging fever, refusing both food and water. Otto had pressed to send for the doctor, but she did not want to hear of it. Gertrude only wanted *me* to tend to her, which I did, dutifully, with cold compresses and herbal brews, special prayers, and a few chosen symbols drawn upon the walls. Sometimes I even brought Kate along to aid me. She mostly seemed bored, however, standing over Gertrude's bed. She never much cared for those who could not somehow serve her.

Although not much of a churchgoer, Gertrude Vandle was still a fierce believer and seemed to take great comfort in my cures—so much so that she found a little light and strength and slowly started eating again, just as her coughing abated. Soon enough, Gertrude became well again, and I was immensely pleased with myself. Gertrude, too, was brimming with praise and felt I had indeed saved her life.

The issue was the payment.

I had of course not presented a sick woman with a figure, but I had—as was within my right—expected some compensation for my constant care. I had not thought that it would be a problem either, as Gertrude had clearly benefited from my attention. I had saved her life, she said. I never thought that she would refuse to pay me.

"It was nothing more than any neighbor would do," her husband, Otto, said one time when I went there to try to collect. "It was your Christian duty, nothing more."

"You yourself have benefited from my knowledge many times, Otto," I reminded him. "How come your joint aches have lessened and your sleep is undisturbed? I'm as skilled as any physician, and certainly deserve payment for my trouble."

"Quackery and witchcraft." He all but spat the words. "My wife is a simple woman, but I am not so easily fooled. I only partook in this nonsense to please her, but I do not believe your reeking salves to be worth much more than the mud in my pigsty."

Gertrude herself seemed swayed by him and refused to speak against her husband. "Maybe he is right," she said, "and it was all God's work, not yours."

"Isn't that one and the same?" I asked.

"You are hardly God, Elvira, and it's a sin to think of oneself as *his* equal." That was clearly not what I had meant.

"You are doing me a great wrong," I warned her, but that did nothing to change her mind.

Having tried thus to persuade the Vandles for a while, I finally asked for William's help. He, too, was furious, of course, that the couple would cheat us in such a manner. Even Kate had wanted to come with us when we went to confront them. She would stay out in the wagon with me while the men went inside to get our money from Otto Vandle.

The Vandle house was dark that night, but for a stub of a candle on the windowsill, and I thought perhaps Gertrude and Otto were already in bed.

"If so, they better rise again," William said. His brow was furrowed and his jaw set, his anger barely contained. Mayhap it all reminded him of Pennsylvania and the unkind treatment of us there. Mayhap he had been angry for a long time, just waiting for an opportunity to unleash his righteous wrath.

Whatever the reason—things did not go as anticipated.

William and John left one of the lanterns behind so that Kate and I would have some light when they went in to confront Gertrude and Otto. We sat in silence and watched as they approached the door and knocked with closed fists. For a good long while they stood there, banging on the door, crying out for Otto to open. When he finally did, his face was already red with fury, and he complained loudly about the disturbance at such an ungodly hour. My William did not heed him, though, and he and John shouldered their way inside, ignoring the frail man's attempts at barring them from entering. I remember feeling proud then, that my man would not falter but speak my case.

For a moment, there was silence again, though we could see more candles being lit in there. Then there were voices: Otto's, of course, and William's, but Gertrude's, too, loud and shrill. She was frightened, I thought, and I deemed it well deserved. She had proved to be such a poor friend to me that I did not wish her any good.

Then her voice turned from shrill to screaming, and the men's voices, too, rose to shouts.

"What do you think they're doing in there?" Kate was halfway off the seat, about to jump down and enter the house. Even the horses before our wagon moved restlessly and twitched their ears.

"No," I told Kate and placed a hand on her arm to stop her. "Let William and John deal with it."

"But it sounds as if something has gone awry," said my daughter, not without delight.

"No." I was stubborn. "Let the men handle it, Kate."

Now it sounded as if things were being thrown in there; heavy objects hit the walls. Fear for my husband flooded my veins like a rush of cold water as my calm fled like a bird from a cage. Maybe Kate *should* go and check on them. I dearly wished that we had a rifle in the wagon.

Then all was suddenly calm again, and nothing more happened before one window suddenly filled with haze, and an acrid scent of burning seeped out into the yard.

"It's burning, Ma," Kate informed me, though I could see that quite well. "William must have set it on fire," she deduced, though I had not yet reached that conclusion myself, being too absorbed by the sight before me, the licking flames that could now be seen, and the dark smoke that came welling out from every window and every crack in the wall.

Kate was half off the seat again and pulling me with her when

the men appeared in the door, coughing and cursing. They ran toward the wagon, where Kate had already taken the reins.

"What happened?" I cried. "What happened in there?"

"Nothing good," William muttered as he and John climbed in.
"Go, Kate!" he commanded. "Go as if you have the devil on your
heels!"

Kate went; the lanterns danced on the sides of the wagon, and
the men lay in the bed of it, smelling like a bonfire and with soot
stains upon their brows. "What happened?" I asked again, shaking
all over.

"We got your money," William said, and held up a glass jar filled
with coins and bills. Otto Vandle's savings, for sure. Behind him, John
started laughing. It was a quick and nervous sound, like a titter. I
could tell, even in the dim light, how William's hands were red.

"You killed them?" I asked, although I already knew they had.
"Are you out of your minds?" I scolded. "Everybody knows we had
an argument with them!" Behind us on the road, the burning house
lit up the night sky, and the sound of the crackling fire filled the air.

"I *am* sorry," William said, but he sounded oddly calm. "He just
did not want to give up what he owed."

"And Gertrude?" I asked.

"She was the first to go," said John, just as calm as his father.

"I lost my temper with that one," William added. "She kept
screaming so loud that I could barely think."

"They'll *know* it was us!" It was a peculiar feeling, to see everything come tumbling down again. Now we would hang for sure!
"You fool!" I cried and took my fist to William's cheek. "Now you
have ruined it all!"

He laughed then. *Laughed!* "No, dear wife, I have not." He shook
the heavy glass, leaving smears of blood and ash. "Why would we

even want to stay when we finally have the money to settle some-where else?"

I knew it then, without asking, that William had *known* that Otto had savings. Maybe it had come up as they played a game of cards, or maybe—just as likely—Kate had figured it out as she went snooping around the house while I was tending to Gertrude. She might very well have told her stepfather where to find the jar.

Nothing had been the same since the Vandles, and I could not let it go on. Not even the thought of another farm like the one I had lost—a home where I could settle and prosper as my bones grew brittle and old—could cheer me anymore, for the husband was ru-ined and so was I, and there was nothing much left for us now.

Nothing but to settle the score.

30.

KATE

WHEN I WAS with Nicholas and his family, time curved in on itself and became one perfect sphere. At the Morrin farm, there was happiness, harvest, and corn boiling in a pot. There were the girls, cherubic and beaming, their laughter like music; and there was him, Nicholas, who embraced me with love and kindness, whose kisses fell like honeydew and fire on my lips, whose patience and conviction never wavered.

With him, I thought, the hunger in me would surely be sated. I could achieve all I had dreamed of and *be* that woman up on the stage with a fur stole and a jet brooch. The extraordinary circumstances in which we had met would only add to my allure, and why would I need to let the blade cut deep if I had a life that did not cut *me*?

Such a marriage would take care of everything. I would no longer nurture thoughts of blood and murder. I would redeem myself and become exactly who I wanted to be. Surely the darkness could be put to rest—and surely I could find true happiness.

I was never a good cook, but Nicholas was, and he showed me. Together we made roasts and corn bread, porridge, soup, and biscuits. He had a new, well-equipped range and several pots and pans. He even had an icehouse out back. Rosie had grown accustomed to the place and made it her own. She was rarely far from the girls' warm laps.

It was only me we were waiting for.

"How long will it take for Mr. Brockman to overcome his pain, do you think?" Nicholas often asked me in a voice thick with longing.

I could never give a satisfying answer to that, of course, as Brockman was not the one who stood in our way. The problem resided much closer to home. "I just worry for my parents if Brockman ends his partnership with them. The inn barely earns as it is." I kept to the story I had given him.

"Surely the man can be reasoned with," Nicholas argued. "Mayhap if I spoke to him—"

"Oh no! Please, don't." I placed a hand on his arm. "I would rather not disturb the peace. If we only wait for just a little while longer . . . My parents speak of moving away from here, and if they do, there will be no more need to appease Brockman." I so wished that they would. That they would get enough cash and go.

"What about John?" Nicholas asked, and something cold slithered into my chest. "Would he go, too, or would he stay on to run the inn alone?" He had often asked about John since I confided in him in the barn, and I was pleased to see how the seed of suspicion had touched fertile soil. It might serve me well in the future.

"Oh, he would go, too, I suppose." I gave him a reassuring reply.

"That would solve all our problems, then." Nicholas sounded relieved.

"It surely would," I agreed. "Pa is not well, and John will have to take care of him when he leaves." It was what I told myself, that John would choose his father over me, and not remain here as a millstone around my neck. "We should get married before they leave, though. I would like for my mother to be there on the day."

"Of course." He smiled with warmth and squeezed my hand. "The sooner the better, as far as I am concerned. I think it's strange to be held hostage like this by another man's jealousy," he noted, as a dark frown settled on his features. The fact that he spoke of Brockman did not make the statement any less true. "Had not your family's predicament been so dire, I would not stand for it."

"I know," I replied and kissed his lips. "That's why I love you so."

For a moment there, I actually believed that I could have my way: that I would marry Nicholas and my family would leave and take the darkness with them—that John could safely be blamed for the murders, should they ever be discovered—but as I rode home that afternoon, it all came tumbling down.

I had been riding for a quarter of an hour when it happened, just as the mare took me down a road where nothing but tall prairie grass and a few gnarled trees marred the endless horizon. There was a chill in the air as autumn had settled, and winter would soon arrive. We had not killed a man for some months, but the darkness did not bother me as it had before. I vividly remembered the disappointment I had felt after we'd killed Mr. McKenzie, and I had come to fear that the next slaying would be equally drab. I blamed it all on my family, their confusion and endless complaints. Not even the darkness could survive among *them*, it seemed. It boded well for my future, though, if all that was to remain of my hunger for blood was a box of single buttons.

It was then that I saw him coming toward me. I recognized the wagon at first, the rickety gait of it. Then I saw the horses and noted with a chill how one of them was Henry McKenzie's beast. This act was beyond reckless. John—for I figured it was he—should never have taken the gelding from the stable but should have shot it and left it in the quicksand pit many weeks ago.

Next, my rage at his recklessness turned into concern, for what event could possibly have made him act in that way? Had another search party arrived at our doorstep and found the dead men in the orchard? Had Pa been confused again and done something outrageous—like harming Ma?

I spurred the horse on and rode as fast as I could to meet the wagon, then hesitated when I saw the look on John's face. I knew that expression of quiet rage all too well.

"What are you doing out here?" I asked when we met. "And why are you driving as if the devil is chasing you?"

"I wanted to know if it was true." His reply startled me some, as did the tears that had welled up in his eyes, and which he angrily wiped at with his hand.

"If *what* is true, John? Why are you out here?" I did not even think to ask how he had found me.

"I had to know if you were really seeing him—that widower! Have I been a fool, Kate, for believing it was nothing more than rumors and lies?" His wet eyes pleaded with me.

"Of course not." I lifted my chin. "I'm helping Mr. Morrin speak to his dead wife. You know that. *Everybody* does."

"Giving him *cures*, huh?" Something ugly had come into his face and made him look like a snake. "I cannot believe that I was so gullible," he complained. "After Brockman, I thought we were done with this nonsense." He wiped at his eyes again.

"John." Impatience tugged at me, overriding all concern.

"There's nothing between Mr. Morrin and myself, though even if there were, it's nothing to you."

"How can you even *say* that, after all we have done?" His knuckles around the reins were as white as chalk. "How can you say that after all the blood we have shed? We're not fit for anyone else but each other now, Kate. Can you truly not see that? We have supped and dined with the devil—"

"Have you been talking to Ma?" It certainly sounded like her mother's words.

He straightened up and looked almost haughty in that rickety wagon. "She told me all there is to know about you and this *widower*—" He spat the last word.

"Ma knows nothing," I hissed. I could not believe she would tell on me—she *knew* how John would get.

"Ma knows more than you think," John retorted. "She said it's been going on for some time now, with you riding out here instead of seeing to the sick with cures, as you said. It is *he* who gives you the ham and honey you bring home." His face was almost as white as his knuckles at that point. "What is it he is paying you for, Kate?"

"That's not for you to worry about," I tried again. The horse beneath me had become uneasy from the shouting and was moving a little sideways.

"Like hell it's not my concern!" he bellowed, setting my mare dancing. "I would kill for you, Kate—you know this! I've already done it!"

"I know you have," I said when I had gotten the horse back under control. My voice was very quiet as the threat in his words became real to me. "You must leave Mr. Morrin and his daughters alone."

"Why do I *have* to do that?" He sneered. "What is another body to us? We have nearly a dozen to account for already."

I quickly looked around. Even if nobody but us was on the road, it was still foolish to speak of our secrets so openly. "You will leave Mr. Morrin alone," I said again. "I will not speak to you again if you don't." It would ruin everything if he harmed Nicholas. If he killed him, everything would unravel—and should he merely scare him away, my dreams would still be forfeit.

"I think I'll take my chances." John shrugged. "He means an awful lot to you, though, for being just a sitter." His eyes were narrow with suspicion; he did not believe me at all.

"I've said a thousand times that I won't marry you, John." That was, after all, what lay at the heart of his ire.

"I need no priest to tie you to me," said he, sounding awfully smug. "The blood already did that. We belong together now."

"*Not* if you hurt Mr. Morrin," said I.

His eyes when he looked at me were calculating and cold. "Perhaps I should tell him about Emil Zimmerman," he said.

"He would never believe you." The thought was absurd.

"Yet, there would be suspicion—one that he might find it hard to shake. Perhaps I should tell the other townspeople as well. They won't offer you a stage then, Kate. They won't offer you anything at all!"

"You wouldn't," I snapped. "I could tell stories of my own!"

John only shrugged. "What is it to me?" he asked. "I'm not hankering to make a name for myself. Ill rumors are nothing to me—we're all about to leave soon anyway, and then I can take another name. You, though . . . you'll be stuck with yours."

I just stared at him as if I had never seen him before. I had not thought such cunning to be a part of his nature—but then perhaps he had watched and learned.

"You *will* give him up," John stated, "or you won't ever make a name for yourself. Mayhap the law will even come looking for you, just like Ma says."

"Maybe it's you they'll come for!" I shot back, but my ammunition was not up to par. What little groundwork I had lain with Nicholas was hardly enough—yet—to blame John for the whole debacle. I found myself caught in a trap, and I did not like it at all.

But then, I should perhaps have seen it coming.

When we had first arrived in Pennsylvania, John was a lanky young man of seventeen. He was sullen and a loner already then. I had perhaps thought that he was moldable; that he was like the dough Pa was beating every morning, something that could be fashioned to my liking. The first time I got an inkling that it was not so, that I had been wrong about the depth of his feelings and the strength of his anger, it had to do with a cow.

John had always brought the cattle out to pasture; they were beautiful animals with dun-colored hides, large black eyes, and horns like ivory rising from their brows. He had named every one of them and treated them better than he did people. His favorite among the small herd was a silken-smooth cow called Lorelei.

He doted on that cow; he always brought her the best hay first and made sure she got a spot in the shade on hot days. Quite often, I would catch him scratching her between the eyes and whispering into her ear. I would make fun of him then, but he would only shrug it off, as had always been his habit. Lorelei, in turn, would reward his kindness by coming toward him whenever he entered the pasture, and she would lay her large head on his shoulder in trust. I thought him so very foolish to nurture such a bond with a beast.

Then there was our bull, Victor, a large creature, wide across the back, and with mighty horns that swung up against the sky. Victor took a liking to Lorelei and would court her in breeding season. Pa had been eager for it, too, as he thought the pair of them would make a strong calf.

John had not been thrilled at all.

At first, he withdrew into himself and became even quieter than before. Next, a certain expression settled on his features like a mask; his face appeared smaller, somehow, and his eyes narrowed to slits. Even at night, as we were all relaxing inside the house, he wore that uncanny expression on his face.

Then one day, as I came into the pasture, looking for John as it happened, I was met with the sight of blood adorning the lush green grass. John sat cross-legged in the middle of the meadow, while the cows moved around him, keeping their distance, warily, as they chewed. Even Lorelei avoided him that day, preferring to stay safely within the herd. At the edge of the meadow, close to the fence, stood Victor, shivering all over. His horns were broken, I could tell it even from a distance, and his head was covered in blood. It was not hard to tell that the animal was in pain.

I did not approach John. He looked uncanny to me: a solitary figure among the budding flowers, staring down at the ground before him, still with that dark expression on his face. Instead, I turned and ran back to the house in search of Pa.

It turned out that John had crushed Victor's horns with a rock and hurt his eye beyond repair. Victor had to be slaughtered that very day, and John got a bloody beating for wasting a strong bull, but that hardly remedied the damage done.

What must doubtlessly have pained John's sour heart, though, was that Lorelei's belly was already swelling, and she had a strong calf come fall.

Pa named the young bull Victor.

John had grown sharper teeth since then—surely strong enough to bite—and as we traveled home from the Morrin farm, that truth weighed heavily upon me. I had known it ever since we came to Kansas, but I had not wanted to admit it.

I had become John's Lorelei.

I had become that cow.

31.

KATE

Labette County, Kansas
1873

BY THE TIME the New Year arrived, we had already suffered through a long and terrible winter. It was not as much the weather that made my days intolerable, but being forced to stay inside with nothing much to do but drink.

The thought of what I had lost kept tormenting me. I barely even took sitters anymore, let alone healed anyone. It seemed so utterly pointless all of a sudden.

Nicholas had been confused, to say the least; one day, we had been as good as married, and the next I had refused to even see him. He even showed up at the inn one day, dressed in his Sunday best. I had so dearly wanted to go out to him, to throw myself at his mercy and beg him to take me away, but that would do no good. John would surely see to that.

It was he who went out and spoke to Nicholas in the end. What exactly was said between them I did not even want to know. Later, John asked me to pen a letter of parting, though, telling Mr. Morrin that the spirits had had a change of heart and no longer thought me the key to his happiness.

I did no such thing, of course.

As much as I resented John, I hated Ma even more. I could not for the life of me figure out why she had tattled to John about my secret. Did she so dearly wish to see me fail that she would risk *all* our lives and reputations?

I confronted her, of course, shortly after that fateful day on the road. We had been alone in the house at last. Pa had gone hunting and John had gone with him to make sure that it was the prey he aimed at. I had spent the morning upon the bed with my pamphlets and a bottle.

"How could you tell him, Ma?" I had yelled at her. I was still feeling raw from the ordeal then, was still grasping for ways out, a glimmer of hope. "How *dare* you meddle in my affairs!"

Ma did not look very upset by my outburst, but looked up at me from her chair with a smirk on her lips. "It's just not for us, Kate. Not anymore. You forfeited your right to a wholesome life the very first time you used that knife." She nodded to the grandfather clock, where Pa's knives were stored with the cash.

"Oh, and you're the one to judge, is it so?" I stood before her with my fists clenched at my sides, swaying a little on my feet from the drink. "You are the one to grant or deny?" I could not believe her gall!

"I'm doing it for those girls." She pursed her lips and lifted her chin, looked every bit the disapproving schoolmarm. "You will bring nothing but trouble to their doorstep. Even if you can curb your temper, our sins might come to light, and it sure won't do if those girls get caught up in it—"

"Since when do you care about the welfare of little girls?" I could not believe that she was trying to act the righteous one with *me*. I, who had tasted the broom many a time and spent hours locked in the cupboard. "You sure didn't bother when *I* was a child—or is it just your own children you despise? Telling John was reckless, Ma! It could have caused worse damage to their household than any dead man in the ground . . . You know *well* how he can be. You put Mr. Morrin—*and* his girls—in *danger*—"

"Yes," she replied, looking all sly. "But then you saved him, so there's that."

"What about your farm, Ma? Don't you want that anymore?"

"How would you dallying with Mr. Morrin ever help you pay me back?" She sounded quite amused.

"Is *that* why you did it?" How little she understood! "I cannot live on as John's prisoner," I cried, loudly enough that Rosie ran behind the canvas curtain to hide. "You should never have told him about Nicholas Morrin."

"Well, someone had to, and it was better that it was me," she said, and finally stopped her eternal knitting. "If he had learned the truth from someone else, Mr. Morrin might not have lived to see another day." She explained it to me as if I were a child. "It couldn't be contained, Kate. You had been *seen* over there—been careless . . ."

"I think you just want to see me hurt," I accused her in a hoarse voice.

Ma only shrugged. "Maybe you deserve it," she quipped. "I mostly thought of those girls, though." She sniffed and lifted her knitting, held the unfinished garment close to her eyes so she could see the patterns she had made.

I wanted to hurt her, but I did not think I could explain it to anyone's satisfaction if Ma was to come to harm with only me around. I got my shawl off the peg, the bottle off the bed, and went out to the barn with Rosie instead. There I found the cigar box and the treasures inside, sat down in the hay, and played with the buttons until the darkness purred like a milk-sated cat and my breathing was calm again.

I suppose those little trinkets reminded me that there was still power to be had in this world, and that I would not be shackled forever.

It just felt like that—like endless torment.

Inside me, the darkness roared with hunger.

"I should have taken my chances," I said to John another night. I was sitting on the bed with a deck of cards and a bottle, while he sat on the floor—guarding me, I thought. "Nicholas is a capable man. He could have defended himself against you, and he would never have believed a word you said."

John looked up at me. "I would rather see you hanged than with another man," he stated quite calmly. He had pulled up his knees and was dark around the eyes as he sat there leaning his head against the back door. He did not sleep much either.

"So you would rather give me up to the law than see me happy?"

John snorted. "There's no happiness for you—not with a man like that. The darkness in you is too strong."

"If *I* hang, we *all* hang," I reminded him.

"Be as that might." John shrugged. "I will still not give you up."

"You would kill us all just to punish me?" I gave him a wry smile. It was such a childish notion. "Maybe I'll get to *you* first."

The thought had certainly occurred to me—it seemed the obvious solution. But then I would be burdened with Ma and Pa, unless they died as well, of course.

IT WAS STILL early in the year when Mr. Longchor stopped by. He was a tall, slim man, cleanly shaven and with a head full of thick blond hair. He was plainly clothed but had a scarf of a dusty pale violet wound about his neck.

Mr. Longchor was also marked.

My mood had been foul for days prior to his arrival. The walls around me seemed to come closer by the hour. It was all becoming too much: Pa's howling in the bed, shouting about men coming to take him; John with his little smirk upon his pale visage and a look of triumph in his eyes, because he thought that he had bested me at last. Ma in her chair, humming German psalms, as if she had not given me up to John and set the destruction of my future in motion.

I could not stand it—I could not!

I drank excessively because it pained me too much to have a clear head. I kept thinking that mayhap we would always be there on the prairie, living in the midst of our ruin. It was *not* what I had seen for myself.

At least, I thought, I deserved a nice scarf.

While Mr. Longchor haltingly bartered for dry goods with Ma at the store counter, I slipped behind the canvas curtain and found Pa upon the bed. He was not mad then—not restrained—just resting after his latest bout.

"Pa," I whispered, bending over and steadying myself against the bedframe. "The angels have spoken to me at last. They say the man who is out there now is concealing some money on his person."

Pa looked up at me with doubt in his eyes. "It's not a good time, Kate. The ground is still frozen."

"Is it, though? I think the weather must have turned." I was swaying on my feet when I straightened up.

"Is he staying to eat?" William asked me.

"Not unless we invite him to." We did that sometimes to make them linger. No man on the road will refuse a free meal.

"Does Ma have something in the pot?"

I shook my head and sneered. "Her pots are rarely in use these days, but we can do a simple meal of bread and cheese."

William thought for moment. "Are the angels *sure* this time?"

"Oh yes," said I, nodding with much vigor. "Quite clear."

"All right," he said and made to rise. "I'll go and find John in the barn, then."

He went out the back door, and I walked up to the store counter, offering Mr. Longchor the simple meal to strengthen him for the road. At first he looked doubtful, but soon enough he relented and let me guide him to the table.

"We have had some quiet days," I told him. "It's nice with some company other than ourselves." I wholeheartedly stood by that statement. Ma watched me all the while, with that viper gaze of hers. Mayhap she could tell from my sweetness alone that another kill was about to occur.

"You're drunk," Ma accused me in German.

"You're vile," I shot back and sniggered a little.

I was a little taken aback when Mr. Longchor refused to drink more than half a cup of cider. He seemed restless at the table, and his gaze kept drifting to the door.

"Could we leave the door ajar?" he asked. "I have valuable cargo in the wagon." He added a lopsided smile, looking somewhat abashed.

"For sure," I said, perking up at the news. I quickly swung the door open, ignoring the freezing cold that seeped inside. "Better now?" I asked.

He nodded with gratitude. "I should not stay long," he said. "I better get going soon."

"Oh, we won't keep you overnight," I said, "though I'm sure it would have been a pleasure." I gave him my sweetest smile, but he did not seem to rise to the bait.

Mr. Longchor ate well, so the offer of a meal had been timely. I saw with satisfaction that he had removed his scarf and placed it on the table before eating, so at least that piece of cloth would survive. I also could not help but notice the unusually fine ivory buttons of his coat—one of them was surely destined for my box. For the first time in months, I felt excited.

Longchor barely twitched when John struck him from behind the curtain, and he slid easily down into the cellar when we toppled the chair. I held the knife steady for the cut and felt the familiar jolt of pleasure when he died—it surely brightened my mood.

Ma only snorted and rolled her eyes when John helped me climb out of the cellar, as if we were nothing but children doing mischief.

"This might be the one Pa has been waiting for," I told her, panting from the exertion and dizzy with excitement. "He admitted to having valuable cargo in the wagon."

"Let's have a look at his wagon, then." Pa fetched the lantern from the table, as dusk had come creeping while we murdered the man.

I was ahead of the men out the door and almost danced across the yard with Mr. Longchor's pretty scarf looped around my neck. I felt more alive than I had in a long while. Inside me, the darkness swam like a fish, whipping its tail and caressing my soul. The sense of power was as strong and poignant as the scent of fresh blood in my nose.

I had not anticipated what we found in the wagon.

In a nest of woolen blankets and hides lay a girl, no more than a year. Her fine hair, blond like her father's, spilled out around her face, and her thin eyelids fluttered as she dreamed. In her hands was a doll, wooden and crude, but doubtlessly loved. Her rosebud mouth let out soft puffs of air.

She was Mr. Longchor's valuable goods.

"Oh no," I muttered. "Oh no . . ."

Neither of the men said a word; both were taken aback by the sight before them.

"What are we to do?" I spoke as loudly as I dared. "What are we to do with her?"

"What do the angels say?" Pa asked. Something frantic had come into his voice. "Didn't they warn you of this?"

I shook my head. "They didn't mention her at all." My heart raced and I felt faint—a little sick, too. I thought that I might retch.

"Fetch Ma," Pa said to John, and the latter raced, fast as a weasel, back into the house. He was happy, perhaps, to be rid of the sight of the child.

Ma came out then, moving slowly, and with a grim expression upon her face. John must have told her what we had found. She had wrapped the gray shawl about her, but the night was coming in fast, and puffs of air rose from her lips as she spoke.

"Look what a mess you have made of things," she scolded while peering down at the girl. The latter suddenly moved in her warm cocoon, and her blue eyes blinked as she came out of her sleep.

"I did not know!" I defended myself. "I would not have chosen him if I—"

"Well, you *did*," Ma said in a clipped voice, just as the little girl gave a wail, recognizing no one around her.

"She can't stay out here." Pa looked around the darkening yard with fear in his eyes. Without any further ado, he grabbed hold of the blankets and hoisted the girl out of the wagon. She started crying of course, but he did not heed it, just placed the child against his shoulder and marched back into the house. Ma and John followed in tow, while I stayed outside to retch.

When I finally stepped across the threshold with my mouth tasting of bile, the girl was with Ma in the rocking chair, sucking on a sugar lump. She looked up at me with eyes so wide and innocent that I could barely stand it.

They were speaking of the wagon.

"I don't care *where* you take it," Pa said to John. Both men were seated at the table, where Mr. Longchor's empty plate still rested. "It has to be dealt with, though, as soon as can be."

"If only you had not shot at Jack," John complained. "I don't know where to take it!"

"What about the girl?" I did not care about the wagon. I looked at the child, sucking greedily on the sweetness, and my stomach lurched again. "What are we to do with her?"

Silence settled in the room, and I sat down in a chair—the very one Mr. Longchor had been in when he died. It was a robust piece of furniture and it had never bothered me using it before, even if it was where the men sat before they landed in the cellar. Now I found myself inspecting the grain for bloodstains.

"Could we keep her?" I asked, looking between their faces. "Could we say she is a cousin?" I could take her with me, I thought, when I took to the stage. I could travel with her as my young niece.

"We could." Pa sounded doubtful. "But this is hardly a house for children."

"Mr. Morrin, though," I suggested. "I could tell him that she's an orphan, and that Andrea wants him to look after her in place of Lavinia, the girl he lost." I spoke so quickly that I stumbled on the words.

"Damn Mr. Morrin," John's voice snapped.

I could see that the girl had fallen asleep again on Ma's broad lap and thought it a little peculiar, as she had just slept in the wagon and was among strangers, but perhaps she was merely exhausted. Ma kept stroking her downy hair with her dry, gnarled fingers.

"Maybe she has a mother somewhere?" I mused. "Perhaps we could send word, somehow? Maybe we should leave her by a church in the city?"

"All full of nice suggestions, aren't you?" Ma croaked.

"Maybe it would be easiest to say that she's a cousin," said Pa. "We could tell *her* that as well, as she grows up."

Something warm erupted in my chest. "Sure, Pa." Suddenly, I so dearly wanted to keep her. "We could tell her that for sure." It was then I noticed how the girl's lips had gone blue, and how her rosy pallor had turned quite white.

"Ma!" I cried out, bolting from the chair and over to them. "Ma, what is wrong with her? Is she ill?" I knelt on the floor by the rocking chair and touched the girl's tender neck.

I flinched when I could feel no pulse.

"She is with God now," said Ma.

"What did you *do*?" I was back on my feet. "Ma, what did you do?"

On the floor between us lay the lump of sugar the girl had been sucking on, slipped from her sticky fingers. I did not know what Ma had laced it with, but I knew it was something for sure.

Repulsed, I kicked it away so it flew under the stove.

"I did her a favor," Ma barked. Her voice sounded raw. "I merely saved her from this life. She is better off with her pa, at peace."

"Ma, no!" I could not believe it—the beautiful girl was gone!

"What were we going to do with her? Raise another devil?" Ma gave a hard, sharp laugh, and the dead child shook in her lap. "At least now her soul will remain pure!"

"You said that we still protected children in this house," I reminded her. "Do we no longer live by that rule?"

Ma shrugged and looked down at the girl with something like wistfulness. It troubled me greatly to see it. "We do not deserve something as good as a child," she uttered in a broken voice.

"But surely *she* deserved to live!" My head was spinning badly.

Ma sighed. "She had bad luck—she met wolves on the road, and *they* hardly ask if their prey is deserving."

"I think you have gone mad," I accused her. My own voice sounded faint to my ears.

"We all have, Kate." Her gaze met mine. "We all lost our minds quite some time ago."

32.

ELVIRA

OH, HOW I mourned that girl!

I knew it at once, that snuffing out that little life—that little light—would surely be the last drop. Such an offense against God would be our damnation for sure.

I welcomed it with open arms!

Kate did not understand my reasoning at all. She raged at me in the following days, saying that I thought myself all high-and-mighty for making such a decision, but she ruled over men's lives all the time and was surely no better than me.

"But a *child*, Ma! A *child!*" she cried. As if children do not die all the time—I should surely know, having buried a handful of my own. The only one left was *her*: red-haired and brutal; utterly wicked—a payment for all my sins.

I had no words to give her in reply. It was a matter between mightier powers and myself. I had made a bid for freedom by sacrificing that lamb. Such an unnatural assault would surely not go unnoticed, and it was not a life worth living, what we had.

We all suffered for the things we had done—and rightly so.

I cannot say just when I had ceased dreading our exposure and came to long for it instead, but I think it was about the time when William lost his bearings. I saw it all so clearly then, how I would never have that farm again, how wrong we had been to spill innocent blood. No one can live with a cellar that reeks of rot and iron and not take damage to the soul.

Yet, days and weeks passed after the little girl died in my arms, and no hammer of God came bearing down. There was only ours, rusty and hidden behind the canvas curtain. No justice was there but the one decided between a madman, a brute, a hag, and a devil. Not even William spoke of angels anymore. It would seem we were allowed to do just as we pleased, and that there truly was no watchful eye tallying up our sins.

Then, when I had all but given up, justice finally arrived at our door. Not swift and hard as a hammer blow, but slithering and slow, like a snake.

DR. WILLIAM YORK was tall and healthy-looking, though he appeared a little gaunt, from travel perhaps, or from the injury that had him limping slightly as he sat down at our table. Being of my profession, I did not much like doctors, and they loathed me in return, but I did have some soup that day since John had come and handed me a chicken, plucked and all, and it seemed a shame to let the meat go to waste. I served the doctor some in a bowl.

It should have been an easy transaction; some coins for the food and he would go off. Kate's "angels" had not made any unwelcome appearances, so John had no reason to lurk behind the canvas curtain. Kate was in the room but, like me, she became wary around men who claimed to own the truth. She was curt but polite and made idle conversation about the weather while the doctor consumed his soup. Dr. York was quite safe with us, for, all the madness and devilry aside, my family were no fools, and they would never dare to take on a man of such high standing.

I sat in the rocking chair, minding my own business, only occasionally tossing a wary look in the doctor's direction, listening with only half an ear to their gibberish speech. Though I understood quite a lot, and even more since we came to Kansas and opened the inn, it was still hard to follow when they spoke with some speed.

Kate poured the man cider. She did not sit down with him at the table, though, but retreated again behind the store counter. I kept working on the scarf I was making for John.

I cannot tell just what it was that caught my attention. Maybe it was how Kate's voice suddenly rose a little and her laughter became brittle. When I turned my head to look at her, I could see that her smile was no longer relaxed, but seemed frozen upon her face.

It was then that I heard the man say the name "Longchor."

He said it several more times after that, while gesturing with his hands. I stepped up my speed and the knitting needles flew as I listened in on their conversation.

I could tell that they spoke of a wagon and figured that had to be Longchor's, which we had abandoned, but it took me a little while to figure out just why the doctor was concerned with that. Eventually I pieced together that the wagon had belonged to Dr. York before, and he had recently sold it to Mr. Longchor. Now the doctor had been called upon while traveling to identify the vehicle. Something he had done with certainty.

A current passed through me when I learned that. If it was of dread or anticipation, I simply could not tell.

Behind the store counter, Kate shook her head, and I figured she denied any knowledge of the man *and* his wagon. I could also tell from the crease of her brow that she was not very pleased.

"Ma, will you mind the counter?" she said. "I should like a word with the men in the barn." She wanted to warn them for sure.

She donned her shawl and off she went, leaving me alone with the doctor.

"German, huh?" The doctor asked, polite enough, with the spoonful of soup hovering between the bowl and his lips.

I nodded and plastered on the feeble smile that Kate much preferred that I wore.

"Do you like it out here?" He continued his queries, though I would have liked it better if he kept his mouth shut.

Again, I nodded and smiled. In my lap, the knitting needles kept moving.

"It can be hard," he tried again. "In winter."

"Very cold," I agreed. "Hot, too, in summer."

"You have a nice piece of land," said he, but I thought that he said it mostly to be kind.

It was then I put down my knitting. I looked out the window to make sure that Kate was not yet on her way back, and then I shuffled in behind the canvas curtain and opened up my trunk. There, under the false bottom, my hand easily found what I was looking for.

The thing my family had not even thought to ask for.

When I reentered the room where Dr. York was finishing his soup, my heart was thundering in my chest, and my hands around the item I had fetched were slippery with perspiration. I thought that I might faint before my mission was complete.

I thought for a moment to forget all about it, to go back to my rocking chair, sink down on the seat, and pick up the knitting, but then nothing would have been won. Nothing would lie before me than more of the same ordeal.

That girl would have died in vain.

Knowing full well that it might come to nothing—mayhap he would think me just a foolish old woman, up to strange antics—and yet with a quivering hope in my chest, I placed the Longchor girl's doll on the table, just next to the doctor's chicken soup.

At first, he did not seem to recognize it at all. It was a crude thing with barely any features, and it had no hair but a flowery scarf tied to the skull. Mayhap, I thought, when seeing his incomprehension, men like him did not pay much heed to children's toys.

Then it was as if a light came on in his eyes, and he drew a sharp breath as he picked up the doll and inspected it from every angle.

A rush of words spilled from his lips next, so fast that I could not follow in my wretched state. I heard him say a name, though, several times: "Anne Marie, Anne Marie, Anne Marie . . ."

The dead girl had a name at last.

Dr. York became agitated at the table. He rose to his feet and stumbled toward me, still with the doll in his hand. He was yelling, and I thought that he wanted me to tell him where the girl was, but by then I had lost all speech. I lifted my arms as if to ward off a blow, and he seemed to calm a little when he saw that, thinking me afraid, perhaps. He paused to regain control of his breathing, and then he asked me again.

"Where are they, woman? By God, you must tell me!" His red face contorted with dread.

I never could, though. I never had time to take him by the hand and lead him out the back door to show him the newly turned soil in the orchard, for in came Kate with John and William in tow. Kate was pale already on arrival, so they must have heard the man's harsh words. They barged inside, William with a blade in his hand, and John carrying a scythe. Kate, for once, held the hammer upright in her lily-white hands.

"Ma!" she cried when she saw the doll. "Ma, what did you do?"

She seemed to have asked me that often of late.

Even William paled at the sight. "Elvira!" he burst out. "Have you lost your mind?"

He was one to speak!

Dr. York did not at first seem to realize how his life had become imperiled. He kept shouting about "George" and "Anne Marie," waving the doll around. Now it was William who got the brunt of his anger and fear for being the eldest man.

He did not stop talking until John rammed him with the scythe in the legs, and then he buckled to the floor.

They moved as if they were only one creature. They went at him with all they had: hammer, blade, and scythe, and did not stop before his screaming ceased and his blood ran red across the floor, swallowing up Kate's celestial designs: Mercury, Venus, the sun, and the moon.

Finally, Kate cut one fine silver button out of his coat, and then they were quite done.

When the man was in the cellar, I was back in the rocking chair, humming to myself as the knitting needles moved in my lap. I pretended not to hear Kate as she went at me.

"A man like that doesn't just disappear! They will look for him, Ma, and thoroughly!" She paced the floor furiously, barely avoiding the blood. John was digging out back, while William had gone for water. "Do you *want* us to hang now, is that it? It's bad enough that

Pa is losing his mind, but *you*, Ma? I thought you were made of sturdier stuff than this. It's weak, Ma! Weak and foolish—and it was *you* who murdered that girl!"

I hummed as she shouted. Eventually she came and took my knitting away.

"Don't think I won't lock you up in the barn if you don't behave," she hissed, just inches from my face. Her hair had come undone and tumbled down over her shoulders. Her arms were red to the elbows and her purple dress was stained in several places. She would have to soak it overnight, and that might not even suffice. "I won't think twice about locking you in there with the chickens and never letting you out."

I shrugged and resumed my humming.

I was disappointed that nothing more had come of my bravery than another dead man in the orchard. I thought the doctor a fool for not taking the doll and running for help, instead of just standing there, waving his arms around.

"Do you know that his brother is a colonel?" said Kate. "He told me so himself! You have called all sorts of torment down on us now!"

I had not known that, but I was certainly pleased. Let them come, those men, to look for the doctor. Let them come and tear the place apart.

"Good," I croaked at last, just to stop my daughter's foul mouth. "In torment is where we belong!"

33.

HANSON

THE MEN CAME to the trading station well before noon, one day in late March. There were five of them, led by the colonel himself, dressed in a dark uniform with polished brass buttons. His face looked appropriately severe, set in grim lines around a combed and trimmed mustache. He did not laugh or smile much, and his eyes seemed as blue specks of ice in his tanned and lined face. I thought that was because he had seen much suffering, or perhaps it was due to his brother being gone.

Of the men who rode with him, two were from Cherryvale, farmers both, and of good reputation. The other two were men the colonel had brought along from Fort Scott. I thought at least one of them was a military man, though he did not have a uniform. It was just something about the way he sat in his saddle, and how his movements all seemed so measured and correct. The colonel's party all wore thick coats against the chill and wide-brimmed hats. They were also carrying rifles. They had stopped by the trading station to speak to Mr. Brockman and Mr. Ern, who dutifully appeared on the porch and proceeded to offer the men a drop of whiskey and hot coffee before they moved on.

I made myself useful by carrying out tin cups and pouring from the kettle, but really, I was only listening in. The men being there made me feel immensely relieved. It was as if I could finally breathe again after a bout of pneumonia. Finally, I thought, someone of importance had come to put an end to the disappearances. I did not think that way to put any blame on the county trustee, Mr. Dick, but the truth of it was that many men had gone missing, and no one had seen neither hide nor hair of them since.

The trading station had been abuzz with speculation for months, and many people thought that the murderer responsible for the corpses found on the prairie and in the river had simply found another, hitherto unknown, place to rid himself of his victims. Mr. Brockman, seemingly well recovered from John's beating and finally somewhat at peace with the fact that he would likely never marry Kate Bender, was often a part of those conversations, pouring generous helpings of whiskey to his patrons as they gossiped over the counter.

I could hardly participate in those talks but sat on the stool by the oven to do some cleaning of a harness or some such. I could not find it in me *not* to listen in, as *not* knowing what was being said about the matter was somehow more frightening than staying well-informed. My stomach always pained me, though—ached in a sickening way—whenever the disappearances were being discussed. I often felt weak and clammy after, as if I had gone through an ordeal.

Though I no longer envisioned a blood-drinking fiend, what I did imagine was somehow much worse—so bad, in fact, that I had forbidden myself to even think the thought through. Yet it was there like a writhing thing inside me, something alive and vile, like a rat.

"How long has your brother been missing?" Mr. Ern asked the colonel. He had taken off his glasses and was cleaning them with his handkerchief, as was his habit when he did not know what to do with his hands. Some of the colonel's party sat on our log, while others stood around him, holding the steaming cups. Mr. Brockman still lingered on the porch, holding the whiskey bottle by the neck.

"He left our parents' house a few weeks ago," the colonel grumbled. "His wife is awfully fretful, and his children are as well. We fear that he has met dangerous men on the road, but we will not think the worst just yet."

"Of course not," muttered Mr. Ern.

"It can be a rough landscape," Mr. Brockman said from the porch.

"Dr. York is well used to traveling in such terrain," said the colonel. "He did have an injury to a foot, though—a cut that would not heal. He might have taken shelter if the damage took a bad turn."

I thought to myself that this seemed a feeble hope, especially in an area where travelers were wont to go missing. I did not say it, of course, none of us did, though the knowledge lay thick on everyone's faces.

This was not a search bound for a blissful reunion.

When the men were back on their horses and started toward the Bender place, I followed on the mule. No one had told me to, but no one had told me *not to* either, and I figured that the men could need someone with them who had a particular knowledge of this stretch of the road.

I had not visited the Benders for months. I had been driven away by my own unease and Mrs. Bender's warning. I had even ceased to look in the house's direction, pretending as well as I could that it did not exist. I could make that work for a time—days, even, because the partnership between the inn and the trading station had fallen to the wayside over the winter. Mr. Ern no longer sent me to collect the money, and neither did we stock their shelves. The Benders, in turn, did not come to either collect or deliver, and so it suddenly was as if we were not neighbors at all.

Mr. Brockman, on his side, did not even want to speak of the Benders. His lips became a grim, thin line whenever their name came up, and his eyes became dark with shadows. I knew without asking that it was not as much the memory of John's fists that bothered him, but that of Kate's betrayal. She had never told Mr. Brockman "no" in words, but as her silence had stretched out, he seemed to have come to his senses at last, and what love he had nourished for her before had turned into a painful sort of shame.

I had been reminded of the Benders' presence, though, from time to time, no matter how much I tried to pretend that they did not exist. A whiff of acrid smoke would come drifting from the inn's direction, or my friends, the Weissbrods, would share another tale of witches and their tricks, but I did not voluntarily turn my head to the Bender place, even if I had helped build the house. I knew that if I did so, I would wake up the rat that wriggled in my stomach—or risk seeing something I rather would not—and so it was better to act as if the house were not there at all.

The mule and I entered the Benders' yard behind the others, on account of us being the smallest, and also on account of not wanting to be seen. I had thought it would feel bad to go there again, that my stomach would act up, but I felt safe behind the colonel's broad back. It was as if those shiny buttons were dazzling charms of protection, and nothing bad could possibly occur when traveling with someone with such clout. Furthermore, he seemed to me a man of action, and that was surely needed in these parts. It was bad for business and bad for all with the way people dropped off the road. Just recently, a little girl had gone missing. Her father's wagon had been found abandoned and had been recognized by Dr. York himself, which led a slew of people to believe that he had learned something about the murderer that had gotten him into trouble. I had not slept well on the nights since I learned about the girl. Before she went missing, all those we knew of who were lost or dead had been grown men, and it had been terrible to learn that not even the truly innocent were safe.

I no longer slept in the barn at all, much preferring the dusty floor inside the trading station, where Brockman and Ern were at hand, although neither of them would be very useful in a fight.

The Bender home looked bleak that day; gray smoke wafted from the chimney, and a few scraggly chickens sprinted across the frozen ground. Rosie ran about the horses' feet, yapping something fierce. Everything seemed to have taken on a gray cast, though it was likely just the lack of sun that made everything seem washed-out and old.

A jolt of pain did erupt in my belly when I saw Kate coming out of the house. She, too, seemed tired that day, as she strode toward us while wrapping the brown shawl about her chest. Her dress was new, I noted, made from green-checked gingham. The bell of the skirt flowed from her waist all clean and pristine, though her red hair had not been pinned up, and some grime had settled on her neck. She met the approaching party with a smile on her lips, but it did not reach her eyes. They remained cold and gray in the bleak, dusty light.

"Is this the Bender place?" the colonel asked when she came up to his horse.

"Sure is." Kate nodded.

"I am Colonel Alexander York of Fort Scott," he introduced himself. "Is Mr. Bender around?"

Kate shrugged. "He is, but in a bad shape. The winter has been rough on him, and he does not always know what day or time it is."

The colonel looked surprised at this, but I, for one, was not. Mr. Ern had cited this as one of the reasons why we should no longer work with the Benders, claiming that Mr. Bender had often been seen outside with his rifle, shooting at men who were not there. The Weissbrods, too, had seen it with their own eyes when they went looking about the place. According to them, he had been naked and screaming about thieves in the orchard. I had heard gunshots myself many times, both late in the evening and early in the day. The rumor in town was that he had lost his mind. I had figured at the time that it was a good thing if it was so, because then, whatever had happened at their place—whatever reason they had had for digging in the night—it could have to do with Mr. Bender's loss of reason, and nothing more.

"Is there someone else I could talk to?" the colonel asked. "I come about a grave matter."

"Well." Kate shrugged again. "You could surely talk to me. I am the only one here with a decent grasp of the English language, so I suppose I am your best option anyway." It amazed me how calm and aloof she was, even when faced with all those shiny buttons.

The colonel then explained about his missing brother. He mentioned how he'd looked and when he had traveled. Kate listened to all this with a thoughtful expression. "I cannot tell for sure," she said. "We have a lot of travelers stopping by, and one man looks like the next to me. I can ask my parents and my brother, but they probably won't remember, either. There's a band of bandits roaming, though," she added. "My brother saw them just the other day, by the creek. I suppose they're your best bet if he disappeared around these parts."

I, too, had heard about those bandits, but the rumors had been very vague, and I had thought it mostly a thing folks said to explain why people disappeared off the road. The news brought me a ray of hope, though, because if the bandits were about and had done the wicked deeds, there was some hope that I could get rid of the wriggling rat as well. I therefore listened eagerly as Kate went on to describe a band of maybe ten men, all of them rough-looking, who had set up camp in the wilderness.

"They've been good at staying out of view," she said. "My brother thinks they have escaped prison in another state and live mostly like wild men. We have had things go missing from the yard as well, poultry mostly, but also some feed, and even some of my underthings drying on a line." The colonel looked suddenly uncomfortable at that particular piece of information. "I can ask my brother to take you to the creek if you want to see for yourself where he spotted them," she offered.

At this, the colonel perked up, and he and his men slipped off their horses and gathered in a circle with the reins in their hands to discuss among them, deciding what to do.

It was then Kate noticed me.

"Hi, Hanson," she said in greeting and lifted her hand in a half wave. She sauntered toward me with the skirt of the new dress swinging about her ankles, and I could not for the life of me decide if her approach made me feel uncomfortable or delighted. "How are things at the trading station?" She reached out a hand to pet the mule.

"Oh, the same as always," I mumbled, unable to rightly meet her eyes.

"We so rarely see you anymore," she noted, and guilt came

flooding in at once, swift and merciless. "Is it because Mr. Ern will no longer ply his goods here?"

"I don't know much about that," I muttered, feeling my cheeks redden with shame. Suddenly, I felt like it was very wrong of me to harbor that rat in the first place. The Benders had always been good to me.

"Is it because of what Ma said to you?" she asked. "She only worried because of Pa. He had not been well, and she feared that he would frighten you." She laughed a little. "He even frightens *me* sometimes, so it's not so strange that she worries."

"What is wrong with him?" I asked.

"Some people lose their bearings in old age," she said. "It's a shame when it happens, but not unheard of."

"Can't you cure him?" She *had* said she could cure all sorts of diseases.

"Oh, I have tried, Hanson, believe me, but some rot runs so deep that it's hard to root out. Besides, not all sickness is meant to be cured. No one would die then, and there wouldn't be enough land for all of us." She gave another short laugh.

"Did you hear about the girl?" I burst out, although I had not planned on bringing her up.

Something dark flickered in her eyes. "The little one? Yes, I did. Such a shame. I do hope they find her."

I wanted to ask if she and her father had stopped by the inn, but just then, the colonel and his men were done with their discussion and drifted away from each other. The colonel moved toward Kate with his horse in tow.

"We would like to have a look at the creek, if your brother is willing," he said.

"I shall ask him promptly," said she, then turned her back and started toward the house. There was not a man in that yard who did not watch her go.

Next it was John who came shuffling out of the house. He looked a little more stooped than before, as if he were carrying a heavy weight, and a wicked little part of me hoped that it was due to the treatment he had given Mr. Brockman. His hooded eyes were dark when he glanced at me before placing his hat on top of his head and shuffling over to Colonel York.

Kate came back outside as well, but she paused by the door, seemingly not inclined to go farther. When the door behind her opened again, I was expecting Mr. Bender, as it would be natural for the master of the household to come and see about things, but Kate had clearly not been lying when she said he had taken a bad turn, because it was *Mrs.* Bender who came outside to hover alongside Kate.

She was the one who had changed the most since I had been there last, looking as if she somehow had shrunk. She reminded me of dried fruits, plums or apples, not because she had become very wrinkly but because it seemed as if she had lost all her juice. She looked almost like a forlorn child as she stood there, next to her daughter, with her gnarled hands folded over her belly. Mrs. Bender looked around her as if bewildered, and I briefly wondered if Mr. Bender was not the only one whose mind was scrambled. If so, I surely did not blame Kate for looking a little tired.

John was done with talking to the colonel and was walking alongside the latter's horse as we all set off again. It was not far to the creek, and John made good pace, but I wondered why he had not brought a horse of his own. Mayhap he was in a hurry, I figured, and had no time to saddle up. Mayhap it was that his father needed him at home. The women would surely want another man around if Mr. Bender went at it with the rifle again. When John turned his head to look back toward the house, I could see that his face looked strained and worried.

The men I rode behind did not speak much to one another. I thought that was due to the serious business at hand. They probably did not think it the time for idle chatter when Dr. York was missing, and more men besides. I did not mind, though, but quite enjoyed riding in silence. A ripple of wind sent the prairie grass swaying and the clouds rushing across the sky. I thought of the upcoming search with equal parts dread and anticipation. I dearly hoped that we *would* find evidence of a cruel band of bandits—even if it would bode poorly for Dr. York—as it might silence my wriggling rat, but a dark voice inside me told me it was not so. We would not find a thing at the creek, it said, even if John ran like a rabbit to get us there, seemingly as eager as anyone to bring the evildoers to justice.

When we arrived at the creek, where John said he had spotted "seven or eight men," the colonel's party dismounted their horses and gathered near the water's edge to strategize. I dismounted, too, though I stayed close to the mule so as not to draw attention to myself. Now that we were there, I felt like I was sticking out like a sore thumb, seeing that no one had asked me to participate in the search. Still, I figured it would be a lively story to tell my friends, the Weissbrods, who always seemed to go on such daring adventures.

The men split up next, setting off in different directions. Some took their horses, but others did not, and so I got a chance to prove my usefulness at last, when the colonel asked me to stay put and look after the animals. I received the order with a sense of gratitude.

It was a long and uneventful wait, though, as the men quickly vanished, leaving me behind. Some walked farther down the river; others rode across the brown water to explore the other side. Soon, it was just me, the mule, and three horses left, as John, too, had been assigned a direction and disappeared alongside a man from town.

I tried to make the time count by scanning the horizon for bandits of any kind, but I saw nothing but the occasional bird flying by. I amused myself by throwing rocks across the water to see if I could hit the other side and talking to the horses, which were amiable creatures. I watched the sun to keep track of the time and felt a sense of relief as it crept toward the agreed-upon hour when they would all come drifting back, hopefully with uplifting news.

When they did, there were no smiles on their faces, though; rather, they all seemed disappointed, and the colonel most of all. His jaws worked under his skin, and his sharp gaze seemed somehow diminished. Only John seemed just as before, untouched by the day's ordeal, but for a blister on his heel that he complained about loudly in his halting English. I did feel a little bad about that, as I knew he had to walk all the way back again, and thought of offering him the mule, but she was not friendly to strangers, and so I thought it was safer not to.

He did keep an impressive pace, though, for someone claiming to be in such pain.

When we came back to the Bender place, Kate was still outside. She had brought out one of the wooden chairs and was cleaning out some sooty pots. She rinsed them in a tub of water placed before her feet and had pulled up her new skirt to well above her knees so as not to get it wet or dirty. Even I could tell that it looked unseemly, and I could see no reason for it other than to confuse and befuddle, as Kate had no lack of suitors even with her skirts pulled down.

I could tell that the colonel's party appreciated the sight, though. They exchanged sly looks and put on silly smiles. I myself only reddened with shame and looked away, knowing full well that I was not among her intended audience.

When we approached, she dropped the pot into the water, rose to her feet, and came toward us. She reached the colonel first. John had fallen far behind and was next to me by then, panting and cursing in German.

"Did you find anything?" Kate greeted the colonel.

He shook his head in reply. The men came riding up beside him, one by one. All but me and the mule, who stayed behind the line of horses.

"Whomever your brother saw, they weren't there now," said Colonel York. "Neither did we see any traces of Dr. York."

"That's a shame." Kate folded her arms over her chest and shook her head with a furrowed brow. "I had so been hoping you would find them. We would much have appreciated some help in getting rid of those bandits."

"Well," the colonel said, "you should always have your rifle at the ready." He sounded a little curt. Perhaps because Kate had forgotten to express worry over the missing doctor.

"Oh, we do. We sure do," Kate exclaimed. Then she corrected her mistake. "I just wish you would have found them for your brother's sake. They may have kept him around, with him being a medical man and all." Only I, who knew her, would hear the light mocking in her voice. I knew from our conversations that Kate did not much like real doctors.

The colonel, however, seemed to perk up a little at her words. "You think they may have use of him?" he asked, just as John passed them by. He was red in the face and went directly for the barn. To collect himself, I figured.

"It's dangerous, living on the prairie," Kate said in a knowing way, though she had only been with us for two years and did not really know much. "I'm sure even bandits can be taken ill with the ague, or sprain a leg."

The colonel nodded and seemed to be considering it, though I could not say for sure as I did not see his face.

"I could help you find out," Kate offered, lifting her chin a little. "I have helped to locate many missing men before."

"Have you, now?" Colonel York sounded both surprised and amused. "Then why haven't you found my brother already?"

Kate shrugged a little. "No one has asked me to, and it's hard and difficult work. I would have to enter a trance, for one, to contact the spirit world. That is my profession, you see. I speak to the dead to earn my keep." She gave him a lopsided smile, as if daring him not to believe her. "It also helps to have a relative or friend of the one we are looking for nearby," she continued. "Someone who remembers the person vividly—like a brother."

The colonel sounded as if he was starting to laugh, but then abruptly stopped himself. "A medium, huh? On the prairie!" Now he did laugh, a short, sharp bark. "Well, who knows . . . all my other efforts have surely been in vain. I suppose you'd want me to pay for such a service?"

"Of course." Kate was still smiling. "All the others have done right by me." She lowered her eyelids as she gazed upon him. "You're hardly the first one to stop by the Bender place to ask about loved ones, Colonel, and I assure you I have found every one of them."

"Is that so?" He sounded suspicious, but tempted, too, and I supposed that was only natural, as he fretted so for his brother.

"You can ask anyone," Kate continued. "My reputation around

here is spotless. I am no more nor less than what I say I am, and I feel strongly that I can help you find Dr. York, *if* you will let me."

"For a price?" he asked again.

"For a price," Kate confirmed.

"Well, Miss Bender." Colonel York sat up straight on his horse, readying to leave. "I sure know who to come to, then, if a more *mundane* search yields no results."

"That you do." Kate was still smiling. The men flanking the colonel laughed a little between them, but it sounded nervous to me. "I don't think he's far at all," Kate continued, and the rat in my belly did a flip. "He might have been right under your noses all along."

WHEN MR. ERN and I were tending the livestock in the barn that night, I turned to him and said, "Mr. Ern, don't you think there should be another search of the farms?"

Mr. Ern gave me a surprised look. He was holding a very heavy bucket of water, which he put down by his feet before answering, while simultaneously pressing a handkerchief to his glistening forehead. "Whatever for, Hanson?"

"To look for the missing men—and the girl."

"But they already searched the farms, Hanson. They did that before Christmas."

"But I think they should do it again," I said. "I think they should go into the houses and check all the cellars, and see if anyone has done some digging out of season." My heart thumped painfully as I said that last part.

Mr. Ern gave me a puzzled look. "Why, Hanson? Have you heard or seen anything?"

"No," I lied. "It's just so that people can feel safe around their neighbors." A chill passed through me. "So we can be sure that none of the people we see around here is the murderer." When Mr. Ern still did not look convinced, I added, "They did not search very carefully last time. No one thought it could be one of us, but now that Dr. York is missing—"

"But didn't you just look for bandits about the creek? Surely it's them."

"Oh, I don't know." I grabbed the shovel I used for the muck from its place by the wall. "I haven't seen any suspicious characters around, and neither has anyone else but John Bender." My voice dwindled into nothing. I kept my gaze glued to the ground. Never before had I been so close to voicing what I feared the most, and my face flushed hot from the shame of it while my belly turned into an aching knot. "They might have been just passing through, those men he saw," I added, as if to soften my words. "It could have nothing to do with the missing travelers at all."

"It *is* curious that no one from town has gone missing," Mr. Ern admitted. "It *could* lead one to believe that the culprit resides among us."

"Yes," I agreed wholeheartedly and nodded with much vigor. "Just that, Mr. Ern. Which is why I think there should be another search."

Mr. Ern chuckled a little. "You sure have many serious thoughts in your head, young man—and you're persistent, too."

I chose to take that as a compliment. "I just don't want anyone else to go missing from the road." I started cleaning out the muck from under the cow. "It's bad for business, you said so yourself." Again, I could not rightly look at him, and my mouth felt so dry that it was hard to swallow. My belly ached worse than it had all day; the rat was dancing a jig down there. "We ought to make sure. So we can feel safe."

Mr. Ern nodded with a thoughtful expression. "You may have a point," he admitted. "I'll see what I can do about that."

"Thank you," I croaked, though my insides were in turmoil, shifting every second between gratitude and fear. "I feel a little sick," I said, and vomited down on the dirt floor.

34.

ELVIRA

KATE PACED THE floor in a most annoying way: back and forth, back and forth, before the window. Occasionally, she would glance outside, up the road, waiting impatiently. The hem of her new dress brushed the floor and had already taken on a gray hue; it would not last long, that piece of unwarranted luxury that she had insisted on, citing that she refused to "live in squalor."

"Stop fretting, Kate," I said, when the grandfather clock had counted out another half hour. "They'll be back when they're back. You staring up the road like a lovesick maiden won't make them come home any faster."

"Be quiet!" she snapped over her shoulder. "Don't you ever again dare to tell me what to do!"

"Well, watching you right now gives me a headache. You do nothing but wear out the floorboards, ruining all your fancy designs." I nodded to the circles she had carved on the floor.

"Well, go somewhere else, then, or maybe not—it's perhaps better if you are where I can see you. Pick up your knitting, Ma. Keep your hands busy so they won't do mischief. What you've already done is bad enough!"

It had been thus ever since I gave Dr. York the doll. Her coldness toward me was constant and complete. I did not mind it much, as I had been expecting no less, but the animosity between us sure had its challenges. I would no longer eat the food she gave me, for instance, or drink the tea that she brewed, as I did not trust her not to have tampered with it. She, in turn, did not consume anything from *me*, so our eating arrangements were complicated.

We both feared to die at the other one's hand.

"It's hardly I who have put us in this position," I reminded Kate, though my voice was weak. This was not a new discussion between us, and I did not expect something of value to come of it. Yet I felt that it had to be said.

"*I* did not kill that girl," said she, as I had known she would.

"Didn't you, though? We would not have started down this road at all if it had not been for you. It was *you* who turned our home into a slaughterhouse, Kate, not I."

"And yet you've proven yourself such a capable butcher." Her voice dripped with icicles and searing cold.

"*You* poisoned the well, Kate. You bloodied the hearth!"

"Oh, stop that nonsense, Ma!" The cold in her suddenly erupted into fire. "The men's hands are just as red as mine—they have dark hearts, those two."

"Sure." I nodded in agreement. "But they are weak and in need of a devil like yourself to guide them."

"Oh, Ma." She paused her pacing to shake her head. "Must you really blame me for everything? *I* did not kill Anne Marie—*you* did!"

"It was better if she went right away," said I. "She would not have survived with you anyway."

"That's a poor excuse—and *wrong*. We could have raised her like we said—"

"And made another devil out of her? If you live with wolves, you become a wolf. That is the way of the world."

"Well, I suppose that explains the darkness in *me*." She had placed her hands upon her hips and was looking at me quite sternly. Her hair—never pinned up anymore—fell around her face in greasy tendrils; the brown shawl was haphazardly thrown about her form and tied at the back. On her hands she wore a pair of fingerless gloves against the chill. She looked much like a street urchin in New York, had it not been for the new gingham dress.

I could see why she had wanted that new garment.

"I should have put you out on the prairie the very same night we did in Dr. York," she said. "I cannot fathom what foolishness possessed you—"

"My reasons are my own," I cut in.

"And look at where they have brought us!" She stomped her foot, though it did not make much noise, and thus had very little effect. "Now it may all come tumbling down," she said. "We may hang for this, Ma—*hang*!"

"That *is* often the fate of a murderer."

These words only enraged her more. "I cannot believe how you can sit there so calmly when our very *lives* are on the line. Don't you even want me to live?" Her eyes went large and pleading for a moment and for just a blink of an eye, she was five years old again, begging for her ma's love.

I had none to give her.

"They might come for us already tonight," she fretted, her eyes drifting back to the window and the road.

"Now you sound like Pa in one of his fits," said I. "It's only a town meeting; it doesn't have to mean anything. They shall only discuss what to do. You cannot blame people for not being thrilled about men disappearing."

"But now that the colonel is involved, they might actually *do* something." She wrung her hands. "He seems like a determined sort."

"What is it you fear he'll do?" I asked.

She shrugged a little. "Oh, I don't know . . ."

"He put the fear in you." I chuckled. "Not so much the high-and-mighty Professor Miss Katie Bender now, are you?"

"Oh, Ma," she said again. "You're vile!"

IT WAS LATE when the men finally arrived back home. We could see them come from far off, the wagon's rickety wheels spinning up a cloud of dust. The horses were soaked in sweat when they pulled up in front of the house. William climbed out and came staggering to the door. He had that wild look on his face that meant he had taken a turn, so at first I figured that was why John had been in such a hurry to get home.

Then I caught sight of my stepson's face below the brim of his hat. It looked to be made of stone for how gray and unmoving it was.

"What?" Kate stormed toward the wagon, having seen the same as I. "What, John?" Her new skirt danced around her legs. "What happened? Tell me!"

William had reached the door, where I stood at the threshold, and suddenly he started to laugh. "Jack Handsome's men are coming for us," he exclaimed with much glee and started dancing on the spot, kicking up some dust of his own.

"I am sure that's not right, William," I said, as I thought that highly unlikely.

"I need to get my rifle." He pushed past me, and my heart sank. I envisioned another night of sudden gunshots and startlement; of wrestling him onto the bed to have his hands secured to the brass tubes while he shouted in our ears about horse thieves and vigilantes. I hoped John would hide away the weapon again.

"He slept all the way through." John pointed at his father's receding back with the horsewhip. "He fell asleep right there on the bench, and slept through the whole town meeting. He doesn't even know what happened, I think."

"What *did* happen?" Kate's pretty face was distorted with impatience.

"Well." John looked dazed. "There will be another search, a thorough one, of every farm—they'll even search the grounds for turned soil. It was Mr. Ern, of all, who insisted, though I am curious as to why. I'd think he would rather not let the whole town know where he's digging down their whiskey bottles."

"What can we do?" asked Kate; her eyes were wild. "How can we turn them away?"

John shrugged. "Maybe we can blame Pa?" he suggested, though it sounded feeble.

"Can we dig them up?" Kate had lowered her voice. "Can we move them away, perhaps?"

John shook his head with a slight smile. "It's far too late for that, Kate. They'll see that the earth is moved."

"For saplings," said she. "We can use the plow again; make it all look the same." She had closed her hand over the worn wood of the wagon's side, and her knuckles had gone all white.

"You'd better dry off the horses and come inside," I said to John. "This is not a matter to discuss under the open sky."

I still had some decency left in my bones.

As the night fell, they sat by the table, John and Kate, sharing a bottle of brandy between them. I was back in my rocking chair, while William sat in a chair by the window, clutching the rifle in a tight grip.

"You should not have brought Pa at all," Kate scolded John. "He could have said or done *anything* at that meeting."

"But they wanted all the landowners there," John said, defending himself. "It would have seemed suspicious if he was not there— and hardly anyone speaks German."

"Well, there's Mr. Ern, for one," said Kate, sighing deeply. "What could have spurred him on to make such a request?"

"It's bad for business," I croaked from my chair. "He doesn't want the road to be deemed unsafe."

"The road has *always* been unsafe," said Kate.

"But they are talking about it now," said I.

By the window, William jolted and aimed the rifle, thinking he had seen something.

"We must leave, then," said Kate. "Leave at once!"

"They won't be coming tonight," I protested.

"We don't *know* that," said Kate. "Perhaps they have a suspicion."

William turned back to her from his place by the window. "We need one more," he said to her. "One more with a heavy purse, then we can go."

"It's far too late for that, Pa," she retorted. "Now all we can do is save our own hides—though perhaps we ought to leave you and Ma behind to rot, for all the help you have been of late." She sent me a look black with anger.

"We have affairs to settle," said John. "Animals in the barn . . ."

"No time," said she. "We ought to be far away by the time the search party arrives. The more distance we can get between us and this place, the better." Her forehead had gained a sheen of sweat. I quite reveled in seeing her so distraught. It seemed that it was only lately that she had felt the reality of the noose swinging ever closer to her neck.

She might have seen me smiling. "This is all your fault!" Her pointing finger found my face. "If only you had left that little girl alone—or refrained from gifting Dr. York her doll—"

"If only we had not filled the orchard with dead men!" I replied. "If only you had not been such a snake!"

"Ma can make some poppets." William spoke meekly and looked at me with his childlike eyes. "She can make poppets like she used to in Pennsylvania, and burn them in the oven to make all our enemies go away."

"No, William," said I, but he was already shuffling to the door, on his way out to look for suitable wood for such things, and since he left the rifle behind, I thought it was better to just let him. At least he was not speaking of angels—or Jack Handsome.

Kate was still fuming at the table. "We were all in on the slaughter," she said when the door had closed behind William. "None of us carries more blame than the rest."

John sighed. "Forget about the blame, Kate. We have to find out *where to go.*"

"Well, *she* keeps accusing me!" Kate exclaimed. "Even though it is *she* who has set us up to fall!"

John gave me a lingering look, as cold as Kate's had been before, and then he shifted his gaze back to her. "If she bothers you so, I can kill her for you. I can put her in the ground with the rest."

I suppose he meant to make me shiver, but I only chuckled. It did not seem like a poor ending—fleeing with the pack of wolves seemed worse. I think it was in that very moment I first realized how deeply I longed for death.

"Do what you must," I said, "but for *that* slaughter I will not take the blame."

"Maybe we ought to leave them *both* in the orchard," said Kate, staring right at me. "They've only been trouble of late."

"There is room enough," said John, but then I could see something waver in his gaze.

"You won't," I said. "We're blood." Pack. "We take care of our own; the rest can fend for themselves."

Surely, they would not take the hammer to their own.

William came back inside again with a few pieces of wood. He sat down on the stool by the stove and set to carving.

"We have no time for it," Kate told him. "We ought to ready the wagon."

"We won't have to go once this is done," William replied solemnly; his gaze was on his handiwork: the crude human shape that he coaxed out of the wood. The chips fell about his feet like hail. He sure felt the urgency, only his agenda was wrong.

"Bring out your herbs and letters, Elvira." He spoke to me. "We shall still protect ourselves from Jack Handsome and his ilk."

"Sure, husband." I nodded and even went to the back to find some crushed herbs from my trunk. When I came back, Kate and John had gone outside to ready for our departure. "They said they were to kill us," I told William. "But I don't think they would."

"Who?" He looked up at me through a curtain of tangled gray hair. "Kate and John? *No*, it's that colonel, and the trustee, Mr. Dick—they are the ones that will kill us. They will hang us by the neck, Elvira!" He spoke as if he revealed this to me for the very first time, but at least he got the villains right and did not rave about Jack Handsome.

I chuckled a little as I sat back down and placed the herbs in my lap. "We'll see who gets to us first," I said.

"No one will," said William, placing the finished poppet in my hands. It was barely human-shaped, as he had been in such a hurry, but he had remembered to hollow it out a little, so I could place the cure inside. "Your poppets will see to that."

It was a mighty trust he placed in me, and I did fill the poppets as he asked and placed them in the fire, but I did not name them and I did not read over them, and I did not have any matter from our enemies either, so in the end they were nothing but wood.

35.

HANSON

I SHOULD HAVE seen it sooner, and for that, I blamed myself.

If I had not gotten in the habit of turning my gaze away from the Bender farm, I might have noticed how the chimney exuded no smoke and how the travelers turned around at the door. I might have noticed how the paddock was empty of life.

But I did not.

Ever since I joined the colonel's party when they searched the creek, I had been in a foul and restless mood, which was usually not my habit—and I *did* blame the Benders for it, every twinge of unease in me and every sleepless hour. I kept telling myself that it was hardly fair, as I did not know for certain if the Benders were even guilty of foul play, or if it was just a construct in my head—one so wicked and terrifying that I barely dared to think the thought through. But my mind was not one to listen to reason; only my belly spoke, with twinges and aches.

And so I had not looked at the Bender house for quite some time when Silas Toles came rushing into the trading station on the second of May, white in the face and fuming with indignation.

"They have left them to starve!" he cried just as I entered behind him, having been summoned by his loud voice as he shared his discovery with Mr. Brockman and Mr. Ern behind the counter. "The hog is lethargic, and the calf is dead, I think!"

"I have not heard of the Benders going away." Mr. Ern removed his glasses to clean them. "Mayhap there was an emergency—"

"I did peek my head inside," said Mr. Toles. "The place is in disarray; their belongings are strewn everywhere. I think I ought to tell Mr. Dick and Colonel York . . . Something foul might have happened to them!" His drooping yellow mustache quivered with the strength of his emotions.

I could tell from my vantage point by the door how both Mr. Brockman and Mr. Ern took his words to heart, and their faces became worried. Their brows creased and their eyes widened.

"Is their wagon still there?" Mr. Brockman asked.

Mr. Toles shook his head. "It's gone, and so are the horses."

"They might have left of their own volition, then," Mr. Ern mused.

"It could just as well have been at gunpoint," Mr. Brockman argued, looking a little queasy at the news. "They wouldn't have left the animals in such a helpless state," he said.

"Well, the cows were loose in the barn," said Toles. "Not that it helped much, as there was no feed. The hog looked to be sick with hunger, and I swear that calf was already dead."

"We ought to go and get them, then," I said, brave for a moment, as I did not much like to think of animals suffering. "Was Rosie there? Kate's dog?"

Mr. Toles shook his head. "I didn't see any dog."

Mr. Ern came out from behind the counter and went out to the back for his rifle and his coat. "Bring out the horses, Hanson, and we'll see about moving the creatures to our barn."

This I was more than willing to do, though even in that dire hour, I still could not help that the rat in my belly wriggled and snapped its tail at the thought of going over to the Bender place.

"Mayhap that band of bandits came for them?" I heard Mr. Brockman say behind me, fearful and concerned, as I slipped out the door.

Mr. Ern and I ended up taking the wagon to the Bender place so we could move the hog. This turned out to be a good idea, as the animal was surely starved and could not move around much. It was the worst day of my life up until that point, walking into the Benders' barn, into the foul stench, and seeing the suffering eyes of the animals greeting me. Mr. Toles had not exaggerated—of which I had held out some hope—but had been truthful in his account.

When Mr. Ern and Mr. Toles had to shoot a cow for the poor state we found her in, I went out of the barn and drifted toward the house I had helped build. I felt that I had been another person back then, one with less of a burden on his shoulders, and an easier laugh. Something was wrong, though; I saw it as I came closer to the silent house. The sign that had always hung above the door, spelling out *Groceries*, was gone. It seemed to have been ripped from the wall, leaving nothing but empty holes in the grain.

The inn was truly and utterly closed.

Mr. Ern came up beside me, cleaning blood off his hands with his handkerchief while looking at the house.

"They wouldn't have just left," he mused. "Not without telling anyone."

"They might if they had cause to," I said, thinking of the meeting in the schoolhouse where Mr. Ern had spoken up about a new search of the farms. It did not pass me by that the Benders seemed to have left shortly after that decision was made. I felt sick again from thinking of it, and groaned as I pressed a hand to my belly to try to stop the hurt.

Mr. Ern placed a hand on my shoulder. "We don't know anything for sure, Hanson," he said in a quiet voice. "The colonel and Mr. Dick will sort it out. You don't have to fret."

But of course I did fret. I had been fretting for a long time already.

"We'll have to get the animals back to ours," I said, forcing myself to think of what was urgent. "They'll need water if they aren't to perish."

"You should gather up the chickens—those that are left."

"They took Rosie with them." The little dog's absence was as good as proof to me that the Benders had left of their own accord.

"She might have run off," said Mr. Ern, reading my thoughts. "She might have gone in search of food."

Mr. Toles joined us then. He, too, was bloody from the barn.

"I'll ride to town now," he said, giving the house a dark look. "Mr. Dick will want to know about this." His face was grim-looking—as was mine, I reckoned. "I will send someone to help with the animals."

Mr. Ern nodded absentmindedly. "Hanson and I will take the first ones up shortly."

"We ought to bury the dead ones," I said, though the thought of turning soil on that land almost had me heaving for breath.

"You don't have to help with that, Hanson." Mr. Ern's voice was gentle.

When Mr. Toles had left, riding up the road in a cloud of dust,

Mr. Ern spoke again. "Do you want to look inside, Hanson? Perhaps there is some clue to their whereabouts that can put your mind at ease."

I thought it was rather he who wanted to ease his mind, but I still nodded. I knew there would be no peace for me unless I had looked inside that room. I would be wondering forever what it had looked like after they left; it would keep me awake and torment me. What I wanted to find, I could not say—signs of a struggle, perhaps, as that would suggest they were not the villains. Perhaps I just wanted to confirm to myself that this was still the house I had helped build, where I had taken many meals and played countless games of cards—that there was nothing for me to fear within its walls.

Mr. Ern pushed the door open and a terrible stench came rolling out.

"What is that smell?" Mr. Ern complained and fanned around his nose with his hand as if that would make it go away.

"Maybe they left some meat out?" I suggested as I entered on shivering legs. Before I knew it, I was standing in the middle of Kate's magical circle on the floor. The design looked just the same as before, but somehow it now seemed strange rather than reassuring. Maybe because everything else was in such turmoil.

"Oh God, I hope it's not the dog that smells!" Mr. Ern rushed past me and farther inside the house.

The house really was in disarray. The floor was strewn with pots and pans and cutlery; the shelves behind the store counter were cleared—just a few cans littered the floor, as if the one who had done the clearing had been in a hurry and dropped a few. I went over to the stove and opened the door to make sure there were no embers, and the ashes were stone cold. There was something peculiar in there, though: two pieces of wood, crudely carved and half burned. I reached my hand inside and pulled the one piece closer to me, and could tell it had the shape of a man. It might just as well have still been on fire for how quickly I dropped it again.

"Did you find Rosie?" I called to Ern in a shivering voice. He had disappeared behind the canvas curtain, and I was reluctant to follow.

"No," he called back. "Just a stripped bed and empty cupboards. Some clothes in a jumble."

I looked over to the opposite wall, where the grandfather clock stood silent and with a gaping belly. I knew they had kept their money in there. Mr. Bender had brought out the purse and counted out coins for me many a time when I came on business.

"Do you see a trunk back there?" I called to Ern. "It's a large one."

"No," he called back. "No trunk—no meat either."

It was then that I knew it for sure. Mrs. Bender's trunk with her secret book and herbs was gone, and so, by extension, were the Benders.

Mr. Ern reappeared in the outer room, pressing the handkerchief to his nose.

"Mayhap they'll be back," he said as if to comfort me, but I knew for a fact that they would not.

IT WAS A few days later when Mr. Brockman came inside the barn as I was doing the milking. It was very crowded in there in those days, with the Benders' few remaining animals standing alongside our own. I thought that they should survive their ordeal with the exception of one cow who did not seem to perk up, and was perhaps better off slaughtered.

"The colonel has come to the Bender place." Mr. Brockman's eyes were wild-looking. He also looked to be sweating profusely. I thought that he might have a rat like me, scurrying about in his abdomen.

At once, I lost my zest for the task at hand. "Only him?" I asked. My heart was beating rapidly.

"No, Mr. Dick is there as well, and some other men from town." Mr. Brockman repeatedly wet his lips with his tongue.

"They didn't stop?"

He shook his head. "They proceeded directly to the Bender place."

The knot in my belly was pulled taut.

"Climb onto the roof, Hanson," he urged me. "Perhaps you can see something from up there. Don't worry about the milking—I'll do it."

I did not ask why he could not climb onto the roof himself, as it sure would look unseemly for a grown man to do such a thing.

I watched from the barn roof for quite some time, as the men down there milled about the place, entering the house and the barn. Even from that distance, I could see the gleam of the colonel's brass buttons. It was hot, though, and I had to pull my hat down to shield my eyes from the sun's fierce glare, yet I sat up there, vigilant, as the sun slowly traveled to noon.

"Has anything happened?" Mr. Brockman came climbing up the ladder with some bread and cheese for me, which was very kind of him.

"No." I inched across the wooden tiles to take the bread from his hand. "They are mostly just looking around." Mr. Brockman handed me a flask of water, which was highly appreciated.

"Well, let me know if you see anything worthy of note," he said before climbing back down again.

"I will," I swore, and inched back onto my perch, loaded with much-needed sustenance.

It was just when the water had traveled by the flask's half mark, and the bread was all consumed, that something of note happened at the Bender place.

I had watched as the colonel climbed back onto his horse, and had figured by the way they were all acting that they were about to leave and go back to town, but then the colonel raised his hand and pointed—straight to the orchard.

My heart stepped up its pace as the colonel climbed down from the horse again and strode toward the patch of dirt. More men came to walk beside him, as he kicked about the soil behind the inn. Soon a few men went into the barn and came back outside carrying shovels.

The rat in my belly set its teeth into my innards.

I could barely breathe as they started digging, and I hardly noticed how I dropped the flask so it went sailing across the roof and disappeared over the edge.

Suddenly, I could not stay up there. Suddenly, the need to know was so fierce that my whole body shook when I went for the ladder.

"Mr. Brockman!" I called before I had even set my feet on solid ground. "I'm taking the mule to the Bender place!" It was a sentence I had said before too many times to count, but never with as much urgency as on that day.

Mr. Brockman came out on the porch. "Did something happen?" he asked, sounding breathless.

I nodded. "They are digging," I said in a strangely hoarse voice. "They are digging for bodies in the orchard."

Mr. Brockman drew in a sharp breath and reached out a hand to steady himself against the doorframe. I had no time for him, though; I was already headed for the paddock and the mule.

"Did they find something?" I heard Mr. Ern behind me, as he, too, entered the porch. I did not take the time to answer him.

I had to know what they would find.

It did not take us long to get there. I wisely kept my distance, standing close to the road, and was painfully reminded of when I had stood in just a similar fashion looking on the construction of the house. As I watched the six grim-faced men in the orchard, hard at work, with their shirts glued to their skin, the thought of my friendship with the Benders made me feel just as filthy as their shovel blades, smeared with thick, fat soil.

It did not even help to remind myself that there was no way I could have known if there was something unsavory about them. Suddenly, I was angry with them all over again, for leaving me behind in such a wretched state, and for causing the scene before me: the men working so hard and fast that their faces became red and their chests heaved with the strain.

When I closed my eyes, I saw the bobbing lights in the night again, and heard the back door open and close.

When the first yell reached out over the dirt, and the man next to the caller bent over and retched, I could not stop a sob from ripping from my lips. Without me even noticing, my cheeks had turned slick with tears.

I had known—had I not?—all along.

36.

HANSON

THEY CAME FOR Mr. Brockman a week later. It was in the morning, just as the sun came up.

They were a band of men from town, people who we knew, who had bought their beef and tobacco from the trading station's shelves. Several of them had rifles. Others carried knives.

I had slept inside as usual in those days, and was ripped from my sleep by the door crashing into the wall as the men came pouring in. Shading my eyes against the glare of dawn, I sat upright on my mattress, just as Mr. Ern came striding in from the back, loudly demanding to know just what the ruckus was about.

"Where is he?" the men yelled in response. I could see Mr. Weissbrod among them, and Mr. Toles, too. Even Nicholas Morrin was there, white-faced and dark-eyed.

Mr. Toles spoke for them all. "Brockman must come out at once!" he demanded.

"Whatever for?" Mr. Ern said, confused.

"He has a lot to answer for!" Mr. Toles let us know.

"Silas?" Mr. Brockman came out just then, and I knew it at once that this was a mistake. I could not see how arguing with these angry men would do any good. Tensions had run high ever since the discovery of the bodies at the Bender inn—nine men in all, and one little girl—and the townspeople were angry that the Benders had gone. The Weissbrods had generously shared with me rumors of co-conspirators and "people who had known." It was perhaps not so strange, I had thought then, that people looked for culprits, with the bodies lined up and no one to punish.

I had not thought they would come for Mr. Brockman, though, as the animosity between him and John had been well-known in town.

Yet, there they were, armed and beset with fury.

"You better come outside, Rudolph." Silas Toles's face was a grim mask.

"What for?" Mr. Brockman asked while pulling on his waistcoat. "What is the meaning of this ruckus?" He continued speaking without waiting for Mr. Toles's answer. "Cannot a man get a decent night's sleep without being accosted in his own home?" I could tell that Mr. Brockman was afraid; his face was quite the study in masonry, as hard and unreadable as marble.

"Gentlemen, please, be calm!" Mr. Ern walked toward the men with his hands held up, palms out. "I am sure we can figure this out."

Mr. Weissbrod roughly pushed him aside to get to where Mr. Brockman stood. I rose to my feet then as well, looking around for the poker or something else I could hit them with, but then I caught Mr. Ern's warning gaze from across the room. He had been pushed up against the counter as the men stormed past him, toppling over barrels and boxes on their way. He silently shook his head at me, and mouthed the word "no."

I could only watch as they manhandled Mr. Brockman outside and pushed him to the ground in the yard. Mr. Ern and I came outside last, dithering on the porch like nervous chickens.

When the first blow fell, Mr. Ern cried out, "For God's sake, stop! Have you all lost your minds?" No one even heard him. They were too busy with Mr. Brockman—with forcing a confession out of him.

"How could you not have known?" one of the men cried and grabbed a fistful of Mr. Brockman's hair and shook his head by it.

"You are a liar!" another one exclaimed.

"They gave you some of the spoils, didn't they? So you would keep sending men down there!"

"She had you wrapped around her finger, didn't she, that little bitch?"

"How many men did you help them bury?"

Mr. Brockman, of course, only shook his head, knowing nothing and sharing none. Not even when the blows rained down upon him did he plead or beg, though I wished that he would have. It did not seem right to take a beating for something he had not done.

When his nose erupted with blood, I made to step forward and come to his aid, but Mr. Ern grabbed me around the chest and whispered in my ear. "You better not get involved, Hanson. I cannot tell where this will end."

It sent a fresh chill through me.

In the yard, the men kept yelling and cursing, saying how Mr. Brockman could not have meant to marry Kate without knowing what her family's business was. It sounded reasonable enough, but I knew it was not true. Mr. Brockman had not known. No one had known—but me, near the end. I thought to tell them that but could not see how my voice could cut through the ruckus, and then Mr. Ern and I were roughly pushed aside as some of the men entered the trading station again, to search for evidence, they said. They treated us as if we did not even live there anymore. They had completely overtaken the property.

I could hear them inside the house, throwing things around. They went into the back first, to riffle through Mr. Brockman's belongings, and Mr. Ern's, too, for sure.

I twisted in Mr. Ern's grasp, as I wanted to go inside and make sure they did not ruin Mr. Brockman's things, but then the violence in the yard kept me enthralled, and so I would not have been able to leave the porch anyway.

When the men who had been inside came back, one of them held a stack of folded papers in his hand. His eyes shone with triumph, and he held them high in the air as he approached the other men, as thrilled as if he had found a cache of gold.

It was the notes from Kate, of course. The ones I had delivered.

A German man among them, Mr. Biedewolf, was tasked with translating the letters, as they were hoping the words would prove Mr. Brockman's affiliation with the murders. Mr. Biedewolf only chuckled as he read, though, stating that it was nothing but sweet nonsense.

They had also found the ring Mr. Brockman had had engraved for Kate, and held it up to the sun to read the words inside the slim band.

Curled up on the ground, Mr. Brockman cried. The tears left grimy trails in the bloody dust that coated his face, and it pained me so to see it that I had to look away.

I relaxed a little in Mr. Ern's grip then, thinking that when they could find no proof, they would surely let Mr. Brockman go, but this hope, it turned out, was in vain.

Instead of letting the crying man be, they went at him again with kicks and curses, and suddenly there was a rope there, being passed from hand to hand.

Behind me, Mr. Ern hissed and cursed. I could feel how his body tensed up against my back.

"They won't *hang* him, will they?" I whispered, aghast.

"Of course not," Mr. Ern said in a raspy voice, but I could tell that he did not mean it. He feared it as much as I did.

It was my turn to cry when they dragged Mr. Brockman to our one gnarled oak and threw the rope over the sturdiest branch.

The rope was already made ready, tied into a noose.

I felt as if I could not breathe myself when they slipped it over Mr. Brockman's head and tightened it. Behind me, Mr. Ern's string of German curses intensified.

Then Mr. Brockman went up in the air.

There were five men who pulled the rope, so the ascent was swift and easy. Mr. Brockman's limbs flailed about as he struggled with his hands to loosen the noose, but it was to no avail. It simply was too tight.

"No!" I cried out as Mr. Brockman's face turned from white to blue; as his legs kicked wildly and he soiled himself, staining the fabric of his pants.

Mr. Ern held me even more tightly, pressed me to his body to control my straining limbs. "Don't look at him, Hanson," he said into my ear. "Close your eyes, boy! Don't look at him!"

But of course I looked. How could I not?

I watched as his eyes started to bulge, and his tongue came creeping from between his lips. Then I cried out in horrified relief as the men abruptly let the rope go, and Mr. Brockman crashed to the ground.

Again I strained against Mr. Ern's arms; again he warned me to be cautious. "They might leave now, just you see . . . Don't do anything foolish, Hanson . . . I'd rather not see *you* up in that tree . . ."

Yet I howled when the men grabbed hold of the rope anew and hoisted Mr. Brockman back up in the oak. His color, which had become red while he was on the ground, turned blue again in an instant.

"I'll get my axe," I muttered, not even knowing quite what I was saying. "I'll get my axe, and I'll kill them all."

"No," Mr. Ern said, quiet and firm, "you will do no foolish thing like that."

"It was *I* who was their friend," I said, panting. "It was *I* who saw them digging—"

Mr. Ern's hand closed over my mouth, bottling up the damning words. "It does not matter," he whispered to me. "They don't want justice, they want revenge; don't be a willing lamb for their slaughter."

I wriggled and I fought, but Mr. Ern held me firm, even when the men secured the rope to the tree trunk and went for their horses. He held me thus even after the men had entered the road, afraid, I believed, that I would somehow make a nuisance of myself and make them all come back.

Mr. Toles came riding up to us before he went away. "You better keep your house in order, Mr. Ern," he said with a finger to the brim of his hat.

It sounded like a warning to me.

When they had finally gone, Mr. Ern loosened his hold of me, and I slumped down on the porch, sobbing and shivering.

Mr. Ern had no time for me, though. He ran across the yard with his knife at the ready to cut Mr. Brockman down. When Mr. Ern had sawn through the rope, Mr. Brockman fell down with a thump, sounding like nothing but a sack of grain, lifeless and heavy.

There was life, though, just barely.

By the time I got there, Mr. Ern was rubbing Mr. Brockman's neck and bade me run for water. Mr. Brockman, on his side, was gasping for air. He no longer looked so purple in the face, but his eyes were red and swollen.

When we carried him inside later, we had to make up the bed first, as everything was in disorder in there. The floor was strewn with letters and photographs, trinkets and mementos from Mr. Brockman's life. They had trampled all over it, and we did, too, in our eagerness to save him.

Kate's ring was gone, though, and none of us laid eyes on it again.

I never did learn for sure if the townsmen had *meant* to let Mr. Brockman live, or if it was just luck and happenstance that saved him. He *did* live, though, and even if I later would come to regret it, I was glad for it on that day.

It was as if the hanging broke something in me, and I could not fix it no matter how I tried. I was not frightened, though, not anymore; rather, I always expected the worst, and so it never came as a shock if something went awry.

I no longer struggled to sleep at night—the rat was gone from my belly—but neither did I feel much joy, and I no longer craved other people's company in the way that I had before. Whatever trust in my fellow men I had nursed before the Benders was gone by the time we cut Rudolph down from the tree.

Mr. Ern said that I had grown—matured. He said that a lot in the weeks it took us to get Mr. Brockman back on his feet. Mr. Ern said it as if it was a good thing, but I rather missed who I had been before. I missed not having to think so much about what was hidden behind a smile—and what other people were capable of.

I still saw the Weissbrod brothers, though in secret, as none of us had anything to gain by letting our continued friendship be known. As the summer moved on, we sometimes met behind the barn, where I knew neither Mr. Brockman nor Mr. Ern would want to go, due to the unhappy view.

The Weissbrods craved the Bender place, though. They salivated like dogs over a bone whenever it came within their sight. They had been down there since the findings, of course, many a time, and even pried boards off the walls to sell to travelers and suchlike. Everyone, it seemed, wanted a piece of the Bender place; it was being picked apart before my very eyes. The rear part close to the orchard looked almost like a wooden skeleton already, with all the flesh cleaned off. I could see that the prairie was doing its best in reclaiming the cursed plot as well, and there were already heaps of dust and sand covering what was left of the floorboards.

The chimney had become the home of a crow.

I thought that to the Weissbrods, it was my friendship with the Benders that was my saving grace, as I was no longer much in the way of company. I could tell stories, though, that no one else could, since I had been there so often and had been welcome at their table. Not that they really needed more stories—they already had enough to choose from.

Late in summer, it was the rumors about Kate's death they spoke of the most.

"She tried to get away, you see," Bruno said with glee in his eyes. We were all sitting on the plow's sturdy frame, perched there like spring birds. Twittering like ones, too. "She shot back, too, once or twice," Bruno said, "but since she was injured, she didn't have the strength for a proper fight. By the end she was crawling on the ground like this." He demonstrated eagerly. "When they got to her, they shot her in the head, at close range, five times." He finished his story with rosy cheeks and a wide smile.

Max did not believe in that story. "They weren't shot," he said, smacking his brother at the back of his skull. "They were hanged, and then their bodies went into a sinkhole. Kate died last of all; she kicked and hissed like a cat when they strung her up."

The rumors of the vigilantes had been there from the start. They appeared as soon as the Benders' wagon was found abandoned in a creek, horses and all—even Rosie. There had been no trace of the family, though, and even if the manhunt was excessive, no one had seen hide nor hair of them since they left the inn. Mr. Dick and Colonel York were convinced that the Benders had abandoned their vehicle to continue by train, but others—the locals—claimed to know better.

"They were a band of ten men," Bruno had told me the week before. "They overtook the Benders even before the bodies were found. As soon as they heard of the abandoned animals, they knew that wickedness had been afoot, and set out after them to see justice done."

"And split the loot," Max had piped up. "They thought the Benders had to be carrying great valuables from their robbing."

"*Mostly* it was to see justice done," Bruno insisted, annoyed with his brother. "They didn't trust the law to do it, you see. Then they swore each other to silence."

"Why?" I had asked.

Bruno had shrugged. "Maybe they're just noble men who don't want any honor."

"It seems like a cruel thing to let Mr. Dick keep searching, though," I argued. "If the Benders are already dead."

"Well," Bruno said, straightening up, "such vigilante bands are not always appreciated by the law."

"It is because of the loot," Max insisted. "They split it all between them."

"Do you know what happened to the dog?" I asked, as that was what was at the front of my mind. But no one could tell me what had happened to Rosie after she was found in the wagon.

By the end of summer, the rumors of Kate's death had taken on more grisly details.

"Her skull was blown in half by the second shot with the rifle," Bruno said on another occasion. "She cursed the men with her dying breath."

"I heard that she tried to run away," said Max. "Then she was shot in the legs, and was bleeding like a pig when they strung her up."

"Ma says there has never been a woman as vile and foul as she," Bruno said.

"She used witchcraft to make people turn a blind eye," Max concurred. "She deserved it, everything that happened to her."

"Sure she did," I said, but, unlike the Weissbrods, I frequently read the newspapers, and knew that the search was still on. Outside of the prairie, no one seemed to have learned about the Benders' violent deaths at the hands of righteous men.

"She was a witch and a whore." Max spat down on the ground. His spittle was brown with tobacco.

"Pretty, though," said Max, which earned him another smack on the head.

"Don't let Ma hear you talk like that," Bruno warned him. "She'll have your hide for sure!"

Though I was angrier with Kate—with *all* of the Benders—than I had ever been at anyone in my life, I could not revel in those stories of torture and blood. Perhaps there had been too much of it already. Mayhap it had left me numb.

Then, once in a while, I would remember something good about them: Ma's stew, the sugar lumps, Kate's laughter, or John's clever card games, and I hated how those memories would slice through the coldness I had built around them and unleash the grief all over again. I felt weak for seeing something other than the rest, for *my* Kate had not been a witch and a whore, but smart and funny and fearless.

She had told me I would be a newspaperman.

I could never imagine her gutted and hanged, or shot to pieces by burly men. She had simply been too alive for that—too strong to die so wretched.

I would never tell a living soul, but ever since the hanging, a part of me could not help but hope that Kate was indeed alive. I thought that was the curse of having seen the ugliness of man, that you clung to whomever could protect you from it. Kate, I knew, could handle such men as those who had hung Mr. Brockman. She could handle them and put them in the ground and never even think twice about it.

She became a source of comfort to me in those first few months after it happened. A dark angel to sit on my shoulder and guard me from the world's wickedness.

She became the secret comfort of my soul.

Epilogue

I LIFTED MY skirt just a little to keep the hem of my silk widow's garb off the dusty city street. It had been a long time since I was comfortable wearing stained dresses, and the thick black silk had cost me quite a bit.

I moved as fast as I was allowed with the people crowding me on every side: workers in plain clothing with tired eyes; delivery boys burdened with parcels; an elderly woman with a hand-drawn cart; and mothers with clutches of children in tow and magnificent hats balancing on top of their heads sprouting exotic feathers. The horses were everywhere, pulling simple wagons and carriages alike. On each side of the cobbled street were tall buildings of brick, sporting dusty front windows with printed signs and samplings of the establishments' goods: rolls of fabrics, binoculars, gloves, medicine bottles, books . . .

The noise was overpowering at first, but one got used to it quite easily.

I hardly ever lost sight of the man in the brown leather coat as he hurried on in front of me, with his hat pulled down low over his brow. When he did disappear for a moment, stepping around a corner or behind a sidewalk stall, he was quite easy to spot as he reappeared, on account of him being so tall.

I would have recognized that boy anywhere—at any time. The years that had passed since last I saw him did not mean a thing. It was still him, hiding within that lanky frame, behind the mask of curly beard. I caught up with him in front of a confectionary store, where he paused to peruse the newspapers on display in the window; mayhap he was looking for his own name emblazoned on the page. Perhaps he was not looking at the newspapers at all, but was about to step inside for sweets or tobacco when I came up beside him, adjusting my veil, and spoke to him for the first time since Kansas.

"Hello, Hanson." Behind the veil, I was smiling. I found it such a strange thrill to stand there beside him like a ghost made flesh—it was dangerous, though, I knew that as well, but it was a part of what made it so exhilarating.

I never could resist a spot of danger.

Hanson turned his head to me with a questioning look on his face. Close up, I could detect a certain hardness on his features: a clenched jaw, tight lips, eyes that gave nothing away. I thought that he had not fared so well, and I was sorry for it.

"Do I know you, ma'am?" he asked in a well-modulated yet startlingly dark voice. I suppose I had expected him to still have the sweet voice of his youth.

"It's me," I said from behind the veil, just as my heart picked up its pace. "Kate." I tasted the name I had not used in quite some time, and it felt strange and unfamiliar on my tongue.

A bitter smile flashed across Hanson's lips for a moment before it vanished as fast as it had appeared. "Kate, huh?"

"Oh yes. Professor Miss Katie Bender, at your service." I cocked my head a little and made a slight bow.

He laughed then, but it sounded joyless. "If you only knew how many women have come up to me and given that name . . . You are hardly the first, ma'am, and won't be the last." His face became serious. "I know it is not my place to tell you how to conduct yourself, but claiming to be Kate Bender is hardly the way to fame and riches. Even if I could, I would not offer much for an interview with you; the world is awash in Kate Benders."

"Yes," I agreed. "So I have gleaned from the newspapers." I nodded to the display. "It must be said, though, that I am no longer traveling by that name myself." I had been prepared for some reluctance to believe, and so I opened the little purse that dangled from my wrist, embroidered with beads of glass and jet. "I have a present for you," I said as I brought out the little flower I had made out of a newspaper page. "I gave you another one just like this before, do you remember?"

He certainly did. His face went pale and his eyes widened. "Kate?" Now he *did* look like he had seen a ghost. "How can this be?" He lowered his voice and looked around on the busy street. "How can you be walking around like this? Someone might see you!"

I knew then that Hanson was no enemy to me.

I pressed the newspaper flower into his hand and his fingers closed around it, brushing against the silk of my glove. "I'm careful," I told him. "I wear my widow's veil, and I am no longer young. It's easy to pass unnoticed if you're a woman past her prime."

He scrutinized me with his gaze, trying to look through the

sheer fabric that guarded my face. "I can't believe it," he said. "It feels like a dream."

"A good one, I hope," I said with a smile. "Though I expect it to be a nightmare." There was no point in pretending otherwise.

"If you only knew." It was as if the large man buckled before me, though he was still standing on his two feet. Perhaps it was something inside him that broke.

"I came because of Brockman," I told him. "Well, I was passing through, and I knew from your bylines this is where you reside. I wanted to ask you what happened to him."

"You have read about it, then?" He gave me another dark look.

"That I have. I was surprised to learn of his crime."

Hanson nodded; his face regained the hard, distant look that was so different from the soft openness I remembered.

"Walk with me." I did not much like standing still. If someone with ill intent were on my trail, I would rather not be a sitting duck.

We weaved our way up the street side by side. We had to walk close to even hear what the other one said. He held out his arm to me, and I took it with some surprise. I had not thought he would be so polite to me after everything that had happened. Perhaps it was only in his nature—or perhaps it was so he could make sure I did not vanish again.

"He was not the same, after you left," he told me. "The townspeople tried to hang him in the aftermath, but you may already know that."

"Yes, I read about that as well. People can be cruel when frightened."

"Well, it was *your* punishment he took." He said it like it was, and I found that I appreciated his honesty.

"It was not my intention."

"I know that." He sighed. "He never fully recovered, though, not from that ordeal. Mr. Ern and I stayed for as long as we could, but when he married, we moved away."

"And now he has been hanged *again*."

"Seeing how that happened, I would rather they had succeeded the first time." Hanson's voice held an edge of despair.

"I never thought him a violent man."

"Neither did I—he was not before, and yet he killed his own daughter by the cruelest means." He spoke as if he could not rightly believe it, which was quite a feat, considering all that he had seen. "She was only sixteen," he said. "The hanging, this time, was just."

"And he will not be revived this time."

"No," Hanson said. "He is quite dead. I saw it happen with my own two eyes."

"Do you blame *me?*" I wanted to know.

"How can I not?" He glanced down at me. "He was a broken man after you left, and his girl, well—she might have had some of you in her. Mayhap she was a willful child, beautiful and strong . . . I cannot tell as I never saw her."

"I'm sorry for the child," said I.

"Yes," said Hanson. "So am I."

We had reached a park on our wandering and slipped in through the wrought-iron gates. It was better there, shaded and secluded. Though there were some people wandering about, it was quiet and calm as we drifted on the path below the oak trees.

"I think Mr. Brockman never truly survived that first hanging," Hanson said. "I think a part of him died on that day."

"And you?" I asked him. "Did a part of you die as well?"

He paused before answering. "Not then, perhaps, but earlier, when they dug up the crop in your orchard."

I nodded behind the veil. "I'm sorry about that as well. I always cared for you, Hanson. I hope you can appreciate that."

He did not reply. "What happened?" he asked instead, with some urgency to his voice. "Where did you go when you left?"

"Oh, I went south, then north again. I never stayed long in one place."

He gave me a puzzled look. "You traveled alone?"

"Well, Ma and Pa died, shortly after. They never even made it out of Kansas."

I could feel his arm go rigid under my hand. "What happened to them?"

I did not reply.

"What about John?" His voice had gained a shiver.

"John is dead, too," I replied, not without a smile. "These days, there's only me."

Hanson kept silent for a moment, digesting the news. "Is it them you are wearing black for?"

"No, I wear that for myself."

Another puzzled look then. "Did you die as well?"

I shrugged. "Widowhood suits me. It keeps people away."

"The Kate *I* knew loved people."

"Then maybe I *did* die, a little—or maybe I just don't want them prying. Surely you can understand that."

"Have you—" He struggled to find the words. "Have you kept out of trouble since?"

"Oh, Hanson." I gave his arm a squeeze and recalled the current weight of the cigar box. "You don't have to worry about me." My free hand fluttered to my chest to touch the jeweled brooch that resided there.

He swallowed visibly, still struggling with my news. "I'm sorry to hear they're all dead—though I suppose Mr. and Mrs. Bender were old anyway." I could tell that he was battling his emotions; his arm jerked a little in my grasp, as if he feared the hand that held it.

"It became too much." I sighed. "Believe me when I say it was for the best."

We walked in silence for a moment. His brow was furrowed with the weight of my news. "I will not write about this," he said after a while, as if to belatedly assure me.

"I know you won't," said I. It is easy to make demands when people fear you. "It's best to let Kate Bender stay dead, don't you think? Nothing good ever follows in her wake."

"And who are you now?" He looked at me.

"Whomever I like," I replied.

Author's Note

WRITING A NOVEL about the Bender family was not an obvious choice for me. We don't know *anything* about them, for one. They arrived in Cherryvale in their rickety wagon like something out of Grimms' fairy tales, set up house and did unspeakable things, then suddenly disappeared again when the ground started burning under their feet. Where they came from and where they went is still unknown (though theories abound), and what life really looked like inside the family home, no one can say for sure. This book, therefore, is mostly just fiction—both my own and other people's—and a lot of my research has consisted of crafting a story from fragments, rumors, and assumptions.

Here are some more things we don't know:

Ma's name is still a mystery, sometimes given as Elvira, other times as Kate Sr. Her last name could have been made up as well—a common theory goes that John's real last name was Gebhardt. We also don't know for sure how the family was constructed. Some say that Kate and John were married; others say they were siblings. I opted to go for the third alternative, namely, that they were stepsiblings. Since John allegedly fought Brockman for Kate's affection, I thought it unlikely that they were brother and sister.

As for their origins, there *was* a rumor that they came from Pennsylvania and had been forced to leave, either because William had killed someone or because the women had been caught practicing black magic. We don't know if any of this is true, but it inspired my own Bender origin story. They were also rumored to have been responsible for the murder of the Vandles in New Albany, but this was never proven.

As for Kate's suitors, it is true that Brockman was in business with the Benders and engaged to Kate (though she kept putting the wedding off). It is also true that a mob attempted to hang him after the Benders had fled (though I have taken some liberties with the mob's identity), and that he later killed his own daughter. Nicholas Morrin, however, is mostly my own invention. Kate was rumored to have had an affair with "a farmer," but we don't know anything more than that. On the subject of my own inventions, I'd also like to note that young Hanson is entirely my own, and that old Cherryvale may not look exactly like the real thing did.

As for the victims, only those who were found buried by the house can be tied to the Benders for sure; the other three are assumptions (though widely attributed to the family). I would also like to note that I have changed some of the victims' names for editorial purposes, and bestowed a few names, too, where there was no known identity.

The Benders' spirituality is another question with many answers. We know that Kate tried to establish herself as a medium and a healer, and several people claimed that the family was very religious, especially the older Benders. Some thought the whole family were spiritualists. Kate also gave "spirit talks," which at the time meant to channel a spirit who did the actual talking. Although some have suggested that Kate's business was just a front to draw people to the inn, I find it more likely that she saw it as another source of income. There is also, of course, the possibility that she was a true believer and honest in her attempts to talk to the dead, but that's not the option I chose for this book.

It also must be said that half of what we think we know about the Benders is details we have gotten from people who were believed to be Benders, or who pretended to be Benders. In the first years after their crimes came to light, there were Bender sightings *everywhere*, and several arrests. In the most famous of the latter, a woman called Almira Griffith and her daughter, Sarah Davis, were so strongly believed to be the Bender women that they were shipped from Michigan to Kansas to be identified—and several citizens of Cherryvale *did* confirm their identity. The whole case fell apart, however, when it was revealed that Almira Griffith had been in prison at the time of the murders.

There was also Henry Deutchmiller, an elderly man who was arrested on the belief that he was William Bender, who freely spoke to the press in exchange for tobacco and oranges, and "Mrs. Gavin," a bordello owner in Rio Vista, California, who insisted on her deathbed that she was, in fact, Kate Bender.

For a while, there was so much confusion that the press started making quips about it: "It is a humiliating fact that, though John Bender the Kansas murderer has been arrested in nearly every enterprising town in the West, he is still at large," and, "Old man Bender, the Kansas murderer, who is the worst arrested man in America, has had this service performed for him again—this time in Salt Lake City," shortly after followed by, "And now they have arrested the old man Bender again—this time in Arizona."

In the end, they never caught the Benders—although the residents of Labette County would say that was because the family was already dead. As rife as reports of false arrests and sightings had been, there were almost as many accounts of the Benders' deaths at the hands of vigilantes. For a period of time, there were several deathbed confessions where the dying would claim to have taken part in the vengeance killings. There were so many confessions, in fact, that if all of them were true, it wouldn't have been a band of ten men, as many of them claimed, but more like a small army. Even Laura Ingalls Wilder, author of the Little House on the Prairie series, was so caught up in this idea that she once stated that her father had been one of the vigilantes. This, however, proved to be untrue, as the Ingalls family had already left Kansas at that time.

What truly happened to the Benders is still a mystery.

In addition to all this uncertainty and lack of reliable sources, my own interest in true crime is very specific: I'm fascinated by the half-forgotten female serial killers of yore, and though Kate Bender fits that bill, she comes with her whole family attached, and half of them are undoubtedly men.

So why did I still choose to write about Kate?

At first, I think I was drawn by the fact that she was so different from my last murderess. In my first historical novel, *In the Garden of Spite* (*Triflers Need Not Apply* in the UK), I wrote about Belle Gunness, a ruthless killer and stone-cold sociopath who did the bulk of her killings in her forties, after several disappointments in life. Kate, in contrast, was young and had her whole life ahead of her; she also killed as part of a group, while Belle worked alone. Kate and the other Benders didn't appear to have had the same patience and cunning as Belle had (while the latter ran her operation for years, the Benders' crashed and burned within a year and a half) but seemed to belong on the more disorganized side of the sociopath sliding scale. All of this was intriguing to me, as it made for a whole different character with a whole new set of motivations and challenges.

I had also come across Kate's story several times over the years, and had noticed how she was usually portrayed as the Bender family's mastermind and most vicious killer ("the beautiful throat-cutter," as one book put it). It was a slow process, but finally, while reading yet another account of the Bloody Benders, it dawned on me that Kate had perhaps carried the brunt of her family's crimes, just for being beautiful, bilingual, and an extrovert. Even though there were four people in that house, the rest of the family was rarely given much space, even if there's really nothing to suggest that Kate was any guiltier than anyone else.

Through my research, I had also read several accounts—told by grown men—of how Kate was allegedly killed by vigilantes, and I thought there was something almost unsavory about how they detailed her gruesome death (always last, always worst), that just didn't seem to be there when they recounted the other Benders' alleged demise. This suggested to me that it was not just about getting rid of a criminal, but also about punishing a pretty woman for stepping out of line—through murder, of course, but also by speaking in public as a medium (good women were silent at the time; speaking in front of people was associated with promiscuity), and by generally drawing attention to herself. The fact that the stories about her death were most likely fantasies only made it worse, somehow. There were also the witchcraft rumors and the demonization of the Bender women (that just didn't include the men), which only added to my impression of misogyny at work.

All of this happened a long time ago, and Kate Bender was undoubtedly a terrible human being, but because of the reasons listed, it became important to me to try to give a more nuanced picture of the Bender family dynamics, and perhaps also of Kate herself.

I admit to also being fascinated by Kate's chosen profession: spiritualism was popular at the time, but also controversial, so it seemed like a weirdly bold move for a serial killer to draw attention to herself in that way. I was also pretty amazed by the witchcraft rumors, as they seemed oddly displaced in space and time, detailing practices mentioned in transcripts from sixteenth-century witch trials, like the remote milking by rags and the cat alter ego. There were also the rumors of the wooden poppets found in the oven, the occult carvings on the floor of their house, the story about Ma and Kate dancing with the devil in the graveyard, and the "pricking" of the witch by barbed wire. A little research revealed that the rumors mostly came from the Weissbrods (who did exist but are embellished in this book), and that a lot of the old European folklore still lived and thrived in German immigrant communities at the time. Several of the stories surrounding the Benders find their counterparts in Pennsylvania Dutch folk magic.

The story goes that both Ma and Kate sold "cures"—folk remedies and spells—and that might very well be true, but there is another interesting possibility as well: it wasn't entirely uncommon back then for spiritualism to be confused with witchcraft, as speaking to the dead had traditionally been something only witches did. It could, in fact, be that it was Kate's work as a medium that caused the rumors in the first place. In this book, I opted to embrace both possibilities, as I found the contrast between old folklore and modern (at the time) spiritualism intriguing.

Finally, I was baffled by the Benders' apparent ability to draw out the worst in their fellow human beings. The destruction that followed in their wake with lynch mobs, murder, and vigilante justice (real or invented) only goes to show that regular people, too, can be capable of despicable acts under the right circumstances. That thought, more than anything else, kept me awake while writing this story.

As for Kate herself, if she lived out her days using another name or died at the hands of vigilantes, she would undoubtedly have been pleased to know that the impression she left lives on.

Acknowledgments

I did not make this book all by myself, and much gratitude goes out to the following:

To my wonderful editor, Sarah Blumenstock, and the team at Berkley; this book would have been so much poorer without you. Thank you for letting me benefit from your brilliance and insight.

To my agent, Brianne Johnson; it has been a pleasure, as always, to work on this story with you.

A big thank-you to Liv Lingborn for reading early drafts and being the perfect sounding board. I don't blame you for letting out a breath of relief when I typed "The End."

I would also like to thank a younger me, for taking an interest in divination, witchcraft, and spiritualism, so that this world felt familiar to me from the start. Yes, it was smart to spend my teenage years learning cartomancy and palmistry and reading about the Fox sisters (the very young founders of the spiritualist faith).

I went through a lot of books and articles while working on this novel, but would especially like to highlight *Pioneer Women: Voices from the Kansas Frontier* by Joanna Stratton, a collection of personal accounts from nineteenth-century Kansan women gathered by the author's great-grandmother Lilla Day Monroe. It was a fascinating eye-opener for me, and filled in a lot of details about the weather, food, and day-to-day hardships of living on the Kansas prairie.

Also, a thank-you to my son, Jonah, the epitome of patience.

Discussion Questions

1. Why do you think the novel is called *All the Blood We Share*?

2. The Benders operated at a notoriously violent time in history when there was very little law enforcement. Do you think something like this could have happened today?

3. At one point, Kate initiates a relationship with a local farmer, Nicholas Morrin. Do you think she could have succeeded in turning her life around, or is Elvira right when she says that Kate's own nature would have gotten in the way?

4. Although money was the Benders' main motive for murder, it might not have been their only drive. How would you describe each character's motivations?

5. In the years following the Bender murders, Kate has been sin-

gled out as the "mastermind" behind their operation. Why do you think that is? How would you describe Kate and her role?

6. Kate and her mother, Elvira, have a complicated relationship. How do you think Kate's upbringing shaped her?

7. What do you think drew Kate to spiritualism?

8. Why do you think Elvira gave Dr. York Anne Marie's doll?

9. How does Kate from the early chapters compare to Kate by the end of the novel? Has her personality changed?

Lene J. Løkkhaug

CAMILLA BRUCE is a Norwegian writer of speculative and historical fiction. She has a master's degree in comparative literature and has co-run a small press that published dark fairy tales. Camilla currently lives in Trondheim with her son and cat.

CONNECT ONLINE

CamillaBruce.com

CamillaBruce_Writing

MillaCream

Ready to find
your next great read?

Let us help.

Visit prh.com/nextread

Penguin
Random
House